T0323898

Praise for Abbie Williams

"Williams populates her historical fiction with people nearly broken by their experiences."

— Foreword Reviews (Soul of a Crow)

* Gold Medalist - 2015

— Independent Publishers Awards (Heart of a Dove)

"Set just after the U.S. Civil War, this passionate opening volume of a projected series successfully melds historical narrative, women's issues, and breathless romance with horsewomanship, trailside deer-gutting, and alluring smidgeons of Celtic ESP."

— Publishers Weekly (Heart of a Dove)

"There is a lot I liked about this book. It didn't pull punches, it feels period, it was filled with memorable characters and at times lovely descriptions and language. Even though there is a sequel coming, this book feels complete."

— Dear Author (Heart of a Dove)

"With a sweet romance, good natured camaraderie, and a very real element of danger, this book is hard to put down."

— San Francisco Book Review (Heart of a Dove)

ALSO BY ABBIE WILLIAMS

⮞ THE SHORE LEAVE CAFE SERIES ⮜

SUMMER AT THE SHORE LEAVE CAFE

SECOND CHANCES

A NOTION OF LOVE

WINTER AT THE WHITE OAKS LODGE

WILD FLOWER

THE FIRST LAW OF LOVE

UNTIL TOMORROW

THE WAY BACK

RETURN TO YESTERDAY

FORBIDDEN

⮞ THE DOVE SERIES ⮜

HEART OF A DOVE

SOUL OF A CROW

GRACE OF A HAWK

Winter at the White Oaks Lodge

a SHORE LEAVE CAFE *novel*

Abbie Williams

central
avenue
publishing
2017

Published by Central Avenue Publishing, an imprint of Central Avenue Marketing Ltd.
www.centralavenuepublishing.com

WINTER AT THE WHITE OAKS LODGE

978-1-77168-108-7 (pbk)
978-1-77168-013-4 (epub)
978-1-77168-057-8 (mobi)

Published in Canada

Printed in United States of America

1. FICTION / Romance   2. FICTION / Family Life

THE PAST IS ALIVE, ALL AROUND US...

Chapter One

"ANY DAY NOW, SWEETIE, ANY DAY." GRANDMA'S WORDS were accompanied by her hand on my back, patting me between the shoulder blades as I leaned on my palms against the edge of the kitchen sink and attempted to draw a deep breath.

It wasn't that I was trying to be melodramatic; I truly could not get enough air into my lungs, courtesy of the enormous pregnancy that belled out my stomach. When I lay flat on my back, which I couldn't do for more than a minute these days or I felt crushed, my belly resembled the dome of a cathedral.

"I keep reminding myself that," I said, relaxing my shoulders as she rested her hand upon me, with familiar, tender comfort. On the counter beside me, coffee percolated with a cheerful burbling. I grumbled, "It's not fair. Aunt Jilly looks adorable, and she's almost as pregnant as me. But she never complains."

Grandma said, "That's not true. Everyone complains at this stage of a pregnancy. It comes with the territory. Just be glad it isn't summer and there's no air conditioning in your house."

I smiled at her over my shoulder, my grandma, Joan, who'd lived in this same house since her childhood. The walls here had surely witnessed their share of pregnant women, including my own mother. As long as I could remember, we came to Landon from Chicago for summer break; never in my wildest imaginings had I pictured myself living here as a pregnant and single teenager. On the old timeline, the one I'd known and trusted in before last July, I would be finishing up my senior year of high school, at home in Chicago. I closed my eyes, unwittingly dragged to the afternoon I'd sat trembling on the edge of the tub in the bathroom upstairs, gingerly clutching the end of the world as I'd known it—a plastic pregnancy tester with a purple plus sign on the indicator.

"That's right," I whispered, acknowledging Grandma's words about no air conditioning. "Mom and Aunt Jilly were both born in August. But at least you didn't have to worry about slipping on the ice."

I lived in mortal fear of falling since the first frost at the end of last October, warily traversing the slippery sidewalks of Landon as my belly finally outpaced my breasts in size. It seemed to me that the high school was the last place in town that was plowed or de-iced. I thanked God that, at the very least, I was done with school for now; Landon High was a study in small-town bias against the (and I quote) "slut who got Noah Utley in trouble."

It was irony of the worst sort, as I was truly the least slutty girl I knew. Of course evidence would suggest otherwise, as here I stood, eighteen years old and well into my eighth month of pregnancy. It was a poor excuse, I understood this, but last June and July, under the magic of the hot summer moon, I believed that Noah Utley loved me. Classic idiocy, revoltingly cliche, too stupid for words. Thinking back on it now, I compared myself to a puppy seeking affection; when Noah complimented me, I all but wriggled with the pleasure of it, believing every word he spoke, all his seemingly-sweet and heartfelt words, without any question. He may as well have scratched behind my ears. And, as anyone besides me could have predicted, here I was without him and carrying our baby. I had not seen a glimpse of him, nor heard a word—not even a phone call—since he returned to college last autumn.

"That's true, it's a trade-off either way," Grandma said, on the subject of inclement weather and pregnancy.

"Good morning," said Aunt Ellen, Grandma's older sister, tying her bathrobe as she joined us, reaching immediately for the coffee pot. "Camille, what's the story? Is she coming today, or what?" And she kissed my cheek before pouring herself a steaming cup.

"Who knows?" I asked, unable to keep a note of cynicism from my tone. The way it seemed right now, my daughter was planning a permanent residence in my uterus. But then I was assaulted anew, with pure terror, at the thought of having an actual infant in my arms, a tiny living person who would be solely dependent upon me. Grandma sensed the thought as its impact struck my face, as she resumed patting my back at once.

"It's all right, sweetie, we'll be here to help. You won't be alone," she assured me for the countless time, and I felt warmth slice across my heart, replacing some of the anxious fear. I knew Grandma meant those words, and I was well aware I should count every last blessing. Probably it was better, worlds better, to have two women with decades of experience in child-rearing at my side, rather than Noah Utley, who'd primarily been an expert at getting me out of my jean shorts. My mouth tasted bitter and I pushed aside any thoughts of my baby's errant father.

"I know, Gram," I said, easing to a standing position, drawing a slow breath. Grandma's familiar eyes were the exact same color as Mom's, a perfect blending of golden and green, with a darker ring surrounding her irises—the Davis family eyes, as Mom always said. I chose to live with Grandma and Aunt Ellen rather than with Mom and my sisters, who moved last summer into a rental house just across town. At first I missed them so much that my chest hurt when I lay awake night after restless night, plagued by a continual flow of anxious *what ifs*, but I'd slowly adjusted. And I saw Mom and Tish and Ruthie almost every day anyway, at the cafe. It was an understatement of gigantic proportions to say that things had changed for our family since last May—not the least of which being my parents' divorce. To be fair, my dad's cheating was the catalyst that ended their marriage, and despite Dad's efforts to beg Mom's forgiveness last summer, he was currently married to his co-worker Lanny, the two of them living in our old townhouse in Chicago.

In the meantime, Mom fell in love with Blythe Tilson, a man Grandma hired last spring to work at Shore Leave. Blythe is very good-looking, which is hard *not* to notice, but more importantly, he really loves my mom. When I first met Blythe last May, I wouldn't have believed in a hundred years that by Christmas he would be my stepdad. He is nothing but polite in my, Tish's, and Ruthie's presence, but I'm observant, and the expression in his eyes—which follow after my mom like a compass seeking north—tells me everything I don't exactly want to know. He can barely keep his hands from her when we're around, so I can't even begin to imagine how it is in private. That's another reason I would much rather live here at Shore Leave, in my own space.

It's just the same with my Aunt Jilly and her new husband, Justin Miller; the two of them make out all over the place, but then again, Aunt Jilly isn't my mother. It doesn't bother Clint, my cousin, one bit; honestly, I don't think Clint even notices, and like Mom, Aunt Jilly has been so happy since last summer, even while recuperating after her terrible car accident in September. Since then, Aunt Jilly and Clint moved across town to live with Justin in his house, and the idea is that I'll inherit Aunt Jilly's old apartment, the little two-bedroom space above the garage. No rush, in my opinion. I would rather be in the same house as Grandma and Aunt Ellen right after the baby comes; the thought of being alone with an infant, even close to assistance (as in, down a flight of steps and across the lawn), is a scary one. Besides, I wouldn't want to use those narrow stairs leading to the apartment, not with my bulging belly throwing off my balance; it was hard to imagine having to use them while lugging an infant car seat, but that would be my reality soon enough.

Aunt Jilly's and Uncle Justin's baby is due just two months after my own, and according to Aunt Jilly we are both having girls. Everyone in our family knows to take Aunt Jilly's Notions for truth. So at night in the darkness of my lonely little bedroom, I curl around my belly on the twin bed made up with the same flowered sheets that my mom used in high school, and contemplate holding a little bundle wrapped in pink, my very own daughter. No matter how incessantly I picture her, I know she won't exactly resemble my imaginings, though in my mind she looks like me—nothing like Noah. It hurts so much to imagine him as part of her. What if she looks like him? What if I can't bear it? These are the kinds of thoughts that plague me as I lay there watching the moon rise in the long, skinny dormer windows in my room. On clear nights, of which there are relatively few in a northern Minnesota winter, those windows are at a perfect angle to observe the moon. When the moon is new, and invisible, I watch the stars, caressing my belly and whispering to my daughter.

"Besides, she'd be early if she came today," I reminded my grandma and my great-aunt.

"Jo and Jilly both came early," Grandma said. "And you're so close to forty weeks now, there's nothing to worry about." She leaned to kiss my cheek before reminding Aunt Ellen, "Don't forget we have the whole crew tonight, for Valentine's. And Liz and Wordo are joining them."

"So we'll have the triplets, too," Ellen understood. "We'll be a full house. I better get baking."

Shore Leave Cafe was operational during the winter months, though on a limited schedule. We were closed Sunday through Wednesday, opening during the rest of the week for lunch and dinner. Our business in the winter months was typically limited to locals and the occasional hunters, ice fishermen or snowmobilers who braved the biting cold, snow, and driving wind. The cafe was closed tonight, even though it was Saturday and Valentine's Day, since most people sought a fancier restaurant for the big romantic night out. I almost rolled my eyes at the thought of having all the kids here, not in the mood. But then again, I missed my sisters and Clinty; since I wasn't attending school any longer, I didn't see them as much. Maybe we could roll out the Monopoly board? As they were so prone to of late, my eyes welled with hot tears.

"I don't know why I'm crying," I moaned, tipping forward. The baby performed what felt like a series of donkey kicks, as though in response. I felt so cumbersome, bloated as a milking cow, my ankles swollen along with just about every part of my formerly slim, agile body. Two huge pimples bloomed on my forehead, which was a pasty, midwinter white, my summer tan long since faded. I looked like something straight out of a birth-control manual: *Thinking about having sex? Take a gander at what pregnancy really looks like and see if you feel the same!*

"Camille," Grandma gently chided, and rested her cheek to my shoulder, rubbing my back in small, comforting circles.

"It's only natural," Aunt Ellen said calmly. The radio on the fridge was tuned to the local country station, as usual, and Dolly Parton sang softly about love. I wasn't a huge fan of country music, certainly not classic country, but living with Grandma and Aunt Ellen since last summer worked a spell over me; these days I found myself singing along with Loretta Lynn and Merle Haggard.

"I know," I sobbed, my throat full of shards. How could I admit that if I allowed myself, I would probably cry from dawn until dusk on a daily basis, and then the whole night through, burdened with guilty misery? I loved my baby already, there was no question, but I was so disoriented, disillusioned in all other regards, so often assaulted by thoughts of what my old friends from my former life were doing, back home in Chicago. How at this point in that life I would be writing college entrance letters and polishing my resume, with no more pressing decisions than which campus I might visit over spring break. On the current timeline, in which my life had sharply deviated from its intended path, I was learning about how it's difficult to go more than an hour or so without needing to find the nearest bathroom, how difficult it is to monkey an infant car seat into place, and that mothers find it absolutely necessary to inform a pregnant girl about how painful their own labors were—and how long.

I was a full forty pounds heavier than I'd been last summer; other than my sisters I was friendless, and my future seemed bleak—gray and lonely, peppered with uncertainty. College was out of the question, at least for the next foreseeable five years, surely more. Last spring I'd spent time contemplating if I would rather teach English or history at the high school level. The latter probably, as I'd always been intrigued with the little details that make up a series of events, the primary history found in letters and journals and old photographs. The Civil War era was my favorite and once upon a time I had envisioned myself as that cool, easygoing sort of teacher, my curly hair tied up into a bun and semi-sexy horn-rimmed glasses perched on my nose, creating meaningful and interesting lessons for an avid group of students who hung on my every word. This plan seemed within reach back then, and was currently as far as a star from Earth, and every bit as tangible.

You're a smart young woman, Camille Gordon were the words of nearly every teacher in my past. *You'll go places.*

Yes, I thought now. *As in to the grocery store for another box of diapers.*

"Why don't I make you some of that hot chocolate you like?" Aunt

Ellen asked as though I was a little girl, but I'd be a liar if I didn't admit that it comforted me deeply; letting her baby me a little felt good.

"And…" Grandma pursed her lips and tapped them with an index finger. "There's that old trunk I found in the attic. You wanted to look through it, remember?"

I brightened at this reminder, swiping away the messy evidence of tears. Not long ago Grandma came across a little leather trunk in the attic, crammed full of Davis family mementos. She had mentioned it last night, but I'd been too tired to trudge up there and take a look.

"I carried it downstairs so you don't have to manage those attic steps in your condition," Grandma said. "It's in my room. Why don't you go have a look and we'll finish up breakfast down here."

I nodded, hugging both of them before collecting the afghan from the back of the couch, draping it around my shoulders, and then climbing carefully up to the second floor. Grandma's room was dim in the early morning light, so I clicked on the bedside lamp. This space was comforting in the same way that smelling the scent of my mom's robe would be, familiar way down deep in my soul. Grandma's bed was made with her favorite old quilt, a tattered patchwork that her own grandmother, Myrtle Jean, had pieced together decades ago. Grandma's mother, Louisa, who we kids called Gran, passed away last summer, and I continued to miss her every day in some small way. None of us had yet grown accustomed to being at the cafe without seeing Gran sitting at her usual table, drinking coffee or an occasional cocktail, motoring around with her cane and dishing out advice a wise person would know to cherish. A word from eighth-grade vocabulary suddenly flashed across my memory.

Unflappable. The ability to maintain composure in all circumstances. This word perfectly described Gran—and all the women in my family, really—not counting me these days.

I saw the trunk near the foot of the bed, centered on the braided rag rug adorning the otherwise bare planks of the wooden floor. A beat of anticipation vibrated through me; the trunk looked old, overflowing with intriguing secrets, and I lowered myself with care, settling so that my lower back didn't bear all my weight. My baby pressed outward with her heels. I looked down at my belly, able to see the tiny points under my skin, moving along as though she meant to break free. I would never get over how incredible it was to feel a living person inside of me; I pushed gently upon the little protrusions, easing her into a more comfortable position.

"Look here," I murmured to her as I liked to do, but only if no one else was around. "It says 'Davis' on this trunk. That's our family's name."

With reverence, I ran my fingertips over the single word, which some-one had long ago carved into the leather buckling strap; from the look of it, with a knifepoint. The hinges creaked and once the lid was open the scent of leather was released, like a jinni from a lamp. With a grow-ing sense of wonder I studied the contents, debating what to touch first. Pictures, I decided. There were several small frames, one resting upside down, its black backing cracked with age. Finding myself drawn to that one in particular, I lifted it and parted the sides of the old hinged frame. I stared at the image. My lungs compressed. Immediately I turned the frame over, searching for a way to free the photograph. I released the tiny metal clasps and slid loose the old photographic paper, slightly alarmed at my haste. I only knew that I wanted to see it as fast as possible. There was a date scrawled on the back, and the words *Me & Aces*. Beneath that, *Carter* and *1875* were written with the same strong hand.

"It's you." The whisper rose from my lips like smoke from an ancient fire.

I flipped over the picture, which was so fragile that the edges were yellowed and curling; there was no protective glass in the frame. I would be sure to find a dictionary or some other equally weighty book in which to press it tonight, to flatten it out a little. I studied the image at close range, with complete absorption. I felt an unexpected rush of giddy an-ticipation, the way I used to feel as a little girl when Tish and I were into mysteries, and tried to find crimes to solve.

"Is Carter your first name, or last?" I wondered softly, tracing his face with gentle fingertips.

The photo was almost haunting in its simple beauty, sunset some-where in 1875. Here? Near here? It was tough to pinpoint a location but I was certain it was evening, as the long beams of a gorgeous setting sun backlit both man and horse. Something about his face, captured for all time in a half-grin, made my heart swell with an ache I could not begin to understand; my tendency to romanticize, I figured.

"And your horse," I murmured, my fingers still lingering on him.

Perhaps five years older than I was right now, he stood with his left arm hooked over his horse's neck, regarding the animal with an expression that was both fond and unconsciously sexy. Hatless, sleeves rolled back over lean forearms, he exuded a casual grace that was apparent even in the photograph. The image was rendered in muted browns and whites, with the yellowing tint of age, but I painted the colors from imagination—dark hair, blue denim, his horse a lovely auburn. As my eyes lingered on the man's face, I felt a jolt of what could only be acknowledged as physical attraction.

Wow, Camille, that's just great, I thought, with sharp-edged sarcasm. *The first time you feel drawn to someone in months and it's a man from 1875, even more unreachable than Noah Utley.*

"Who are you?" I whispered, reluctant to part with the photo. At last I relented, wanting to continue exploring the contents of the trunk. If anyone knew who he was, it would be Grandma and so I set aside the photograph with utmost care, angled so that I could look over at him and Aces, his horse, posing at sunset on that long-ago evening. Who took the picture? What was happening just outside the edges of the image? Who was with him as the sun sank? Curiosity flowed in my blood. My baby kicked and stirred as though to insist that she was besieged by the same desire to know more.

"We'll keep looking for answers," I promised, patting my belly. With my free hand I rummaged, with great care, elated as I withdrew a letter, folded three times as though to slide into a business-sized envelope. The paper was heavy, soft and browning with age, though the ink appeared crisp. I didn't think I was imagining that the handwriting looked the same as that on the back of the photograph. Heart hammering, I unfolded it.

"Oh *no!*" I was startled at the level of distress in my voice. The entire middle of the letter was ruined, a pinwheel of indecipherable black ink. I held it up, attempting to read beyond the edges of the spill.

July 16, 1875 - Bozeman, Montana

Dear Lorie-Lorie,

I cannot begin to tell you how much I miss everyone. I am ever so sorry I am not there for your birthday. I'm thinking of when we rode on the wagon from Missouri, sitting there talking about hoop snakes and how hard you laughed at my stories. It seems like yesterday. Aces is familiar at least, and I'm right glad he's with me, far as I am from home. I just wrote Boyd as well, but give kisses to everyone for me, please do. I'll be home by next summer, I do believe. I'll do my best. What I'm hoping for seems within reach for the first time since

"Since when?" I gasped. "Since what?"

The letter was a blurred mess after this word, until the very bottom, where he'd written his name with such a flourish that, try as I might, I could not tell what followed the letter *M* except loops and swirls.

"It's you, isn't it?" I demanded of the photograph, snatching it back into my grasp, not feeling foolish for addressing him in this way. "It's you and you were far from home. Why? What were you doing? Who's Lorie-Lorie?"

"Milla! Your hot chocolate's ready!" Grandma called from the kitchen.

"Coming!" I rolled to my knees and then used the edge of the mattress to help me stand, collecting the photograph and letter and waddling back to the kitchen, trying not to compare myself to a mama penguin. The Davis trunk had been loaded with other things but I possessed the two I wanted most.

Grandma stood at the stove frying bacon; I could smell toast and percolating coffee. Aunt Ellen was on the phone, sitting at the kitchen table with her feet propped on the adjacent chair.

Showing Grandma the photograph, I all but begged, "Who this is?"

Grandma tipped her chin and squinted, forehead wrinkling as she studied the image. She said, "He's cute, that's for sure. I have no idea under the sun, sweetie, sorry. Does it say on the back, maybe?"

Eagerly I showed her the words and then presented the letter, tucking the photograph under my chin in order to use both hands.

"I can't make out his name," I said. "Something with an *M*..."

"It says 'Carter' on the back," Grandma mused. "You know who to ask is Dodge. Or better yet, ask Bull the next time the Carters are in here."

"But that might not be until next week!" I protested, and Grandma raised her eyebrows at my tone. I took my voice down a notch and explained, "I'm just really curious is all."

"We'll see Dodge tonight when he brings the triplets. We'll ask him," Grandma said, referring to Dodge Miller, Uncle Justin's dad who had run the filling station around Flickertail Lake since before I was born. He also helped out at Shore Leave, performing a number of the heavy tasks that proved too much for Grandma and Aunt Ellen, such as mowing and hauling the dock out of the water before the lake froze; although these days Blythe and Uncle Justin took care of most of those duties.

"Did you ever get over to see White Oaks, like you were planning?" Grandma asked.

I shook my head, thinking of the image of the lovely old lodge which I'd swiped from the calendar that hung in the cafe, a locally-made one featuring Beltrami County businesses. Back in June, before getting pregnant, I'd wanted to visit White Oaks, parts of which had been built in the nineteenth century. Bull Carter, whose family originally settled the property, had been excited to show me around; according to Mom, he'd always been a history buff, like me. And now, more than ever, my interest in visiting the old, restored lodge was renewed.

I spent the day helping Aunt Ellen bake desserts, accompanied by the radio and a pot of coffee; we made two dozen snickerdoodle cookies, six lemon loaves, and a pan of banana bread. I ate nearly half of the first lemon loaf straight out of the oven, slathering each slice with butter before it completely cooled. (There was no question why I'd gained so much weight). Before evening fully advanced, I changed from navy blue sweatpants into gray ones and tugged a clean maternity t-shirt over my size double-D bra, as I'd accidentally dribbled grape juice on myself. At last I collected the bristle brush from my nightstand, from beside the picture of M-something Carter and his horse, which I'd propped against my reading lamp. For the hundredth time today I paused to study them, tracing my touch over the letter, likewise nearby. Yet again I touched the man's handsome, half-smiling face, caressing him, shivering a little.

I dragged myself away, finding Grandma to ask if she'd braid my hair.

"Of course." She paused in her task of wiping down the counter, seating me at the kitchen table and working the brush through my curls. Her hands conveyed love and the touch sent prickles along my nerves, sweet relaxation. I loved being touched this way, with such tenderness. She said, as she always did, "You have such beautiful hair."

Grandma was so dear. She never bitched at me for eating too much, or suggested that I refrain from drinking coffee. She brushed my hair almost every night and told me stories about her own pregnancies and the days when Mom and Aunt Jilly were little, her voice lulling and comforting, keeping me sane.

"Thank you," I murmured, eyes drifting closed.

The sky had darkened from a silvery tin to pewter-gray as evening came creeping. Snow mounded along the sides of the house and the cafe, in great rounded drifts taller than me in some places, with no sign of retreat anytime soon. Flickertail lay cloaked in still silence, a solid blue-white expanse of ice, dusted with powdered-sugar snow. Pam Tillis sang on the radio. I'd never spent the winter in northern Minnesota; we'd always returned to Chicago after summer. Winter here meant snow on a daily basis, venturing out only when necessity dictated, such as periodic trips to the local grocery store, but at times I found the isolation oddly peaceful. Proof that I was either acclimating to my new surroundings or slowly losing my mind.

No more crying, I thought as Grandma braided with skillful fingers. *Everyone will be here soon and you can't act like a child.*

Another part of me wailed plaintively, *But you* are *a child, really. You're not a mother, not by a long shot. You fooled around last summer and this is what happened. And you're stuck with it. And that son of a bitch is off at college in Madison as though none of this happened.*

It stung like hell, I couldn't pretend otherwise. Despite that fact that Noah's parents, Curt and Marie Utley, were kind to me and made an effort to stop out to Shore Leave at least twice a month, I had not received a word from Noah. After I told him the news last summer he showed signs of immediate retreat. In one of the most insulting and cowardly displays I'd ever been forced to experience, he told me he would pay for an abortion. He didn't want the responsibility of a child, he said, refusing to listen to why I wouldn't consider that option, disregarding my feelings on the matter. To Noah, the suggestion and subsequent offer of money were the easy way out; I had never confessed to anyone that his words that day sent cold spikes straight to my toes. For the first time in my life, I felt I understood what it meant to be called a whore, even indirectly.

"I'll make him disappear," Clint, ever chivalrous, told me. "Seriously, Milla, I will. I'll find a way."

Tish was part of this vengeful plot as well, chiming in with, "We'll figure out a way. No one will ever know."

Now, eight and half months into the realities of pregnancy, I found myself wishing that I'd taken them up on their offer. Although it wouldn't get me any closer to providing my child with a father.

The baby has you. You're who she needs, not him. Fuck Noah, I thought, with bitter pain; it was cold comfort, at best. At least my own father had stuck it out with my mom, for many years. They'd been teenaged parents but at least Dad stayed around. It may not have been a match made in heaven, so to speak, but they'd tried.

"Jo's here!" Aunt Ellen called, breaking the train of my dark thoughts, peering out the front windows as headlights beamed down the long, icy driveway. Grandma finished braiding, patted my head, and went to welcome everyone. Moments later the house was inundated with the bustling, busy chatter of Mom, Tish, Ruthie, and Blythe. My sisters raced to me, Ruthie kneeling to address my belly, as she liked to do, Tish hugging me around the shoulders; her soft curls tickled my face, the scent of her strawberry shampoo filled my nose.

My sisters always acted like they hadn't seen me in ages, which melted my heart, even though I pretended to be annoyed as Tish inadvertently stepped on my toes. Tish was the only one of the three of us without the golden-green Davis eyes. Instead, hers are like Aunt Jilly's, electric-blue and long-lashed. Her dark hair had grown out since last summer and currently hung just below her shoulders, curling like coiled springs. Ruthie, my youngest sister, crouched near my chair and smiled up at me. Her summer freckles had faded away and she was as adorable as ever, would always be my baby sister despite the fact that she had turned thirteen in January.

"Milla, you look pretty," Ruthie said, and I rolled my eyes in pretended exasperation.

"Not really," I disagreed. "I look like a whale with zits."

"Jake came, too," Tish leaned close to murmur, and immediately I felt my teeth go on edge.

"Seriously?" I yelled in a whisper. I knew Mom liked their neighbor boy Jake McCall, but these days it was as though he'd been inducted into our family. Tish joked that he was our personal Theodore Lawrence, like from *Little Women*, but I didn't share this opinion or find that funny. The worst thing was I knew Jake liked me—and nothing, including my pregnancy, my terrible attitude, and my habit of working to discourage any such feelings, had dissuaded him yet. I raged, still quietly, "Where's Mom?"

I meant to accost my mother in private but when she came into the kitchen to hug me, all of my irritation drained away. Instead I marveled at her, this woman I'd known my entire life looking like a gorgeous stranger, dressed in a big black parka with a furry hood. Her golden hair spilled over her shoulders and she wore a short, apple-green skirt and high-heeled black boots. It was her overwhelming happiness, I realized, that altered her appearance, radiating outward from her face, making her seem young and carefree; it wasn't that she hadn't been happy all the years I'd been a part of her life—it was just that I'd seen her as a mother, nothing more, certainly not a sexy-looking woman with the same wishes and desires as any of us. I still grappled with these thoughts; no matter how much I believed I'd grown up in the past year, I understood I still had fathoms to go.

"Hi, love," Mom said, rocking me side to side in her puffy-coat arms. She drew back and smoothed hair from my face. "How are you feeling today? I like how Grandma braided your hair."

"Fine," I said succinctly, and opened my mouth to complain about her hauling Jake along without even asking when he came barreling into the kitchen carrying a LIFE game box, grinning widely as he spied me.

Jesus Crimeny, I thought, while realizing how mean and uncharitable I was acting.

"Hey there, Camille."

"Hey," I said lamely.

"How are you doing?" he asked next.

"Fine," I said again, with no answering smile.

Tish, facing away from everyone else, sent me a message with her eyes, clearly communicating, *Lighten up!*

Blythe came into the kitchen behind Jake just as the front door opened again, emitting a blast of cold air along with Aunt Jilly, Uncle Justin, and Clinty. Clint threw his scarf and stocking cap to the side and darted into the house to grab a handful of snickerdoodles.

"Hi, guys," he said, mouth full.

"Hey there, little buddy," Blythe said, catching Clint around the neck and knuckling his head, with pure affection; everyone loved Clint. Blythe towered over all of us despite Clint's recent growth spurt, wearing faded jeans and an indigo-blue coat. He was growing out his hair again because Mom liked it that way. Of course his eyes were on Mom, admiring, though he managed to pull his gaze away to say, "Hi, Camille."

"Hey," I responded as the door slammed open once more and the final guests arrived, Uncle Justin's little sister Liz, her husband Wordo, and their triplets, Fern, Linnea, and Hal, who were Ruthie's best friends in Landon. Dodge, Justin and Liz's dad, arrived with them, roaring like a bear about something in the entryway. I smiled a little, despite everything. Our household was never quiet for long.

"Camille, I dreamed about you last night," Aunt Jilly said, squirreling through everyone and into the kitchen, moving gracefully in spite of her protruding belly. Aunt Jilly was smaller than Mom, though otherwise they resembled each other closely. She was a pixie, small and pretty, her silky golden hair having grown enough to brush her jaw on either side. She took my face lightly in her warm hands and I felt a little jolt. With soft certainty she said, "You've met someone. Or..." She cocked her head and narrowed her vivid blue eyes, as though in speculation. "Or, you're on a course to meet someone. Something's changed."

"I don't exactly get out much," I reminded her, though my pulse had already started increasing. Immediately I thought of the photograph. I considered replying, *Yes, I've met the perfect man. Problem is he's been dead for probably more than eighty years.*

Aunt Jilly bit her lower lip, considering—I felt as though she'd just read my mind, to the word—and finally saying, "Doesn't matter."

"Doesn't matter that he's dead?" I whispered.

Her eyes narrowed further but she didn't seem startled. She only shook her head.

"Honey-love, I can't find the tickets," Uncle Justin said, coming behind Aunt Jilly and catching her around the waist. He wore a black stocking cap with a tassel on the top, bending down to rest his chin on Aunt Jilly's shoulder. He said, "Hi, Milla. You look ready to pop."

"So sensitive, this one," Aunt Jilly responded, reaching to smack his ass. "But I love him anyway."

Years ago, Uncle Justin had been badly burned in an accident in his mechanic shop, leaving his face scarred all along the right side, but I'd been around him long enough that I barely noticed his scars anymore. Like Blythe, Uncle Justin was a really good guy; I could only dream of finding a man who looked at me the way that he looked at my Aunt Jilly. I could almost feel the residual heat from his gaze as he regarded his wife with a lazy grin.

"Heaven knows where I'd be if you didn't, baby," he said to her.

"We'll see you in the morning," Mom said, popping back into the room, coming to kiss my forehead. She knew I was annoyed that she'd brought Jake, because she whispered, "Try to have fun tonight."

All the adults other than Dodge, Grandma, and Aunt Ellen proceeded into the snowy night to enjoy a Valentine's celebration. They were driving into Bemidji for dinner and drinks. And apparently something that required tickets.

"Who wants to play?" Jake asked the room at large, hefting the LIFE box high into the air.

Clint, Ruthie, and the triplets all galloped after him, setting up the board on the kitchen table while Grandma loaded cookies and banana bread onto snack trays. Dodge followed Aunt Ellen into the kitchen. He boomed, "Camille, sweetheart, haven't you had that baby yet?"

"*Ugh,*" I groaned at his question, the last thing in the world you ask a pregnant woman; but because it was Dodge, I couldn't be too annoyed. I stood, Tish lending me both hands, and Dodge wrapped me into a bear hug. Something about his arms reminded me of my own dad, back home in Chicago with his new wife Lanny, and I felt an unexpected stab of homesickness. As much as I was glad to be in Landon, I still occasionally missed the big city, experienced a twinge of longing for our spacious townhouse with its view of the glittering Chicago skyline.

"Hey," I asked, shoving aside the thought, turning to Tish. "Can you run up to my room and grab the picture and the letter on my nightstand?"

Tish shrugged and said, "Sure," darting away while I tried not to let myself be too jealous of her lithe body and ability to move unencumbered.

"Camille found a photograph that you might know about," Aunt Ellen told Dodge.

"It's from 1875," I said, helping myself to yet another snickerdoodle. I poured a huge glass of milk and then leaned against the counter to dunk my cookie in small increments.

"I love the horse! Lookit!" Tish enthused, racing back into the kitchen, brandishing the picture. "Remember that one time Dad took us horseback riding near here? That was great. I wasn't afraid at all. You were."

"I was not," I disagreed. "I was just uncertain."

Dodge reached for the photograph and studied it closely, flipping it to examine the words on the back. He finally said, "Bull would probably know, hon. His family has been around the Landon area since just after the Civil War. His great-something granddaddy built White Oaks, initially. Most people don't know, but the main structure of the building was constructed in the late 1860s. Of course they've updated and added on since then. But that little entrance and the porch off the side are original."

"That's what Bull told me last summer," I said, aware of the tinge of excitement in my voice. "Can we drive over there tonight and ask him?"

"Right now?" Tish asked skeptically, crowding Dodge's elbow. "Like, who cares that much?"

"I do," I insisted.

"Milla, you're in your pajamas," Dodge observed. "And in no condition to be out and about in this weather."

I didn't bother to explain that I wasn't wearing pajamas...that this was just how very pregnant women dressed all the time. I knew I wasn't about to win this one, so with complete reluctance I agreed, "All right, but I want to talk to him soon. Gram, can we have lunch at White Oaks tomorrow?"

"We'll see," was all Grandma said; like all kids, I'd learned long ago that this was the sort of answer used to pacify, not promising anything. I would likely be using it regularly for the next eighteen years.

Tish asked, "You wanna play LIFE with those guys?"

"Not really," I said, swishing my cookie through the glass of milk. "Let's just watch."

My sister and I joined everyone at the table, drawing up chairs at the far end where we could chat in relative peace. I was buttering another slice of banana bread when Tish said, "Everyone at school is wondering where you are, and wondering if you've had the baby. I told like ten people yesterday to quit asking me."

My experience at Landon High had proven a sharp contrast to that at River Dell, the plushy private school we'd attended in Chicago. At River Dell I was part of a tight-knit circle of friends and involved in a medley of resume-boosting activities, such as student government and soccer. Here in Landon, my formerly shiny reputation was so severely tarnished that it was more than a relief to drop out last week, under the excuse of maternity leave. Jake was unfailingly kind to me, even though I hadn't seen him much at school; we didn't have any classes together.

The girls at Landon High had whispered about me—and not always behind my back, making snide remarks I was meant to hear; the basic consensus seemed to be that I was the big-city girl who'd gotten popular, innocent Noah Utley into trouble. The cruelest of them was named Mandy Pearson, a tall, intimidating girl with unforgiving eyes. As if she had any right calling me a slut, when everyone knew she gave head under the bleachers at football games. But so it goes. I knew Mom and Grandma expected me to go back and finish classes, graduate in June or perhaps into the summer. I hadn't yet broken the news to them that I was not about to set foot within that high school ever again.

"You don't have to tell anyone anything," I told Tish, with more bite in the words than I'd intended, shifting so that my belly didn't cut off my air supply. Dodge had given the photo back to me and I placed it on the table with great care. Before I knew what I was doing, I began stroking M. Carter's face.

"I know," Tish responded, forehead wrinkling as she observed me caressing the old photograph. She didn't comment on that, but I heard concern leaking into her voice as she asked, "Are you lonely all day here?"

I shook my head. "Not exactly. It's not like I'm alone."

"Are you going to work at the cafe this spring?"

"Yeah, that's the plan."

"What about school?" she persisted.

"What about it?" I asked. "I'm not going back there. I'll get my GED or something." And then, at the reality of those words, I could have cried until my throat was raw.

Tish studied me, her face set in an expression that suggested deep concentration; though she was not particularly observant she often read my mind with impressive clarity. Being closer to me in age, Tish and I shared more memories and consequently fought over things far more often than Ruthie and me. I couldn't remember the last time I'd bickered with Ruthie about anything, but then again I couldn't remember a time before Tish, who knew me better than just about anyone. A trade-off for all the fighting, I supposed.

"I worry about you," Tish said at last.

I held her familiar gaze, marveling at the blue depths of her irises; she, Clint, and Aunt Jilly shared those gorgeous, long-lashed eyes. It touched me that she would be worried.

"What if my baby never has a little sister or brother?" I heard myself whisper, as though it had just occurred to me. In truth this notion plagued me, clamping about my heart like a cold fist. "I can't imagine what my life would be like without you, and Ruthie…"

"She will," Tish said, infusing her voice with conviction. She saw that I was not convinced and repeated, almost sternly, "She *will*. It'll be all right."

"Thank you," I whispered, swallowing away the urge to cry.

She reached to place her palms against the roundness of my belly and I noticed that her fingernails were painted bright red and forest-green, every other nail; I wondered how Ruthie had talked her into that. She marveled, "I can't get over how firm it feels, like a basketball under your shirt." She rubbed her hands in big, sweeping circles and teased, "No, I'm wrong. It feels more like a beach ball."

"Jesus *Crimeny*," I grumbled, using my go-to phrase of exasperation; I couldn't help but giggle, eyeing the enormous swelling that currently comprised my front side. My breasts were the size of honeydew melons and still didn't come close to outpacing the beach ball of my stomach.

Down the table everyone was leaning on their elbows, intent on watching Clint spin the needle on the game board, but Jake looked up at that moment and caught my eye, offering a warm smile. I forced myself to return his smile; my low mood was hardly Jake's fault.

"Well, doesn't it?" Tish persisted, patting the roundness of my stomach as though it was a puppy on my lap.

"I'm *pregnant*," I muttered.

She leaned closer and with a startling change of subject whispered, "Hey, you should be nicer to Jake."

I felt my eyebrows draw together as though magnetized; I didn't even have to utter a word for Tish to retract the comment.

"*Re-lax*," she grumbled, drawing the word into two distinct syllables; recognizing that my patience was dangerously thin she leaned toward the activity of the game, demanding, "Who's winning?"

No crying, I ordered harshly.

I'd never considered myself a vain person. Last summer was the first time I'd actually gone out of my way to get someone to notice me, that someone of course being Noah Utley. The first week we were in Landon, last May, he'd been hanging out with a group of teenagers at the beach and their group merged with ours. Clint, who had never lived anywhere other than Landon, knew everyone and introduced Tish and me around. Noah and I talked for an hour that afternoon, and exchanged numbers; I'd been so giddy with nerves at his attention that I could hardly sleep that night. Mom was in her own world last summer and so it was with very little difficulty that I was able to see Noah on an increasingly regular basis.

I loved his kisses, and the way he touched me—we'd spent many evenings fooling around before we'd gone all the way. But that was his end goal, I understood clearly now, the reason he pushed a little more each time—*Let me take this off*, he'd murmur, kissing my neck as he eased down my bikini top to cup my breasts. *You'll like this*, he'd insist, unzipping my shorts. And as the lowest blow of all, *I love you, Camille. I love you so much*—this he'd spoken as he spread my thighs, kneeling between them and with a few jerking shoves, taking my virginity. Looking back now, knocked up and alone, I realized that he was playing me all along, telling me he loved me so that I would let him have his way.

I was basically inexperienced, even still. Noah and I had sex probably about ten times, and I was so nervous about getting caught that it hadn't been exactly earth-shattering on any of those occasions. The first time, I'd bled all over the place in the backseat of his car, so embarrassed. He said he couldn't believe I was a virgin, even though I told him so, as though I would have lied about it. I didn't know which occasion led to the baby, as we'd used a condom every single time. Now when I considered the concept of sex I nearly cringed; at present, it seemed repulsive. Besides, who in the world would possibly be interested in dating a single mom without so much as a high school degree?

Tears burned the bridge of my nose. Under the guise of getting more milk, I escaped to the fridge and that's exactly where I was standing when I felt a strange shift in my lower belly. I made an inadvertent noise of alarm, bending forward, and then a sudden soaking wetness flowed from between my legs, darkening my sweat pants. I stared wordlessly, uncomprehending. It wasn't until my knees started to tremble that I managed to whimper, "Grandma…"

Grandma, Aunt Ellen, and Dodge were in the living room and didn't hear me. The only person who did was Jake, because he was watching me from the table. I saw the concern that lifted his eyebrows and he was at my side in an instant, getting his left arm around my back.

"Did your…are you…" He sounded like a little kid, his voice wavering with uncertainty.

"Yes," I answered. My knees would not stop shaking and I gripped Jake's other arm, clinging to him. He was tall and lanky, but strong enough that I felt as though I wouldn't topple him straight over; I probably outweighed him by twenty pounds. We were attracting attention now; Ruthie bounded over with her eyes round as silver dollars.

"*Grandma!*" she yelped, and this time the cry generated action.

"Is the baby coming?" Tish cried, everyone crowding around me as though I was a new attraction in the zoo.

Grandma came around the corner like a woman on a mission. She took one look at me and called over her shoulder, "Dodge, get the truck running! Camille, sweetie, your water just broke."

I started to cry, in pure terror, and Ruthie and Grandma moved to hug me; squashed between them and Jake, I could hardly breathe. Grandma nudged Jake to the side and said quietly, "There's nothing to cry about, dear one, it's all right." She turned and began issuing orders. "Tish, run and grab your sister a clean outfit. Her hospital bag is at the foot of her bed. Jake, you stay here with the kids while we get Camille to the hospital."

"Yes, ma'am," Jake said instantly. His eyes were somber with the responsibility of it all.

"Ruthie, call your mom and Aunt Jilly, tell them to meet us in Rose Lake," was Grandma's next command.

"Can I come with?" Ruthie begged, her right arm laced through mine.

I looked down at her, flooded with a rush of tenderness. I swiped at my tears, nodding. It still hadn't quite sunk in that my child was on her way, that very soon, maybe even before morning, I would be holding my daughter. My knees jittered even more fiercely.

"Of course," I told Ruthie. I looked at Tish, standing near Clint, both of them regarding me with wide eyes. I asked, "You want to come, too?"

She shook her head at once. "Sorry, Milla, I'd rather see the baby after."

"Patricia!" Grandma ordered, using Tish's full name. "Get hustling, child!"

Less than ten minutes later, I sat belted beside Dodge in his quarter-ton pickup, Aunt Ellen, Grandma, and Ruthie all crammed into the tiny backseat. Grandma kept one hand on my shoulder as Dodge expertly navigated the snowy roads.

"It probably will take a while, once we get there," Grandma warned. "First babies are notoriously inconsiderate."

I was bundled into a coat and boots, my entire body shuddering now, despite the heat churning from the dashboard vents.

"Are you having contractions?" Ruthie inquired, almost bouncing with excitement. "What names are you thinking of, Milla? You'll have to pick one so soon!"

Just as she asked a knife-edged band of pain encircled my hips. I hissed a little, leaning forward, and Dodge patted my left knee. "Hang on, hon, we'll get you there."

"We'll think about names later," Grandma told Ruthie.

The pain rippled outward and I groaned, hunching around my belly. "It hurts, Grandma. I'm so scared."

"You're just fine," Grandma said, cupping my shoulder with her warm hand. She insisted, "Just fine, Camille. It's a baby, not a dinosaur."

I giggled a little at her words, before another contraction seized my insides. I tried to breathe like the nurse explained during my last visit.

"They're coming fast," Grandma said. "You know what, you may just have a Valentine's surprise."

Mom and Aunt Jilly arrived in the room just as the nurse handed me the newly-bathed bundle of my daughter. I lay there in the hospital bed, sweating and depleted, tears streaming even as I felt a smile stretch across my face. Ruthie had been a trooper, witnessing the entire messy miracle without a shudder; Grandma had not left my side. Noah Utley did not cross my mind once during the ordeal.

"Camille," Mom said softly, from the foot of the bed. She and Aunt Jilly both wore their parkas, having sprinted inside from the snowy night. As one, they moved to join Grandma and Ruthie. Mom leaned to kiss my forehead, smoothing hair from my temple as tears washed over her cheeks. She murmured, "Look at you, look at my girl. You did so well, sweetheart, so well. Look at your baby." She bent to kiss my daughter's tiny, wrinkly-red face.

Aunt Jilly whispered, "You're a mother. I can already foresee lots of trouble-making between her and this one," and she indicated her own belly. "Lots of shenanigans."

"I'm so sorry we weren't here." Mom's voice was rough with emotion. "How was everything? I'm so sorry I didn't get here for you."

"Mama, the baby was practically born already by the time *we* got here," Ruthie explained. "The doctor said Camille must have been dilated for the past few days. She was at eight by the time someone checked."

"Listen to this expert," Aunt Jilly joked, catching Ruthie into a hug. "So, what do you have to say about the whole thing, little one? Was the birthing experience everything you thought it would be?"

Ruthie giggled, detailing the past hour for Mom and Aunt Jilly while I studied my daughter, tucked into a soft pink hospital blanket. She weighed an even eight pounds and I couldn't stop marveling at how perfect she was, down to her little curly toes. And her fingernails! I lifted her miniature hand and examined the bitty nails; they were too tiny to contemplate. I still couldn't settle on what color I thought her eyes were, though Grandma said that you couldn't really tell for a few days, if not weeks. Her cheeks were round and pink, her scalp covered in silky black hair already at least two inches long. ("Did that tickle you on the way out?" Ruthie had asked, in all seriousness).

"What are you going to call her?" Mom asked, stroking the baby's chin with a gentle finger. She crooned, "Hi there, little girl, what a sweet little baby girl. Oh, Camille, she looks just like you did."

"I was thinking I'd call her Millie Jo," I said, clearing my throat in an attempt to force away the lump of emotion. "Millie Joelle, but we'll call her Millie Jo." Mom's eyes flashed to mine and I felt a catch in my heart. I whispered, "Was this how you felt?"

She nodded, pressing a kiss on my temple; her tears were warm on my skin, combining with mine. She whispered, "That's a lovely name, sweetheart."

"It suits her," Aunt Jilly agreed.

"Everyone decent in there?" Uncle Justin asked from the hallway. "We're all out here dying to see the baby!"

"Come in," I told them. From the waist down I was safely tucked under a hospital blanket and Blythe, Dodge, Aunt Ellen, and Uncle Justin all crowded into the room to meet Millie Jo.

Chapter Two

March, 2004

"GRANDMA, SHE WON'T STOP CRYING," I MOANED. I WANTed to sink into my bed and not stop crying either. My head swam with dizzy exhaustion, an insistent pounding centered behind my right eye. My breasts were probably larger than regulation footballs, my nipples at last beginning to adjust to the constant demand upon them. During the first week they not only dribbled milk but cracked and bled, to the point that I cringed every time Millie Jo latched on to nurse. Which was about every fifteen minutes or so, give or take.

"Let me walk with her for a minute," Grandma murmured, collecting my squalling daughter from my arms. I sank to the rocking chair positioned near my dresser. It was three in the morning and a full-scale snow storm raged outside. It was a late-season blast of ice and snow, the snow especially heavy and wet, and I felt as though it would never be spring again, in both Landon and in my heart. Just now my entire life was centered upon a seemingly never-ending winter, in which I was claustrophobically trapped within the house, tethered to a baby that would not stop screaming unless she was eating.

Grandma bobbed gently up and down as she walked the hall; she made a circuit with Millie Jo, coming back into my line of view every ten seconds or so. I felt just this side of insane as I sat there in a stupor and studied the slice of light thrown by the overhead fixture in the hallway. My hair was scraggly and dirty, jammed into a messy bun; I'd worn the same pair of sweatpants for the past three weeks, my nails were bitten to the quick and my child seemed to hate me. I couldn't reconcile her unceasing weeping in any other way.

I hate this, I thought, and then cringed away from the piercing guilt. *No, I don't mean that. I don't hate my life. I just hate that I'm so tired and nasty-looking right now. I hate that I can't think straight and that my baby won't stop screaming. Why? What's wrong with her?*

I slipped a thumbnail between my teeth before realizing there was nothing left to bite. It took me a while to comprehend that Grandma had managed to quiet Millie Jo; the absence of sound pressed on my ears, seeming unfamiliar.

"Is she..." I whispered, hardly daring to breathe as Grandma crept back into the bedroom.

She nodded and deposited Millie Jo onto the bed, where she'd slept with me since the night we brought her home from the hospital. Anxiety pressed at my spine as I waited, anticipating the wailing of the fire engine that were my baby's vocal cords, but she curled up on her belly like a plump little puppy and blessedly continued sleeping.

"Thank you," I murmured to Grandma, tears collecting in my lashes, and she hugged me, patting my back.

"Rest a bit," she insisted, and I didn't need to be told twice; with great care, as though settling near a bomb that would discharge at the slightest movement, I curled beside my tiny daughter. Grandma went back to her own room, neglecting to click out the hall light, but I was too exhausted to get up and turn it off myself. Instead I let my gaze touch the photograph of M. Carter, just visible in the dim amber glow.

Who were you? Oh God, tell me who you were. I need to know. What were you hoping for? What's your full name?

My thoughts were disjointed, fuzzy, almost the same experience as being high, which I had been exactly one time in my life, back home in Chicago, sophomore year. I drifted for a time, dreaming but still vaguely aware of my surroundings. Sometime later I felt a small stirring, low in my belly. M. Carter suddenly seemed real, as though I was peering through an open window rather than at a still photograph; as I watched, he looked up and outward, right at me, the half-grin becoming a full-scale one. The sight of it caved in my chest and I leaped out the window and to the earth below, bathed in the slanted beams of that long-ago sunset. The ground was dusty and warm beneath my bare feet as I ran. I felt welcome sun all along my hair and shoulders, dusting over my cheekbones like caressing fingers; the coppery quality of the summer evening made my throat ache with need, which swelled as swiftly as a flooding creek—a need for *him*. The air was scented by a recent rain, sharp and immediately recognizable.

You're here. Overjoyed at the prospect of holding him close, I absolutely threw myself into his open arms. Behind him, Aces, his beautiful chestnut horse, made a soft whickering noise. He laughed, spinning us in a circle as I clung to his neck, my cheek against his collarbones. My feet were off the ground. I was so happy that laughter and tears closed off my throat.

Of course I am, he whispered against my hair, halting our slow spin and letting me to the ground. His body fit against mine as though we'd been carved from a single piece of wood. It was where I belonged, and I understood this as pure and simple truth. He spoke my name then, not Camille, but somehow I knew he meant *me*, his voice husky and warm, and so very familiar.

On the bed in my chilly little room in wintertime Landon, eyes tightly closed, I twitched, heart throbbing, skimming both palms over my belly and then lower, where I applied pressure. A passionate force built within me, spiraling outward.

I've missed you so much, I told him, pressing closer, hearing the bass grumble of thunder on that distant summer evening, echoing the wild pulsing in my heart and between my legs. *Where have you been, Malcolm? I've been so worried!*

He took my face in his hands and his eyes beat into mine, intense and heated.

Tell me! I begged. Happiness gave way to accelerating fear. *Where? Tell me! I'll find you!*

Cold rain began to fall, striking my eyes—and dissolving him.

No! Malcolm! I screamed, fighting to hold onto him, sliced to the bone with terror. He was disappearing, literally before my eyes, being washed away by the increasing rain, and there was nothing I could do to stop it. My hands fell through empty air, clutching at the space he had only just occupied. Thunder detonated and I flinched awake, the cold rain-splatter on my face becoming hot tears that gushed over my temples as I woke to winter darkness, clamped in the grip of a terrible, sharp-edged nightmare. Heart in panic mode, I floundered to the side, straining desperately to cling to the heart of what I'd been dreaming…

What was happening?

It's important…

I can't remember, oh God, I can't remember…

The nightmare flickered like a candle flame in a mounting wind and then blinked from existence, settling to dust as I lay there in my charcoal-tinted bedroom, hearing the rise and fall of my baby daughter's breathing.

"Can I hold her again?" Ruthie begged, gliding her fingertip over Millie Jo's satin cheek. It was a Saturday night late in March and basketball championships played on the tiny television behind the bar. Aunt Jilly and Mom were busy taking care of the crowd, Aunt Ellen behind the bar while Blythe and his step-grandpa, Rich, manned the kitchen; Grandma sat at the till near the front door, going over receipts. Outside the snow appeared dense, a thick, cream-cheese frosting causing tree limbs to bow beneath its weight, but it had melted at least six inches. Within a few weeks we might even be able to see the porch boards.

"Here, but be careful," I ordered, passing Millie to her.

Ruthann grinned big enough to showcase nearly all of her teeth and cuddled her niece close, resettling on the booth seat opposite me. Tish, on Ruthie's right side and closest to the window, leaned over and poked her index finger at Millie's nose.

"God, Tish, *don't,*" I bitched. "What are you doing?"

"Hi, pretty girl," Ruthie murmured. She looked up at me and declared, "She's going to have your eye color, I can tell."

"You think?" I'd been speculating the same thing lately. So far Millie didn't look much like either me or Noah. Her hair was crow-wing black and her skin had mellowed from bright red to a softer pink. She'd gained weight in the past month and was truly adorable—at least when she wasn't screeching.

"Have you heard from Noah at all?" Tish asked.

I said, with quiet resignation, "Has the answer ever been different? You asked me last week, too."

"But his parents have come to see her, right?"

I nodded.

"Does he give you money?" Tish persisted.

"His parents are going to take care of it until he's done with college," I said, wounded to my core with the shame of this. "I told them I didn't want their stupid money…well, I didn't say it *exactly* like that…but they insisted." Tears threatened but I swiped them angrily away, not about to cry over the pathetic situation; it irritated me that since becoming a mother, all emotional response seemed connected to my tear ducts.

"Aren't they embarrassed that their kid is such a deadbeat?" Ruthie asked, her eyes on Millie.

"I would hope they are," I said. "They've apologized for him about a hundred times. Apparently his program at college is *stressful* and that's why he hasn't called me."

My sisters heard the venom in my voice and both studied me with varying degrees of caution. I let my gaze drift out the window, framing an evening sky the gray of an old tin washtub; by contrast, inside the cafe it was cozy and warm, full of the bustle of a Saturday night crowd. The dining room smelled like fried fish and fried potatoes, perking coffee and beer.

I exhaled a slow breath and ran one hand through my uncombed hair; I'd tied it back in a ponytail but the rubber band had broken and I didn't have the energy to dig through the junk drawer behind the counter for a replacement.

"Well, you've got us," Ruthie said, ever the sweetheart.

I managed a small smile for them, noticing at the same instant that Jake McCall was here, pushing through the front door to the tinkle of the bell. He caught sight of us and zeroed in like a homing pigeon, grinning with apparent happiness. He wore a red parka and a battered Twins cap, and moved to sit down with no invitation whatsoever. Having little choice, I scooted over to let him squeeze onto the bench beside me.

"I just got my acceptance letter to the U of M," he said with unmistakable excitement, referring to the university in Minneapolis.

I should have been happy for him, I knew it, but instead felt only double swellings of jealousy and resentment; such things should have been arriving in the mail for me. Immediately my gaze fluttered to Millie, guilt assaulting like a fist to the solar plexus.

I love you, baby. I sent her the silent message with all my strength. *I really do. It's not your fault my life is hard right now.*

"Good for you," Tish said to Jake, leaning over the table on her elbows. She wore an old sweater of mine, striped green and cream; I saw that it now bore a tiny hole in the right shoulder. Oh, well; it wasn't as though I would be wearing any of my old clothes in the near future. Tugging as unobtrusively as possible at the wide strap of my heavy-duty nursing bra, I felt destined to be this overweight and dumpy for the remainder of my life.

Jake said, "It was my first choice. I can't wait to live in the city." He really was fairly clueless, as he turned to me and asked, with clear enthusiasm, "Where would be your top choice, under other circumstances?"

Instead of completely losing my cool, as my instinct dictated, I bit back a sigh and admitted, "I always wanted to go to Northwestern, in Chicago. It's where my dad went."

"And now you're stuck here," he observed, clearly intending to empathize; I shrugged noncommittally. "In a few years, maybe?"

"That's where I want to go to law school," Tish said. "But I'd like to get my undergrad degree at the U of M." And I had no doubt she would accomplish both of these things; Tish was nothing if not determined.

"How's Millie Jo?" Jake asked, peering at her in Ruthie's arms.

"She's getting bigger every day," I said.

"She's beautiful." Jake nudged his left shoulder against my right, adding, "Just like her mom."

I felt the twin beams of my sisters' smiles at this statement; they adored Jake, and had pestered me about dating him ever since last autumn.

I forced myself to reply, "Thank you. That's nice of you to say."

He smiled sweetly and I supposed I should say something complimentary in return. I studied him for a moment, his familiar face under the brim of his cap. Like all of us, his summer tan had long since faded, which made his long-lashed eyes appear all the more chocolate-brown, by contrast. Jake *was* cute. I was fair enough to acknowledge this, but he also possessed an unfortunate habit of licking his lips; consequently, they always seemed chapped. Half the time I found myself imagining passing him some lip balm.

"Camille, the Carter girls just came in for a drink," Mom said, approaching our table. Her golden hair was twisted high off her neck, her cheeks flushed. She held my gaze and I could tell she intended to silently communicate something to me but my mind was not at capacity, as tired and washed-out as I felt.

Her words, however, activated my heart.

Tina, Glenna, and Elaine were the grown, married daughters of Bull Carter of the White Oaks Lodge, my connection to the photograph. I had not yet managed to venture around Flickertail Lake to pay Bull a visit; that his daughters were here at Shore Leave seemed like a sign and I felt my flagging spirits catch a faint breeze, lifting from down around my ankles to somewhere more mid-level.

"Ruthie, watch Millie Jo for a sec, all right?" I asked, and nudged at Jake's shoulder to get out of the booth, explaining, "I need talk to them quick."

But first I darted through the snowy, slushy yard under the lowering evening sky. I was much more agile than a month and a half ago, though nowhere near my old self. My body, when viewed naked in the ancient bathroom mirror, resembled a stranger's, in no way connected to the girl I used to know. My breasts were so heavy that they were painful on my chest, and still occasionally leaked milk, to boot. My formerly carnation-pink nipples now appeared the color of raspberries, and had swelled to the circumference of vanilla wafers. I couldn't even begin to discuss my belly, soft without its pregnant girth, my stomach that last summer I'd shown off with such naïve pride, flaunting its smooth, tanned surface in my teeny string bikini.

Quit it, I reprimanded, dashing up the steps to my room, slightly out of breath at the unexpected activity. I grabbed the picture, kissing M. Carter's face as I had been doing rather ritualistically lately, and then slipped back into my boots for the return jog across the yard. Once inside Shore Leave, enveloped within its cheerful noise and commotion, I scanned the crowd for the Carter girls, which everyone still called them, despite the fact that they all had married surnames these days. I spied Glenna, the middle sister, just claiming a barstool, her sisters removing their coats and fluffing their hair before taking seats. I slipped through the crowd and elbowed up beside Glenna; I knew all of them fairly well, as they came often to the cafe in the summer and autumn months, usually bringing their husbands and kids.

"Girls' night out?" I asked.

"Camille! Hi, sweetie!" Glenna said, turning on her barstool to give me a hug. "Congratulations on your little girl! Mom said you called her Millie. That's so darling! How are you doing?"

"Thank you. I'm great," I said, feeling the warmth of their personalities as tangibly as something I could cup in both hands. They reminded me of my sisters, unwinding their long woolen scarves, giggling and at complete ease with each other. I indicated the booth over in the dining room as I said, "She's over with Ruthie and Tish right now. How are you guys?"

"Drinking away the winter blues!" Tina said, wiggling her eyebrows up and down. The girls all resembled their mother Diana, a petite redhead. On the three of them, the color translated into varying shades of ruby and russet; it was like a visual of the word *red* in a thesaurus. Tina, who was Aunt Jilly's age and just as blunt as my auntie, added in a conspiratual tone, "Hon, you don't have to pretend for us. Those first months of motherhood are hellacious. No sleep, no sex, no sanity." She lifted a strand of my hair and gave it a companionable twirl, enthusing, "You look great, considering!"

I laughed a little. "Thanks, I'll take that as a compliment."

Elaine said, "Dad was just talking about you, Camille. He said you hadn't stopped out to White Oaks like you'd wanted to, last summer."

"I actually have a question for your dad." All three regarded me with undiluted interest in their eyes and I rushed to explain. "Grandma found this old trunk in our attic and there was a letter and a photo that I'm hoping your dad can tell me about."

"Ooh, let's see it, is it a dirty picture?" Tina teased, reaching for the photograph, and I relinquished it to her hands.

"Oh wow, it's really old," Glenna said, crowding beside her sister. Elaine leaned the other way to catch a glimpse of the back.

"'1875,'" Elaine read aloud. "And 'Carter?' That's really interesting. If anyone would know, Dad would."

"Let me call him," Glenna said, fishing her cell phone from the depths of her purse. She added, "If he's not walking his trap lines, he'll want us to come right over!"

"This guy is absolutely adorable," Tina said, tilting the photo this way and that, using her thumbnail to gently smooth flat a curling corner. "He must be a relative!"

"He makes me miss Matty," Elaine said. "Doesn't this guy kind-of look like him?"

"Our baby brother," Tina explained, even though I was vaguely aware that they had a little brother; Mom or someone must have mentioned him at some point. "He moved to Minneapolis to go to college and we're afraid the big city is going to steal him away for good, aren't we, girls?"

"He has more sense," Elaine said, though there was a note of doubt in her voice.

Glenna was talking to Bull on her phone.

"Look here, his horse was named *Aces*. I love this. What a great find. I hope Dad knows something about it." Tina's smile reappeared as she ran a thumbnail over the long, pale stripe on the horse's nose.

Glenna hung up and told us, "God, Dad is *all* fired up. He wants us to drive over there right now, just like I said." She giggled and added, "He thinks it might be from the original Carters here in Minnesota. They got here in the late 1860s and a couple of them built the original lodge. Their homestead cabin is about a half-mile from the lodge, still intact. If you're into history you'll absolutely love it, Camille."

"I'm sure I would," I agreed. "I meant to get out there last summer and check it out."

"Remember how Matty used to camp out in that old cabin when he was a kid?" Elaine asked her sisters; Glenna nodded, grinning at the memory, stashing her phone back in her purse.

"Come out and see it when it starts to thaw, Camille," Tina said. "We'll give you the grand tour."

"Dad says to bring the picture as soon as you get a chance," Glenna said. "He would love to see it and he has a bunch of old things from our ancestors. Shit, he'll talk your ear off, I'm just warning you. Plan to spend an entire afternoon!"

"I wouldn't mind a bit. I love history. I thought I might be a teacher one day." I couldn't quite contain the wistful undertone in my voice. I was tempted to agree to drive over to the Carters' house right at this second, but Tina's observant gaze flickered over my shoulder.

She said, "I think your guy is headed this way with the baby."

A small firebomb seemed to explode in my gut at these words; I thought she meant Noah. But it was just Jake, carrying Millie, who was fussing; my nipples prickled with milk at the sound. It took me a second to draw a full breath, to calm down. I'd been certain I would turn to see Noah approaching me, for the first time since last summer.

"Oh, let's see her," Glenna said. "Can I hold her a minute, Camille?"

Jake reached us, smiling with bashful apology. "Millie misses you."

I collected my daughter and kissed her forehead, settling her over my right shoulder. I asked Glenna, "Do you mind if she's crying?"

Glenna rolled her eyes. "Honey, I have three daughters and they were all colicky as hell when they were babies. It's fine."

The girls each took a turn cuddling Millie; Jake wandered back over to Tish and Ruthie, who'd been joined by Clint and Liam. Aunt Ellen was busy taking an order from a five-top and so I darted behind the bar to grab drinks for Tina, Glenna, and Elaine.

"What would you like?" I asked.

"A pitcher of Honeyweiss will do nicely," Tina ordered for them, lining her forearms on the edge of the bar. In a softer tone, she said, "Camille, seriously, you have the prettiest eyes I've ever seen. They're gorgeous."

Her words were heartfelt and I was a little self-conscious as I replied, "Thank you. It's nice of you to say so."

"I'm serious. I know it's hard to remember your old self once you become a mother," she said, lowering her voice a little, leaning forward. Her sisters were enraptured with Millie, allowing us a small slice of privacy, and Tina asked softly, "Has he seen his daughter?"

An ice chunk lodged in my throat, so I shook my head slowly, like I wasn't sure of the answer. I knew she meant Noah this time; everyone in Landon knew he was Millie's dad.

Tina's lips compressed and her expression spoke depths of understanding. "I know how that feels. My oldest, Beth, has never known her father. I got pregnant senior year, too."

I chewed on the inside of my right cheek, studying her blue eyes, afraid I would start crying and I didn't want that; I didn't want to seem as immature and unstable as I felt. Tina reached and squeezed my hand, just briefly, but it was enough to stave off any tears. The bridge of my nose stung but I managed a smile for her. She smiled in response and whispered, "I know it doesn't seem like it now, but you'll be all right, hon."

And I wished so badly that I could believe her.

Chapter Three

June, 2004

"Noah is home from college," Mom told me as we rolled silverware. School had let out a day ago, and since then the atmosphere at Shore Leave had been one of pure chaos, total joy at the prospect of three months of freedom. The weather, by contrast, had been a complete downer, featuring intermittent rain for the past three days; it was currently drizzling, echoing my depressive gray mood. It was the month and year that I should have graduated high school but no diploma was in my possession. Mom remained upset with me for refusing to return to Landon High for spring semester. I staved off her concerns by hinting that I would work on earning a high school equivalency degree in the next year—but as low and unmotivated as I often felt, it was an empty promise at best.

"Good for him," I finally said, speaking of Noah, carefully avoiding Mom's watchful gaze. Lunch rush was over for Saturday, the cafe empty of all but us and Rich, back in the kitchen running a load of dishes.

"I just thought you ought to know." Mom folded her hands above the stack of silverware and napkins on her side of the table.

I let my gaze wander out the window, seeing Flickertail pockmarked with droplets. I was honestly at a loss to describe my feelings at knowing this information. I lifted my right hand almost instinctively to my mouth, in order to chew at my nail.

"I thought you grew out of that habit," Mom said.

I withdrew my hand, tucking it under my thigh, and met her eyes at last. Mom tried not to let the worry she felt flicker too overtly over her face. I said, "It's all right, really. I don't care that Noah's home." My tone indicated that I might be stretching the truth just a little.

Mom let my lie slide, to my enormous relief, and took our conversation on a more welcome path. "So, I heard from Grandma that Bull Carter gave you the full historical tour of White Oaks last week."

"It was really incredible," I replied, a candle-sized flame brightening the interior of my heart as I recalled. "When I showed him the picture and letter back in March, he told me he would do a little research and that I should come back when the weather was nicer, so we could walk in the woods out there."

"That's what you said," Mom mused, again rolling silverware with her fingers flying, a skill we all performed with perfect muscle memory. "I remember being out there for parties now and again, back in high school. White Oaks is such a grand old lodge. How many rooms do they rent out these days?"

"Only five," I said. "Bull told me that the main room, where the check-in desk is, was built just after the Civil War. His great-something grandparents originally built White Oaks, and raised their kids there. Bull thinks that my picture might be of the younger brother, named Malcolm." A sharp jolt skittered over my skin—even if Bull was mistaken about the man's name, I'd called him Malcolm ever since. *Malcolm Carter.* Just the thought of his name sent chills leaping from the base of my spine. His picture remained propped on my nightstand and surely I was compromising the integrity of the old paper with my constant touching, but I could not restrain this urge any more than I could have pressed my hands to a storm cloud to prevent rain from falling.

I continued, hearing actual enthusiasm in my voice. "Bull doesn't know what became of him, but I would love to find out, Mom, maybe do a little research." I refrained from mentioning that I was obsessed with discovering the truth. "And then Bull showed me the old homestead cabin down the road from White Oaks. It's in decent shape, considering how old it is, and it's *so* pretty. It's surrounded by pines and has this adorable little porch. Really peaceful. I just love putting my hands on something that was built so long ago. I like to think about all of the people whose hands have touched the same things between then and now."

Mom studied me intently, her expression caught somewhere between somber and relieved. "It's so good to hear you excited about something. Motherhood isn't easy." And then, softer still, "I've been so worried about you, Milla-billa."

Rather than being irritated by the little-girl nickname, I acknowledged, "I know. I do."

Mom continued to study me and a silent understanding flowed between us, more powerful than any words. She recognized in a way that my sisters, no matter how much they loved me, could not; Mom had been there. Mom had raised her own newborn daughter with very little help from any man, and now she was watching me do the same. Granted, I had plenty of support from Grandma and Aunt Ellen (far more help or patience than Noah Utley would ever have offered in a hundred thousand years). But still.

Mom whispered, "Being a mother is not something that can be explained. You have to experience it. One of the most profound instances of sink or swim in existence, I'd say."

"Do you think I'm swimming or sinking?" There was a husk in my throat.

Mom dropped the bundle of silverware she held and immediately reached for my hand, curling together our fingers. "You are swimming and then some, sweetheart. Believe me."

"I don't feel that way." Tears overspilled and I used my shoulder to swipe at them. I admitted, "I know it's stupid, but sometimes I really miss Dad."

Mom skirted the table to engulf me in her arms. I clung to her unashamedly, inhaling her familiar scent: the peach-scented lotion she favored, Prell shampoo, and what I could only describe as the essence of her skin. I thought about how my own daughter was learning my scent as I held her close while she nursed, absorbing these memories of me through her senses; someday I might be comforting her when she had her own baby at age eighteen.

Jesus Crimeny. Don't get ahead of yourself now, I thought.

Mom's arms felt good and I tipped my forehead to her shoulder. She rubbed my back and murmured, "It's not stupid. He's your dad. You can call him anytime. I know he misses you and your sisters, too. He wants to come and visit this summer. Or you and Millie could always go to Illinois to see him. He'd love to have you, I know." My parents didn't talk with any sort of regularity, instead confining their communication to an occasional email. I knew Mom was right but the idea of driving all the way to Chicago with a fractious baby in the back-seat made my stomach cramp with anxiety.

"I know." I drew back and scrubbed at my face. "I'm just so emotional these days."

"It comes with the territory. Don't be hard on yourself. Grandma told me that you cry at night."

"I didn't think she could hear me," I said, embarrassed at this revela-tion, as Mom took her seat again. "It hasn't been as much lately. Millie Jo has been sleeping a few more hours each night. I feel a little more human when I get at least four in a row. Not so much like crying."

"I still can't believe that my baby is a mother." Mom's eyes appeared in danger of misting up, but then a smile graced her beautiful face. "But you are doing a wonderful job, my Milla, I promise you I wouldn't just say that."

Later that evening I wrapped into the old afghan from the back of the couch and went to sit alone on the end of the dock. Alone with Malcolm Carter's picture, that is, sitting and staring off to the left, in the general direction of White Oaks, which was built on the opposite shore of Flickertail. If one of our canoes was handy, I could paddle over there and see it firsthand, the old log cabin in which Malcolm may actually have lived. I'd considered that very possibility as Bull took me around their property, marveling that Malcolm could have pressed his palms to the same porch railing; surely he'd walked along the porch boards, slept within the same walls. I imagined him sitting on the shore of the lake (did they call it Flickertail Lake back then, I wondered) and watching the moon rise over the water, studying the ivory path it made across the dark surface, undulating with the slightest motion on or below the water. I found myself creating a personality for Malcolm Carter, imagin-ing him as somber and thoughtful; an observer, naturally tenderhearted. Somehow, I was sure he admired the moon just as much as I did.

As I had so many times, I whispered like an incantation, "*Malcolm.*"

I slipped one foot through the black silk of the nighttime water and swished a disturbance into the otherwise glass-smooth surface. Mosquitoes were thick as strawberry jam around me, so I withdrew my foot and tucked it back under the afghan.

"It's so pretty here," I said aloud, keeping my voice soft because I could hear Mom and Aunt Jilly up on the porch of the cafe, talking and laughing about something. I reflected that I really did love it here in Minnesota, when just a year ago I'd never conceived of living anywhere outside of Chicago. I'd considered myself a city girl but clearly a piece of my heart had always been here, in Landon, a result of all the summers spent at Shore Leave as a girl. And now it seemed that this little north-woods town would be my home for the visible future.

"It's not so bad," I whispered. For at least a few minutes I set aside all my fears, the whole slew of gnawing doubts about what I would do when Millie Jo started asking about her father, wondering why he wasn't a part of her life.

Another question surfaced, one I tended to avoid the way I would a sore tooth. What about finding a father for her, eventually? Though the thought seemed mildly repulsive now, given my appearance and current living conditions, probably someday I would want to date someone. Doubt surged anew; what man in his right mind wanted to chance a relationship with a single mother? I knew it was a terrible, let alone judgmental, thought—but one I couldn't help wondering. Guys my age were starting their first year of college, worried about dorm life or who would buy them beer, what hot girl would pay attention to them at a house party, or that they had a research project due. They wouldn't look twice at a girl with a baby of her own, unless it was to speculate that they might get laid, because probably it meant that she was easy.

My shoulders sagged beneath the weight of my ugly thoughts.

As I had too many times to count, I brought Malcolm Carter's picture to my lips and gently kissed him goodnight; I knew it was crazy and that anyone observing would think so, but I didn't care. I cradled him and Aces to my heart and whispered, "Thank you for being here," and then tucked the photograph safely under the afghan, where it would stay warm against my skin. For reasons I could not explain, speaking to him made me feel measurably better. I knew I couldn't linger down here on the dock and so climbed the little incline to the cafe. It was late and Millie would be waking for her first nighttime feeding in just a little while, back at the house with Grandma.

"Noah's here," Aunt Jilly said, bending to my ear as I sat at table three the next morning, eating breakfast with Clint, Tish, and Ruthie. Her words were laden with compassion.

A flash of what felt like boiling water hit my heart and then proceeded to churn through my body, but I kept everything I felt from my face. Clint and my sisters immediately stopped eating and stared as though expecting me to turn into a werewolf, with lots of writhing, bursts of hair, and ferocious snarling. I felt like I could start foaming at the mouth and immediately cursed myself for even caring.

"He could have called first," Tish said, echoing my thoughts exactly.

"What a *dick*," Ruthie contributed, and Aunt Jilly laughed in one surprised huff at this unexpected comment.

Clint cracked his knuckles. "I'll take care of him. Seriously."

Aunt Jilly raised her right eyebrow at Clinty. "That's a nice thought, son, but he's not worth getting in trouble for."

"You want me to tell him to get lost?" Tish asked, rising from her seat, scraping the chair along the floor like fingernails on a chalkboard; or maybe things just seemed amplified because my adrenaline was rushing.

"No, I'll talk to him," I said, rising unsteadily. At least I'd showered last night, so my hair was relatively tame this morning, held back on my neck with a large tortoiseshell barrette. I wore baggy faded jeans and a Twins t-shirt that once belonged to my dad, so I looked as fabulous as usual, but what did I care what Noah thought? I ignored the part of my heart that cried out in shame, wishing that his first sight of me in nearly a year involved me looking gorgeous and aloof, giving him only enough attention to suggest utter disdain.

"Here he comes," Tish muttered.

I stood to my full height and spied him crossing the parking lot with his hands tucked in the front pockets of a pair of khaki-colored shorts, in no hurry. He was clad in a yellow, short-sleeved polo shirt and my first thought was, *What an asshole. He even looks like one, a privileged jerk who takes things without asking, without caring how someone else feels.*

What had I ever seen in him in the first place?

Oh, yeah. Possibly the fact that he said everything you wanted to hear last summer?

Aunt Jilly put her hands on my shoulders and suggested, "Why don't you meet him outside, hon, have a little privacy?" Her soft voice was a gentle balm, alleviating some of the pain.

I nodded without words and left the cafe through the porch door; Noah looked up at me as he approached the porch, the heavy clouds in the ashen sky reflecting in his mirrored sunglasses. He did not smile as he removed them. "Hi, Camille."

"Hey." My voice was embarrassingly hoarse as I studied his eyes for any hint of apology. We stood in sickly-tense silence; I was too nervous to clear my throat, or to say anything else. I thought about how he'd had no trouble talking me up last summer.

"Can I see her?" he asked at last. "Mom and Dad have told me all about her. I've seen a bunch of pictures…"

His voice trailed into nothing and my instinct screeched with the desire to tell him to get lost. I studied his pale hair and familiar, lightly-tanned face. He was tall and slim, built like a tennis player. He seemed remote enough to be a complete stranger, certainly not the person who'd taken my virginity last July, who I thought loved me. But in the end I could drum up no logical excuse to refuse him and said, "She's at the house with Grandma."

We walked in silence, a good two feet between our bodies. He smelled the same, like the expensive cologne he favored; I couldn't remember which brand. The scent turned my stomach now.

"Come in," I invited, and found I was actually relieved that he hadn't attempted to apologize for anything. I wouldn't have known how to respond.

Grandma was in the kitchen; I could hear Pam Tillis singing on the radio. Hearing the screen door, not realizing Noah had accompanied me, Grandma called, "Camille, just in time! Guess who's hungry?"

"Noah's here with me," I said in response, and could actually hear the mushroom cloud of surprise that swelled throughout the house at these unexpected words.

Noah looked a little green in the gills but he followed me to the kitchen. Grandma was just lifting Millie Jo from her high chair; Millie was dressed in a pair of bright yellow corduroy bibs, her dark hair beginning to curl these days. Noah stopped dead and stared at her without blinking; I moved forward and Grandma passed her to me. Grandma's eyes were more eloquent than words but she refrained from offering any, only saying, "Hello, Noah," and then leaving us alone with our daughter in the kitchen.

I carried Millie over to him, holding her up on my left shoulder, keeping my eyes from Noah's face. I didn't want to see what was present there, for better or worse.

"She's really cute," he said, and his voice sounded clogged. He cleared his throat and shifted from foot to foot, like a little boy who knew he was in trouble; I swallowed away my disgust. He went on, "Dad and Mom told me how cute she is. They really love seeing her."

What about you? I wondered, but didn't respond, not about to offer him any assistance or support right now. His hand hovered in the air, as though he thought I might shove it away; I remained motionless and Noah finally patted Millie's back, pitifully tentative.

"Thanks for letting them see her," he whispered.

I gaped at him, so offended that I could barely respond. "They're her *grandparents.*"

He ducked his head, longing to be anywhere but here, around anyone but me. My, how times had changed.

"Hi, Millie," he murmured, studying her as she stared right back, her eyes round and solemn. I wished she would spit up all over him in a sticky, smelly spew. Her diaper needed changing, as it felt squishy beneath her bibs, propped on my forearm. I debated passing her to Noah and suggesting that he give it a whirl.

"She's growing really well," I said to fill the dreadfully awkward silent void, grateful that the radio continued playing, a welcome distraction.

"Does she crawl yet?" he asked, attempting to do the same.

"Not yet."

"I'll be around some this summer," he said, a paltry and even laughable offering. "I'd like to see her now and again, if that's all right."

Even though I didn't believe him, I whispered, "Sure."

And that was that; anti-climatic, ridiculous, probably even a little heartbreaking. I couldn't honestly claim that my heart felt broken, not anymore. Rather, despite how much I loved Millie Jo, my heart seemed asleep, in a state of hibernation, closed off for its own protection. I stood on the porch, Millie in my arms, and watched the taillights of Noah's car disappear down the lake road. No apology, no words of regret at having missed witnessing her birth. Instead I was the one apologizing, cupping a protective hand against the back of my daughter's head, caressing the downy curls that twined around my fingers. Sorrow pierced my heart; surely there was internal bleeding in my chest cavity. I whispered, "I'm so sorry, Millie Jo-Jo. I'm so sorry I didn't pick a better daddy for you."

I kissed her round cheek, inhaling her sweet, milky, baby scent. She issued a happy gurgling sound and the sadness gouging at my heart felt partially repaired—I would be here for her; that I could promise my daughter. And maybe one good parent was enough; Gran had raised Grandma and Aunt Ellen on her own, and later, Grandma raised Mom and Aunt Jilly with no help from their dad, Mick Douglas, the grandpa I'd never met. I refused to believe that any sort of ancient family curse (which Tish, Ruthie, and I were not supposed to know about) was to blame. There were surely very good reasons that the Davis women tended to end up single mothers—good reasons for losing the men they loved.

Maybe because we hadn't loved the right ones to begin with, I thought, watching the dust settle in the wake of Noah's tires.

I would raise my child as best I could, and she would know a mother's love. I could never be sorry enough for Noah's attitude, but I would make up for it in every way possible.

Chapter Four

December, 2004

"Do you care if Jake comes to our Christmas party?" Tish asked.

I was helping her decorate the little blue spruce that Dodge had cut down to adorn the bar, same as every Christmas. It was already secured in its stand and decked in candy-colored twinkle lights; Tish and I were in the process of hanging popcorn strings, pretzels tied with red ribbons, and an assortment of gingerbread cookies. I'd already warned Grandma and Aunt Ellen that the ice fishermen, who routinely arrived at Shore Leave drunk and hungry after a day spent on Flickertail, were going to try and eat our decorations but they just laughed.

"Let them," Ellen had teased. "Serve them right to crack a tooth on that gingerbread."

I said to Tish, "No, why should I care if Jake comes to the party?"

"He's home from school and he's been asking me about you until I told him to just call you already," Tish complained. I felt her censuring gaze but kept my own away, dutifully wrapping the red, popcorn-strung ribbon around the spruce, its boughs pungent with the scent of sap and wintertime. In a gentler tone, Tish asked, "Why don't you give him a chance?"

I sighed, debating how to answer that. The real bitch of it was I knew Jake was a good guy. He cared about my family, he cared about me. Last spring he'd made an effort to come and visit me frequently, simply hanging out at Shore Leave, letting me talk about Millie Jo, all without a single complaint. This past autumn he'd emailed me on a regular basis, wondering how Millie was doing and how things were back in Landon. He refrained from mentioning how much fun he was surely having as a freshman at the U, instead lamenting that he missed me and wished I could somehow be there, too. That I would love it, he was certain.

All of these things pressed heavily on my guilty conscience, which nagged at me to give him a chance, unsure why I couldn't like him as more than a friend. Jake was good-looking…tall, sweet smile, nice build. Undoubtedly he would make a far better father for any child than Noah Utley, despite the fact that the last thing Jake was considering right now was fatherhood. As was his right.

"I like Jake," I said, in all honesty. "I just don't like him like *that,* you know what I mean?"

"I guess," Tish muttered, though she was even more inexperienced than I had been at her age, content to be friends with boys but nothing more as of yet. My gaze flickered over her striped wool sweater and I could tell sports bras were still her lingerie of choice, Tish's way of stubbornly denying the fact that her body was curvy rather than athletic. She pestered, "Just maybe go on a date with him or something. I know if you asked him he would be *so* excited."

How could I explain that I didn't want to be the one doing the asking? It seemed vaguely sexist, or at least old-fashioned, to expect Jake to ask me rather than the other way around but that's what I wanted of a guy. I finally settled with, "If he asked me, I might consider it. But it's hard for me to get away anyway. Millie Jo is still nursing and I leave her with Grandma or Ruthie enough as it is when I have to work. I miss her."

"It's really because you're in love with a picture of a *horse,*" Tish said, flicking her forefinger against my shoulder. Go figure. When I least expected it my sister made an uncannily accurate observation.

"Not exactly," I griped, shrugging away from her teasing. I thought of the way I nightly traced my lips over the words Malcolm had written on the back of the photograph, imagining his hand touching the same spot. "I'm just interested in finding out more about him. *And* Aces. There doesn't seem to be much information anywhere, or evidence. It's a dead-end."

My only clue seemed to be the fact that my family and the Carters had been connected with each other since the nineteenth century, proof being Malcolm's picture and letter stored in the Davis trunk in our attic. Had they been friends? Neighbors? Bull had stopped out to Shore Leave just to see me last July, bringing a bunch of photographs he had unearthed, but when I'd asked about the connection between our families, he was not entirely sure, either.

"Camille, you want a job out at White Oaks, you just let me know," Bull told me last summer, on that visit. From the first time I'd met Bull I liked him, a balding, stocky, perpetually good-natured man with a very muscular torso, making it clear just where his nickname originated. His real name was Brandon and in addition to running White Oaks with his wife, Diana, he was a volunteer firefighter for Beltrami County. Much like Dodge, Bull had a roaring voice and loved to joke, but beneath this exterior there lay a kind and considerate soul.

"If I wasn't so busy at Shore Leave, I would love to work there," I'd responded. "But thanks for the offer." Then I added, only half-kidding, "Maybe I could rent that old homesteader's cabin from you."

"That place needs more work than I can manage before it's livable, sweetie. It's falling down," he said. "The boy had a mind to fix it up before he left for college. I guess I keep hoping he will, someday."

Bull rarely referred to his son by name; apparently *the boy* was earning a business degree and planned to settle in Minneapolis. Bull made it clear that he was upset by this decision.

"The boy has it in his head nowadays to stay on in the Cities," Bull told me, and I heard the deep regret in his tone. "He's always had an independent streak a country mile wide, which I admire, I truly do. I just hate that he's so far away."

"The Cities aren't that far," I said; up here, that's what everyone called Minneapolis and St. Paul. "It's less than, what, four hours?"

"You can be the first to tell the boy that," Bull grumped. "He can't even make it home in the summers to see his mother! Busy at his job, he says."

I got the sense that the youngest Carter was maybe a little bit spoiled; Tina, Glenna, and Elaine had all referred to him as either immature or crazy at one point or another, but not without affection. But, then again, I was more than a little crazy these days, talking to an old photograph, considering renting a homesteader's cabin from another century. I'd loved the little structure upon sight last spring, tucked as it was in the woods, the surroundings peaceful but the cabin somehow lonely, its chimney cold and missing stones when it should have been cheerfully streaming smoke. Waiting for a family that would never return, I supposed. I'd battled the urge to hug the front door, certain that Bull would think I was cracked.

"Are you paying attention?" Tish complained, drawing me from my woolgathering. The country station we always tuned in on the radio behind the bar was playing "White Christmas" for about the two-hundredth time since the beginning of December.

"Sorry, what did you say?" I refocused on my sister.

"Mom is planning the party for this Saturday night. Grandma's going to close the cafe. Doesn't that sound like fun?" Tish was actually gushing.

"It does," I said, mostly to pacify her.

"Wear that red sweater Dad just sent you for Christmas," Tish insisted and I gave her a suspicious look, narrowing my eyes.

"Why is that?"

"You look so pretty in it. And you've lost a bunch of weight since last winter. You almost look like yourself again."

At least I could count on Tish's honest opinion at all times. I realized that she meant this as a compliment. "Thanks."

"Except for your boobs. They're huge! You look all out of proportion."

"Oh my *God*, Tish," I groaned, shoving her shoulder. "Seriously? I'm nursing my child." And then I couldn't resist needling her. "I could always wear a sports bra, I suppose."

Tish glared at me and I smiled sweetly.

"Just wear the red sweater," she insisted, taking a bite of a stale gingerbread cookie without thinking, then spitting it right out onto the floor. I laughed at her expression.

"You're cleaning that up," I told her, as the radio switched to "O Holy Night."

"I will. Wear the sweater."

"We'll see," was all I would settle for.

Saturday night there was a blizzard warning in effect for greater Beltrami County but that didn't deter anyone from showing up to the Christmas party. In the past, the big deal party at Shore Leave occurred in August, for Mom and Aunt Jilly's birthdays, which were one day apart. This past August, however, Mom had been pregnant and Aunt Jilly nursing Rae, and neither of them claimed to be in the mood for a blowout summer occasion. Mom was still pregnant but past the morning-sickness phase, and so she agreed to let Grandma host a Christmas party instead. Shore Leave dazzled with holiday decorations, from the trees in both the dining room and the bar (the dining room tree was adorned with silverware wrapped in red and green ribbons, candy canes, and tin cookie cutters) to the glittery red-and-silver tinsel that Grandma had draped along the edge of just about every horizontal surface in the place.

The crowd was boisterous; Eddie Sorenson and Jim Olson, who were called upon to provide music at nearly every local occasion, were situated in the bar, at the moment strumming out "Jingle Bell Rock" on their guitars, while everyone in the vicinity sang along. Drinks were flowing, and ceramic pans of every conceivable shape and size lined the counter, along with serving spoons and oven mitts. The party was a potluck and I'd already helped myself to a large paper plate, loading it with green bean casserole, tater-tot hotdish, au gratin potatoes, baked chicken with wild rice, and three kinds of Christmas cookies, including the ones that looked like miniature wreathes, made from corn flakes and marshmallows and a lot of green food coloring. I had managed to shed some pregnancy weight but planned to pig out tonight; eating good food was one of the few pleasures in my life. I didn't mean to sound pathetic; it was just the plain truth.

I settled comfortably in the corner booth, the windows near it blotted out with a thick, swirly frosting of snow, content for a moment to watch everyone from afar. Mom and Blythe sat at table three with Rich, Liz,

Wordo, and Aunt Jilly, who was holding Millie Jo. Mom sat on Blythe's lap, his hands resting on the mound of her growing belly; she was due with their first baby in March and we'd never seen Bly so excited. He and Mom planned to begin building a new house this spring, only a few hundred yards into the woods from the cafe. Blythe carried on about having six or seven bedrooms and filling them all with kids, until Mom was forced to sit on him to contain his emotion. Literally, she would plop onto his lap and cover his mouth with both hands, teasing him.

"I'm glad you're so willing, sweetheart. Do you want to carry each of them for nine months, too?" she joked.

"Baby, if I could, I would," he said, and I had no doubt he meant these words; it truly made me happy to see how much Blythe loved my mother. Even if the happiness was simultaneously tinged with a sort of strange, low-grade pain, the realization that Mom had never exuded so much joy when married to my father, not in all the years they'd been a couple. I wanted to talk about this with Tish and Ruthie but hadn't yet drummed up the nerve; besides, to what end? It wasn't as though such a truth negated our happy childhoods or tarnished our memories. I believed that Mom had loved our father once—it was more the 'what if' that troubled me; what if Mom had never met Blythe Tilson, had never known how happy she was capable of being?

The bite I'd just taken seemed to turn to dust in my mouth.

Aunt Jilly, sitting to Mom's right, was eating an enormous piece of chocolate ribbon pie, which I'd helped Aunt Ellen make just this afternoon. Millie Jo reached her chubby hands for the fork with each bite and Aunt Jilly obliged her about every other. Uncle Justin was toting Rae around the party; both babies wore matching red velvet footie pajamas that declared *Baby's First Christmas*. I'd already taken a hundred pictures but there was Dodge snapping a few more of Millie Jo with chocolate all over her chin. Tish, Clint, Liam, Ruthie, and Liz's triplets were crowded on the barstools to listen to Eddie and Jim play. The Carters were here, Bull and Diana, Tina and Glenna along with their husbands and kids; Elaine and her family were on a cruise. Jake was around, too, chatting with Grandma and Aunt Ellen behind the counter. Poor Grandma couldn't relax long enough to stop making coffee and checking crock pot temperatures, ensuring that everyone had plenty to eat and drink.

Jake looked good, I could not deny, dressed in a maroon sweater with a turtleneck collar, his dark hair cropped short; he seemed slightly more mature than when he'd left for college in August. He gave me a big hug when he arrived. I saw Tish and Ruthie observe this from afar, elbowing each other. I hadn't worn the red designer sweater from Dad but instead a baggy old North Stars sweatshirt, my faded jeans, and mukluk boots. As a concession to politeness, I'd combed my hair and borrowed a little mascara from Mom, fishing out the wand in her purse. I couldn't remember the last time I'd even considered using cosmetics. I was so exhausted these days, and puffy-eyed, that make-up would not be a flattering addition to my face. Jake looked my way and I thanked the powers that be for the fact that at the same moment Glenna and Tina came from the bar, martinis in hand, and zeroed in on me sitting alone.

"Camille, what're you doing over here all by yourself?" Tina asked, sliding into the bench seat opposite. Her martini sloshed over the edge of the glass and she grumbled, "Shit."

"Hi, guys." I was genuinely glad to see them, and sat a little straighter. "I'm not trying to be a party pooper, truly. I just like to watch what's going on."

"Dad is so excited that someone is actually interested in our family history," Glenna said, nodding in the direction of the bar, where Bull and Diana sat listening to the music. She used her cocktail napkin to help Tina wipe up the spilled gin.

"Your dad is so great," I said around a bite of casserole. I swallowed before elaborating, "Primary history, letters and pictures or journal entries, are my favorite way to learn about the past, and your dad has all sorts of things like that from the Carters. It's a treasure trove."

"Hon, you sound just like Matty," Tina said, grinning at this mention of her little brother, using the toothpick in her drink to eat an olive. "You want to teach history, right?"

"I did once," I said, plucking the chocolate kiss from the top of a peanut butter cookie.

Glenna made a scolding sound. "You're so young, hon. There's plenty of time to get a degree. BSU is close enough that you could commute."

"Maybe someday," I hedged, unable to imagine having the energy for college-level classes anytime in the next few years.

"Camille, you sound so defeated." Tina set aside her martini. "We worry about you."

I was touched at this news, and a little embarrassed. "I'm just fine."

Both of them continued studying me, clearly not buying what I'd just said, concerned and wishing to make me feel better. They were both so pretty, their scarlet hair shining in the Christmas lights, Tina's full with waves, Glenna's flat-ironed straight. Their eyes were a dark, stunning shade of blue. Glenna had freckles, Tina wore sparkly silver eyeliner; their lips gleamed in a similar shade of magenta, as though they'd shared a lipstick.

Tina said softly, "It took me a long time, but I don't hate Beth's dad anymore." She reached and gently squeezed my forearm; her nails were at least an inch long and painted a merry, holly-berry red.

Glenna nudged her sister's shoulder and added, "And if he'd stuck around here, you never would have given Sam a chance."

Tina brightened, beaming. "Sam and I have been married for over a decade now and I've never been happier. I wouldn't have my younger two girls without Sam." She paused, searching my eyes, and finally concluding, "The point being, hon, things don't ever work out how we think. But sometimes, they work out better."

"Thanks," I whispered, nodding a little in acknowledgment. I drew a breath and heard myself admit, "I just get so lonely. I mean, I have Grandma and Mom, my sisters and Aunt Ellen. I'm grateful for my family every second. But I feel…I feel so…" I trailed to silence, not exactly sure what I intended to say. That my body sometimes longed so badly to be touched that I could hardly stand it; that my own hands on my skin would not suffice, and that I wanted something I couldn't even begin to explain. Sex? No…not just that. Much more than that.

I want Malcolm Carter, I thought, and then almost laughed at my own absurdity, at what they would think if I were to speak this desperate, obsessive yearning aloud.

"We understand completely," Tina said, and somehow I believed her. She invited, "Come and have Elaine read the cards for you. She does that on the side and it's so fun to see what she turns up."

"She does?" I was intrigued.

Glenna nodded. "It's all in good fun. Elaine takes it a little seriously but we can laugh her out of it. Usually."

"Here comes someone who wants your attention," Tina noticed, tilting her head at Jake as he made his way through the crowd to our booth. She leaned closer to me and murmured, "Jake's cute. And nice. What about him?"

Before I could reply, Jake was upon us. He shoved both hands in his pockets. His eyes were almost painfully earnest. "Hi, ladies, care if I join you?"

I hated to relinquish this time with Glenna and Tina but I could hardly refuse Jake; I hadn't really talked with him yet and the Carter girls exchanged a sisterly glance, the kind that conveys an entire conversation with one look.

Tina said, "We'll give you two a little privacy, c'mon, Glens. We'll talk soon, Camille."

In their absence I looked up at Jake, remembering Tish's words. With that in mind, I said, "You look great, Jake, you really do. It's good to see you."

He flushed all across his pale cheeks, ducking his head as he smiled. "Thanks. It's great to see you, too."

"It sounds like you're loving school."

"I am. I love the city. There's always something going on, any night of the week."

"Not much like Landon." I attempted to force my lips into a smile.

At the exact same moment he asked in a rush, "Maybe, if you'd want, we could go have dinner this week sometime? I have time off from school until the second Monday in January."

"That would be nice," I said, which was such a puke answer. But I didn't know what else to say.

"You mean it?" His eyebrows lifted. A grin spread over his face and I all but writhed with discomfort.

"Maybe tomorrow, since I don't work," I said. *Besides, why delay it?*

"If we're not snowed in," he replied, still smiling. And then, serving to effectively punch me with guilt, he enthused, "I can't wait."

"Me, too," I lied, hating myself.

"If we're snowed in, we can watch a movie at my house," he offered, and my stomach cramped worse than ever. He nodded at my empty cup. "Do you need a drink? Maybe a hot chocolate or something?"

"I do, but I'll go get it. I was going to listen to the music anyway."

I snagged a mug from the kitchen and used the hot chocolate machine near the coffee makers; it made a noise like a chainsaw and thirty seconds later I held a steaming cup. I sipped gingerly, scanning the crowd from behind the counter. Jake had grabbed us a couple of seats in the bar. I caught Mom's eye; she waved me over, appearing flushed and merry, her belly round as a pumpkin beneath a white sweater covered in tiny blue reindeer. I realized something and went to stand by their table, giggling even as I scolded, "Mom, *no*, you don't. Come *on*."

She knew exactly what I meant and started laughing, resting her head on Bly's shoulder as she said, "We're cute this way."

"You *match!*" I groaned. Bly was wearing the same sweater, in a reverse color scheme.

"I told them it was completely barf-worthy," Aunt Jilly said, still cuddling Millie Jo. My daughter saw me and grinned, showcasing her new tooth.

"Hi, baby," I cooed to Millie, setting my mug on their table and lifting her from Aunt Jilly's lap, covering her face in kisses.

"I picked them out," Blythe informed me, pretending to be offended. "You don't think we're cute this way?"

"Oh, *please*," I groaned. "At least don't make a habit of it."

Uncle Justin appeared with tiny, adorable Rae. "Jilly-honey, I think we should get the same set."

Aunt Jilly flicked a finger against his lean belly and he laughed, snuggling Rae. He said to his daughter, "Your mama is a little temperamental, isn't she, baby girl?"

Tish ran up and snagged my hand. Just loud enough for me to hear she hissed excitedly, "So you and Jake have a date tomorrow night?!"

Mom sent me a questioning look, clearly perceiving something was up, but I was not about to announce this news in front of everyone. Instead I bounced Millie on my arm and asked her, "You want to listen to the music, baby?"

Tish dragged us away; Jake saved a barstool for me and asked immediately to hold Millie, exclaiming over how big she was, while I claimed my seat and tried to pretend there wasn't a leaden feeling in the vicinity of my heart.

"It was terrible," I muttered. Beside me on the mattress, curled beneath her own downy-soft quilt, Millie Jo slept on, oblivious to my woe. She had nursed for a few minutes before dozing off, leaving me alone here in the darkness, only the moonlight coming through the windows to lend me an ear. What I really needed was a shoulder, upon which to cry. But I hadn't wanted to disappoint Grandma and Aunt Ellen, both of them delighted as I prepared to go out for dinner with Jake earlier this evening. When he dropped me back home, hours later, they were waiting up at the kitchen table with cups of decaf, clad in their bathrobes and obviously expectant, and so I lied, "We had a great time."

"He kissed me," I whispered into the silent gloom of my bedroom, shifting to lie flat on my back and draping a forearm over my eyes. "It was like kissing my brother. If I had one, that is. Dammit to hell, why did it have to be that way?"

Sweet Jake had tried so hard that I felt like an ungrateful bitch for my current thoughts. He picked me up just on time, drove us to dinner at the Angler's Inn, which was Landon's only hotel, situated across the street from Eddie's Bar. Jake mentioned wanting to go somewhere in Bemidji but the weather was uncooperative, stranding us in Landon. We ate snow crab legs and Jake told me all about his classes, and the various foibles of his professors, and some of the more memorable fellow students he'd met since August. It was interesting, and on the one hand we talked really easily. I enjoyed that part of him, the friend. It was later, sitting buckled in the passenger seat of his car and thanking him for the date that I felt unease creep back into my stomach

"I'll walk you to the door," he'd said.

"That's all right. Thank you for dinner, Jake." I climbed out of the car, hoping he wouldn't follow.

But he did.

"No problem." He studied my face as we stood in the sphere of yellow cast by the outside light. I looked up into his eyes, which were the color of melting chocolate, and willed myself to *want* to kiss him, to put a little heart into the effort.

He took this for an invitation and bent down, barely touching his lips to mine. I lifted my chin, and then...

"He put his tongue right in my mouth," I whispered. I felt crazy, lying here talking to myself, my child snoozing a foot away. Probably this is exactly what I should get used to; surely this was my future. Soon all I would need were six or seven housecats. I continued, as though dictating a diary entry, "He tasted like seafood. It was *awful*. Oh God, I hate myself."

Far worse was the fact that Jake did not find the kiss awful; he'd taken me into his arms, gathering me firmly against him. He wanted to keep kissing me, I knew, but I ducked gently from his embrace and muttered, "I should get inside. See you!"

Tears seeped over my temples now, hot and fast.

"Dammit," I muttered again, digging my fists into my eye sockets, rubbing until I saw a checkerboard pattern in oranges and blues; probably I shouldn't press so hard. It had been a long time since I'd cried at night but I couldn't hold back my pathetic sobs, try as I might. It was two nights before Christmas, four nights before my nineteenth birthday, and I felt utterly lost, riddled by doubt...like I stood at the bottom of a well, peering up at a distant moon I possessed no hope of ever touching.

Chapter Five

June, 2005

"WELL, THE BOY GRADUATED. WE ALL DROVE DOWN THERE for it." Bull was busy tugging at the weeds which grew densely along the foundation of the little porch. He paused to swipe the dirt from his big hands onto the sides of his jeans, before saying, "Now he's looking for a job in the city. Got himself a prissy little girlfriend. More poodle than woman, I tell you. I don't understand it at all."

"Are you sure you don't mind if I explore out here a little while?" I asked, biting back a smile as I changed the subject; Bull was rather prone to rants.

It was a humid, overcast spring afternoon and I'd driven over from Shore Leave to pick up something Bull found for me; he was delighted that I was so interested in the Carter family history and its connection to our own. Millie was napping and so I told Grandma I'd be back within an hour. Once at White Oaks Lodge, Bull said I could check out the homestead cabin if I wanted; he was busy, but took the time to walk me through the woods to the right clearing, and then unlocked the front door so I could poke around inside. The little cabin was constructed of interconnected logs, perfectly square and consisting of one room with a tiny loft. The hearth was positioned directly across from the front door; on my first visit, back last spring, I'd advanced immediately to admire the mantle, running my fingertips over the polished maple. Someone had carved interlocking pine boughs upon its surface.

"This is gorgeous," I'd marveled.

I was about to ask if Malcolm Carter had done this carving when Bull said, "The boy has a fair hand with the woodworking. The old mantle had rotted away so Matty whittled a new one."

Now, a year later, I recalled that conversation as I stood in the same place near the hearth, again touching the wood that Bull's son had once carved. Even with dead leaves covering the wide floor planks, the musty smell of bat droppings and over a century of disuse, I thought the little cabin beautiful. I was illogically happy to be inside its walls. There were two windows, one missing the glass in the bottom right quarter-pane, neatly patched with a piece of fitted cardboard and duct tape. For whatever reason, I wanted to touch it and pressed my fingertips to the window frame that had been repaired.

"Matty fixed up that window back when he was a teenager and it's still holding. Huh. And I don't mind you being out here one bit, sweetie," Bull said. "Explore all you like. Just padlock that door when you leave, otherwise the local kids get a notion to hang out in here, do some drinking and necking, if you know what I mean."

I giggled at the old-fashioned expression. "I will. Thanks, Bull."

"Anytime you want a job at White Oaks, you just tell me," he said again, tipping the brim of his baseball cap as he took his leave.

In his absence I walked around the entire structure, trailing my hands on the logs, at one point pressing my palms and then forehead against the wood, not understanding what motivated this action, only that I was compelled. At last I settled comfortably on the top porch step and inhaled the scents of the forest, hanging heavy in the air along with the humidity; my hair was wild with curling frizz. I fantasized about putting a hammock between two slim oaks adjacent to the porch, as they were a perfect distance apart. It was peaceful here, away from the hustle of the lake and its springtime boat traffic, both tourist and local. The tree branches were decorated with jewel-green leaves, grapevines curling all along the ancient porch railings, as though I was sitting in a tropical jungle rather than northern Minnesota. Bull had given me an old, yellowed envelope containing a telegram, which I brought up to my lips, holding it there and closing my eyes for a couple of heartbeats. With great care, I lifted the outer flap, mindful of the fragile paper, and carefully withdrew a smaller rectangle—the telegram itself.

"1876," I noted, my eyes darting over the old handwriting, inked with all capital letters, as if the sender was shouting the words:

SEARCHING STOP UNABLE TO RETURN HOME STOP SENDING MY LOVE STOP MISS YOU ALL SO MUCH I HURT STOP REGARDS MALCOLM A. CARTER

My heart seemed to stop each time the word appeared on the telegram; I knew that it simply indicated a pause in the transmission over the old telegraph wires but it struck me as creating an even greater sense of urgency in the message. One would have been charged money for each word, so that explained the succinct nature of it, the awkward syntax. At first, all I really noticed was the name *Malcolm A. Carter*. What was the 'A' for? For what was he searching, and why was he unable to return home, especially when he said that he was hurting? He missed his family so much he hurt.

Oh, Malcolm, sweetheart. I brought his words to my lips, picturing his face, and then my heart was what hurt, intensely so, as if suddenly stuffed with thorns. I held the telegram close, transferring it next to my heart, clutching it to the increasing pulse behind my ribcage. Somewhere in 1876, Malcolm had dictated this message to be sent to Minnesota. I understood the handwriting was not his but instead belonged to whatever clerk took the message at the telegraph office, well over one hundred years ago.

"What was happening? What were you looking for? Tell me." Then, so quietly it was almost inaudible, I begged, "Please, Malcolm. *Please*."

A breeze stirred the birch leaves near the cabin, sending a restless whispering into the air. I shivered, my imagination seizing hold.

"I want to find you so much," I said to the trees, but of course I meant Malcolm, surely just a step from being totally insane, sitting here fantasizing about a man from another century and wondering if his spirit was maybe hovering near. I had not yet gone to have Elaine read the cards for me, as Tina had invited last winter; I was typically skeptical about such things. But at this moment the air seemed alive with mystery and magic. Malcolm had lived here in this very cabin, had walked through this forest, had surely fished in Flickertail Lake. I swore I could sense him, and wrapped into my own arms. I whispered my final promise, "I love you. I will find you, sweetheart."

Millie would soon wake from her nap and so I bid the little cabin farewell and retraced my footsteps through the forest, cradling the telegram, emerging into the parking lot of White Oaks Lodge. There I stood, staring with outright admiration at the lodge itself, a lovely, sprawling, A-framed building, with curving balconies placed high and low, the structure spacious and grand, situated a few hundred feet from Flickertail Lake. And for the first time, I seriously considered taking Bull up on his offer of employment.

Three weeks later Jake was home from college and called me to ask if I was free Saturday night.

"I have to work," I said, which wasn't a lie. He and I had continued emailing, all winter; I was the coward who didn't usually answer the phone when I saw that he was calling. Now that I knew he was home, however, it would only be a matter of time until he stopped out to Shore Leave to find me.

"I'll come and hang out there," he said, anticipation in his voice. We'd never declared ourselves as a couple, not even close, but he was surely on the verge of asking me to go out with him, to consider him as my boyfriend. I cringed away from that thought.

"Maybe if it's not too busy," I said, pacing the dock as we spoke, using the cordless phone from the cafe, which we'd bought to replace the one Mom threw in the lake two summers ago.

"I've really missed you," he replied. "I can't wait to see you."

And it was with those words that a crawling chill seized my spine; I suddenly recognized in his voice the tone once prevalent in my own, almost two years ago now, when I'd first dated Noah. That puppy-dog quality, that pleading to be acknowledged, and I hated myself for recognizing it in Jake. I knew I wasn't wrong and it was up to me to stop this from progressing, if for no other reason than respect for him. I said, "Jake, I'm not ready to date anyone. I'm just not. Please understand."

"I'll wait until you're ready," he insisted, though gently. "I don't mind waiting."

Don't do this to yourself, I silently begged. *Don't you have any self-respect?*

I may have been directing a little of that at myself, though long after the fact.

"I'll be working up near International Falls this summer," he said, changing the subject when I remained stubbornly quiet, vacillating between resentment and guilt. Then, softly, "I really will wait until you're ready, Camille. I don't want to rush you."

I sank to the glider at the end of the dock, closing my eyes and trying not to think. I'd just finished a dinner shift on this Tuesday evening and Millie Jo was busy playing with Rae out on the front lawn, Ruthie keeping an eye on them. The glider creaked beneath me, familiar and immediate, and I opened my eyes, studying the lake, which lay flat and smooth as the sheared-away top of a polished agate. The blues and the golds combined to make a dazzling display on the water and a part of me reflected how much I loved this place, that just the sight of the sun sinking behind the trees across the lake brought me a sense of peace, if fleetingly. This evening, the branches of the pines over on that side were backlit with a burning, peach-tinted glow.

"Are you still there?" Jake asked.

"Yes," I whispered. "And I really mean it when I say I can't date yet. Please understand."

"I do. I really do, Camille. Can we maybe just hang out?"

"Of course." I felt a slight easing of guilt; we could be friends. I'd made it clear that this was all I could handle…if only he hadn't kissed me last winter.

"See you soon, then," he said.

"All right," I whispered, and disconnected the call.

"Milla! You down there?" It was Mom, bracing her hips on the porch rail to call to me.

"You can see me down here, can't you?" I responded. I was especially irritable today, having heard from Tish (who'd seen them around Landon) that Noah was dating Mandy Pearson. Tish claimed she was only guessing but I was sure it was true; as far as I was concerned, those two deserved each other. I didn't care one bit. I covered my face with both hands, thinking, *Not one bit.*

Mom called, "Come on up and help me roll silverware! You snuck out of it, you little weasel, you."

Dammit. I was hoping she'd let me get away with slacking off, at least for tonight. But then I reminded myself that Mom was surely even more tired than me; her and Blythe's son had been born only two months ago. They'd named him Matthew Blythe and he was adorable, a chubby and complacent baby; I couldn't help but feel as though I'd done something wrong because my own baby cried so unceasingly for the first four months of her life.

"I'm coming," I sighed, reflecting that this was my life and so I better get used to it, let alone appreciate it. Rolling silverware, chasing my toddler hither and yon, nursing her to sleep at night; nursing was so much easier than preparing a bottle and I loved snuggling her close, letting her drift to sleep cuddled warm against my side.

Ruthie and the girls sat at the picnic table near the porch, playing with a plastic tea set. Rae and Millie Jo had crackers on their plates and Millie was busy pouring water into Ruthie's cup. I said, "Hi, everybody."

"Hey, Milla. You look pretty," Ruthann said, as though on a mission to make me feel better; I rolled my eyes, prompting her to insist, "You really do."

"Pwetty Mama," agreed Millie, giving me her special grin, the one that crinkled up her eyes and wrinkled her nose. Everyone said how much Millie looked like me, and she did, with dark curls and the golden-green Davis eyes, but to me she was so very much *herself*, my sweet baby who made each day unique simply because she was a part of it; she had taken her first steps back in February, just after her birthday, and now tore around everywhere. I lived in mortal terror of her falling in the lake.

I said, "I love you, my silly girl."

"Wuv you, Mama," Millie replied.

Rae silently offered me a crumbling, half-chewed cracker.

"Thanks, Rae-Rae." I accepted this gift and pretended to eat a bite, making a lot of noise. She smiled happily at my efforts, clapping her sticky little hands.

Ruthie said, "I can watch them longer if you need to help Mom."

"I do, and thank you," I said, leaning to kiss the top of her head. Ruthie smelled exactly as she always had, of her favorite strawberry-scented conditioner. I smoothed a hand over her soft curls. "I'll be done in a few minutes."

Inside, Blythe was changing Matthew on the diner counter, Grandma hovering near and offering advice.

"Not so much powder," Grandma said. "For heaven's sake, Bly."

"This has to be against health code," I teased, even though there were no customers at the moment except Clint's best friend Liam, and he was practically a family member anyway.

Mom sat at table three with a tub of silverware. She said to Grandma, "Mom, Matthew has such a bad diaper rash. I remember with the girls that cornstarch always helped…"

"I think it looks a little better," Blythe said, and for just a second I allowed myself to covertly admire him, still somewhat in awe that someone who looked like him was technically my stepdad. Little Matthew appeared utterly content despite the fact that his bottom was the main topic of discussion, holding his toes in his chubby hands.

I sat on a stool near the action and stroked a finger along his satin cheek, murmuring, "Hi, sweet little guy. Aren't you the cutest little thing?"

"My little man," Bly said, bending to kiss Matthew's tiny feet, one after the other. To Grandma he added, "Joan, I swear he goes pee way too much. I mean, every hour or so his diaper is full. And he's peed all over me about fifty times already."

Grandma and Mom just laughed and laughed.

"Don't even get me started on the other stuff in his diaper," Bly added, grinning in response to our amusement, snapping up Matthew's onesie and scooping his son into his strong arms. He held Matthew up on his shoulder and kissed the baby's cheek. I happened to glance over at Mom as he did, and the expression on her face flew like a small dart to stick in my ribs; she watched Blythe holding their baby with love pouring from her eyes, her face a picture of quiet joy. As a mother, I understood that overwhelming rush of love for your baby; as my mother's daughter, a selfish and childish part of me ached as I wondered, *Did she ever look at me in my own dad's arms that way?* And then I simply acknowledged that she was happy, and didn't allow anyone to see the sudden surge of stinging tears.

Two nights later Elaine, Glenna, and Tina showed up at Shore Leave with exciting news. At least, to them it was exciting. I leaned one hip against their high-top table in the bar, in between orders as I waited for a second pitcher of beer for another table, watching with private enjoyment as the three sisters bickered with good-natured ease.

"He *finally* broke up with the poodle-girl," Tina informed me. She was a little drunk already; apparently tomorrow was her birthday and the girls had taken her out for some pre-party partying.

"Your little brother?" I asked, distracted as I noticed Jake come into the bar from the corner of my eye. It was the second night in a row he'd stopped out to Shore Leave, just because. Last night we sat on the porch with Clint, Liam, Tish, and Ruthie, playing Monopoly for almost three hours just like the old days, the kind of high-stakes game in which you couldn't even leave the action to go to the bathroom because you might get robbed by another player. All of us except Ruthie became heartless scavengers once the Monopoly board appeared, and Ruthie had her hands full attempting to keep us on the straight-and-narrow, non-cheater path. We'd played until moths swarmed the outside light and mosquitoes nearly carried away the game board, while Millie Jo snoozed in her playpen in the cafe. Jake said not a word about anything even remotely related to dating but I felt his eyes lingering on me time and again; he didn't think I noticed this, it was obvious.

"Yes, and it's about time," Elaine elaborated, drawing my focus gladly back to them. "But he still thinks he should stay in Minneapolis."

"He has a good job there," Glenna countered.

"But he's not a *city boy*," Tina groaned. "He used to spend all summer in the old cabin, without any electricity or hot water, like a crazy person. He even camped out there in the winter, when he'd walk his trap lines! *That's* crazy."

My heart skittered at the mention of the homesteader's cabin. I was happy to hear that someone occasionally lived within its walls; I felt strongly that it needed a family.

Talk about a crazy person…

"Yeah, it's not like he didn't wander home when he was hungry, or needed a shower," Elaine remembered, smiling.

Aunt Ellen set my table's pitcher on the bar and I was forced to say, "I need to grab that. You guys all right for now? Tina, that round of shots is on me."

"I just fucking *love you*," Tina said, winking at me. "Thanks, Camille."

At the bar, I said, "Hey, Jake."

"Hey," he replied, all smiles. "How's everything?"

"Good," I said, purposely keeping busy so that I didn't have to meet his adoring gaze. "What are you up to?"

"Nothing much." His chocolate-brown eyes caressed my face, there was no mistaking. I felt my heart give an awkward thump, studying him with a frown nudging my forehead, almost *willing* myself to fall for him. He was good-looking and kind; I knew he liked me far more than he would admit. But there was no point in admitting anything. It wasn't as though he planned to stick around Landon; he'd told me numerous times how much he loved Minneapolis. Besides that, he was no older than me at nineteen, nowhere near ready or inclined to be someone's stepfather.

"I'm pretty busy," I said, trying not to compare the expression on his face to the one I'd surely worn when I looked at Noah two summers ago, rampant with adoration, wishing so badly for attention in return. At least I wouldn't take advantage of that with Jake.

"You want to watch the sunset later?" he asked with absolutely no guile, leaning on his elbows over the bar. He wore jean shorts and a junky white t-shirt, sandals with straps; he'd undoubtedly been out on Flickertail today. He liked to fish.

"Sure, if it hasn't set before I'm done." I caught up the pitcher and nodded in the direction of my table. "I gotta go."

Later, I collected Millie from Grandma before joining Jake on the dock; the three of us caught the tail end of the sunset together. I held Millie on my lap, keeping her close since she wasn't wearing her life jacket, repeatedly smoothing her hair from tickling my face as the light breeze caught her curls. The sunset glowed electric-pink this evening, my favorite, and I felt a small measure of contentment.

"Millie Jo, what's your favorite animal?" Jake asked; he'd been keeping a running commentary with my daughter.

"Doggie!" she yelped, then giggled, covering her mouth with both hands.

"She looks so much like you," Jake noted, looking between us.

"I'm glad," I said, then immediately regretted the comment; it was the kind of thing I could never speak in front of Millie, especially when she grew old enough to understand that, however indirectly, I meant I was glad she didn't resemble her father.

"Does Noah see her much?" he asked, low.

"Not since last summer." I kept my eyes on the western horizon. I sighed as I said, "But his folks still send me a check every month. I've been putting all of it into a bank account for Millie."

"I'm sorry, Camille," Jake said with quiet sincerity, and his left hand twitched a little, as though he intended to reach for my right; to my relief he didn't and my shoulders relaxed again.

"It's all right," I responded, just as quietly. And then, to Millie, "What do you say we go read a bedtime book?"

"No, Mama!" she cried, flailing against me; *no* was her favorite word these days.

"And that means it's time to call it a night," I informed Jake.

"Camille, I'm going to work up near International Falls for the rest of the summer," Jake said then, a small catch in his voice. He touched my wrist, but only briefly; I paused, keeping Millie in my arms even though she was struggling to get loose.

"Millie, hold still," I ordered.

"I'm doing some stuff with the Forestry Department up there in Koochiching County. A couple of other guys on the volunteer fire squad hooked me up with a job."

At that moment the porch door clacked open and Mom called down, "Millie Jo, come give me a hug good-bye!"

"Go hug Grandma," I said, walking her to the place where the dock met the grass; she scampered up the incline and I watched Mom hold open the porch door to let her inside, before turning back to Jake. The air around us was no longer tinted pink but instead the gray of advancing night. In this gloaming light, Jake studied me with serious eyes.

"Can I kiss you good-bye?" he asked. "I know we're not together like that...but I...but we..."

I was blindsided by a rush of pity and tenderness. Without saying a word I stood on tiptoe and put my hands on his shoulders, suddenly determined to give it a second chance. He caught me instantly close, kissing me with so much enthusiasm that I felt terrible all over again. His lips were warm and he tasted sweet this evening, like spearmint gum. His tongue was in my mouth, his arms around me, and yet there wasn't one firework exploding in my brain. Instead, I found myself analyzing what brand of gum he'd been chewing earlier.

When he drew away, he said at once, "I know you're not ready to date, I really do. But promise me the second you are, you'll call me. All right?"

I nodded weakly.

Jake collected me near once more. His neck, where my nose was pressed, was warm and smelled like the lake. He kissed my hair. "I'll miss you, Camille." There was nothing accusatory in his voice but his words still hurt. He whispered, "And I'll never quit hoping that sometime you'll miss me a little bit, too."

Chapter Six

November, 2005

"Bull asked if I could help out at the bar at White Oaks this winter," I told Grandma a week before Thanksgiving. "He said through New Year's, if that's all right with you. I think a change of pace would be good."

Grandma said, "I know you like it out there, sweetie, of course it's all right with me. How many nights a week?"

"Just Fridays and Saturdays. So I can still pick up lunch shifts at Shore Leave. What do you think, Grandma?"

"I think you look excited about it." Grandma cupped my shoulders, rubbing with her thumbs. "And that's enough for me. You don't get out enough. I worry that you don't visit with any young folks."

"Tish and Ruthie," I countered. I knew Grandma was too kind to acknowledge that I had no real friends in Landon.

"You know what I mean," Grandma said, and hesitated before asking, "What about Jake?"

I had not seen Jake before he left for college in August but we continued to email on a fairly regular basis; he wanted to get together over winter break. I remained somewhat stunned that he hadn't yet found a girlfriend at school. At last I said, "I like Jake so much, Gram, but not...I don't..." I stumbled to an awkward halt.

"I know," Grandma said. She studied me without blinking, her eyebrows and lips set in compassionate lines. She finally said, "Why don't you tell Bull that you've agreed to take the job?"

I started at White Oaks the very next evening, Bull leading me through the entire lodge, talking up a storm while I listened with rapt attention. He told me about each part of the structure, and which Carter ancestor had added what. The original building, constructed in the 1860s, now housed the check-in desk, which Diana managed.

"Camille, it's wonderful to have another history buff around," Diana said. "Bull would talk the hind leg right off a mule if we let him." Diana was an older version of her daughters, with beautiful dark blue eyes and long, auburn-red hair, hers shining with a silver thread here and there. She regarded her husband with a fond smile. "And we've heard all your stories, haven't we, babe?"

"You love them," Bull rumbled, winking at his wife.

Tina and Elaine also worked in the bar on the weekends, especially during the busy holiday season, and Elaine showed me the ropes that first night. The bar and adjacent dining room were housed in the section of White Oaks built in the 1960s, by Bull's father. It was designed to resemble a nineteenth-century saloon, the bar top a gleaming expanse of polished oak built over rough-cut logs, similar to the walls of a cabin.

Each barstool was handmade and unique, as were all of the sturdy chairs in the dining room, upholstered with varying shades of leather in brown tones, from coffee to caramel. According to Bull, the floor was constructed of reclaimed barn wood, and a long rectangle of a mirror, complete with beveled glass, graced the wall behind the bar, along with all of the top-shelf liquor. The tables were covered in creamy linen, arranged around a massive limestone fireplace—one in which you could grill up an ox, Bull had joked.

The best feature of all was closed off for the season, the west-facing wall of floor-to-ceiling windows showcasing the wide front balcony that ran the entire length of White Oaks and offered a panoramic view of Flickertail. Even now, with snow dominating the landscape, the view was dazzling, the setting sun igniting red sparks along the icicles and throwing fire over the glittery, frozen surface of the water. I sighed a little, with simple pleasure, and Elaine followed the direction of my gaze. "It's lovely, isn't it? I've lived here my entire life and I've never grown tired of the view."

"I know exactly what you mean," I said. "I mean, I didn't grow up in Landon but the past few years have made me appreciate that I live here now."

"Yeah, it's not exactly a hotbed of activity, but I wouldn't change it for the world." Elaine looked my way and smiled. "We'll be busy in an hour but since it's quiet now I'll show you a few things."

White Oaks was booked with guests through New Year's but was also a destination for the local crowd. I didn't recognize the two families currently seated in the dining room and so figured they must be guests. *Out of towners* was the expression people around Landon used when describing tourists.

"We've got a lot of specialty drinks," Elaine said. She was the youngest of the Carter girls, a fact which she rubbed in with a great deal of glee on the eve of Tina's birthday, while they were at Shore Leave. Unlike her sisters, who were energetic and talkative, much like their father, Elaine was quieter, more observant. She regarded me in the saffron glow of the bar lights, tapping an index finger against her chin, and finally asked, "Can I tell you something?"

"Sure," I said gamely.

Elaine tipped her head to the right and pursed her lips as though fishing for the way to best express her thoughts. At last she settled for, "Tina told you that I read the cards, right?"

I nodded.

"I do, but I also get these strong senses about people. I can't quite figure out what I'm sensing with you…" She let her voice trail away and a shiver crept its little cat feet up my spine; my arms broke out in goosebumps, which Elaine noticed. "See, you get what I'm talking about! All I can speculate is that there's a…this sounds weird, but it's what I'm getting, so work with me…there's a *tearing* in your soul. An old one, from a long time ago, so probably not this lifetime. And it needs to get stitched back up."

For a split second my vision wavered, as though I'd submerged my head in Flickertail. I blinked, fighting the sensation, forcing my focus back to Elaine.

"I know it sounds crazy," she was saying. "See, your soul, like everyone's, has been around forever, and it—"

The phone near the till rang, interrupting whatever it was that Elaine was about to say, and there wasn't another moment to talk about non-work-related subjects the rest of the evening; the bar grew busy shortly thereafter. So it wasn't until I was home in bed that night that I was able to fully ponder Elaine's words about the tearing in my soul, the one that needed stitching. I was not normally hooked by those kinds of abstract comments; I was the one who had scoffed at my friends in Chicago when they got all excited about their horoscopes and birth signs.

But you believe in Aunt Jilly. Her Notions are never wrong, so there is certainly far more to the world than you can see.

I acknowledged these truths as I lay curled on my side, my favorite afghan tucked around my legs. Millie snored beside me, clutching her stuffed panda, and I stroked through her glossy curls, attempting to form a concrete opinion. Elaine had meant past lives, suggesting that my soul had been wounded (or the equivalent…I didn't know if a soul could actually receive a wound, like flesh) in another lifetime. But when, and how? Perhaps most importantly, *who?* Elaine had seemed certain but I could forge no connection with any sense of a past self, at least not as I lay awake, trying. Were multiple lifetimes possible? Was I crazy for entertaining the idea that they were? I let my eyes sink shut, concentrating on the shifting, muted color patterns present on the backs of my eyelids, speculating that a soul must look somewhat similar—amorphous, colorful, ever-changing.

But in the end I fell asleep before reaching any sort of conclusion.

The mountains.

I could see their jagged peaks on the distant, hazy horizon as I plodded along, my feet bare, the ground beneath them proving more painful with each step. Tall, swaying grass on all sides and the chilly sun about three hours past noon. I was so thirsty that my tongue seemed twice its usual size and I was having trouble thinking of anything other than water. Even my own despair, brutal as a whip cutting chunks from my skin, seemed minimized by the desire for liquid.

Where are you? I begged, my slow forward progress stalling to a full stop. I directed this unspoken question to the enormous sky that arched, silent and impassive, above the prairie. I wavered, afraid to lose focus; it seemed the sky might suck me into itself, my body lost forever in that unending blue. My legs begged permission to sink to the ground; I battled this growing temptation. If I sank, I would not rise again. The air rippled as would the surface of a river in a brisk wind and I wrapped into my own arms. I was cold down to my bones.

Don't stop walking. You cannot stop walking. Stopping means death.

I can't die. He's looking for me. I know this.

Ragged sobs swelled in my center. I bent forward, agonized, rendered immobile.

He won't stop searching. He will find me. Goddammit, keep walking.

The sky pulled at my head. The ground tugged at my feet.

I sank to a crouch.

I jerked awake, thrashing free of the covers, nearly knocking Millie Jo from the bed. Startled by my sudden movements my daughter began fussing, rubbing her eyes with both fists, though I could hardly hear her over the roaring of my pulse. My mouth was dry as campfire ashes—a shuddering convulsion overtook me, almost like a small seizure.

"Stop," I commanded, my voice rasping over the word. I meant to address the panic clutching my midsection but Millie cried harder, thinking I meant her, and I forced myself to sit up, sweaty and horribly disoriented, the afghan falling to my hips. Even though my jaw was numb, I whispered, "Come here, baby, it's all right," and gathered her close, gradually comforted by the normalcy of feeding my daughter. And after a time my heartrate decreased, my blood slowed its frantic pace. I drew up my knees, holding Millie Jo close as she nursed, blinking into the silvery dimness of an early winter morning. Beside my bed on the nightstand, the picture of Malcolm Carter, along with his letter and telegram, were still front and center; the photograph had been in that exact place for nearly two years now.

Without questioning my actions, I reached and tipped it facedown atop the nightstand.

Chapter Seven

December, 2005

"HONEY, CAN YOU TAKE THE TEN-TOP IN THE BAR?" Grandma asked as I hurried through the front door of Shore Leave, shivering and cold, wishing I could manage to take orders wearing my mittens. She explained, "Jillian is swamped in here."

"Sure, Gram." It was much busier than a usual Thursday night this close to Christmas, laughter and chatter spilling from both the dining room and the bar, serving to thaw me a little. The decorated trees and twinkling lights strung festively along the counter also worked to ease my low mood. Both White Oaks and Shore Leave had been jam-packed this entire week, as Landon's annual ice fishing event (Bull and Dodge called it a "convention" but it was really just an excuse for men from across Minnesota and Wisconsin to gather and drink beer, all the while sitting on tiny stools in their ice shacks on the lake) was in its third day, and subsequently in full swing. Flickertail resembled a community of refugees, dozens of icehouses of every conceivable color clustered near its center.

I felt a lightening in my shoulders as I hung my puffy down coat on the hook behind the front door, the party-like atmosphere working a little magic, and brushed melting snow from my face. Grabbing my server apron from the drawer behind the counter, I asked Grandma, "Has the ten-top been here long?"

"No," she said, as I stashed a few extra pens in my apron pocket. "It's Eddie and some of the other fishermen. They just came in from the lake and it's one fish story after another in there. I don't know how Ellen stands it." She worried her lower lip between her teeth before saying, "Jake's here with a couple of his friends. I thought I better let you know."

I knew Jake was home, as Tish and Ruthie kept me well informed, though this would be the first I'd seen him. I straightened my spine and managed a smile as Aunt Jilly breezed past with a tray of draft beer. Her golden hair was pinned up with a sparkly poinsettia barrette; clad in a red-and-white striped sweater and with flushed cheeks, she looked like a Christmas pixie.

"Sweetie, can you manage Eddie's bunch?" she called.

"Yes!" I called after her retreating form.

"Hi, Camille!" heralded Clint, rounding the corner from the bar at full speed, hot chocolate mug in hand. He wore a green felt hat meant to resemble an elf's stocking cap, which Tish, on his heels, was grabbing for. She bumped his hot chocolate and it sloshed on her sweater sleeve (an old one of mine, I noticed).

"Give it back!" Tish yelped, giggling, standing on her tiptoes to reach for the elf hat.

Both of them were giddy—with the Christmas spirit, I hoped, and not stolen sips of booze. Even though I didn't live in the same house with my sisters I felt pretty confident that they would tell me if they'd engaged in any illicit behavior; besides, Tish was determined to earn a scholarship or two, not about to let something like underage drinking ruin her chances at law school.

"Hiya, Clinty," I said. "Nice hat."

"Eddie's table is thirsty, you better hurry," Tish said, abandoning her effort to seize the elf hat, ducking behind me to help tighten the strings of my apron. I used the opportunity to covertly smell her breath, but detected no hint of alcohol.

"I'm hurrying," I insisted, twisting my hair into a knot high on my head, securing it with the rubber band I'd slipped around my wrist before leaving the house.

I felt a little sloppy, since I'd washed my hair but hadn't done anything in the way of styling it this evening; it had grown long and unmanageable. The one beauty salon in town only seemed to be open when I was at work and I'd not yet taken up Aunt Jilly on her offer of a trim. I wore a red flannel shirt that hadn't fit since before I was pregnant, a soft, fitted one; I was elated by the fact that it buttoned over my chest again, though it remained snug across my breasts. And wonder of wonders, in the last few months I'd been able to zip into a couple of old pairs of jeans.

Light at the end of the tunnel, I thought, cautiously optimistic. When I stood naked after showering these days, giving myself a critical once-over, at least *parts* of my body resembled their former selves.

"Milla, for real! I was about to take their order and I'm not even on shift!" Tish nagged. Satisfied that she'd secured my apron, she turned to the jukebox that Grandma had found at a discount store and dumped a couple of quarters into it. "Rockin' Around the Christmas Tree" blared joyously forth as I hurried into the bar, which glowed with mini twinkle-lights, fake icicles, and shiny tinsel; the blue spruce that Dodge had chopped down for us was festooned with edible ornaments in the far corner, as usual.

Jake sat at a high-top with two of his friends that I recognized from Landon High; he broke into a happy smile at the sight of me but I could do little more than wave as I navigated my way through the boisterous bar crowd.

"Hi, sweetie!" said Eddie Sorenson as I reached their table, rowdy with at least ten ice fishermen. I stopped near Eddie, my right hip at his shoulder. He enthused, "Just in time, we're *dying* of thirst!"

"So, you didn't get the plaid shirt memo?" I teased, noting that he was the only one not wearing some version of checkered flannel. I indicated my own shirt with my pen. "Even *I* did!"

Eddie and everyone near him laughed, and he flung open his Carhartt jacket the way a flasher would, to reveal a green-and-black check on the shirt beneath.

I giggled, flipping open my order pad. "Are you guys eating or just drinking this evening?"

"Bring us two baskets of onion rings—" Eddie began.

"Shit, Ed, that's not near enough," said someone down the table and my eyes flickered toward the sound of a voice I didn't recognize.

I thought I knew everyone in Landon by now, especially anyone who would be sitting at Eddie's table; Eddie and his little bar on Fisherman's Street were such fixtures in Landon that guidebooks probably listed them as landmarks. This guy was holding a menu, regarding me with a lazy half-smile, and for the length of two heartbeats our eyes held completely still and steady. I was only aware of my heart at that moment because it delivered a solid punch to my breastbone. I blinked and looked immediately away from him, back to Eddie; my right hand, holding the pen, trembled a little.

What the hell?

I injected as much good nature into my tone as I could manage as I addressed the table at large. "What else, guys? A couple more pitchers, too?"

"Give us two more of the High Lifes and then five baskets…" Eddie paused and made a point of addressing the stranger—though he didn't seem to be a stranger to anyone but me—teasing, "Is that all right with you, buddy-boy?" With a grin, Eddie concluded, "All right, five baskets of onion rings and how about two fried mushrooms. And tell Rich light on the salt!"

"Coming right up." I tore off their order and retreated to the kitchen, where Rich and Blythe were busy keeping up with the unexpected crowd. I didn't notice Jake until he caught up with me at the dining room counter.

"Camille," he said, enveloping me in a hug. I was glad to see him but wished that he wouldn't feel compelled to hug me. Drawing away, he added, "You look *incredible*. Don't be mad at me for saying so."

I shook my head, smiling a little in spite of myself; it was tough not to at such a genuine compliment. "Thanks, Jake. How's school been this fall?"

"Great," he said, as I went to the ticket window to pass Rich the order. "Couple of appetizers, light on the salt for Eddie!"

"You've been working at White Oaks, Tish was saying," Jake continued.

I turned to face him as he straddled a stool at the counter; he was tall enough that with him sitting, we were nearly the same height. I couldn't help but think that surely there were girls at the U who would be thrilled to date him. "I have, yes."

Jake leaned on his elbows. "How have you been? How's Millie Jo? I've missed you guys." He spoke with such sincerity that I squirmed, rolling to my toes and then back down.

"She's getting bigger all the time. And she's really excited for Christmas." Because Jake seemed inclined to carry on a long conversation, I added, "I better get that beer for Eddie's table."

"You need help?" he asked immediately.

I tried to tease him a little. "I'm the server here. You're supposed to be relaxing."

He flushed. "Right."

I was poised to fly to the bar but my gaze flashed to someone beyond Jake's shoulder at that second, some instinct setting off an alarm in my mind. The breath I was about to release lodged in my lungs. I suddenly found myself trying desperately to act normal, a sure-fire sign that attraction raged like a drug through my bloodstream. It had been so long since I'd experienced such a feeling that it was almost surreal.

Quit it right now. I was truly furious at myself. *Quit staring at him.*

Before I could quit staring at him, however, the stranger from Eddie's table stopped right beside Jake and clapped him on the back in a companionable, if drunken, fashion. And then, to my amazement, he absolutely grinned at me; I felt the intensity of it like a burst of summer sunshine. He said to Jake, "Hey there, McCall. Long time no see."

"Hey," said Jake, distractedly; I could tell he didn't like that my attention had been diverted. "I heard you were home."

"I would *love* an introduction to you," the stranger said, offering me another radiant grin, one that I felt straight to my tailbone. I realized he was pretty damn intoxicated as he added in a teasing way, "But first, I gotta use the pisser."

Jake shot him a look that clearly asked, *You're talking this way in front of a girl?*

Irritated at myself for finding this stranger so attractive, I snapped, "The little boys' room is that way," and jerked a thumb over my shoulder to indicate, earning a look of amusement rather than the embarrassment I was secretly hoping for.

He was probably a few years older than Jake and me, with the kind of build you'd expect on maybe a construction worker or a firefighter, one who handled large, heavy things on a regular basis. His flannel shirt was a blue-on-black check, rolled back at the sleeves so that the cords of muscle along his forearms were clearly displayed, along with a lot of dark hair. The deep navy blue of his shirt almost exactly matched his irises. He had thick black hair and what was probably a good day's worth of scruff on his jaw and he was, as Grandma would say, as handsome as the devil. There was a dimple in his right cheek.

I felt shivery-hot, full-body flushed, all the damn way to my toes.

"Thanks," he murmured. Our gazes held and my stupid, stupid heart splattered against my ribs. My nipples were ready to slice through my nursing bra. I shrugged in a heroic attempt to convey disdain and his grin only deepened, along with his dimple.

Oh, holy Jesus. Don't even think about it, Camille.

Unable to draw a full breath I muttered, "Excuse me," and escaped to the bar, ashamed for such a ridiculous reaction to a complete stranger. Because Aunt Ellen already had her hands full with drink orders I ducked behind the bar counter and collected two pitchers, tilting one after the other beneath the beer tap. When I turned around, Tish was elbowed up to the bar wearing the green elf hat.

"You foamed those perfect," she said, nodding at the pitchers, each with a perfect inch and a half of froth at the top.

"Where did you guys get that dumb hat?" I asked, and then rolled my eyes as the jukebox kicked in with Bing Crosby crooning "White Christmas."

"How many times do we have to hear this song this week?" I groaned.

"Like we're dreaming of a white Christmas around here," Tish joked.

"Are those for us?" And there he was again, obviously back from the bathroom, leaning against the bar beside my sister and pinning me with that same grin. He indicated my full hands with a tilt of his head.

"Hey," Tish said cheerily, as though they were longtime buddies, so totally Tish. She asked him, "Are *you* dreaming of a white Christmas?"

"Experiencing one," he corrected, dark eyebrows lifting as he regarded her cockeyed hat, with amusement. Instead of commenting on it, he said, "I just played the song, though. I love this one. Isn't it great? God, I love Christmas."

"This is our favorite, isn't it?" Tish asked me, giggling.

I almost smiled at that. I bit the insides of my cheeks.

"So, I'll help you carry those if you tell me your name," he offered, dimple appearing.

My heart panged, the sound of a hammer striking an anvil. Breathing became an effort. *Oh dear God, you are gorgeous*, I told him without speaking; our gazes intertwined again, perhaps for no more than a few seconds, but it was enough for my blood to sizzle beneath the surface of my skin; I swore I could observe the same thing happening within him. I reminded myself, taking no prisoners, what had happened the last time I'd been so stupid about a guy, and it was with true determination that I vowed, *And I will not notice that from this moment forth. In fact, I plan to steer clear of your path altogether.*

"I got it," I said, not quite brusquely but not far from it, and carried both pitchers to the table, where they were received with extreme gratitude. I collected a tray of empty glasses and on the return trip didn't even make eye contact with him, attempting to appear steely and unapproachable.

It's for the best, I insisted. But then…

"So, who is that?" Here I was casing Tish not fifteen seconds later, back at the bar. I was such a hypocrite.

"Who, Mathias?" she asked, looking over her shoulder at Eddie's table.

"*Shh!*" I hissed, refusing to look that direction.

Tish whipped around to roll her eyes at me. She said knowingly, "He's got a girlfriend. And it's Tess French. At least, that's what Clint and Liam told me."

Of course he has a girlfriend. And then, pretending there wasn't a chorus of dismayed, falling notes in my mind, I thought, *Tess French?* I remembered Tess as a popular blond girl who'd been friends with Mandy Pearson—Mandy, whose goal it had been to make my days at Landon High miserable.

"Who cares about that?" I asked, surely making it entirely obvious that *I* cared about that. Heading back to the dining room, I persisted, "Who is he, though? I've never seen him before."

Tish followed me and claimed a stool at the counter. It was just as busy in here as it was in the bar, the tables all crammed full. Aunt Jilly was leaning one hip against the corner booth, where Justin, Clint, and Rae were all seated, along with Dodge; Rae was perched on her grandpa's lap, brown eyes wide and full of wonder as she observed the noisy crowd.

Tish said, "He just moved back from the Cities. His name is Mathias." I nodded at this news, repeating his name in my mind. *Mathias*. It sounded old-fashioned. My sister added, "Mathias Carter. Like, from White Oaks."

"Wait, Bull's son? No kidding?" My heart hammered anew, this time with outright surprise. "I've heard all about him from his sisters. I thought his name was Matty." I was babbling and felt Tish angling me a speculative look. I snapped my mouth closed.

"Camille, order's up!" Rich called, and I looked over to see the entire window full of onion ring baskets.

"I'll help," Tish offered, even though she wasn't technically on shift this evening. She took a second to band her curly hair into a ponytail and then together we carted the food out to the ice fishermen.

And as much as I tried to pretend I didn't notice Mathias Carter, it was a flat-out lie.

So here was Tina, Glenna, and Elaine's baby brother, the workaholic and dater of poodle-like women, visiting from Minneapolis. I'd heard so much in the last two years that I felt like I already knew him. He sat with one elbow curled over the back of his chair, tipping it onto two legs as he listened to one of the other guys, but as I deposited the food and the ketchup and double-checked their beer pitchers, purposely keeping away from his side of the table, he looked right over at me. I refused to return his gaze.

"Another pitcher?" I asked Eddie, who was always the unofficial leader.

"Yes, ma'am!"

Thirty minutes later Shore Leave had mellowed to its usual crowd. I hid out like a coward, avoiding the bar, soliciting Tish to cash out their tickets for me. Tish was willing to help and thankfully didn't question my motives; she was currently holed up in a booth with Clint and Liam, playing poker with a pile of individually-wrapped dinner mints. Dodge and Jake had joined the ice fishermen, most of them now sipping coffee and chatting. Mathias Carter was still in the exact same spot at Eddie's table—he hadn't ventured out of the bar to use the bathroom, I'd noticed. I pretended that I was not completely aware of his exact location.

Grandma was wiping down the counter in the dining room while Aunt Jilly rolled silverware at table three; Justin had taken Rae home to bed. I was just moving to help with the never-ending task when Mom came from outside, the bell above the door tinkling in her wake. Her golden hair hung loose over her shoulders. She was wearing her warmest sweater, a deep green one that matched her eyes, a gray wool scarf that I knew was Blythe's, gray leggings and big furry boots, carrying Millie Jo, who was bundled in her snowsuit.

"Millie missed you," Mom explained.

"Hi, baby," I said to my daughter, her little round face peering out from behind the furry rim of her hood. I collected her into my arms, lowering her hood, peppering her cheeks with kisses.

Blythe came from the kitchen at the sound of Mom's voice. He said, "C'mere, sweetheart, you look cold," and wrapped Mom into his embrace, where she snuggled close.

"Aw, I was hoping I'd see Millie before I left," Jake said, from behind me. But when I turned around I had eyes only for Mathias, who was draping a scarf around his neck as he walked in a group with Dodge, Eddie, and Jim Olson. All of the men were clad in their winter outer gear, clearly preparing to leave; Mathias tugged a gray wool hat over his coal-black hair and our eyes met.

Before I could stop it, I thought, *Please don't go. I haven't even talked to you yet.*

Jake patted Millie's back. "Hey there, Millie Jo."

"Say hi to Jake," I prompted my daughter, dragging my gaze from Mathias. I figured he would walk past but to my stun he came right over, abruptly re-centering all of my focus, like a magnifying glass would the light.

"What a sweetheart you are," Mathias said to Millie Jo, his dimple appearing as he grinned; the joyful expression seemed to come naturally to him. With the ease of someone accustomed to little kids he took her hand into the tips of his fingers and gently bounced it, seeking my gaze, which was already fastened upon him. He guessed, "Your little sister?"

"Her daughter," Jake corrected, before I could reply. Irritation prickled through me that he would answer for me that way.

Oh, Mathias said, without sound, dark eyebrows lifting. He carefully removed all traces of surprise from his face; I watched it happen. Then he added, "Well, she's adorable." He addressed Millie, asking, "What's your name, little one?"

"Millie Jo!" she answered, giving him her biggest crinkly-eyed smile, practically flirting. In the next instant she spied Tish and squirreled down from my arms, running to tug on Tish's sweater, begging to be lifted up.

"And what's yours? You *still* haven't told me," Mathias said next, his eyes holding mine.

I damned my heart for thrusting so fiercely, beset by a sudden, powerful urge to touch his face. He was probably about five inches taller than me, and I could see his resemblance to Bull, the black hair and incredibly powerful shoulders. But his eyes were purely Diana's, the sort of intense dark blue you see in primary-color blocks. For an odd and overwhelming moment, I forgot my name. At last I all but stuttered, "Camille."

"I should have introduced you guys, I'm sorry," Jake was apologizing. "Milla, this is Mathias Carter. He graduated three years before us."

"Nice to meet you," I said, and my voice was thin and reedy. Determined not to continue sounding like a moron, I asked, "You've been living in the Cities?"

"Wait, you're Camille?" Mathias asked, not answering my question. "Camille who's been working at White Oaks?"

"Yes, I've been helping out in the bar—" I started to say, but Mom interrupted, however inadvertently, coming over and giving Mathias a fond hug.

"Welcome home," she told him. "Your mother is so relieved that you're back in Landon, I can't even tell you."

Mathias grinned gamely at her words. His cheeks were flushed and his scarf just slightly askew; a few dark curls had escaped the back edge of his wool hat. I swallowed and tried to pretend I didn't feel too warm with him so near. I could not pull my foolish gaze from his face.

"I'm home for good now," he explained to Mom, but his eyes were back on mine. "Spent enough time in the city."

Mom commandeered Jake's elbow, tugging him away as she explained, "Blythe had a question for you…"

The noisy bustle of everyone leaving jostled me closer to Mathias.

"Your family was really worried you'd never come home," I said, almost inanely. He had to be experiencing the strange, wordless communication happening between us; I was not just imagining it. We seemed safely lodged in a small bubble of intimacy, even here in the noisy cafe.

"I know they were," he acknowledged, with such tender affection that my belly went light and airy as dandelion seed. "It was time to come back. I lived in Minneapolis for over four years. Three and a half years too many, if you want to know the truth."

"Are you living in the homesteader's cabin again?"

Wry amusement lifted one corner of his lips at this question and my eyes detoured to his mouth; he had what Grandma called a cupid's bow on his top lip, close enough that I caught the faint scent of beer on his breath. Rather than making me want to draw away, it only served to increase my instinct to lean closer to him.

"Nah, the summer is when I used to do that." His eyes crinkled just a little at the corners as he studied my face as though searching for answers to questions only he knew. "But I love that old cabin, always have. The thing is, Dad has been telling me all about this girl who was interested in the Carter family history. *You*, I mean. See, I used to—"

Dodge wrapped a big hand around Mathias's shoulder in that instant and said with a good-natured roar, "Boy, you tell that goddamn Bull he owes me money from last August!"

"I will, Dodge, and you know what he'll say," Mathias replied, leaning a shoulder into Dodge for emphasis. "He'll say that you owe him from that one poker game in '76 or whatever. Shit, I can't keep track."

"Well, we're glad you're home, ain't we?" Dodge said, winking as if including me in this pronouncement. And all I could think was, *Yes. Yes, I am glad.*

"I'm so happy to be back, you don't even know," Mathias said in response, his dimple appearing again, making my heart hitch even worse. "City life is not for this boy. Took me a while to figure that out, but give me the northwoods every time."

"Mathias, you coming?" Jake asked. Even without looking his way, I could tell Jake was bristling with irritation.

"That's right, I need a ride. Thanks, McCall," Mathias said. "Drank more than I intended, but it's a night of celebration, right guys? We're out at eight tomorrow, Dodge. Dad and Sam are coming, too."

"Yessir," Dodge agreed. "Bright and early! We'll stop in for coffee first, Camille."

I said, "It wouldn't be a normal Friday morning if you didn't."

Jake said, "See you soon, Milla," but I could hardly even look at him.

Mathias put one hand on my left elbow for just a fraction of a second before he tugged on a woolen glove and though it seemed like a polite gesture more than anything, heat flared along my skin from the brief point of contact. "It was good to meet you, Camille. I'll see you at White Oaks. And it sounds like tomorrow morning."

I sank to a chair as they left, watching until Mathias was out the door. He looked back just before leaving, catching me staring after him. Wrapping his scarf more securely, he beamed—already I sensed this was a natural expression for him—and lifted one gloved hand to wave good-bye. And I cursed December for its long nights, already wishing it was morning.

Chapter Eight

I WOKE BEFORE DAWN, AFTER A BLESSEDLY DREAMLESS SLEEP. IN THE shower I steamed myself like a bundle of snow crab legs, taking time to shave my armpits and my legs (normally I didn't bother in the winter, but I was struck with a blast of femininity that had been absent in my routine for too long). I studied my face in the mirror after wiping away condensation, leaving a small circle in which to critically peruse, combing wet hair back from my forehead, appraising my pale skin and the undeniable fire in my eyes; there was no mistaking that for anything but what it was—elation at the thought of seeing Mathias this morning at the cafe.

What are you doing? I thought, dismay at once diluting my exhilaration. *What in the hell are you doing?*

But that was a question I could not answer, and so gave up trying.

I brushed my teeth and blew out my hair (Grandma came upstairs to see what the racket was all about, not recognizing the sound of the hot-air dryer) and then left it loose over my shoulders rather than scraping its length into the usual ponytail. My hair was just like Dad's, dark and curly, and I used to consider it my best feature. I ignored what was probably a lot of split ends. My cosmetics supply was meager, if not to say nonexistent, so I settled for applying some lip balm, avoiding my gaze in the mirror. Standing before my closet a minute later, wrapped in a towel, I was assaulted anew with doubts.

Why does it matter what you wear, how you look? It's so stupid, Camille. Mathias has a girlfriend. You are setting yourself up to get hurt. You're as bad as Jake.

The minutes ticked by and I grew edgy, at last yanking a faded green sweater from its hanger; it was soft and almost worn through at the elbows, but it had once been one of my favorites and would subsequently fit over my breasts, which were harnessed into my huge, totally unsexy nursing bra. In the kitchen, Millie stood on a chair near Grandma, helping to roll out biscuit dough on the floured counter. The scent of cinnamon rolls filled the small, warm space. Grandma's long braid hung over her right shoulder; she smiled my way, using the edge of her wrist to wipe a smudge of butter from her cheek, as her hands were covered in sticky flour.

She wondered aloud, "Was that you singing in the shower? I thought it must be a burglar or something, surely not my granddaughter."

I flushed a little, which did not go unnoticed, but Grandma didn't tease me further. I helped myself to a glass of orange juice. "That looks yummy, Millie Jo-Jo."

"Ellen said you're heading over to the cafe with her," Grandma said. "She'll appreciate the company. I don't know how she listens to those fishermen go on and on without stabbing someone."

I giggled and went to kiss Millie's cheek. She cried, "Hi, Mama! Me and Gwandma are making more cinnamon wolls!"

I couldn't believe my daughter would be two years old this next Valentine's Day; it seemed unimaginable. I smoothed dark curls from her soft forehead, studying her golden-green eyes with a sense of wonder. No trace of Noah had yet emerged in her features, as though he hadn't contributed a thing to the conception of her, as though she was formed in my body by me alone. I knew it was silly, and surely vain, but a petty, vindictive part of me remained glad there was nothing of him in her appearance. Noah didn't deserve her, wasn't worthy of a single hair on her precious head. He hadn't set eyes upon her, to my knowledge, since June of 2004. Though Millie knew her grandparents, Curt and Marie Utley, I honestly had no idea if she'd ever heard Noah mentioned in any context. I would ask Marie next time we talked; Millie was getting old enough to wonder about a daddy.

"I don't mind their stories," I murmured, in response to Grandma's comment about the ice fishermen. "They make me laugh."

Grandma's gaze flickered over to me as she rummaged in a drawer for the biscuit cutter. Millie filched a piece of dough and ate it without a sound. I winked at her as we shared the secret and she giggled, hiding her mouth behind both hands and rocking forward.

"I saw that, Miss Millie," Grandma said, and then to me, "Well, be sure to bundle up, hon."

"The high is supposed to be ten degrees today," I said, which was the equivalent of a heatwave. "But I'll grab my scarf."

"Millie and I will be over once these rolls are done," Grandma said.

Aunt Ellen and I walked to the cafe through lightly-falling snow, arm-in-arm. It was a pure white day, both ground and sky taking on the appearance of an artist's blank canvas, against which brown and gray tree branches created a stark contrast. The air was so still we could hear the whisper of the falling snow. I tipped my face and stuck out my tongue, and Aunt Ellen laughed.

"That reminds me of when you girls were little," Aunt Ellen said, hugging my arm to her side. Then she pointed toward the parking lot. "There comes Dodge and if I'm not mistaken, the Carters' big plow truck."

At those words, electricity sizzled through my limbs, leaving my nerves sparking. I followed the direction of her gaze and saw Dodge's big winter truck, followed by a growling blue diesel with a canary-yellow plow attachment, hitched high at the moment to avoid the snowy ground.

"We better get that coffee perking," Aunt Ellen said. She wore a crocheted white hat and matching scarf, and hurried up the steps ahead of me; admittedly, I was lingering to catch the first glimpse of Mathias. From across the parking lot, I watched Bull lumber down from the plow truck; to my dismay, Tina's husband Sam climbed from the passenger door. What if Mathias wasn't with? What if he slept in, or decided it wasn't worth getting up so early on a Friday morning…

But then I saw him bound out of the truck; he'd been in the backseat. He was bundled in heavy-duty Carhartt bibs and the same gray wool hat as last night, and I imagined that the blue of his eyes was visible even with the distance currently separating us. The men met up with Dodge as one more truck rumbled into the snowy lot. Mathias caught sight of me and I saw him grin; he lifted one arm in a wave and I felt another bolt of lightning strike my center. I waved once, quickly, suddenly self-conscious, and darted into the cafe, following Aunt Ellen's footsteps. Once inside, I shed my coat and scarf, agonizing over the static snapping through my hair. I smoothed my sweater and busied myself helping Aunt Ellen with the coffee.

The men clattered in seconds later, stomping their boots, full of loud chatter and excitement over the day to come, spent crouched freezing around small holes drilled into the ice. Some things I would just never fully understand. My gaze was drawn, magnet-like, to Mathias, who hung his coat next to mine (unintentionally, as I clearly understood). Under his snow bibs he wore a thermal-underwear shirt, dark blue and form-fitting, emphasizing the powerful muscles of his arms and torso. The breath in my lungs became suddenly thin and insubstantial.

Camille Anne Gordon. Stop it.

Here he comes.

Jesus Crimeny. Act normal.

"Good morning," he said, straddling a stool at the counter just across from where I stood, pretending to be busy making coffee. His cheeks were flushed from the cold. He was freshly shaved and still wearing his hat, from under which his longish hair was visible. There were curls on his neck; those and his dimple gave him a quality of sweetness that was belied by the devilish glint in his blue eyes. He leaned forward on his elbows and grinned, with absolutely no regard for what this did to my pulse.

"Good morning," I responded, and caught myself as I stood totally immobile, doing nothing more than smiling back at him. I turned back to the coffee maker, bumping my hip in my haste, and said over my shoulder, "This'll be ready in just a minute."

Bull came to join his son and wrapped an arm around Mathias. He roared, "Camille! Hi, darlin'. This here is the boy I've been so goddamn worried about, home at last!"

"We met last night," I told Bull, smiling at him; I adored Bull. My gaze flickered to Mathias, then away, as though he'd radiated a sudden sunbeam directly into my eyes. "Home to stay, it sounds like."

"Gonna start up a plow business," Dodge said, claiming the other stool, his bulk sandwiching Mathias against Bull.

"That's the plan," Mathias said, cheerful and smiley. "At least for this winter. Skid Erickson and I have been talking about it since last spring."

The coffee pot burbled and Aunt Ellen came over with the basket of cinnamon rolls she'd carried from the house. Men that I recognized as the Carter girls' husbands joined them at the counter and I hurried to line up mugs and pour coffee; when I got to Mathias, I felt his gaze on me even though he was talking with his dad. They all thanked me but I remained stupidly tongue-tied and retreated to table three, just behind the row of stools at the counter, where I poured my own mug of coffee; I was just tearing open a second sugar packet when Mathias did a half-turn on his stool so that he was facing me. He pulled off his hat and his hair was a little wild with static electricity; one strand in particular was sticking up from his forehead and I felt my fingers twitch, wanting to touch it…just tuck it back into place.

"Care if I join you?" he asked. The others were arguing about lures and didn't seem to notice when he moved without waiting for my response, settling just across the table from me.

"Not at all." I allowed a little sarcastic teasing into my tone and he smiled again, his dimple appearing.

"So, I've heard about you since last winter," he said, clearly wanting to chat. I marveled at this attention but figured that he was just being polite. And probably wondering why in the hell I cared so much about his family's ancestors anyway.

"I've heard about you, too," I allowed, stirring sugar into my mug. I let myself meet his eyes and tried not to gulp at the gorgeous sight of him in the bright morning light, no more than three feet from me. If only he wasn't *so* good-looking; the feeling of being kicked in the chest might dissipate.

That's a cheap excuse, I thought. *And you're being a moron.*

I gathered my wits and explained, "Two winters ago, when I was still pregnant, I found this picture in an old trunk from our attic. It was taken in 1875 and it was a photograph of a man standing by his horse." I would *not* mention how I'd kept this beside my bed ever since. "The back of the picture said 'Carter,' so I ended up asking your sisters, and then your dad, and we think that the man is maybe part of—"

"The family who originally built White Oaks," he interrupted, and then immediately said, "Sorry, I have a bad habit of that. Keep going."

"Yes, the family who built the homestead cabin, too. Your dad is pretty sure his name is Malcolm, and I also found this letter in the trunk, written by him—"

"Can you bring it to work tonight? You work tonight, right?" he asked, and I was not imagining the note of anticipation in his tone.

"You're interrupting again," I pointed out and he grinned, sending sparks all along my skin. "I do, and I will."

"Sorry, I get carried away. Dad said something about a telegram, too."

"Yes, it's very urgent-sounding and in it Malcolm says that he was searching for something. And that's the last correspondence from him, ever since." I paused to take a sip of my coffee; I debated mentioning that I was determined to discover what happened to him after that telegram.

Mathias leaped in with, "So you're wondering where he ended up, right? That reminds me of why I used to spend all summer in that old homesteader's cabin. My sisters think I'm crazy, but I love it out there and I like thinking about all the people who've lived in that space before me. It's full of dust and bat shit and spiders now, I know, but there's always been something appealing about it. Did Dad tell you that I found an old ring tucked behind a stone in the fireplace? It was the most—"

"You did?" I was interrupting him this time, thrilled at this revelation. And also the fact that he wondered about who came before, the people that lived in the cabin since the 1860s. "Will you show me?"

"For a small price," he said, with slight wickedness in both his tone and the angle of his black eyebrows. Upon seeing my immediate wariness, he rushed to explain, "I'm just kidding. I was going to say that you can't believe anything my sisters tell you about me. That's the price."

I giggled at this, telling him with undisguised smugness, "They've already told me just about everything, anyway."

"Dammit," he muttered, and irritated affection for his sisters was apparent in his voice. He implored, "Don't listen to them. Shit, Elaine hasn't tried to read the cards for you, has she? Don't let her, she'll tell you all sorts of crazy things and then expect you to make sense of them."

"Like what? What sorts of things?" I was fascinated by the animation on his face.

"Like that you have to heal something from the past to make sense of the future, and all sorts of abstract hoo-ha that—"

I was laughing then, interrupting him to demand, "Did you actually just say 'hoo-ha?'"

He ducked his head, laughing but seeming a little shy at the same time, as the skin over his cheekbones flushed. "Yes, yes I did. I try to use embarrassing words like that frequently."

I studied him, completely enraptured, my gaze roving shamelessly over his black hair, his nose—knife-edged and perfect—his lips with their cupid's bow curve, the powerful, sloping curve of his wide shoulders, forearms bared by his pushed-back sleeves and covered in dark hair; his hands—currently wrapped about his coffee mug, capable-looking hands with strong, blunt fingers. His nails were square, his knuckles forming ridges of peaks. I tried to picture this man as a business major, or dressed in a formal suit and striding along a busy city sidewalk, but could not. He appeared so right, here in Landon, rugged and dressed to go ice-fishing. I realized I was being outright rude, staring so openly at him without saying a word. Fortunately for me, Bull, Dodge, and the other men were rising from their seats, thanking Ellen, and Bull said to Mathias, "Boy, you about ready?"

Mathias blinked, his face somber, but then that grin burst through—beaming as heatedly as the noontime sun in July. Grinning just for me; or at least, I pretended that he was grinning for that reason. He finished off his coffee with a gulp and tugged his hat back over his hair, curls still sticking out along the back edge. I bit my bottom lip, hard.

"What time do you work tonight?" He leaned forward over the table to ask.

"At five," I whispered.

"Well, I will see you then." He rose and pushed in his chair; for a moment he curled one hand over the back edge, looking down at me as I stared right back up at him, unable to stop. His eyes were absolutely beautiful, such a striking blue and fringed with long lashes, his straight black brows almost stern above them. I sensed that he was just as caught off guard by this unexpected undercurrent flowing between us, even stronger than it was last night.

"See you later, sweetie," Bull said to me.

Mathias looked my way as he zipped up his coat, appearing nearly twice as imposing in all of his winter gear. I studied him with no smile, just absorbing his expression, every bit as serious as my own. Then he smiled as he wound his scarf and I felt everything inside of me leap, blood and heart and senses, toward him. I watched through the wide front windows as the six of them made their way back to their trucks; I was pressing my fingertips to the glass before I realized what I was doing. Out in the parking lot, Mathias bent down and scooped up an armload of fluffy snow, throwing it over his brothers-in-law. Even through the glass and with the heater running, I heard their shouted threats as he laughed and darted away; Sam clamped him around the torso and they wrestled around, almost tumbling to the snow. I giggled.

"That Mathias has always been crazy," Grandma said, coming into the cafe carrying Millie Jo, stamping snow from her boots, indicating the scuffle in the parking lot.

"Cwazy!" Millie parroted, and I reflected that they were both right, as my heart was going crazy just watching him.

That evening Tina and I were scheduled to work the dining room and Elaine the bar, but when I got there at quarter to five I found the space empty of anyone but Mathias. The bar lights glowed warmly, the radio playing "Little Drummer Boy," with which Mathias was humming along, polishing a glass. He wore faded jeans and a black flannel shirt with the sleeves rolled up to his elbows. The second I came through the swinging door from the kitchen he set aside what he was doing and held out his right hand, with a great deal of ceremony, curled into a loose fist and palm down, all without a word. I stopped in my tracks and everything within me sprang fiercely to life; pins and needles had prickled all along my skin driving around the lake, knowing I would see him this evening, maybe even as soon as I got to White Oaks.

And here he was, not five feet away.

"Hold out your hand," he ordered in the tone of a magician, indicating my hands with a tilt of his head.

I obliged, absorbing every last detail of his face, as though I was only allowed to see it for a limited amount of time. I noticed, secondarily, the way his jeans fit him like a cowboy's and that his dark shirt emphasized his shoulders really, really well, but it was his face that claimed my attention.

How was it that I knew his face? This man I'd only just met—I *knew* his face.

Mathias held his fisted hand over mine and then, to my surprise, caught it from beneath, holding me steady. Watching my eyes, he dropped a small metal object into my cupped palm.

"The ring!" I lifted it between my index finger and thumb, bringing it near to examine. It was a smooth, weighty gold band, no more than a quarter of an inch thick.

"It's engraved." Mathias leaned over the bar beside me and I tipped the band so I could see the tiny words on the inside rim.

"'My heart is yours for all time,'" I read. My eyes flew to his as I breathed, "Oh, wow."

He shook his head, grinning at me as though in jest, but something in his eyes was serious. "All right, I admit I thought it was a little over the top, back when I found it. If you don't mind complete romantic cliches."

"Cliches!" I repeated, almost indignantly, letting it rest on my palm, tracing the rim in an endless circle. I disagreed, "No. This is heartfelt."

"If you say so." He maintained a light tone but his blue eyes held mine and there was absolutely no teasing present in his expression. "Did you bring the picture?"

"Here," I said, handing the ring back to him, embarrassed at how violently my heart responded at this brief touching of our skin. I lifted my purse and withdrew the journal-sized notebook I'd found to keep the picture from getting bent on the way here. We traded again, me ending up with the ring, Mathias with the photograph, which he immediately scrutinized. Hearing the reverence in my voice that I could not quell, I explained, "His name is Malcolm Carter."

"'Me and Aces,'" he read. "Holy shit, this is a find. I don't mean to be inarticulate, but *shit*. Look at his horse! I love it. This is like everything I wanted to be when I was a little boy."

I smiled to hear such enthusiasm, the two of us leaning together over the bar, completely at ease—and so close that I could smell the scent of him, maybe shampoo or body wash, or a hint of cologne, something very delicious.

"I would really like to find out what happened to him." The ring was pleasantly solid against my right palm. "I feel like—" But here I stumbled to a halt, embarrassed; words seemed to pour from me in his presence, without my intending it.

"Feel like what?" he asked. I felt the warmth of his gaze the same way I would have felt his hand, stroking through my curls. And then I imagined him doing that, his hand bracketing my face, his thumb tracing my lips...

"It's stupid." My voice was embarrassingly hoarse.

"It's not," he insisted. "What?"

Instead of replying, for no reason I could name I slipped the ring over my left index finger; it was a little snug there, not moving beyond the middle knuckle. I admitted, "I feel like I'm supposed to discover what happened to him. I don't know exactly why. I've been a little obsessed since finding this picture. After the telegram, there aren't any other clues."

Mathias said, "It's not stupid at all. You sound the way I used to when I would go on and on about who built what in the homesteader's cabin, like that old fireplace. I fixed up the mantle in there when I was a teenager, I hated to see it in such disrepair. That's how I found the ring, monkeying with the stones in it." He suddenly said, "It isn't supposed to fit on that finger, you know." And as though I didn't understand, he tapped my ring finger.

Without a word I slipped the ring into its proper place, where it fit snugly. Mathias caught it between his thumb and index finger, not exactly touching me, but my breath lodged in my chest, sharp and painful.

"See?" His voice was husky with emotion; he kept hold of the ring and my fingers curled inward without my intending it, so that I held his thumb. Still leaning over the bar, our faces were no more than six inches apart, far too intimate for two people who didn't know one another, who'd only just met. I saw the way his eyes glinted with flecks of topaz in their depths, like gold dust beneath creek water. And just like that, with a certainty that churned in my blood, beyond any control, I knew I'd kissed him before.

"Camille," he whispered.

"Matty!" called his father, and we heard the sound of Bull approaching from the kitchen. Mathias and I turned around at the same instant, toward one another, effectively clocking foreheads with enough force for me to yelp and him to groan. Bull entered through the swinging door in time to spy the both of us bent forward, moaning and squinting, clutching our heads. Bull planted his fists on his hips and demanded, "What in the Sam hell?"

"We…" I found myself ensnared by giggles.

"Are you all right?" Mathias cupped my shoulders, helping me stand straight.

I nodded, putting my fingertips on his forehead before I even realized I'd moved, tracing over the spot where we'd struck. "Are you?"

Mathias grinned even wider, clearly teasing me as he said, "It hurts so much. I don't know…maybe if you held me…"

I laughed harder, shoving at his chest. Bull, seeing that we were just fine, sidestepped us, muttering under his breath, and caught up Malcolm's picture. "Ain't this something? Hi, Camille, I didn't get a chance to greet you, sweetheart. You're so darn pretty you almost hurt my eyes. Look at you."

Mathias said in a stage whisper, "Dad, c'mon, you're stealing my thunder here," and laugher overtook me again.

It began to grow busy after that. Tina arrived for her shift a couple of minutes later, breezing in with an air of merriment that seemed an integral part of the Carter family's genetic code. She hugged her brother tightly. "It's *so* good to have you home, Matty-pants."

"Already with the nicknames?" he asked, sounding pained.

Facing away from them as I topped off the salt shakers on the dining room tables, I felt a smile spread over my face; this family had that effect on me.

"What about *Bratty*-pants? Hah! Remember that one? You were such a whiny little shit." Tina was laughing.

"Why do I put up with this? You want a snake bite?" he responded and I peeked over my shoulder to see Mathias catch Tina's forearm in both hands, as she laughed and struggled against his hold. He said gleefully, "Remember *those*?"

"Sam said you threw snow all over him this morning." Tina freed her arm from his grasp and reached to rough up his hair. "And that you guys caught your limit."

"We did at that," he said, and looked my way; we couldn't seem to stop stealing looks at each other. I felt my cheeks scorch all over again.

"Hey, Camille!" Tina called. "I'll be right there to help you."

The evening was busy and as Mathias tended bar, I was allowed many lovely excuses to be near him, if for no other reason than to grab the cocktails I needed for my tables. I'd never been quite so encouraging of my customers to keep drinking.

"Can I get this one with decaf instead?" I asked him near the end of the evening; the dining room was empty except for a father and son from the twenty-top, lingering over Irish coffees.

"Sure thing," Mathias said, turning away to dump the caffeinated contents down the sink. He caught up a whiskey bottle from the shelf and poured a shot into the mug, along with the decaf coffee, and perused my face, asking, "How's your head?"

"Much better." I shamelessly enjoyed his company, bathing in the warmth of his grin as I would the rays of summer sun after months of hibernation. "How about yours?"

"I've never felt better," was his response, handing me the coffee. He braced the base of both palms against the edge of the counter in the manner of a bartender from an old-fashioned saloon. "I was thinking about taking Aces for a ride after work, if you'd care to join me."

His words, spoken so casually as to almost be factual, struck me in the gut. I sensed he meant to coax a smile, tease me a little, but a bizarre and powerful awareness arose ever more strongly between us, swelling into the space between our bodies. In that moment I believed we actually could go and saddle up the chestnut horse, and gallop out into the woods together. My fingers twitched; his black brows knitted.

"It's been a while since we've ridden him, hasn't it?" I heard myself say, the words falling upon my ears as though from the other end of a long tunnel.

The strangeness was too much, the sense of coming undone, and so I turned away, focusing on breathing normally and delivering the coffee drink to my last table; I spent a minute chatting with them as if this could restore me to normalcy. When I did head back for the bar, I was quite unprepared for the sight that met my eyes; immediately I felt as if someone had rammed a couple of fingers down my throat. This time, however, the feeling was pure jealousy, I could not deny.

Tess French was just settling herself atop a barstool, dressed in fitted jeans, tall black boots, and a vibrant purple jacket. From behind, she actually resembled my mom, with silky golden hair that swung halfway down her back and long, long legs. But then I caught sight of her mean little face and the resemblance to Mom vanished. I supposed a guy wouldn't find Tess's face particularly mean; it was more that her attitude shone through, and I saw only that. Mandy Pearson was one of Tess's good friends; the first time I ever saw Tess was two years ago this winter, when I'd unfortunately bumped into her and Mandy at the Doggetts' gas station. Upon seeing me in line to pay, Mandy whispered something and Tess had responded, loudly enough for me to hear, "So *that's* her."

I remained rooted on the opposite side of the dining room but heard Tess ask Mathias in a purring voice, "So, what are you doing later?"

See there, I reprimanded, furious and hurt, realizing I had no right to feel such possessiveness, had no claim on Mathias Carter; despite Tish spilling the info last night at Shore Leave, I'd apparently forgotten that he had a girlfriend. I wished I was brave enough to stalk over to Tess French and say, *We're taking our horse for a ride, you mean bitch, that's what.*

"Miss?" asked one of the customers at my last table. "Sorry to be a bother, but could I get another shot? I need a warm up."

"Sure thing," I said, echoing Mathias.

Dammit to hell. Now I couldn't sneak out unseen. And then I squared my shoulders and thought, *Stop acting like a child. Why should you feel uncomfortable?*

But it was all worthless bravado; I was strung with tension as I approached the bar, and even more so because Mathias watched my progress, using a bar towel to whisk dry a row of brandy glasses, one at a time. Tess continued gabbing, oblivious to me, but her eyes flickered up and then she looked over her shoulder at what was drawing his attention from her.

"I need one more Irish coffee," I said lamely. "You want me to grab it?"

"No, I got it," Mathias assured, throwing the bar towel over his left shoulder. Tess regarded me as one might a dead bug in a garden salad. Her lips were outlined in a different color than her lipstick, and it looked stupid.

"Camille Gordon?" she asked, over-enunciating the syllables of my name. "When did you start working here?"

"A month ago." I spoke calmly, not about to give her the satisfaction of witnessing my discomposure.

Tess turned from me without a response, asking Mathias, "Can you make me a vodka cranberry?"

He nodded, first filling a mug with coffee and whiskey for my table. When I reached my left hand to grab the drink I realized the ring from the fireplace, the delicate gold ring with its heartfelt inscription, was still in place on my third finger. Mathias noticed at the same moment and his dimple appeared. A hot burst of anger shuddered through me, that he would dare be *amused* by me, and I took the mug without a word of thanks. At the table once more, I said, "Do you guys care if I settle up with you? I'm headed out for the evening."

This way I could sneak away as I originally intended. Without glancing at Mathias or Tess, I retreated beneath the triple-wide arch separating the dining room from the adjacent ballroom that functioned as a reception hall. As I walked, I slipped the ring from my finger; at first it stuck, refusing to slide over my knuckle. Bull and Tina were both in the ballroom, seated at a separate bar used only when the reception hall was rented out, going through a stack of receipts.

Tina was smoking and in the middle of a sentence, but cut short her words as she caught sight of me. "You heading home, hon?"

"I am." After hesitating for a heartbeat, I asked, "Can I give you this? Mathias let me see it earlier and I forgot that it was in my apron pocket."

"Sure." Tina anchored her smoke between her lips and held out her cupped palm for the ring. She studied it and then removed her cigarette to observe, "Wow, this is that old ring Matty found when he was a kid. God, I'd forgotten all about this. He always said his wife would wear it someday."

The tip of my tongue burned with the desire to ask her to give me back the ring—I wanted to tell her that it was mine and I intended to keep it—but wisely I didn't speak such a stupid, irrational thing out loud.

"You need a ride, sweetie?" Bull asked. "Here, I'll walk you out."

"No, that's not necessary. It's not far," I said, but reached impulsively to give him a quick hug. I held tight to his burly torso and he patted my back. I figured that anyone in Bull's strong embrace would feel completely safe and protected; he was solid as a brick wall. I refused to think about how hugging Mathias would be a similar experience.

"'Night, hon, you drive safe," Bull said before releasing me.

Thirty seconds later I stood beside my old truck, the one Dodge outfitted with tire chains for me each winter; it was snowing and the flakes appeared crystalline in the blue-white glow of the single streetlight in the parking lot. I paused, listening to the quiet sound of snow falling; to look straight up during a nighttime snowfall was similar to the sensation of riding a merry-go-round a few too many times, but I looked up anyway. It wasn't as though I could feel much more off-center. I thought, *Malcolm. Did you stand in this exact spot, looking up at the winter sky? Did you ride Aces near the lake and stare out across the water? What were you searching for? I'd give almost anything to know. And to be there with you, riding Aces, safe in your arms.*

At home in my bed, after I'd briefed Grandma and Aunt Ellen on the evening, kissed Millie's cheek as she slept soundly on the couch (she'd fallen asleep looking at the Christmas tree) and then shed my clothes, I covered my face with both hands and thought about the evening. Or, tried to think about the evening and ended up thinking relentlessly of Mathias, recalling the expression on his face when I slipped the ring into its proper place on my hand. His eyes had been very intense. I brought my fingertips to the lingering sore spot on my forehead, thinking of him saying that if I held him, he would feel better…and I wrapped into my own arms, desperate with foolish longing; he had a girlfriend, I was a single mother, and there was no sugarcoating these truths.

I lay naked beneath my soft flannel sheets, restless and hot, twisting to find a comfortable position, with no luck. Though it wasn't close to what I really needed, I slid one palm along my belly and then lower, pressing gently against my flesh, stroking my fingers over the sensitive skin between my legs. A throbbing pulse rose in the wake of my touches; I shuddered with need and for no good reason at all a sob choked my throat.

Chapter Nine

SATURDAY NIGHT WAS EVEN BUSIER, BUT THIS EVENING Elaine worked the bar along with Mathias, while Tina and I managed the tables. I purposely kept away from Mathias, ordering drinks from Elaine's side of the bar whenever possible, and so it wasn't until much later when I was clearing the table nearest the fireplace that he caught me alone. It was hot enough this close to the crackling fire that I'd undone two buttons on my White Oaks server polo, which was black and bore an emblem featuring two oak trees stitched in white, with their branches intertwined. I could feel sweat along my hairline, creating frizz of my curls, but at least I'd pinned my hair into a clip before leaving home.

"Let me help you," Mathias said, moving to do so. He wore a different flannel shirt this evening, the same faded jeans. I watched as he pushed back his sleeves, exposing those muscular forearms, before collecting empty glasses. I tore my gaze away.

I realized I hadn't spoken and replied, "Thanks."

"So Noah Utley is Millie's dad?" Mathias asked next, and I absolutely froze, groping for a response that wouldn't make the tears I could feel prickling in my eyes fall all over my face. *Dammit.* I'd come so far since then. I was very much over Noah. It was just that Mathias caught me off guard.

"It's not your *business*," I tried to snap, but the hoarse quality of my voice didn't quite allow for that.

"Hey," he said, at once contrite. "Shit, I'm sorry. I shouldn't have asked like that. I asked Tina about you, I admit it. I wanted to know. I'm sorry."

I shook my head, unable to look at him, busying my hands with useless motion until I was sure the tears were safely contained. Mathias misunderstood. "Wait, he's not her dad?"

I corrected, "Yeah, he is. I thought everyone around here knew."

"Well, I didn't. Does he see her very often?"

"No," I said shortly, hoping he would drop it.

"That's what McCall said the other night, indirectly anyway." And then he added, "Here, let me take that. It's heavy."

"What does Jake have to do with it?" I demanded, shoulders tensed with anger as I faced him across the table.

Mathias admitted, "The other night I asked Jake if you were with your daughter's father. He gave me a ride home from Shore Leave so I basically had him cornered."

"It's not Jake's business either! How dare you!" Coals seemed to catch fire in my throat.

"I know, I really do know it's not my business. I'm sorry. I don't have a good excuse. I wanted to know more about you, that's all." Mathias stood opposite, watching me; I believed that he was sincerely sorry.

"You could have asked *me*, you know." There wasn't overt rancor in my voice, but I was angry and he knew it.

"I should have asked you, you're right," Mathias said, withdrawing his hands from the dish tub on the table. I watched his intense gaze move from my eyes to my lips and back again. For a moment I forgot that there even was a person named Noah Utley, who once upon a long time ago broke my heart. Right at this moment my heart was more alive than ever.

"Don't do that again," I said. "Don't ask someone else about me, I mean. I *hate* that kind of thing."

Despite my serious words, I swore a smile kindled in his eyes. He dared to say, "Then...that *wasn't* you asking your sister about me the other night at Shore Leave?"

Consternation blazed in my chest, radiating outward. My lips dropped open but I couldn't come up with one justifiable response and a smile elongated his mouth.

"How did you hear that?" I was on the defense now, cheeks scorching.

"I heard her talking to your cousin. She was telling him you asked about me." His smile was becoming a grin. "And there I was, sitting there counting the minutes until I could ask you your name, because I wanted *you* to tell me rather than someone else." He paused, searching my eyes. "You kinda disappeared after you dropped off our food, you know."

I had to bite the insides of my cheeks to contain a grudging smile. Mathias was obviously enjoying this taking me down a notch business. I muttered, "I was just busy, that's all." I regrouped then, clamping both hands on my hips. "Besides, I was only asking Tish your name, not who the father of your baby was. There's a big difference." When he didn't immediately acknowledge this, I nagged, "Wouldn't you agree?"

"I would," he said, subtle humor in his tone. He threw me a curveball then, asking, "How long were you with Utley? He hurt you, I can tell."

My hands were still planted on my hipbones. "How is *that* your business?"

"It's not, but at least I'm asking you."

He had me there. I heard myself admit, "Just for one summer. My grandma warned me about him, but I didn't listen. Of course she was right."

"Does he help you out? I know Utley, I remember him from high school. He was a punk. I'll kick his ass for you. I will. I have no time for a guy who doesn't take care of his daughter."

"You have a lot of experience with those sorts of guys?" I was still irritated but found room to tease him a little. I had already realized that Mathias was a talker, full of energy. If only I wasn't so terribly attracted to him maybe I wouldn't get this trembling feeling in my stomach whenever he was near.

"Not exactly," he admitted, and grinned anew in that effortless Carter fashion, dimple flashing. I released the breath I'd been holding and refocused upon the tabletop, away from the temptation of his face. He carried on, "I will kick his ass though. That's a bunch of shit. You and Millie deserve better than that. What about his folks? Do they see their granddaughter?"

"The Utleys have never been anything but kind to me. Truly. They see Millie as much as they can. I would never keep them from her, no matter how I feel about…" I almost stumbled over his name, and cleared my throat. "About Noah."

A beat of silence passed before Mathias invited, "Sit, let's talk. Will you talk with me?"

I felt compelled to point out, "I'm getting paid for a job here, you know."

"The place is empty. It's practically a blizzard outside. Please sit," he insisted, sliding atop a chair and motioning to another. "I know you didn't grow up around here, but you graduated from Landon High? When did you move to town?"

I relented, claiming the chair across from him, scooting the dish tub to the side and inadvertently bumping the salt shaker. It tipped, spilling salt, and, reflexively, I caught a few grains in my fingertips and tossed them over my left shoulder. Mathias cocked his head to one side and quirked his eyebrows.

"I know it's weird—" I began.

"No, I do the same thing with spilled salt," he interrupted. "I've just never known anyone else to do it."

We studied each other with a sense of accelerating fascination. I'd never seen such dark blue eyes, his irises glinting with those flecks of topaz. I felt that observing this about his eyes was like knowing a secret about him. Never mind how many other women had surely been close enough to learn the same secret. He folded his hands as though to assure me that he was listening with complete attention. His flannel shirt stretched tight over his strong shoulders. His jaw and chin were peppered with dark stubble. I imagined that he needed to shave at least twice a day and found this oddly sexy. He was so much more of a man than Noah.

"My parents grew up here, in Landon," I finally said, turning the salt shaker around and around between my fingertips as I spoke, drawing imaginary circles on the creamy linen. "They moved to Chicago just before I was born and we lived there until 2003, before moving back to Minnesota for good. My dad still lives in Chicago. My parents are both remarried."

"I've been going out to Shore Leave since I was a kid, but your parents would have moved away before I was very old. My sisters remember your mom and of course I know Joan and Ellen and Jilly. You guys always came to Landon in the summers to visit, Tina was saying. It's funny we've never met before now, you and me."

My heart thrust at his words. *You and me.*

"When did you leave for college?"

"I left for Minneapolis in 2001. I would have warned you about Utley if I'd been here the summer you met him. In fact, I wouldn't have let him anywhere near you."

"*Right.*" I infused a gigantic dose of sarcasm into my voice.

"I'm serious," he insisted, his posture conveying an abundance of energy, as if he could hardly sit still. And again the picture of him riding Malcolm's horse, Aces, flashed through my mind; the image was so right I could nearly taste it. I restrained a smile, wondering what Mathias would say if he knew I was taking liberties with my imagination. He was actually saying, "That little punk wouldn't have gotten within a mile of you, if I'd been here."

His words resonated to my toes, sending a slow, warm shiver across my belly. I didn't want him to see that what he said affected me that way and so I confessed, "The thing is, I really liked Noah back then. He was the first guy I ever really dated." Mathias listened, his face set in somber lines, brows knitted and eyes narrowed; in truth, he looked as though he was considering storming out into the night and finding Noah to make good on that ass-kicking. I rushed on, "The point being, I *wanted* him near me. If my grandma couldn't convince me he was bad news, no one could have."

Mathias inhaled through his nose and muttered, "I beg to differ."

I laughed then, a little huff of a laugh. For whatever reason, teasing him felt very natural; I was enjoying our conversation despite its rocky start. "You're pretty sure of yourself."

He grinned and hot sunlight shattered over me. "I'm pretty persuasive."

I worked hard to restrain another shiver.

"And your daughter was born your last year of school?"

"She was born that February. Valentine's Day, actually," I said, my gaze lifting up and to the left as I flew back to that cold winter night nearly two years ago now. There were times when it seemed more like two hundred.

"Was Noah there?" Mathias asked. Gone was the confident, teasing tone. We were both leaning over the table, toward each other, and I eased back just a fraction, my heart beating like a frantic bird at the expression in his eyes. I was caught terribly off guard by the strength of my feelings. I hardly knew this man; it was senseless, even dangerous, to like someone this much that you hardly knew.

But...I *did* know Mathias. I could not explain why he was familiar to me. So familiar, in fact, that a lump of pain formed behind my breastbone, induced by the intensity of my longing to move around the table and let him take me on his lap, let those powerful arms curl me safe and close. My fingers twitched, wanting to dig into his hair and comb through his curls, cup his stubbled jaw and then...

"No," I whispered at last, answering his question about Noah's presence in the delivery room. "But I didn't want him there, not really. To be honest, he didn't even cross my mind. My grandma was with me, and my littlest sister, Ruthie."

"Did he try to be there?" Mathias demanded. When I shook my head he all but yelped, "He didn't even try to show up to see his child being born? What a fucking jerk, seriously, what a little fuck. Excuse my language."

I bit my cheeks again, containing a smile. "Do you get this worked up about everything?"

A slow grin spread over his mouth, crisply defining his cupid's bow. That and his dimple made me all squirmy. I entertained the thought of leaning over the table and gripping his shirtfront, of really kissing him. Since Noah, I'd only ever kissed Jake—poor unsuspecting Jake, being manipulated by Mathias into revealing things about me.

"If it's a good cause, I do," he said. "I can tell you're a sweet girl and Noah obviously saw that and took advantage of you."

A sweet girl. How patronizing. My temper flared and eradicated my enjoyment. I glared at him. "You don't know *any*thing about me."

He was unruffled by my bitchiness, replying calmly, "I know a sweet girl when I see one."

Anger rose, swift as a March kite; I was uncertain if I'd been complimented or indirectly called a fool. Probably a little of both, even if

Mathias hadn't intended that. "You don't know anything about it! You're being presumptuous. What if I took advantage of *him?* What if I—"

Mathias interjected, "I know that's not what happened. He took advantage of you. And I would really enjoy beating him senseless because of that. I'd take pleasure in it, and I'm not even a violent man."

"Will you let me finish!" I all but yelled.

"I'm sorry," he said at once. "I'm interrupting, I'm sorry." He brandished one hand in the way of someone saying, *Go on.*

I exhaled before I could say, "Even if I didn't think so at the time, Noah was a mistake all around. You think I planned to get pregnant at seventeen? I was terrified when I found out. And when I told Noah, he couldn't handle it. He…left." I tried not to grit my teeth. "I haven't seen him since Millie was four months old."

"That was way over a year ago!" Mathias said, as if I was not well aware of the fact. "You haven't seen him since over a year ago?"

"Nope." This truth would never cease to sting. "But I don't care about not seeing him, not anymore. I only care that he makes no effort to see Millie Jo. I don't think he's ever been at his parents' house when Millie has visited."

"What the hell is wrong with him?"

"He's scared. And immature."

"Well, those are *pathetic* fucking excuses. And it hurts you, it's plain as day, even if you say you don't care." His expression became speculative. "Is he home for Christmas?"

"I'm sure," I said, though I hadn't run into him around Landon. I thought of what Tish told me last summer. "My sister heard he was dating Mandy Pearson but I don't know if that's true." Mandy's name tasted bad in my mouth, like a rotten grape. I admitted, "In school she told everyone that Noah got some slut from Chicago pregnant."

"I know the Pearson girls," Mathias confirmed. "They're all slutty, like she should talk. She really said that about you?"

"I could be the biggest slut you've ever known." Bitterness crept back into my tone; I was annoyed at him for acting like he could fix things by threatening to beat up Noah. "Like I said, you don't know a thing about it."

Mathias shook his head slowly, not removing his gaze from my face.

"Are you kidding me? You are nothing of the kind. Shit. Utley took advantage. He saw an easy mark," and when my lips dropped open in stun Mathias lifted both hands, like a traffic cop, clarifying in a rush, "I mean that Utley saw a sweet girl who would believe he loved her so he could get in her pants, that's what I mean. He said it right away, didn't he?" When I stubbornly refused to answer, he said with certainty, "I knew it."

A word from eighth grade vocabulary flashed into my mind, right out of the blue.

Incorrigible. The inability to be corrected or changed.

"I'm right, admit it," Mathias persisted. Incorrigible, indeed.

"Just…shut *up*," I said, but without any malice.

Mathias grinned in response, wide and warm, and the sense of enjoyment returned, the *knowing* between us flowed stronger than ever; I didn't want to crave his company this way—I knew it was foolish, and irrational, all of that. But as our eyes held, there was no denying; I already liked him far too much for my own good.

Bull stuck his head from the kitchen at that moment and called, "Boy, Tess is burning up the wire. Ain't you got your cell phone on you?" And then to me, "Camille, sweetie, you need a ride home?"

Tess. I'd managed not to think of her in connection with Mathias for at least the past fifteen minutes, and the sound of her name now set my teeth on edge; I turned in my chair to tell Bull, "I don't, but thank you for the offer."

Despite his dad's words, Mathias remained seated, his gaze unwavering. "I'll drive you home. It's shitty out there. You left in such a hurry last night I didn't even get a chance to offer."

I met his direct blue gaze and wanted to ask what Tess would think of that—and so very desperately did I battle the image of him meeting up with Tess later tonight, as he surely would after work—but said only, "Thanks. There's no need." And suddenly I was tired and depressed. My breasts were aching and I needed to get home and nurse Millie. My gaze drifted to the tall front windows, framing a black night rife with blowing snow. All traces of my good mood vanished like frost on a sun-kissed windshield.

Mathias insisted, "Let me drive you home. It looks terrible out there."

I felt a renewed surge of anger then, startled at how swiftly Mathias motivated extreme emotions. It was all tangled up with my intense attraction to him, with visions of being held close to his powerful-looking chest and kissing him, letting him do all of the things to me that I'd once let Noah. And look where that had gotten me. I stood and caught up the dish tub, bracing it against my belly, almost defensively. And I looked straight into Mathias Carter's gorgeous, gold-flecked eyes and said, "No."

Once through the swinging door I set the tub near the sink and called good-night to Bull, who I could hear puttering around in the kitchen. I tapped my clock-out code on the computer monitor and hurried into my coat. Travis Tritt sang mournfully from the radio in the bar. I fished the keys from my pocket and was pulling on my wool mittens when Mathias burst through the swinging door.

"Hey," he said, and sounded tight in the chest. "I didn't mean to offend you. I was enjoying our conversation and I was being presumptuous, you're right."

Another rush of pure longing assaulted me, painful as it coiled about my sensibilities. But I was a mother, first and foremost, with no time for such thoughts. Mathias had a girlfriend and no guy in his right mind wanted to date a girl with a baby. I finally allowed, "I know."

"Do you have snow tires?" he demanded. "Tire chains?"

"Both," I whispered. I sensed that he was as reluctant to let me go as I was to leave—that he wanted us to continue talking. I pretended that he wanted us to find Aces out there in the snowy night and ride him somewhere; the location didn't matter so much as the two of us, plus our horse, being together.

Stop it, I thought. *You're crazy.*

"Drive safe," he said and briefly touched my elbow, bent toward him as I put on my second mitten.

Mathias.

I knew I would replay this moment, that gentle touch, over and over as I lay in the darkness of my bed, letting my child nurse herself to sleep.

"Good-night," I whispered, and hurried out into the snowy night.

Chapter Ten

THE NEXT DAY WAS SUNDAY AND I WOKE TO HEAR GRANDMA and Aunt Ellen in the kitchen, making banana pancakes, their winter Sunday specialty. I rolled to Millie's side of the bed (she still slept best tucked in next to me) and found her absent, surely already downstairs sneaking batter from the bowl. I reflected that I was pretty damn fortunate to have the help of my grandma and my great aunt; without them, the last two years would have been unimaginably difficult. I showered and dressed in cozy, baggy sweats, an old flannel shirt, and my warmest slippers, leaving my hair to air-dry, meaning it would be tangled with curls in about a half hour, but I really didn't care. I harbored no plans to leave the house today. I thundered down the steps and had just reached the landing above the living room when I caught a glimpse of something out the front windows that completely stalled my feet.

There's a logical explanation, I thought, squelching an instinctive, expanding joy, with real effort. Maybe it was just Bull, stopping out here to talk to Grandma and Aunt Ellen. I watched, silent and motionless, as the Carters' big plow truck rumbled up to the house and stopped near the garage. And then Mathias climbed out, clad in his heavy-duty snow bibs and gray stocking cap.

It's him, it's him, it's him!

"What in the world?" I heard Grandma ask from the kitchen, and I raced back upstairs to tug on jeans and latch into a bra, frantically finger-combing my hair as Grandma answered the door.

"Good morning!" Mathias sounded cheerful and a wild fluttering happened in my heart. I heard him ask, "Is Camille awake yet?"

"Come on in, Matty," Grandma invited, curiosity in her tone but also genuine warmth; I reflected that she'd known Mathias far longer than me. "The shower was running a minute ago, so I'd say that yes, she's awake."

I tried my best to appear unruffled as I descended the stairs. Mathias looked up at me and grinned, which did things to my insides. Wonderful, heated things. He was dressed as though to go ice fishing, which was probably exactly where he was bound. Still wearing his gray wool hat and all his winter gear, he said, "Hi. Good morning, I mean. I'm glad you're up. I was hoping to steal you away for the day."

You were? Yes, steal me away, oh my God.

"Who's here?" Millie Jo yelled, running from the kitchen in her footie pajamas. Aunt Ellen followed, carrying a cup of coffee.

"Hi, Millie," Mathias said, redirecting his gaze to smile at her. "Does your mama like to ice fish?"

"Eeeeew, *no.*" Millie planted her fists on her hips and turned side to side, belly sticking out. "*Gross.* Dodge said you gotta stick a hook frew a worm."

Everyone laughed and I realized I couldn't hide out up here on the stairs. As I came closer, Mathias looked my way. "I didn't mean to just show up like this. I mean, I could have called, but I don't have your number…"

"Would you like some coffee?" Aunt Ellen asked, and I sensed more than saw her smile as her eyes moved between Mathias and me.

"Thank you, but I've got a thermos in the truck," he said. "I also have a box of scones that Mom made this morning. Camille," and my name on his lips was so lovely, "you forgot your scarf last night and then I realized that I wouldn't be able to give it to you tonight, since you don't work. And then I thought I could drop it off for you, and then I wondered if you might want to join me in the ice shack today. Do you guys have plans today? I knew I should have called…"

He was actually babbling a little, as though with nerves. My heart, already glowing, heated even more at this realization. I interrupted him. "If you give me a minute, I'd be happy to join you."

He grinned again, and the radiance of it burst through the entire living room. A smile spread across my face in response. I asked my daughter, "Millie Jo-Jo, will you mind if I leave for a while today?"

"Mama, Rae is coming to play today!" Millie reminded me. "Don't you 'member?"

"You go and have fun, hon," Grandma said, and in her voice were ten thousand questions that I knew she was dying to ask.

"Dress warm," Mathias ordered. "At least two layers."

"Dress warm for ice fishing, really?" I teased, hurrying back upstairs to don my thermal underwear, a long-sleeved shirt and what amounted to thick tights, both made from a heavy waffle-weave material. Over these I tugged my warmest sweater, jeans, and two pairs of socks. Feeling like a snowman, I was back downstairs in less than five minutes to find Millie Jo busy telling Mathias what she wanted for Christmas, while he listened attentively; I reflected that he had a number of nieces, as Tina, Elaine, and Glenna's children were all daughters. He was munching a rolled-up banana pancake. I smiled at the sight of them as I grabbed my coat from the closet, along with my wool hat and mittens. Millie was almost out of ideas for presents as I stood on one foot to pull on a snowboot.

"Mama, will you be home for supper?" she asked, coming to pat my cheeks as I bent forward.

"I will," I promised, catching her into a hug. "You have fun with Rae today."

"Stay warm," Grandma said. She asked Mathias, "Another pancake?"

"I better not," he said. "But thanks. Oh, here's your scarf."

He was wearing my scarf draped around his own neck; with hardly the blink of an eye he replaced it over my head, with touches sweet and gentle, momentarily near enough that his breath brushed my forehead, and then proceeded to open the front door for me. I waved to Millie, who ran to peek out the front window. She blew me a kiss and I blew one back, and Mathias moved ahead to open the passenger door; the plow truck was a huge diesel, issuing a muted growling as I climbed inside and onto the bench seat. The small backseat was loaded with gear, the cab of the truck toasty-warm and smelling like him, indefinably delicious. The day was a brilliant, glittering white, as so many of the winter days were, and Mathias slipped on a pair of sunglasses as he backed the truck down the driveway. It was lightly snowing, the pines already frosted with a candy-coating of snow. The drifts on the edges of the roadside reached my shoulders.

"What about Tess?" I asked before we'd even cleared the cafe's parking lot. I had to ask.

He looked over at me immediately, removing his sunglasses. "Tess and I dated in high school. When she heard I was moving home, she called me. More than once. She's been..." He paused and I sensed his desire to put things delicately, at last settling on, "She wants to get back together." Probably what he meant was *wants to screw my brains out*, but there wasn't a polite way to express that sentiment.

Thinking of everything we'd discussed last night I admitted, "I know it's not my business. I just don't want her finding out I was hanging out with you and then come after me." I meant this as a joke but Mathias didn't laugh.

He said quietly, "I'm just so glad you agreed to come today. This morning when I realized I wouldn't see you until next weekend, I just... it just seemed like..." Again he stumbled to a halt.

"I'm glad, too." Soft little thrills rippled over me at his words. "Truly. I've never ice fished. What's it like?"

"Have you ever fished in the regular season?" he asked, meaning summertime.

"Yes."

"Then just picture doing the same thing while sitting around a hole about a foot in diameter. It's freezing and your fingers get numb when you land a catch."

I giggled. "That sounds great." Because I was on his right, I could peek over and study his dimple to my heart's content.

He agreed, "It does. If you're with, it does."

I felt the sincerity of his words the way I would have felt his hands cupping my face. I stared in wonder at him; the sense of familiarity I had experienced since the night we met was stronger than ever.

"You also forgot the picture of Malcolm Carter and Aces," Mathias said, and I was stunned to realize he was right—how had I missed this? Every night since finding the photograph, I'd kissed Malcolm's face good-night.

"Did you take care of them?" I demanded, only half-kidding.

"Of course." He sounded surprised that I would even ask. "I probably read his letter fifty times. Who do you suppose Lorie-Lorie was? What was finally 'in reach' for him? And what do you suppose he spilled on it back when? It cuts off right where you're just dying to know more."

I loved that he cared about it as much as I did. "I've wondered that for over two years now. He seems happy in the letter but then, just over a year later, everything has changed. The tone of the telegram is frantic. And so sad." Malcolm's sadness, ancient history though it was, pierced my heart. "I want to know why."

"What was he searching for?" Mathias asked. "I'm curious as hell, too. I asked Dad if he knew anyone else who might have an answer, any sort of clue…"

"Oh God, like a journal," I said, imagining finding such a wealth of information about Malcolm Carter. "Primary sources."

"Right, those are the best kind. Elaine told me that you want to teach history. I could see where that would be really interesting."

"I used to think I would." My gaze drifted out the passenger window. I was embarrassed that I had not yet graduated high school; even though I didn't have the sense Mathias would be judgmental in that fashion, he was a college graduate and I was reluctant to confess my lack of education.

"Not anymore?" he persisted.

"Well, it's a little more difficult now," I pointed out. "I can't exactly make decisions just based on what I want."

"Still, don't give up on it."

"Easy for *you* to say." I hadn't meant to sound so confrontational. "I'm sorry, I don't mean to—"

"Don't apologize," he interrupted. "I mean, don't feel like you have to. You're right, it is easy for me to say. I don't mean to be presumptuous. I have a real problem with that, as you already know."

I smiled at his words, pulling off my mittens and setting them between us on the seat; it was broiling in the cab.

"Shit, I can't stop putting my foot in my mouth. I'm sorry," he said, sounding truly sorry. "Hey, are you hungry? I have all those scones... they're in the tote behind us..."

"I'll get it." I turned to lean over the front seat and retrieved the bag. "So, you're living at home for now?" I unzipped the tote and pulled out a plastic container, opening this to reveal a pile of glazed pastry. "Oh, *yum*."

"Here, pass me one, will you?" he asked and so I did; he used his teeth to yank off the glove on his right hand, keeping his other on the wheel, and our fingers brushed as I handed him a scone. I took one for myself and cupped a hand to catch the crumbs as I ate.

"Yeah, I'm living with Mom and Dad. I've only been home a week but my plan is to move in with Skid Erickson. He rents a room in Pine Ridge, you know, over by Farmer's Market?" He meant the little apartments over by the co-op in town, and I nodded. He continued, "Skid and I are going to start up a business. Plowing and de-icing for now. I know Dad wants me to take over White Oaks eventually, but I want to try and do something on my own first."

We had reached the boat landing, directly across Flickertail from Shore Leave. There were about twenty other vehicles hunkered like freezing animals, and Mathias parked the truck while I looked at the fishing shacks stationed in the middle of the lake, the little structures painted in a variety of colors under the bright-white sky. Men and kids, a few dogs here and there, made the cheerful little frozen community resemble an active anthill from this far away. Mathias collected the tote and another duffle bag, both patched with silver duct tape.

"Let me come and get your door, it's hard to open," he said, and I watched him round the hood with my entire body palpitating; he cranked open the squeaky door and then took my elbow unceremoniously into his gloved hand to help me down.

"Thanks," I whispered. I could see my reflection in his sunglasses but imagined the blue of his eyes behind them. His lips appeared somber, the lower just slightly, sensuously fuller than the upper. I swallowed hard.

"Can I carry something for you?"

He shook his head, shouldering the duffle and shifting the tote to his right hand. I wanted to catch his free hand into mine, but was way too chicken. Besides, this was not exactly a date. We were hanging out, the way friends would.

"Now, it's slippery as shit out here," he warned. "You've got the right kind of boots, that's good. And the ice is deep, so there's no fault lines or anything. Our ice shack is on Snowflake Street."

We navigated the snowy bank, Mathias buffering my elbow with his hand, only lightly touching me, but I felt the heat of it through all the layers of our winter clothes. I giggled and repeated, "Snowflake Street?"

"There are bona-fide streets out here, yes," he confirmed. "It's a little town on the lake. Isn't that the title of one of the *Little House on the Prairie* books?"

"You know those books?"

He angled me a look and reminded, "Sisters. All sisters."

"Right. And no, it's *By the Shores of Silver Lake*."

We were on the ice now, and he ordered, almost businesslike, "Here, you better take my arm."

I tucked my hand beneath his elbow, again with a sense of heat that came from his skin and right into mine. He was so solid and strong, and I recalled the dark blue thermal shirt he'd worn Friday morning, the one that showcased each dip and definition along his powerful arms. I accepted this excuse to touch him as a little gift from the universe. Would people think we were a couple? I peeked up at him to find him peeking down at me and we both looked instantly apart.

As we neared the ice houses, the activity grew boisterous. It was like the downtown of any actual community, men standing around the open doors of their ice shacks, chatting and drinking canned beer, or coffee from large stainless-steel mugs and gas station-issued plastic sippy cups, the kind you could refill for a quarter. Little kids played a racing game on the ice about twenty yards away, running to see who could slide the farthest on their snowsuit-clad bottoms. The ice houses were as unique as their owners, emblazoned with wooden signs and propane-powered lights, Christmas decorations and neon-colored lures, and wind chimes fashioned from empty beer cans strung on fishing line.

Everyone called greetings as we came close, and in the bustle I let go of Mathias. Dodge was there, bundled into his plaid overcoat. He hugged me. "Camille! Fancy seeing you here!"

"Mathias is going to show me how to ice fish," I explained.

"Hey there, kiddo," said Uncle Justin, joining us with a tackle box in his gloved hand. "Rae is excited to see Millie today. And hey, Jilly would be proud to see you out here. Usually she's the only woman in these parts."

"Everyone knows you two only come out here to make out in your ice house," Dodge teased his son, and Justin punched his dad's shoulder.

"Dammit, Pa, that's not polite."

"When have I ever been polite?" Dodge asked, a fair question, but he winked at me and grinned.

"So where's yours?" I asked Mathias, who disentangled himself from a good-natured headlock. It seemed that everyone was glad to see him back in the Landon area. I recognized Skid Erickson, whose family were regulars at Shore Leave in the summer. Skid had probably graduated high school with Mathias.

"This way," he said, taking my elbow this time, carefully, as though I might bolt.

"See you later," I told Dodge and Uncle Justin.

The Carters' shack was two rows over, no bigger than the fish-cleaning shed at Shore Leave, painted barn red, with a corrugated-metal door that would no doubt blind a person on a sunny day. Mathias said, "This is it!" with the air of someone presenting a palace, and opened the door, allowing me to enter first. He cautioned, "Don't step in the hole!"

Inside it was dim with only one small window. There were low-slung camp chairs arranged around the thick-sided hole drilled into the ice, a wooden barrel that served as a counter, a gigantic tackle box and a green propane lantern, which Mathias fired up right away. He left the outer door propped open only about a foot or so, giving us a little privacy.

"Here, have a seat while I get the lines set up," he invited, and we were practically on top of each other in the crowded space. Not that I was complaining. Shamelessly, I put my hand on his ribs, one on either side, as I ducked around him to claim a chair, while he stashed the bags and began rummaging.

"Where's that coffee?" I asked as he clicked on the radio, keeping the volume low. It was the same station we always played in the bar, when the jukebox wasn't running, tuned to the country station out of Bemidji.

"Here." He handed me the thermos. "Cups are right beneath the other chair."

I retrieved these, small and squatty plastic mugs emblazoned with the words *Love to Fish*. I poured us each a cup and then stashed the thermos under my chair, which only cleared the ice by about six inches. Mathias proceeded to bait two lines and then attached them to the reel set-up, arranged so that we wouldn't have to continuously hold the poles. Finished with these tasks, he seated himself opposite me and said, "Thank you," as I passed him the coffee.

"You're welcome," I murmured. I wanted to go and sit on his lap. I let myself very clearly imagine doing that and he must have seen something in my eyes, as his own (he'd removed his sunglasses in here, sticking them on the top of his head) flashed a beat of pure and unmistakable heat into mine. I felt hotter than the coffee in my hand, letting this heady feeling bloom all along my center and infuse my entire body.

Oh God, Mathias…

He blinked then and cleared his throat a little before saying, "So now we hurry up and wait."

I gathered myself together and sipped my coffee, burning my tongue. "I always wondered what it looked like in one of these things. It's really kind-of cozy. Homey, I mean. You even have curtains on the window. Those are nice." Now I was the one babbling.

"Mom made those," he said, glancing over at the ruffled material gracing the window. The song on the radio switched to a country version of "White Christmas," complete with lots of steel guitar, and Mathias began belting out the chorus, making me laugh. He was clearly being silly, but his voice was really good.

"Not bad," I applauded when he finished, and he shook his head.

"Sorry, I get swept away. I was very much tortured as a boy. Tina was especially evil. She liked to dress me up as a back-up singer for her imaginary band."

"Tish and Ruthie and I used to do that, too. Have pretend bands, I mean. We weren't very good. But you were on pitch pretty well there."

"I can hold my own in a karaoke competition. My song…you want to know what my song is?"

"As in, the song you sing for karaoke?"

"Yep. It's 'The Gambler' by Kenny Rogers. It's the one—"

"I know it," I interrupted. "It's a great song. Grandma has that record, actually."

"That one is my personal best," he said. "In college I won fifty bucks one time at a competition."

With a slight air of wistfulness, one I didn't exactly intend, I observed, "I bet you had so much fun in college."

He heard the note of it in my voice and studied me silently for a moment before answering, "I did. I thought for a short while that I could live permanently in the Cities. But I missed home. I missed being around guys who could actually bait a hook. I mean, I know that's probably ridiculous, and I know it's important to be educated. I value that. But I wasn't interested in learning about wines, or brand names, or any of that stupid shit. I know it's judgmental of me, but—"

"No, I get it. I understand completely," I said, and I really did. "I realized after living here that those are the kinds of things that my old friends in Chicago care about. Even my own dad cares more about money, and *things*, than just about anything else. Mom said he always wanted to be rich. Now he is, but he doesn't have her anymore. That's a pretty shitty trade-off, if you ask me."

"I'll say," Mathias agreed softly. "Does your dad see Millie very often? And by the way, she looks just exactly like you. Same wild hair and—"

"What!" I cut him off, unable to let that comment slide. I lifted my free hand to grasp a strand of my hair, as though in defense. I wore my lavender wool hat, patterned with gray snowflakes, and my hair was a veritable static-snapping mess beneath it.

Mathias said fast, "No, wait, that came out all wrong. I like that your hair is wild. I mean, it's really beautiful, *exquisitely* beautiful, actually..."

I allowed, "Nice save."

"I mean it!" he insisted. His eyes stroked all across my face, my hair. I was burning up beneath his gaze and pulled off my mittens, setting them on my lap. He concluded softly, "I'll just shut up now."

"Sing more," I ordered, loving that he could actually seem a little shy. One of my favorite Christmas songs, "The Little Drummer Boy," was playing on the radio.

He drew a breath, closed his eyes, and took up the chorus. I giggled and joined in, softly, on the *pah-rum-pa-pum-pum* part. Mathias's voice was rich and true, and I sang quietly, the better to hear it.

"Jesus Christ, do you take requests or what?" asked a voice from outside, and Tina's husband Sam poked his head in the door. He was wearing a fur hat with earflaps and smiled as he shook his head at us, then implored Mathias, "Hey, bud, come out here and help me quick."

"Sure thing," Mathias said, rising. He asked me, "Will you hold this for a sec?"

I took his coffee mug and the moment he was outside, turned it so that I could sip directly where his lips had touched the rim. Childish, stupid, senseless, I knew. But then I sipped again, from the same spot, closing my eyes and savoring.

I suddenly heard Mathias utter a laughing roar. He yelled, "Bastard!" and I jumped up to see what was going on, first setting the coffee mugs on the barrel; I squinted a little in the brilliant light after the dimness of the shack and then saw Sam stuffing snow down Mathias's collar, holding him around the torso with one arm. They struggled and were attracting attention. Skid Erickson came running and launched himself at them, almost taking everyone to the ice.

Men. I would never understand this basic urge to beat the shit out of each other.

Mathias was laughing hoarsely, thrashing against Sam's hold. He bellowed, "Dammit, the snow is burning my ass!"

"Do you surrender?" Sam demanded.

"Never! Carters never surrender!" Mathias yelped.

I couldn't help laughing as Sam grunted, "Serves you right!" and ducked to scoop another handful of snow, which went directly down the back of Skid's coat. Skid yelped and began floundering to dislodge it, subsequently freeing Mathias, who bent forward, his hat falling off, and groaned.

"Are you okay?" I called.

He straightened, his hat gone and his hair wild, ordering with mock urgency, "Camille! Don't move. It's dangerous out here."

Skid managed to dislodge most of the snow from his coat and then rounded on Sam, declaring, "If you know what's good for you, you better run!"

Sam held up his mittened hands and wiggled them in pretend fright, and Skid bent over laughing. Mathias crept behind Sam and caught him around the neck, yelling to Skid, "Now's your chance!" and Skid tried again to take both of them to the ground.

"Boys! Jesus Christ," Bull yelled, trudging up carrying two twelve packs of Leinie's cans. He wore a knitted red stocking cap and resembled a stout garden gnome. Bull indicated me with one of the packs of beer and bellowed, "You're scaring the lady!"

"Shit, let me free," Mathias gasped out. He looked my way, hamming it up as he cried, "I'm sorry! Don't be scared, Camille!"

I called, "I'm not scared. And you probably deserve snow down your pants anyway!"

Mathias thrashed free of both Skid and his brother-in-law. He bent with deliberate slowness and scooped a large handful of snow, which lay in thick drifts on the solid ice. He began packing it between his gloves, all the while keeping his eyes trained on me.

"Oh, don't you dare," I ordered, catching his intent.

"Deserve to be ambushed, do I?" he asked, coming closer. I squeaked in alarm, darting to the side as he lunged for me.

"Matty!" yelled his dad. "You act like a gentleman!"

I shrieked and slid across the ice in my attempt to escape, Mathias right behind me. He caught me around the waist and it was such a marvelous excuse to touch him; I didn't want to stop touching him, ever. I twisted and struggled, tripping us, but Mathias took us sideways instead of falling on top of me; we landed in a giant snowdrift between two ice shacks, his arms locked around me, my spine aligned with his chest, my puffy coat hampering my feeble, halfhearted attempts to escape him. My hat fell off and I spit out a long strand of hair, laughing too hard to catch my breath.

Mathias shifted so that his arm cushioned me from the snow and put his mouth near my ear to ask, "Do you surrender?"

"Never!" I gasped, feeling his breath on my cheek, the power and heat of his body behind me. Just the scent of him sent longing ripping through me, made my nerves crackle with awareness. I thought of him saying that Carters never surrender.

"Never is a long time," he cautioned, teasing me, his lips at my temple and just skimming my skin with his words; I knew he felt me tremble. His arms tightened around me. Instinctively, as a flower to the sun, my chin lifted toward his mouth. I wanted him to kiss me so badly that I made a small, inadvertent pleading sound.

"Oh God, come here," Mathias whispered, his voice hoarse and fervent, all traces of teasing having vanished, and rolled so that he was sheltering me beneath him. The blinding-white sky created a nimbus around his head, making it appear haloed. Before I knew what I was doing I gripped the front of his coat in both fists, holding for all I was worth; for a split second I'd harbored the terrible sense that he was going to be sucked into the sky, taken from me, and I was not about to let that happen.

"Camille?" I heard then, through everything else, Bull's yelling, and Skid and Sam's roughhousing and raucous laughter; it was Jake's voice, somewhere nearby, and Mathias and I were abruptly returned to reality. Jake's booted feet were no more than a dozen steps away, coming closer.

Mathias swallowed hard, his throat bobbing; for a last second, we stared deeply into each other's eyes. Disappointment sank its teeth as I realized there was no choice but to release my grip on him. He shifted to his feet to help me to mine and we emerged from between the two ice shacks, Mathias dusting snow from my coat and retrieving my hat while

Jake stood there and studied me with an expression I'd never seen on his face, one of complete stun.

"Hey, McCall," Mathias said companionably, not perceiving Jake's anger—but then his eyes were on me, not Jake.

Jake's voice was a sharp little dart as he asked me, "Are you okay?"

"I'm just fine." I was swamped by the familiar burden of guilt. *Don't be like this, Jake, please. Please don't.*

Jake was with a couple of his friends, who were carrying supplies into a shack the next row over. Jake sent me a pointed look of hurt; another dart, this one aimed at my head, but I refused to flinch. Bull stomped over and unknowingly broke the tension, to my relief, grasping his son by the scruff, reaching up to do so, as Mathias was taller than him. Jake turned and walked away without another word and I decided it was best to let him.

Bull blustered, "I oughta take a strap to you, boy," and then politely offered me his arm. "Camille, it's so good to see you out here. I hope the boy hasn't scared you too awful much."

I took Bull's elbow and allowed him to lead me back to the shack, turning over my far shoulder to stick out my tongue at Mathias, who grinned and shook his head slowly, pulling on his hat. Just the look in his eyes made my knees go weak.

A few yards away, Sam and Skid were still exchanging insults and Mathias warned them, "You best be on guard, dipshits. You won't know when it's coming, but it's coming."

They laughed and laughed, and the next thing, all three were wrestling again.

Chapter Eleven

WE SPENT THE REST OF THE AFTERNOON CROWDED AROUND the fishing hole, Bull taking the chair at a right angle to mine. I didn't mind Bull's company one bit, even though his presence kept Mathias and me from being alone together. But Bull was entertaining, and told us straightaway about his cousin out in Montana who might have a lead on Malcolm's "disappearance."

"My cousin's wife, out near Bozeman, found a few letters last year when she was cleaning out their attic for a sale. She'd be happy to mail them to me, she said."

"From Malcolm?" I asked eagerly.

"You mean Harry and Meg?" Mathias asked.

Bull nodded, cracking a can. He offered one to Mathias, who shook his head, holding up his coffee. Bull went on, answering my question, "Yes, ma'am. At least, some of them are from Malcolm."

"Oh, that makes me so happy. Maybe she could read them over the phone to me." I was gushing. "I don't know if I can wait!"

Bull and Mathias both grinned at my enthusiasm, increasing their resemblance. Bull said, "I'm sure she'd be happy to."

"Sounds like a road trip to me," Mathias said, setting aside his coffee and stretching, twisting at the waist; I tried not to stare. "We haven't been out that way since I was in high school. God, it's gorgeous out there in the mountains. Next summer, we'll hit the road."

I wasn't sure if he was asking me to join him or just mentioning this in the abstract but I heard myself agree, "For sure."

It was nearing late afternoon when I told Mathias that I should probably head home; I was reluctant to go, as I didn't know when I might see him again before next weekend. I didn't work until Friday and there was no logical excuse to hang out before then. *Was there?* Today was special; surely we couldn't recreate it every day this week. But I felt all sickly and senselessly deprived at the thought of almost five whole days before we would be in each other's company. Walking back across the ice in the dimming, silvering day, I held his elbow and tried to keep our pace slow to prolong this excuse to touch him.

Seeming to read my thoughts, he said, "I can't believe we've only known each other for a few days. I know it's crazy but I feel like I've known you for a long time. People think I'm crazy anyway, so I guess it makes sense in that regard."

"It's not crazy. I feel the same way." I wanted to say his name and whispered, almost shyly, "I really do, Mathias."

"You do?" he asked.

"Yes," I said, and in response he tightened his elbow around my hand, as though giving me a little hug. I rested my cheek against his coat sleeve for a couple of steps, in as natural a motion as any I had ever made, and actually felt the joy that throbbed outward from him at my action. Eyes closed, I observed, "We didn't catch any fish today."

His voice was full of a quiet happiness. "I don't care about any old fish. That was just an excuse to get you to come with me, in case you hadn't gathered."

Tish called later that night to tell me Jake came over to their house to talk to her; since they were next-door neighbors, this happened relatively frequently.

"He said that you and Mathias Carter were making out on the ice this morning!" my little sister announced, with pure elation.

I restrained a sigh, rolling the other direction and speaking quietly, as so not to wake Millie Jo. I grumbled, "Like that's any of Jake's business."

"So you *were* making out!"

I smiled into the darkness. "We were wrestling a little, maybe…"

"You were?" Tish sounded like she was smiling, too.

I snuggled into my pillow, seeing Mathias's face whenever I closed my eyes. I explained, "We went ice fishing today. He stopped out this morning to see if I wanted to join him."

When he'd dropped me off at home, huge snowflakes were falling, dusting over the windshield, the two of us alone in the warm, insulated privacy of his plow truck.

Kiss me, kiss me, kiss me, I begged wordlessly, refusing to consider what happened the last time I allowed emotions to take such control of my sensibilities.

But this is different. Mathias is not Noah.

"I start my plow route for the county tomorrow," Mathias said. Even in the gathering darkness I could see the blue of his eyes. "And then I'll be moving in with Skid in the middle of the week."

I nodded in response, my mittens stacked on top of one another on my lap; the diesel engine growled softly, the radio turned low. The last thing in the world I wanted to do at that moment was get out of his truck and go into the house without him.

"Do you—" he began.

At the exact same instant I asked in a rush, "Would you want to come over and watch a movie tomorrow night? After work, I mean?"

His answering grin made my entire body weightless, anchored to the seat only by a thin thread. "Oh God, I would love to. I was just going to ask if I could see you again. Friday is way too far away otherwise. Here, call my phone so I have your number, too."

And so I had.

Sitting here in my bed two hours later, I told my little sister, "We have a…sort-of, anyway…a date tomorrow night. To watch a movie."

"Where, at Grandma's?" Tish asked.

"Where else?"

"Well, have fun. Mathias seems like a nice guy. Funny, you know? And he's super hot."

"He is, isn't he?" I marveled, and then giggled at Tish's use of that particular phrase; usually she made fun of girls who used it. After we hung up, I lay flat on my spine and stared up at the dark ceiling. Though the thought of tomorrow night filled me with what could only be described as unbridled joy, my doubts came crawling, nagging and sharp-pointed, needling into my happiness now that it was night and I was relatively alone.

What if he's playing you? What if he thinks you're easy…
He doesn't! How can you think that about Mathias?
But how do you know? *This is all so fast.*
I feel like I've known him a long time.
That's so stupid, Camille, it's not real justification.
It's not stupid! How else would I know that I've kissed him before?
Just take it slow.
Take it slow.

The next evening I fluttered all over the house until Grandma said, "Child, sit down for heaven's sake. You said he won't be here until after six."

"That's what he thought," I said, dancing from foot to foot. I caught Grandma's eye and plunked obediently onto the couch, folding both hands in my lap. "But this is the first time that he's done this plow route, so he wasn't exactly sure."

He had called me around noon, his name flashing across my phone's screen. *Mathias.* It was such a solid name, old-fashioned sounding, and it suited him.

"Hey," he'd said when I answered, his voice all warm and smiley-sounding, just the way I was feeling. "We still on for tonight?"

"We are." I hoped he wouldn't mind if we watched a movie with Millie sitting between us. Or more likely crawling all over me, as she was known to do when I paid the least bit of attention to anyone other than her; but, I reflected, if he did mind such a thing, then seriously dating him was out of the question. But I didn't get the sense that Mathias would mind.

"Will you guys have eaten by then? Should I bring something?" he asked.

"No, and come hungry. Aunt Ellen is making seafood chowder and cheddar biscuits."

"Oh my God, that sounds good. That's one perk of living at home, isn't it? Great meals all the time. I'll see you around six, then."

"I can't wait," I dared to say, and sensed his grin even over the phone.

"I'll get there as fast as I can," he promised.

Drawing me out of my daydream, Grandma asked, "So, you like Matty Carter, then?"

"You sound worried," I observed, my stomach going all at once hollow. From the direction of the kitchen came the high-pitched happy lilt of Millie Jo's laughter; she was busy helping Aunt Ellen make the biscuit dough. The house already smelled wonderful, like yeast and cheddar cheese, and garlic sauteing in butter. I studied Grandma, who saw the sudden gathering of fearful questions in my eyes.

She sat beside me and took my hands into hers. "Your eyes have been shining as bright as evening stars since you met Mathias, sweetie. It makes me happy to see it, but I worry so for you. I don't remember you looking this way with Noah." She sighed, squeezing my fingers. "I would do about anything to prevent you girls from being hurt."

I drew a careful breath. "I know, Gram, I really do. And I won't rush into anything. You know what I mean, right?"

"I'm not talking about sex, exactly," Grandma said. "I'm more worried about your heart getting all twisted up in this. Aw, Camille, it's so difficult to watch from the outside and not offer advice. Remember how I warned you about Noah?"

My blood froze. "Are you warning me about Mathias?"

"He's not the same man as Noah, that's obvious. But he's even more dangerous, and by that I mean that you're falling hard for him, I can see that plain as daybreak."

I whispered, "I can't explain it, Gram. I saw Mathias and felt like I'd known him for a long time."

"Sometimes that's the way of it," she said, and gently released my hands. "I just love you so much. Take it slow with him at least, promise?"

And I promised I would.

The big plow truck grumbled through the darkness of the winter evening at about ten to six. I raced to the door but then forced myself to open it calmly, Millie peering around my knees, her hands on my legs. Mathias bounded out of the truck and waved to us, then reached back inside for something, which he carried to the house.

"Hi, you two," he said, grinning as he approached. He'd come straight from plowing, still in his outer gear, including a fur hat with earflaps, which made Millie giggle. At the sight of his flushed cheeks and stubbled jaw, his gold-flecked blue eyes, I felt aglow with something far beyond my control.

"Hi." I stood aside and held open the door.

"Wow, it smells good in here." His eyes were all over me. I wanted to go up on tiptoe and get my arms around his neck, recalling very clearly the expression on his face when we'd been so close together yesterday, there on the ice. Instead, I reached for the paper bag he carried. He explained, "Smoked salmon, from Dad, and fudge, from Mom. I grabbed it on my lunch break. They said to tell you guys hi."

"Ooh, *yum*. Thank you."

"Fudge!" Millie cried. She peered up at Mathias, and giggled. "Your hat haves ears!"

He laughed with delight, removing the furry hat and placing it on her head.

Millie crowed, "Mine!"

I giggled. "Good luck getting that back." And then to my daughter, "Here, baby, take this to Grandma," and handed her the container of fudge. Behind me, Mathias was in the process of shedding his coat and gloves, and then his boots and snow bibs, shivering a little in the process.

"Dang, it's cold out there," he said, free from his gear. His hair was flattened from his furry hat, his clothes all static-clingy; I'd never restrained the urge to touch someone so fiercely in my entire life. At the last second I couldn't help it; I was just close enough to brush hair from his forehead with my free hand. I didn't even question this action it seemed so natural, and let my fingertips trail over the side of his face, coming to rest along his jaw. He shivered again, this time not from the cold, and cupped my left elbow in his right hand when I intended to withdraw my fingers, embarrassed to be so bold. After all, he wasn't my boyfriend…

He's so much more than that. I don't know how I know this to be true, but I do.

"I can't tell if your eyes are more green or more golden," he whispered, his fingers gentle on my elbow, moving slowly. I felt this touch all along my arm, straight as an arrow to my heart.

"Hi, Matty!" Grandma called, and Mathias squeezed my elbow and then let his hand drop back to his side.

"Hi, Joan!" he called, and then offered, "I can take that," nodding at the paper bag still containing the salmon. I passed it to him and led the way to the kitchen, my elbow still tingling.

Millie was busy putting forks on the table, set with Grandma's Christmas dishes, an old, creamy-white set edged in holly berries, the kitchen cozy and warm, so very familiar to me. Sometimes I could barely picture the spacious, modern kitchen in our townhouse back in Chicago, where Dad still lived. This place seemed more like home than the townhouse ever could have. The ancient woodstove in the corner burned cheerfully, the orange flames flickering through the cutout pattern punched into its cast-iron belly. The table was covered in its holiday cloth, a forest-green one shot through with gold thread. Aunt Ellen stood at the stove, stirring the chowder; the biscuits sat on the counter in the biscuit tin in all their golden perfection. I smiled at the scene before my eyes, feeling immeasurably fortunate, and told the womenfolk, "Bull sent some smoked salmon."

"Holy God, it smells good in here," Mathias said. "My belly thinks my mouth's been sewn shut."

I experienced a strange moment of déjà vu at his words, as though abruptly sunk beneath lake water, sounds and sights temporarily blurred; Mathias moved at once to help Millie at the table. He teased her, "You didn't put a fork by my plate!"

"Did too!" She peeked up at him from beneath his furry hat, still settled atop her head and nearly obscuring her eyes.

"Hon, set out the towel," Aunt Ellen said, returning me to reality. She positioned the steaming kettle on it, while Grandma brought over the biscuits and the butter dish and I poured milk.

"You can sit there, next to Camille," Grandma told Mathias, indicating which chair she meant.

We ate. It was a bizarre kind of first date, if that's what this was; it depended on whether I considered yesterday a date, out on the ice. Rather than being alone and facing one another, Mathias sat to my left at a table crowded with my family, his elbow occasionally bumping mine as we ate bowls of Aunt Ellen's delectable chowder, dipping buttery biscuits and making a drippy mess. Millie proved too excited to remain still, sitting on her legs and bouncing in her chair, telling us all about how she and Rae played in a blanket fort that Grandma built for them yesterday. Then Mathias told us about his plow route and using a truck called a ditch witch to clear out the icy ditches.

"We get right out on County 71 in the mornings, and that will be our main route for now," he explained, wiping his lips with a napkin. "And then we plow out Landon Township. I told Skid we can't neglect those side roads."

"You're careful, aren't you?" I asked, and then clarified, "Of yourself, I mean."

Mathias looked my way with his dimple showing. "We take it easy on those bad roads. No donuts in the plow truck. But in my own truck, we can do a few out on the ice."

"Donuts!" Millie sang.

"You kids want dessert now or later?" Aunt Ellen asked after we'd eaten our fill.

"Later, for sure, I'm stuffed," I said, moving to help her clear the table.

"No, hon, you guys go hang out. I'll get this." Aunt Ellen nudged me aside.

"Thank you." I caught her around the waist and kissed her cheek.

I led Mathias to the living room but Millie Jo clearly had other plans, tugging the bottom of his sweatshirt and inviting, "Come see my fort!"

Mathias gave me a look with his brows raised and a smile on his lips; his eyes clearly asked, *How can anyone refuse this child?*

"Hang on, Millie Jo-Jo," I ordered. "Let Mama make sure our room is clean."

I dashed up the stairs ahead of them, whirling through the room, stuffing bras and dirty laundry into the closet, leaning my hip against the bi-fold door to force it shut before dragging the quilt over the pillows in an attempt to make the bed. I wasn't the worst housekeeper in the universe, but likely ranked in the top ten. I could hear Millie leading Mathias up the steps, chattering nonstop, and almost laughed at the absurdity of him seeing my bedroom, which was an undoubtedly intimate experience, under these circumstances. Mathias paused in the doorway and studied me somberly, certainly thinking something similar. I'd clicked on the lamp atop my dresser rather than the overhead light, lending the room a warm, peach-tinted glow. Millie ran to her blanket fort, stretched between the rocker and the dresser, ducking inside and telling Mathias to follow, but for that moment he remained motionless and our eyes held fast.

I felt a leaping in my blood, an awareness of him that seemed deeper than instinct. Heat sizzled along my spine and over my limbs as I stood near the bed, studying his serious face in lighting that echoed that of a candle's flame. I felt assaulted by need, sharp as a blade and just as insistent, and in my mind he crossed the room with determined strides and took me to the bed, kissing me as though the world would end before morning light. I swallowed hard and he gripped the door frame on either side.

Millie popped back out and I refocused on her, my face scorching. I found my voice and tried for a teasing tone. "Well, this is our room. Probably didn't expect to see it tonight."

"You two share a room?" he asked softly. He stood motionless in the door and his voice was a little hoarse as he asked the question.

I nodded, keeping my eyes on Millie, who knelt on all fours, watching us. "It's easier to get her to sleep if we share a bed."

Mathias crouched down and asked Millie, "So does your mama snore, or what?" and then I giggled, the tension effectively broken.

"Hey now, that's cheap." I poked his knee with my toes.

Mathias was a good sport, crawling into the blanket fort and offering

Millie compliments on its construction. His hair was more static-y than ever when he emerged, resting his hand on the edge of my mattress as he rose back to his full height. He turned in a slow circle and observed, "It's cozy in here."

"Are you gonna watch a movie with us?" Millie wanted to know.

"If you don't mind," he said. "Do you have one picked out?"

Back downstairs we settled on the couch, Millie curling up on my lap, with clear possessiveness. I snuggled the afghan around us; there was about a foot of distance between my left hip and Mathias's right. We watched the first part of a cartoon, truly only aware of one another, and it wasn't twenty minutes later that Millie fell asleep against me, sucking her thumb. I collected her close, whispering, "I'll be right back. Feel free to change the channel."

He murmured, "I'll be right here."

Now it would be up to me to judge the distance between us on the couch; I reflected upon this as I tucked Millie into bed, bending to kiss her round cheek, brushing wayward curls away from her face. I paused on the landing, heart thrashing; what I wanted was to sit near enough that I could put both arms around Mathias, and feel his around me, but of course this was out of the question—though, as I approached the couch his welcoming grin was warm enough that I seriously considered snuggling right onto his lap. I reclaimed the afghan and drew it to my shoulders, fluttery and wishing I hadn't left so much distance between us; twelve inches seemed unimaginably far away from him.

He asked innocently, "It is chilly in here? Maybe it's just me…"

I braved it, and heard myself invite, "You maybe want to share the blanket?"

His eyes shone with that Carter merriment. "If you don't mind *too* much…"

Mathias moved just a little closer, enough that I could feel the heat of him. He drew the afghan to his hips and angled so that his knees were bent my direction.

"What are you watching?" I asked, mostly to banish the desire to move fluidly and straddle his lap.

"I don't know, I can't concentrate on anything besides the fact that you're so close to me."

My eyes flew at once to his.

He went on, speaking in a rush, "I know it's crazy, Camille, I do, but I want to…I feel like…"

"It's not crazy." There was a great deal of intensity in my voice, echoing his. "I feel it, too. I really do."

"I know I never met you before last Thursday," he said, as though trying to reason with himself. "But there must have been sometime… someplace. I know that I *know* you."

I felt an unexpected swelling of tears and his eyebrows rose in concern. I hurried to explain, "I'm all right, it's not that. It's just that…I know exactly what you mean."

"Say my name," he insisted, with quiet passion. He cupped his hands around my knees and begged, "Please, I need to hear you say it."

"Mathias," I whispered, trembling at his touch, his words. I realized that my first instinct had been to say *Malcolm*.

"Camille." His eyes drove into mine, his grip tightening.

"Kids, I'm dishing up butterscotch pie if you want some!" Aunt Ellen called from the kitchen.

I blinked and Mathias exhaled in a rush. My entire body reverberated to a plea I could sense, if not hear. As though something within me was screaming to wake up, to get it, *to understand*, shaking me just shy of violently. My voice trembled. "Do you…"

Mathias took my hands into his, his touch so warm and strong, holding me securely. He brought them to his lips, kissing the back of each in a tender gesture that served to tear at my heart. Studying my eyes, he murmured, "I do."

We joined Grandma and Aunt Ellen for coffee and butterscotch pie, Mathias joking with characteristic ease, the both of us pretending that nothing out of the ordinary hummed like live wires between us. The womenfolk genuinely liked him, I could tell; but by the time they ventured up to bed, leaving us alone in the living room lit by nothing more than the Christmas tree, I felt as though I might shatter with the faintest touch.

"Come here," I whispered. "Come sit with me."

We sat facing each other on the couch, not yet touching, and Mathias admitted, "When I think about you sleeping alone with your little girl it just about breaks my heart. It seems so lonely. And I was down in the Cities all this time, while you were up here alone."

"You had things to finish. And I haven't ever been alone, not truly. My family has always been here."

"I'm so glad," he said. "They love you so much."

"I love them, too." My eyes grew wet with tears. "Besides, finishing college is important. Mathias, I never even finished high school."

"You were raising your child. Nothing is more important than that."

"I know. It's just hard being left behind. It seems selfish, because I know Millie Jo needs me so much, and I need *her*. I don't know what I would do without my girl. But everyone else my age moved on…"

"It's not selfish. You're young to be a mom. It would be hard on anyone. I remember after Tina had Beth and then Beth's dad ditched out on them. Tina and Beth moved back home for about a year, and I saw firsthand how tough it was on my sister."

"I felt so irresponsible for getting pregnant." I wanted to tell him everything that was in my soul. "I mean, I've gotten over that feeling now. But when I first found out, it was like I had the plague. All of my friends just disappeared, not to mention Noah, and I begged Mom not to make me go to school in Landon. But she insisted."

"And then girls like Mandy Pearson were mean to you," he acknowledged.

"It's not like I'm that fragile, but it hurt. I mean, they called me a slut, a whore, like I took advantage of *Noah*. I'm the least slutty girl I know." I shook my head, embarrassed that I had said that. "I mean…" I faltered before concluding, "So many things have changed since then. I don't even know who I used to be."

"Would you have gone back to Chicago that summer, if not for being pregnant?"

I nodded. "We only came up here for a few weeks every July."

He said, "Then I am eternally grateful that you took advantage of poor, innocent Noah Utley and got pregnant as a result." He let that sink in for a beat, before explaining, "Otherwise you wouldn't be here right now. Otherwise, I would still be searching for you. And I can hardly even bear the thought of that."

I fumbled my hands free of the afghan, pulled haphazardly over my lap, and he reached for mine at the same time. And again, as though instinct drove the action more than anything, he brought my hands to his lips and kissed the back of each, closing his eyes. His lips were so very warm and I made a small sound in my throat, of yearning and need. He opened his eyes and kept both of my hands in his left, reaching with his right to tuck hair behind my ear. His fingertips lingered on my cheek. His voice was husky as he whispered, "Come here, come be in my arms."

I couldn't speak as he encased me against his powerful chest. He smelled so good that it was almost dizzying; I pressed my cheek to his thermal shirt and felt his arms come around me, holding me as though he would never let go. The Christmas tree glowed in the corner, again creating a sense of candlelight, of lanterns glowing or a campfire burning, and I snuggled closer, letting my eyes sink shut. A gruff sound came from deep in his throat and he curved his chin over the top of my head, stroking through my long hair with a touch both gentle and passionate. Wordless, we clung to one another. But no words were necessary.

The front windows shone silver with approaching dawn when I opened my eyes next; I blinked a couple of times and realized that Mathias and I were still wrapped together on the couch. He was snoring like a ripsaw and my left arm was numb from being tucked under his body all night; we lay full-length, Mathias curved protectively over me, the afghan tucked around my shoulders. Happiness melted over my soul like warm butter before reality intruded; no matter how innocent, Grandma would not be pleased at this situation.

"Mathias," I whispered, leaning up on one elbow to study his sleeping face, tenderness overflowing in my heart. He lay positioned with his chin tipped up, mouth slightly open as he snored, arms locked about me. He felt so good that I hated to wake him and be forced to move, but Grandma or Aunt Ellen would be up any moment. I relented to the need to caress his jaw, prickly with stubble, letting my fingertips learn the feel of his face. I couldn't resist and traced lightly over his lips, and my entire body vibrated with desire.

He twitched, stopped snoring, and rolled to his front side, almost crushing me in the process. Without opening his eyes he mumbled, "It's morning, isn't it?"

"Yes," I whispered, snuggling against him for the last few seconds we would be allowed this morning.

He groaned a little and then shifted us to the side, kissing the top of my head. He whispered, "Good morning, then. I suppose I better get home before we're in trouble."

"I'm glad you stayed," I murmured.

"Me, too. The last thing I wanted was to go home and be without you last night. Well, now we've slept together, Camille. We better redefine our relationship."

I giggled, muffling the sound against him, and he kissed my hair again, stroking it with both hands, as he had last night. I said, almost shyly, "Maybe it would be all right if I called you my boyfriend."

"Damn right," he said, and reached to lift my chin. In the dimness of dawn, our sleep-smudged eyes held fast; we couldn't stop smiling at each other. Tracing his thumb over my skin, he asked, "Are you free this evening?"

"I am. Will you be back?"

"Wild horses couldn't stop me."

Chapter Twelve

"SO HE'S YOUR BOYFRIEND NOW," JAKE SAID, AND HIS VOICE was full of disdain, clearly masking his hurt. It was Tuesday the twentieth, the first day of winter break for my sisters and Clint, and Shore Leave was packed with people even though we weren't technically open. Grandma, Mom, Aunt Ellen, and Aunt Jilly were drinking coffee and planning what day to celebrate Christmas with the entire family, and at whose house. Rae and Millie Jo played in the corner booth, having a tea party with their dolls. Little Matthew dozed in the playpen near the counter, the one always reserved for the newest baby, bundled in a bright red footie that had once belonged to Millie. Tish, Clint, Liam, and Ruthie were involved in what appeared to be a rather cutthroat game of Uno at table three. Blythe and Uncle Justin were both at work; Blythe worked with one of Eddie's sons on days when Shore Leave was closed, in a woodshop on the outskirts of Landon, where he was learning to make cabinets.

And I sat enraptured in my daydreams, gazing out at the snowy day, wondering just where Mathias was at this moment in his plow truck, and what he was doing, and how many hours would have to pass before I saw him again.

He had texted me almost immediately after leaving the house this morning, sneaking out just ahead of Grandma.

Thank you for a wonderful night.

I loved being in your arms, I wrote back, all shivery and smiley at the memory.

My phone vibrated almost at once and I'd nearly dropped it in my haste to see what he'd responded; I read, *All yours.*

Did he mean his arms? Or did he mean him in his entirety? Both? I could hardly breathe and wrote back, *Tonight?*

His reply read, *No question mark. Tonight, exclamation point (!!!)*

And now my daydreaming had been rudely interrupted by Jake, who'd ridden over with Mom and the girls. I knew Mom was just trying to be kind, inviting him for breakfast, as Jake's own mother worked two jobs and he was often alone, but I really wished he'd just stayed home.

I nodded in response to his question, uncomfortable telling Jake that I considered Mathias my boyfriend. I reminded myself that I couldn't help it if Jake liked me more than I liked him.

You kissed him. Twice.

But that doesn't matter now. It was a mistake, both times.

I would never be so cruel as to admit this to Jake, but the truth remained. He sat opposite me and I slipped my cell phone out of sight beneath the table.

"Isn't it a little fast?" To be fair, he also appeared concerned, not just hurt. "I mean, you just met."

I longed to say, *It's not your business! Back off!*

Instead, trying to infuse a little teasing into my voice, I said, "Thanks, Dad."

He directed at me an exasperated look, lips compressing. "I remember Mathias from back when, working on the fire crew in the summer. He's, like, nuts. I mean, like the kind of guy who'd race into a burning house because someone's picture album was in there."

I sat straighter. "He did that?"

Jake nodded vigorously. "Maybe six summers ago. This lady was freaking out that her wedding album on the coffee table was going to get burned up and before anyone could tell her sorry, it's way too late for any album, Mathias ran back into the burning house and saved it. I mean, it was a little singed…"

"That's *brave*," I corrected, though I hated to think of Mathias in harm's way, endangered for a bunch of pictures. Not even a kid or a pet, but *pictures*.

"It's nuts," Jake repeated. "And he's a total player, Camille, ask anyone."

My temper flared. Of course there was no reason to believe this offensive statement, but a small, insecure part of my brain acknowledged that someone as incredibly good-looking as Mathias could well deserve that description. Then I reassured myself that most rumors like that were not true; I was hardly the slut everyone believed I was, right?

"Look, that's not only mean, it's none of your business," I said at last, and anger seeped into my tone.

"I get that," Jake said. His voice grew pleading. "I just worry about you."

Mom appeared at the table. "Can I steal you away for a sec, Milla?"

I nodded, grateful for this inadvertent rescue. Jake moved to join Tish and Ruthie.

"What is it?" I asked Mom, following her through the arch that led into the bar.

She looked over her shoulder, covertly, as though expecting to have been followed, and then whispered, "I was just trying to save you." Mom ignored the question in my eyes and invited, "So. Tell me about Matty Carter." Before I could even speak, she half-groaned, "*Camille*. You just lit up like a firefly. I *knew* it. What's going on between the two of you?"

"We...we just..."

Mom said, "You like him."

There was no hiding it.

"I haven't seen that smile on your face in a long time," she murmured, reaching to smooth my hair with both hands. "Oh, Milla, sweetheart, I just hope...I mean, I just don't want you to get hurt."

"He's not like that." I recognized how crazy it was to make this sort of statement when Mathias and I had only met last week—when I hardly knew him. But I couldn't explain to Mom that somehow, some way, I'd known him much longer than that. That we'd been searching for each other. Despite a fairly romantic nature of her own, Mom would drag me away by the ear.

"Grandma told me she talked to you. And that you were going to take it slow." Mom spoke this last word with over-exaggeration and I shrugged irritably from her grasp.

"I'm not planning to get pregnant again." My shoulders sagged and I said immediately, "I'm sorry."

"Don't be sorry," Mom said. "And I know you would never *try* to get pregnant..."

"I'm not as naïve as I used to be," I said, closing my eyes.

"Hon, it's not about being naïve, not at all." She spoke gently. "It's about being in love."

"Mom, please understand." I looked deeply into her familiar eyes, the Davis women eyes of green and gold, her fanlike lashes a shade of blond just slightly darker than her hair; I'd always wished I'd inherited Mom's cornsilk hair. I said, "I don't know why, but I trust Mathias. And if it doesn't work out—" My insides seized at these words, but I forced myself to finish. "If it doesn't work out then I'll deal with it. But I'll never know if I don't give it a chance."

Mom didn't reply at once, and I was afraid she was going to contradict my words. But she just said, "You mean *we'll* deal with it."

On Wednesday I helped Mathias move from Bull and Diana's house to the little apartment in Pine Ridge. I loved this chance to see the place where he'd been raised, a sprawling modern cabin on the northern bank of Flickertail, a five-minute walk from White Oaks Lodge. His bedroom was painted a dark, woodsy green and was currently almost bare, his belongings tucked into cardboard boxes and canvas bags, many of which were patched with duct tape, his go-to fixit tool. The bed and furniture had all been loaded into the U-Haul out in the driveway; Sam and Tina were also here to help. Their kids were downstairs in the kitchen with Diana. Christmas music played on the radio and Diana and her granddaughters were baking gingerbread cookies. The Carters never failed to remind me of my own family. There existed the same sense of semi-controlled chaos whenever they gathered; something delicious always baking, kids giggling and running around.

"See, I took good care of them," Mathias said, referring to the photograph of Malcolm and Aces, now carefully tucked into my purse. He caught me around the waist for a sideways hug, his right arm burdened with a cardboard box. He kissed my temple, lingering there and sending spasms of shivers along my skin as he murmured, "Thanks for helping, by the way. I'm glad you're here."

"I hardly did a thing," I said; the men had done all the heavy lifting. And then I could not resist teasing him, my face already hot as I said sweetly, "Besides, how else would I know that you wore boxers with tiny green *elves* on them?"

I'd shamelessly grabbed these from a box of what appeared to be top-drawer things, like socks and t-shirts, and hid them in my pocket, presenting them now with a flourish, laughing hard at his expression of surprise. He yelped and tried to grab for them but I darted away, not about to relinquish this chance to tease him. Other than hugging and cuddling, we'd not yet kissed (I knew Mathias did not want to rush me), and so I hadn't come close to seeing his underwear in person, besides this pair.

"Not reindeer or snowmen, but elves!" I cried, evading him with difficulty in his empty room. He dropped the box and managed to corner me, advancing menacingly, his shoulders curled forward.

I couldn't stop laughing, hiding the boxers behind my back as he pinned me with both arms, one on either side of my shoulders. "Now, give those here and I'll let you free." He lowered his eyebrows with a hint of wickedness and clarified, "For now."

I shook my head and then giggled and gulped at the same time as he leaned just slightly closer, as though executing a push-up against the wall.

"One," he began. "*Two…*"

"What happens on 'three?'" I asked, embarrassed by how breathlessly my voice emerged, as though I'd been sprinting.

"Why don't you wait and find out?" he invited, still grinning, and my heart almost thrust through my ribcage. At the last second I darted, ducking beneath his right arm. He chased after me and we bumped into Tina in the hallway.

"Whoa there, kiddies," she said, flattening against the wall to avoid us. Mathias caught my waist from behind, pulling me against his broad chest, and he felt so good that I only weakly struggled.

"Tina, take these!" I tossed the boxers her direction.

Tina whooped with laughter and held them up by the waistband.

Mathias said to his sister, "Joke's on you. I was just wearing those."

"Matty!" she shrieked, flinging them down the hall. "Eeeeew!"

"He wasn't," I contradicted, and my stomach hurt from laughing.

Tina slapped his shoulder. "Nice one, Bratty-pants. Come on down, Mom's got cookies for us."

The big, farmhouse-style kitchen was warm, scented by vanilla and sugar, cinnamon and coffee, the towering blue spruce in the adjacent living room rounding out the heady aromas of Christmas. Diana hugged her son close the moment we set foot in the kitchen, then roughed up his hair, reaching way up to do so. Her blue eyes, so very much like his, shone with happiness as she said, "It's about time my baby was home for Christmas."

"Aw, Ma," he complained, but his love for his mother was apparent in his tone. It was easy to see that his sisters adored him, for all their teasing, and Diana absolutely doted on him; but then, I'd known that long before tonight. My heart swelled with a quiet joy to watch Mathias with his family, so dear and beloved to them, their son and brother who'd been away far too long.

Diana hugged me next, patting my back, encouraging, "Eat up, everyone, there's plenty."

In the tone of a big sister attempting to get her sibling in trouble, Tina tattled, "Mom, Matty's not wearing underwear." Her mouth was full of cookie and she started laughing even before Mathias groaned and chucked a gingerbread snowman at her. Tina's daughters began shrieking and laughing, yelling, "Gross, Uncle Matty!"

"What's this I hear?" demanded Bull, entering the kitchen. He wore a red flannel shirt complete with suspenders, his torso appearing as powerful as his namesake. I bit back a smile as I imagined that someday Mathias would resemble his father even more than he did now; while Mathias was taller and leaner than Bull, they were in all other ways similar, right down to the dark chest hair visible at their open collars. Bull used a bottle opener on a beer and then slapped at his son's backside. "Are you trying to scare your lady on her first evening here?"

I flushed, immeasurably pleased to be referred to this way. Bull winked at Diana, helping himself to a handful of cookies, while Mathias heaved a long-suffering sigh and lifted the bottom of his sweatshirt, baring a good couple of inches of his lean, muscular belly—my own belly went weightless at the sight—and then proceeded to hook his thumb around the elastic waistband of his underwear, showcasing its presence for his family. By the time we'd all stopped laughing Tina had commandeered my elbow, leading me to the living room for a tour of the framed family pictures gracing the limestone mantle.

"And this is Matty the Christmas when he lost six teeth at once, four on top, two on the bottom. Isn't that hilarious?" she said.

From the kitchen, where he leaned over the counter eating cookies, Mathias called, "Yeah, real hilarious. I couldn't eat anything but pudding and applesauce."

The picture melted my heart away—an adorable little blue-eyed Mathias grinning up at the camera from a toboggan sled, appearing almost completely toothless.

Tina, standing near me, tucked her hand around my elbow and rested her chin momentarily on my shoulder. She whispered, "We're all so happy about you and Matty, I just wanted you to know. I had a feeling about you two, ask Elaine. All three of us girls have talked about the possibility of you and Matty since that night you showed us the picture of Malcolm Carter."

"You have?" I asked, stunned at this revelation; I remembered well that soggy March evening when I'd been so low and sad. Tina had been the one to tell me that I'd be all right and now here I stood, proof that her statement was the truth.

Tina nodded, squeezing my arm. A smile lifted her lips as the lights strung on the tree painted her lovely face with candy colors. "I haven't seen him so happy since I don't know when. And it's all you."

Skid Erickson's apartment at Pine Ridge was a small two-bedroom. The apartment complex was located just outside Landon, near Farmer's Market grocery store, bordered by dense pine forest. By the time all of Mathias's things were unloaded it was well into the evening and I needed to get home. By then it was just us and Skid, who had disappeared into the bathroom while Mathias and I unpacked the last few kitchen supplies he deemed necessary for morning, like the coffee filters. The rest of his things were stacked and scattered haphazardly all across the floor of the adjacent living room.

"I better go," I murmured, catching sight of the green numbers on the microwave display. I tried to deny a prickle of regret; I couldn't even look forward to spending very many evenings here with him, and consequently away from Millie Jo.

Mathias saw the change in my expression. "What's wrong?"

"Nothing," I said.

"Not nothing. Camille, what's wrong? Tell me."

I closed my eyes for a second. "I was just wishing that I could stay here and hang out with you, but I can't. I can't just do those things."

"Then I'll come to your house."

I opened my eyes to his serious expression, his black eyebrows slightly knitted, his lips somber. Though I wanted him to come over more than about anything, I forced myself to say, "No, you have lots to do here. It's all right."

"Will Millie be asleep yet?"

"Not for a couple hours, probably."

"I'll get a few things done here and then I'll come over in time to tuck her in. Will Joan be upset that it's too late?"

"Of course not," I said, and banished the thought that he would eventually grow tired of waiting around for someone with a child of her own; I wanted so badly to believe in him.

Mathias hugged me close, rocking us side to side with his usual enthusiasm. And then he bent forward, bending my back over his forearm as though executing a ballroom dance move. I giggled, shivering and squirming as he rubbed his unshaven chin on the sensitive skin of my neck. Both of us heard Skid coming down the hall and Mathias whispered in my ear, "Would it make you feel better to know I'm still wearing underwear?"

Nearly upside-down over his arm, I was laughing too hard to answer.

I worked Thursday lunch at Shore Leave and then Friday dinner at White Oaks, and basked in the warmth of Mathias's gaze as he tended the bar with Elaine. Tina was also on shift and we stayed busy all evening, as it was the day before Christmas Eve and White Oaks would be closed for the holiday weekend. Bull didn't book guests over Christmas, instead reopening on the twenty-sixth. Before I left home Millie helped me get ready, pinning two glittery red poinsettia barrettes into my hair and picking out gold tinkle-bell earrings that once belonged to my great-grandma, Louisa.

Fastening them into my ears, I imagined Gran doing the same thing once upon a time; the ache of missing her, though having mellowed with time, throbbed like an old, slow-healing bruise, reminding me of its presence. What would Gran have to say about Mathias and me, I wondered, sending him a smile as I hurried between tables, my earrings playing a tiny, two-note refrain, like that of miniature wind chimes. Gran thought very highly of the Carters, this I knew, especially the way Bull, much like Dodge, was always ready for a good argument—or *discussion*, as Gran had liked to say. The old bruise throbbed again, stronger than before, as I thought of how Gran had gripped my hand in hers the night I'd confessed to Mom that I was pregnant, way back in the summer of 2003, offering me wordless comfort and unwavering support.

And then you never got to meet my baby, I thought. *Oh, Gran. You see her from wherever you are, don't you? Heaven or whatever it is that exists beyond. You can see Millie, this I believe.* And then I wondered, not for the first time, *Wherever it is that your spirit now lives, Gran, is Malcolm Carter there, too? Can you see him, talk to him, hug him for me? Does he know that I'm trying to solve the mystery of him, here in Landon, long after his death?*

I wanted to believe this, so very badly.

Later that evening I dallied over the computer monitor as I typed in a last order of mozzarella sticks, mentally riffling through the Santa Claus presents I'd picked out for Millie Jo and considering what I could possibly get for Mathias so last-minute, when he burst through the swinging door that led from the dining room. I looked up in surprise; he was obviously angry.

"Utley," Mathias said through clenched teeth, "just came in here."

"What?" My stomach went all at once hollow and cold. I looked over my shoulder as though expecting Noah to be standing there. I hadn't seen him in well over a year.

"He's at the bar with Mandy Pearson," Mathias explained, tension vibrating from him. "You don't have to go back out there. I'll deal with him."

"He can do what he wants," I said, though unwelcome anxiety flooded me at the thought of the two of them sitting together at the bar. Sweat prickled between my breasts and beneath my arms.

Mathias said heatedly, "You know what I want to do? I want to go out there and fucking slam his head against the bar and then ask him if he knows what his little girl wants for Christmas."

At his heartfelt, if rather violent, words, tears seeped into my eyes.

"Oh God, don't cry, honey. It breaks my heart and I want to kill him even more. I hate that he has this much power over your emotions."

I set aside my order notebook and pen, touched by the fact that he'd called me *honey*, reaching up to put my hands on his shoulders. His blue eyes were fierce, blazing with angry emotion. I said, "Noah has no power over me. But what you said…about him not knowing what Millie wants for Christmas. It just makes me sad for my daughter. That the person who conceived her doesn't even know her."

Mathias wrapped me in his arms. I felt so safe there, tucked close to him, that it was almost too much for me to bear; surely this level of happiness could not last. I could feel his heart, clubbing at a much faster than normal pace, and tightened my grip. He said against the side of my forehead, "You don't have to go out there. I'll take care of that last table for you. Don't give him the satisfaction."

I buried my nose against his chest. It might have been a wee bit off topic, but I murmured, "I like how you just called me 'honey.'"

Even though my eyes were closed, I felt the warmth of his smile. "You do?"

I nodded and he cupped my nape in one strong hand, brushing his thumb over wayward curls on my neck. He whispered, "I feel very protective of you. I don't want you to have to deal with his bullshit, ever."

I stood on tiptoe to kiss the hollow between Mathias's collarbones, so very warm beneath my questing lips. Maybe now wasn't the time, but I thought about all that dark hair on his chest, of which I'd only caught tempting glimpses, and was broadsided by a sudden image of my breasts naked against it. A thrill erupted all the way to my toes and I kissed his chin, pressing even closer. It didn't matter that Noah and his girlfriend were here; I thought, *Noah, who?*

Mathias bracketed my jaw and his eyes blazed with a different kind of heat.

"Is anyone going to take that order? We got customers out there," Jerry, one of the cooks, appeared in the ticket window, sounding as irritable as usual, and I startled as though electrocuted, both of us turning toward this interruption.

"Sorry, Jer, I'll get right out there." My voice was hoarse. Jerry made a noise that sounded halfway apologetic before disappearing into the kitchen. Mathias didn't fully release me, his eyes on my mouth.

"I suppose I better let you go," he murmured, tracing his thumbs over my lips. Some of the playfulness dissipated from his expression as he said again, "I'll take care of your last table."

I moved with sluggish reluctance from his arms, collecting up my order pad and pen and reminding him, "I'm not a coward."

"I know," he said at once. He tried for a little teasing, as though to coax a smile. "But one word from you and—" He slammed a fist into the opposite palm. "I admit I would take pleasure in it. Shit."

I did smile then, a crooked little smile. I admonished, "Quit it. Honestly, Noah probably won't even notice me. He can't possibly know

I've been working here, or he never would have shown up."

Mathias lowered his brows and squared his wide shoulders, appearing truly menacing as he looked in the direction of the bar. "I'll keep my eye on him."

I ducked into the employee bathroom before daring to brave the dining room. A shred of pride remained, buried beneath the weight of my resentment toward Noah Utley. I was going to assume that he didn't realize I was working at White Oaks this winter; surely he would not show his face at Shore Leave unannounced in this fashion, so it seemed reasonable that he couldn't have known to find me at the lodge. At least I hoped he would have more class than to show up with his new girlfriend where the mother of his basically-unacknowledged child worked. Though, nothing should surprise me about Noah, not anymore. I gave myself a quick, critical perusal before proceeding into the dining room.

Immediately I saw that Tess French had joined Noah and Mandy. Even though I knew that Tess's relationship with Mathias was over a white-hot poker of jealousy seemed lodged between my ribs. My feet stalled as I stared at the three of them, sitting on barstools with their backs to me. Mathias looked my way and his expression softened; he stood in an otherwise unmistakably belligerent pose, knuckles braced on the bar, arms spread wide, directly across from Noah. I dragged my eyes away and proceeded to the far side of the dining room to check on my table; Tina had already cashed out and was now chatting with her mother at the front desk in a completely different part of the lodge but I was glad, only wanting to escape at this point, to avoid Noah and what would surely be—at best—an awful, awkward conversation.

Minutes later Mathias caught up with me in the kitchen, his hands full of empty beer mugs, which he deposited with a clatter into the sink. "He doesn't know you're here. He's pretty drunk. He tried to talk to me like we're friends."

"Tess is here, too." I avoided his eyes.

"I can't help that," he said, just as quietly.

A quarter-hour passed. I wrapped up my last table and studiously circumvented the bar, while Noah proceeded to drink two whiskey sours, according to Mathias, who kept me informed. Tess and Mandy continued chatting, giggling, and sipping fizzy drinks with limes on the rim.

Not that I noticed or anything.

I cleared the tables in my section and it was going for ten when I realized that only Tess sat at the otherwise empty bar; Mathias was in the kitchen and Noah and Mandy were not in sight, so I let my shoulders relax. But as I turned to wipe down my last table I heard someone approaching from behind; Noah suddenly said, "Hi, Camille."

My heart twisted up into an icky little knot and for a second I considered just ignoring him. But I would not be a coward. I thought about how his parents had just asked if they could come to Shore Leave for dinner; how much they adored Millie Jo, how kind they were to her. Even Noah's older brother, Ben, along with his wife, occasionally came to the cafe to visit Millie and me.

Chin up, I pretended to hear Gran say, and this afforded me the strength to turn and face Noah Utley, unwitting father of my child. He stood with both hands lodged in his front pockets, looking thoroughly drunk and slightly shamefaced. I let my gaze take in the familiar: his clear, pale-blue eyes and close-cropped golden hair, the cleft in his chin. I sometimes wondered if Millie Jo would eventually have one, too. Noah seemed older, more filled out; he was tall and broad-shouldered in a navy-blue pea coat, with the faintest of goatees, which didn't really do much for fair-haired men, in my opinion. But he was still handsome, I'd once believed that he loved me, and I felt more vulnerable than I would have guessed, even after all this time. I hated that he might think I was still hurting.

"Hey," I finally said. My hands became loose fists before I could stop them. And then I could not believe my eyes; Noah's unsteady gaze roved south, lingering on the swell of my breasts. I was seized by the urge to deck him in the stomach. I thought, *Go ahead and look. You're never touching me again.*

"How've you been?" he asked, rocking back on his heels.

"Millie is getting so big." I cleared away the catch in my voice at once. Noah flinched and I continued, lifting my chin, "She's the sweetest little girl in the world."

Noah prudently ignored this obvious bait. "When did you start working here?"

Over his left shoulder I observed Tess watching us from the bar, her gaze fixed intently, as though no one had ever taught her it was rude to stare.

"I'll stop out and see her," Noah said then, shuffling his feet, directing his gaze at the floor. "I really will, I've just been so busy…" His voice trailed away and I refocused upon him, with real venom.

"*Busy*," I repeated, infusing every possible ounce of sarcastic innuendo into my tone.

"Listen, Milla." He slurred over all the Ls in the words. I hated how he'd used my nickname, as if he had any right, but I recognized that he was intoxicated. For a second I almost asked him if he needed a ride home. But that wasn't my job anymore; I thought of the summer we'd been together, how many beers he'd consumed those nights, how many times I'd seen and heard him act exactly like this—usually just before he offered up his most charming smile and began working on unbuttoning my jean shorts or fumbling with my bikini top.

How could you have let him treat you that way, Camille? How could you not see that he was playing you? Using you?

Anger flared like brushfire; the rest of the dining room receded into a fuzzy gray distance as I yelled in a whisper, "Listen to *you*? What could you possibly have to say to me?"

"Camille." He started over but I didn't let him speak, storming my words right over him.

"You haven't seen your daughter in over a year *because you're busy?!* That's the cheapest, shittiest excuse I've ever heard!" I had stepped closer to him without realizing; we were practically nose to nose. Or we would have been if he wasn't so much taller than me. "You haven't even bothered to *call* and then you waltz in here with your *fucking girlfriend*—"

"Jesus Christ, do you have to—"

"Don't you *dare* scold me!" I shouted, forgetting my intent to keep my voice down.

Tess stalked over, as if any of this was her concern.

"What's going on?" she demanded, eyeing me up and down, standing with one hip jutting. Even from a few feet away I could smell gin on her breath.

All of the resentful fury broiling inside of me for the past two years boiled over; it was perhaps a poor excuse, but in that moment I wielded absolutely no control. I turned on Tess. "It's absolutely none of your fucking business!"

"Don't you talk to me that way, you little slut!" she snapped without missing a beat, driving her pointer finger into my shoulder.

I thought the top of my head might come off; Noah, drunk as he was, still perceived my violent intent and caught me around the waist, hauling me away from Tess and likely preventing me from doing physical damage to her. A tiny part of my brain retained the sense to be grateful that there were no customers present; unfortunately, at that exact instant Mathias pushed through the swinging doors, just in time to see Noah and I tumble over a chair, Noah's inebriated clumsiness and my furious momentum causing him to stumble. We went tail over teakettle, taking a chair with us.

Mathias was at my side before I could blink, let alone collect my bearings. He lifted me from the pileup, clearly astounded. "Holy shit, are you all right?" Mathias eased me behind him and rounded on Noah, his eyes dangerous as he said through his teeth, "What the *fuck*, Utley? Put your hands on her again and you will regret it!"

"No...no...it's not like that," I tried to explain, winded from the fall and with adrenaline pulsing through my veins. "I was...I was just..."

"You're crazy!" Tess said to me, fists on her hips. Her eyes were wide. "You tried to hit me!"

"Stay out of this!" Mathias ordered her.

"*You* stay out of this!" Tess yelped, shoving at his shoulder, and flames burst into my blood yet again.

"Don't touch him!" I cried, and Tess immediately narrowed her eyes, as though in speculation. She shifted her weight to the opposite hip, flicking her long golden hair over one shoulder.

And then, her boozy breath reaching my nose, she purred, "I'll touch him *all I want.* Tell her, Matty. Tell her how we had sex all over your apartment the night you moved in. Just last Wednesday."

Scalding water to the skin would have hurt less than these words. I sensed more than saw the stun that crossed Mathias's face. I wanted so badly to believe that Tess was bluffing.

But what if she's not?

Oh God, oh God, oh God.

He didn't come over until at least two hours later that night.

And it was Wednesday.

How would she know that?

His voice tightly controlled, jaw clenched, Mathias said, "That is not true."

Obviously a few paces behind, Noah muttered, "Camille is not a slut."

Despite everything, I heard Noah's quiet statement. I could feel the shakes starting in my knees but I bent down and offered Noah my forearm, experiencing a small flash of redemption at his words; at least he could acknowledge this about me. I was many things, but I was not a slut.

"Camille." Mathias spoke my name in a quiet but concentrated request for my attention but I could barely hear a thing; my heart roared between my ears. My face was hot enough that I could probably spark a match to life with my skin. Noah gripped my arm and I helped him to a sitting position before the trembling moved into my upper body. I kept stubbornly stiff, refusing to let anyone see this weakness.

"Are you all right?" I asked Noah, but I was the one who wasn't all right; my lips had gone numb.

What did you expect?

So stupid, Camille.

Tess is lying. She's trying to hurt you.

But what if she's not...

Noah used the edge of the table to attempt to get to his feet. I didn't bother to stick around to see if he managed, shoving past Mathias and Tess; her smirk seemed to span my entire vision. Mathias came after me and so I ran, slamming smack into Mandy Pearson, who must have been in the bathroom. She yelped in surprise but I disentangled myself with no explanation and dashed through the swinging door. In that moment, escape was the only option my mind recognized.

"Camille, wait!" Mathias implored, but I did not. I was tripped up at the door, out of necessity, forced to grab my coat and purse so that I could drive home. My fingers had become unbending wooden planks; I could hardly manage to retrieve my things from the hooks by the back door.

See, you've let a guy do this to you again.

Mathias took my shoulders in his hands and turned me to face him. His face had gone ashen, his eyes blue darts aimed straight into my heart. "Tess is lying. She said that to hurt you and it's not true." Even though I fought it, tears wet my eyes; Mathias made a choked sound and insisted, "She's lying because she's jealous. I know it's hard but you have to trust me."

I shrugged from his grip. "I don't have to do anything! Get away from me!"

Stun took him across the face, as though I'd swung a crowbar along with the words. I stumbled blindly out the door and into the freezing winter night, thrusting my arms into my coat. Mathias chased after me as I jogged across the icy parking lot, purse bumping my hip. At my truck he cornered me against the driver's side door, our breath appearing as clouds of blue-white steam in the icy glow of the lone streetlight.

"Don't go," he implored, sounding aghast. "Don't believe her. It's what she wants."

I wanted to trust him but Tess had succeeded at one thing; I looked up at Mathias and whispered, "I don't know what to believe."

"She's jealous." His hands moved as though to cup my elbows but he held back, sensing my intent to bolt. He whispered, "Where are you going?"

"Home, of course," I said shortly. I was about to start crying and didn't want him to know. I studied his face as though I would never see it again, absorbing the intensity in his eyes like a drug, and a sudden hot fury replaced all else. "I can't do this! I can't handle it. Leave me alone!"

"Camille," he whispered painfully. "Oh God, don't leave like this. Please." He had to be freezing. The wind bit into my exposed skin and he wasn't even wearing a coat.

"I just need...to go home."

"I'll drive you." He controlled the panic in his tone, squaring his shoulders decisively. "There's no way I'm letting you go alone."

Mathias, I thought, aching for him to come with me, to believe what he said. But I shook my head, fumbling for the keys in my purse, turning from him to attempt to unlock my truck.

He implored, "Please listen to me," and moved his left hand to the truck door, as though to keep it closed. The wind howled and my tear-streaked face felt like frozen plastic. All I could see was his strong hand, fingers spread against my window, forearm bare to the cold wind, as his shirtsleeve was rolled back. He whispered, "Please."

At last I succeeded in unlocking the door, so aware of him standing there that I struggled to draw a full breath. "I have to," I said and the words were no more than harsh whispers.

Wordlessly he removed his hand from the door and I climbed inside as quickly as I was able, because if I continued to stand here I would relent to the desire to believe him. He didn't move from the side of the truck, watching me. I started the engine and drove away into the snow; I could see him in the rearview mirror, standing motionless where I had left him. I turned left for Shore Leave and the streetlight shone through the image of his hand against my driver's side window.

Chapter Thirteen

I SAT IN THE CANDLE-GLOW OF THE CHRISTMAS TREE FOR over an hour, nursing my daughter to sleep with the comforting background cadence of Grandma and Aunt Ellen in the kitchen drinking coffee and chatting; I kept my mind carefully blank. At times like these I felt as though I was channeling Mom, picturing her curled in the same position, the exact age I was right now, holding me to her breast as she sat in this same living room and thought about where the hell her life was going. Even though I knew my parents had been living in Chicago by the time I was Millie's age I pretended that Mom had sat here on the carpet near the old Christmas tree, watching the silver tinsel spin little light webs as it moved in the gentle draft created by the forced air of the furnace.

There wasn't an ornament on Grandma's tree that was newer than probably the 1970s, the most recent being ones made by Mom and Aunt Jilly in elementary school. My eyes roved over the blown-glass bulbs Mille and I had helped Grandma and Aunt Ellen hang at the beginning of December, fragile as eggshells and painted in cheerful colors like cobalt and scarlet, sprinkled with gold glitter; these had belonged to Grandma's grandmother, a woman named Myrtle Jean. The tree was also graced by a chorus of a dozen china angels holding little hymnals, their china mouths wide in song. And my favorite ornament of all, placed in its spot of honor at the front of the tree—a clam shell once plucked from Flickertail Lake, cleaned and polished to a glossy sheen, open two inches and decorated with rickrack ribbon and fake fluffy snow, a gleaming pearl centered on its bottom curve. When I'd asked Grandma where it came from she said she wasn't entirely sure; it had always been one of their traditional decorations. After a long time my gaze roved to the couch where Mathias and I had fallen asleep together, where we'd snuggled and talked these past nights when he came over after work.

It's crazy to feel this way, Camille. Crazy doesn't begin to cover it. You met him hardly a week ago. Jesus Christ. You can't let yourself feel this way. You know this. Better to just let him go now, before you like him more than you already do.

I refocused on my daughter, studying her little cheek, moving as rhythmically as a chipmunk's as she drew sustenance from my body. My breasts remained as fully rounded as halved cantaloupes, my nipples the size of miniature marshmallows. I marveled at this sight almost every time I bared them; it was like looking at a stranger's body superimposed over my own. Millie's head wasn't quite so dwarfed by my breasts as it used to be; she'd grown so much. Her eyes were currently closed, her long lashes fanned against her flushed cheek. I stroked the tip of my index finger into her downy hair, curling the same strand repeatedly.

Millie Jo. I love you so much. I wouldn't trade you, baby. It's just so hard. I don't know if I'm doing this right.

Almost against my will, I thought, *Please come over, Mathias. I didn't want to leave, but I'm so scared. I'm so scared to let myself trust you...*

Millie Jo sighed and detached from my nipple, smacking her little rosebud lips as warm milk glided down the bottom curve of my breast. I swiped it away and then bent to press a kiss to her temple, my tears falling on her sweet face; I used the edge of my pajama sleeve to gently wipe her dry.

"I love you more than anything," I whispered to my daughter. "I want you to know that. I hope you always know that."

I rolled gingerly to my knees and then carried her up to our bed, drawing the quilt to her shoulders, kissing her silken forehead. And then I sat on the floor, bringing the nightstand lamp with me, only clicking it into existence once I was certain that Millie remained soundly asleep. With the devotion of one clutching a talisman, I held the picture of Malcolm Carter to my heart for a long time; later, I softly kissed his face.

Studying the yellowing, black-and-white image, I whispered, "I love you, sweetheart. I love you even though it's completely crazy and everyone I know would think so. I know that once, somewhere, you and I rode Aces together. Somehow, we did."

My heart hurt. I sat on the floor for hours, holding Malcolm's picture, wishing that there was some way he could respond to me. At last, my fingertips chilly and my back cramped from sitting too long in the same position, I snuggled near Millie Jo in our bed, where it seemed we would continue to sleep alone together for the foreseeable future.

I put on my bravest, most cheerful face all the next day, Christmas Eve. It was as picturesque as a snow globe outside, all horizontal surfaces decorated with a layer of delectable snow frosting, the house redolent with the constant baking. Christmas Eve dinner ended up being held at Uncle Justin and Aunt Jilly's house, but Grandma and Aunt Ellen insisted upon bringing their specialties, olive-cheese bread and pecan pies. I couldn't think about eating a bite, and only managed to get dressed and feign enjoyment because of my daughter. This was an important day for any child and she was so excited, dancing all over the house, thankfully claiming everyone's attention. If Grandma or Aunt Ellen noticed anything amiss with me, neither said a word; I was unwilling to consider explaining how short-lived my time with Mathias Carter.

Grandma only mentioned him once. "Will Mathias be joining us this evening?"

"No, he's got family stuff of his own," I said, forcing a cheerful smile.

I survived the evening at Aunt Jilly's, playing cards with the adults while the little ones ran wild, even though I crept into the empty kitchen to throw away my plate of food. Lucky for me, everyone was too preoccupied with celebrating, boisterous with the holiday spirit, to notice that I was trying too hard; safely hidden in the quiet room I covered my face and wondered what Mathias was doing right now, surely over at his parents' house, full to the brim with his sisters and their husbands and kids.

Would anyone ask where I was? And what would he say? By the time we got home and I managed to coerce my over-stimulated child into bed, I felt as though I might crumble apart at the seams, like an old ragdoll. Grandma helped me arrange presents under the tree as soon as Millie Jo fell asleep; I begged off when Grandma suggested we make some hot apple cider and talk.

"I'm just so tired," I said, and retreated to my room, where I lay in the darkness and caressed my phone, wanting to call him. Dying to hear his voice.

But at last I fell asleep without managing to dial his number.

It was hours later that I woke to the hall light and Grandma's sleepy voice. "What in the world?"

I sat up, hearing a low growling sound coming from the snowy night; the quilt fell to the floor as I stumbled to my narrow bedroom windows, seeing headlights headed up the driveway. From the living room I heard Aunt Ellen announce, "It's the Carters' plow pickup."

I flew into my robe and raced down the stairs.

"It's Mathias," Grandma confirmed, having joined Aunt Ellen at the window. They peered through the curtains and then looked back at me with almost comical unison. Grandma muttered with quiet certainty, "I told you that boy was crazy."

I nearly fell over attempting to get my boots on my bare feet. I heard the big truck's diesel engine as he drew near, the headlights beaming right into the front room. It was probably three in the morning, it was snowing buckets' worth of big, fluffy snowflakes, and my grandmother and great aunt were bearing witness to everything. Aunt Ellen clicked on the outside light.

"Is he drunk? Camille, if he's drunk I'm calling Bull," Grandma complained.

I swung open the front door just as Mathias climbed from the cab of the truck, leaving it running. He wore his brown Carhartt overhauls and steel-toed snow boots, his gray stocking cap, and his cheeks were flushed with the cold. I could tell that he hadn't shaved since sometime yesterday and his black hair stuck out from beneath his hat. He pulled off his big gloves with his teeth, tossed them back on the seat, and then walked with determination, coming to a stop just in front of me.

"I came to tell you not to be scared to trust me," he said, eyes serious upon my face. "And that the thought of not seeing you is more than I can bear."

I couldn't speak, unable to describe the relief that overflowed within me. In that moment I understood that he'd told me the truth.

Mathias saw this on my face and smiling joy lit his eyes and lifted his lips. He braced one hand on the doorframe near my head and leaned a little closer. "I also came to ask you if you'll go on a date with me Monday night."

"Matty Carter! Are you drunk?" Grandma appeared right behind me, the afghan from the couch wrapped around her shoulders.

"No, ma'am," he said at once. "I apologize for waking everyone but I needed to ask your granddaughter something." His blue eyes came back to mine. "So, will you?"

"I will," I whispered, and his dimple appeared as he grinned, his relief nearly palpable.

"Can I...is it all right if I hug you?" he asked, and Grandma snorted. But I nodded and wasted not another second, leaping into his arms. He smelled of snow and winter, and of himself. He crushed me against his chest, made almost twice as big with all of his winter gear in place. My toes came off the ground. My lips were just at his left jaw and I kissed him there—once, then twice—with exuberance, where his skin was warm and prickling with stubble. He squeezed, rocking us side to side before letting my feet slowly back to the ground.

"It's freezing with this door open," Grandma scolded. "Camille, you're in your bathrobe for heaven's sake. Come inside."

But we couldn't take our eyes from one another. My heart thudded against his and I asked, "Can you come over later tonight, too?"

"Nothing would make me happier," he said. And then to Grandma, "I would love to come in right now, but I have to finish my plow route."

His arms stayed locked around me. I reached up and smoothed hair from his forehead and cupped his cheeks, our breath making clouds in the freezing air. I caressed his chin with my thumbs, wanting to kiss his lips but way too chicken with Grandma standing right beside us.

I implored, "Be careful on the rest of your route."

Mathias hugged me one more time, with characteristic enthusiasm, and then caught my hands into his and brought them to his mouth, kissing the back of each. His face was chilly but his lips were so very warm, and I shivered anew at the contact. He promised, "I will, and I will see you later."

"Yes." I was all tingling and mushy-gushy, and didn't care one bit who saw it.

He climbed back into his truck. The engine growled as he reversed and cranked it around. He rolled down his window and called back to us, "Merry Christmas!"

"Crazy," Grandma muttered, wrapping her arm over my shoulders.

"Crazy for Camille," Aunt Ellen corrected, and my face about split with a smile. Aunt Ellen put her arm around me from the other direction and squeezed.

I was so buoyant that morning that Millie Jo said twice, "Mama, sit still! You gotta watch me open my pwesents!"

Grandma and I traded off with the camera, snapping Millie tearing into her Santa Claus gifts, eating pancakes shaped like Christmas trees; at least, that's what Aunt Ellen had been trying for. Mathias texted around nine and for a moment I thought about how a text was almost like getting a telegram, only without the word *stop* in place of end punctuation.

Merry Christmas. I can't wait to see you later. I have a present for you.

A present? I wrote back. And then I corrected, *I mean a present, exclamation point!!!*

Haha. It's a good present. If I do say so myself. But I can't show you until Monday.

I can't wait that long.

I'll be over at 5. I'll bring us a picnic.

A picnic?? If you say so.

After a day spent playing with her new toys and eating her weight in fudge and Christmas cookies, Millie Jo fell asleep in the late afternoon and was still snoozing when I saw the plow truck, its plow attachment lowered to remove the snow from our driveway. I watched as Mathias spent minutes backing up and driving forward, in a steady rhythm, displacing the snow to the side. At last he parked and I swung open the door as he hurried over the snowy path through the silver dimness of this winter twilight.

"Merry Christmas," I said. "Thank you."

He stopped just in front me. "Merry Christmas. And no problem."

He was clean-shaven, his eyes bright as blue stars, wearing a black parka instead of his usual Carhartt work gear. The sight of him, the immediacy of him here before me, took my breath away. He'd left his gloves in the truck; his hands were bare and warm as he reached and cupped my face.

"I'm *so* glad you came this morning," I whispered.

"I would have come right away." He traced his thumbs over my chin. "I hope you know that. But I needed to gather my thoughts. And you needed to gather yours."

I nodded, acknowledging this, and invited, "Come inside."

"Aw, did Millie have a fun morning?" Mathias asked, catching sight of the mounds of wrapping paper piled around the tree. It looked like the aftermath of a tiny tornado.

"She did. She got a new train set that she wanted. And lots of doll clothes." I saw that he was still wearing his coat and offered, "Here, let me take that."

"Wait, the northern lights," he said, and I lifted my eyebrows, slightly mystified. He explained, "They're gorgeous. I saw them on the way over here. Plus I have a picnic for us. You want to get bundled and come see them with me? Is that terrible to ask? I mean, I know it's Christmas Day—"

"No, it's not terrible at all. Let me tell Gram and get my coat," I interrupted, and five minutes later we were heading back down the driveway. At the end he turned the truck around, shifted into first and then second and the engine growled as it took us over the snowy lake road.

He said, "I'm just so glad to have you right there on the seat beside me, you don't even know."

I studied his profile, crisply defined against the driver's side window. The sky was black as charcoal even this early in the evening, courtesy of winter's short days. I admitted, "I do know. I was so happy to see you this morning." I paused, choosing my words with care. At last I said, "I don't believe what Tess said the other night. I want you to know that. She just caught me off guard."

"She's jealous. But that was cruel even for her. God, I'm so sorry she said that shit. Please know it's not true."

"I do. I just…the whole thing was so surreal, with Noah…"

"Yeah, what exactly happened there? I thought he hurt you and I was ready to kill him."

"He actually stopped me from launching myself at Tess. She called me a slut."

"God, I'm sorry, Camille."

"It's not your fault."

"After you left White Oaks on Friday night, I drove around for hours. I almost came to Shore Leave about a hundred times. Camille…" He paused and inhaled deeply. "I want you to trust me. I want that so much. I'm not Noah and I know you probably can't help comparing us. When I tell you things I mean them, and I want you to know that."

I reached my left hand across the seat. He caught it within his and lifted it to his lips, where he gently used his teeth to free my hand from the woolen mitten. Once bare, he curled his warm fingers through mine and then settled our hands between us on the bench seat. I sat there, struck to my core at this small gesture's power to affect me. I tightened my fingers around his, loving how his hand felt within mine, hard and strong.

"You look gorgeous, by the way," he said, tightening his fingers in response. "I wish I was better at giving you compliments. Like the way your eyes are green and golden at the same time. I can't stop thinking about your eyes."

My voice was soft with shyness at speaking my thoughts so openly. "I think about you all the time, too."

"You do? What parts of me?" he demanded, with so much eagerness that I laughed.

"Your eyes and your hands," I admitted; I thought, *Your lips...*

"Really?" he marveled, caressing my skin with his thumb. "What else?"

"And your dimple." I couldn't believe that I had dared to speak the thought aloud. Because I'd already dug myself into a hole and also because I wanted to really, really badly, I whispered, "I was hoping I might kiss it later."

He said, "Hold on," and then braked the truck so that it skidded to a stop on the shoulder, before throwing it into park. He started to ask, "How about—"

But I was one step ahead, already unbuckling the seatbelt and sliding across the bench seat; before I lost my nerve, I cupped his jaw in my hands, my right still clad in its mitten, and kissed the dimple in his cheek, softly as the brush of a bird's wing. Electric shocks jolted my lips, flaring outward at this contact with his skin. I wanted to straddle his lap and keep right on kissing him, though my intent had been to dart back to my own side of the truck, but he caught me around the waist and insisted, "I get to kiss you back now, it's only fair."

"Fair's fair," I tried to whisper, my blood pounding so fiercely that I could hardly manage coherent words.

"Come here," he whispered, tugging me gently closer, and I could smell his breath and feel his hands against my body. Everything within me was sensitized, responding to him; I could see the blue of his eyes in the dash lights. He murmured, "Right here," leaning forward and pressing his lips to the corner of my mouth, just lightly, scarcely touching my skin. "And then right here," doing the same thing to the other side, and I made a small sound, I couldn't help it, as he touched a final kiss to my lower lip and a pulsing beat thrummed between my legs.

"Camille," he whispered and there was so much heat between us that sweat trickled down my spine.

Headlights beamed at us then, from the opposite direction, and the driver of the other car honked his horn with two angry beeps, as though we were doing something illegal. Mathias blinked and then refocused his attention to the road. He said, "Shit, we better move," and I scooted back to my side of the truck, pulse still churning.

Once we were driving again, I asked, "So you made a picnic?"

"I did. A winter picnic." He took my left hand back into his right, linking our fingers. He added, "I stole the idea from my sister Glenna's husband, I admit it. But it's a really great idea. I brought all sorts of good stuff. I have hot chocolate and a thermos of chicken noodle soup, and a whole container of those sandwich cookies you make with crackers. I thought we could eat in the truck and watch the northern lights. They've been really amazing the past few nights. I saw them last night before I talked to you and all I could think of was how I wish you'd been with me. And now you are." He paused and then said in a rush, "I mean, it's not fancy or anything—"

I interrupted at once. "Honestly, I think a winter picnic is the most romantic thing I've ever heard of."

He looked over at me as though uncertain I was serious. A grin nudged his lips as he murmured, "I even have a box of mint chocolate truffles."

I lifted his hand to my lips and kissed the back of it, as he was so fond of doing to mine. Then I tucked our joined hands on my left thigh. Desirous to learn everything about him, I asked, "What's your middle name? When is your birthday?"

"James and May twelfth. Taurus is my sign. Stubborn, bull-headed, quick-tempered."

I was smiling long before he asked, "What about you?"

"Anne, like my mom's, and December twenty-seventh."

"Capricorn," he said assuredly. "Elaine reads horoscopes for people, which is how I know this. Cool, calm, collected. Slow to anger. We're both earth signs. Wait, so your birthday is in just two days?"

"It is," I affirmed, before asking, "What's your favorite song?"

"I honestly couldn't pick just one. I love country music, always have. When I was little I had a huge crush on Dolly Parton."

"I like her, too." I giggled at his confession. "I love that one old movie she's in with Burt Reynolds...you know..."

He was already grinning. "*The Best Little Whorehouse in Texas* you mean." To my amazement, he broke into the first lines of "A Lil' Ole Bitty Pissant Country Place."

"How do you...have that memorized?" I was laughing so much I could scarcely ask the question, bending forward over my lap. I was so happy to be here with him that my heart was about to burst apart, nearly unable to contain such joy.

"I grew up in a house with sisters, might I remind you? So there was a lot of watching of musicals and singing of dumb songs. And there was always mascara and curling irons and talk about boyfriends. And periods. Jesus, I know all about PMS. Don't get me started."

I couldn't reply since I was laughing too hard and he continued the song, totally off-key, taking Dolly's part.

"So what's *your* favorite song?" he asked when he'd finished singing and I caught my breath.

"I liked when my dad would play his old records. I like a lot of classic rock. But I love country music, too. It's always on the radio at our house."

"Do you like living with Joan and Ellen?"

I nodded. "When I first found out I was pregnant I decided I wanted my own space for Millie and me. That's why I stayed at Shore Leave when Mom and Blythe moved in together, with Tish and Ruthie. It took me a long time to get over missing my sisters, at night especially. I was so used to talking about stuff after we went to bed."

"That's hard to get used to," he agreed. "When I lived in Minneapolis I missed my sisters so much I couldn't stand it. Even though they used to baby me and treat me like the little shit I was."

"They love you like crazy. As you well know. You should've heard them worry over you before you came home."

"Glenna told me the first night I was back that I should date someone more like you," he informed me. "They all like you and that's some pretty heavy-duty praise. They can be real bitches."

I giggled again, thinking of what Tina had said. "I'm glad they approve."

"So you're close with your sisters?"

"It was really hard on them when I got pregnant, Tish especially." I studied the snowy road as it appeared in the headlights. Mathias tightened his fingers around mine as he listened. "She felt betrayed, like I was leaving her behind. She couldn't believe that I was stupid and irresponsible enough to get knocked up, and told me so. She didn't like Noah from the first, to be fair."

"Yeah, I pretty much hate him, too," Mathias said. "I was ready to snap his neck on Friday."

"*You* were?" I scoffed, and then sighed a little. "But then I remembered that I don't give a damn what he thinks, or what he does. It's embarrassing that I *ever* cared. Now I just hate that he won't be a part of his daughter's life. What will I tell Millie when she's older?"

"Does she ask about him?" I could tell he was keeping his voice neutral with effort.

"Never yet. But she has met him a time or two, once at our house and another time at Curt and Marie's place, Marie told me. Millie loves her grandparents. And they're good to her, I can't say they aren't."

"God, I could just kill him," Mathias said, almost as though thinking out loud. "For hurting you and lying to you, and for being such a shitty father to your little girl. And mostly because—and this is so selfish, I'm sorry, Camille, but mostly because you loved him once."

My heart stuttered at these words; I didn't know exactly how to respond. Finally I whispered, "I thought I did."

Mathias turned to look my way before his gaze went back out the windshield. He said quietly, "But you said that to him and he used it and I fucking hate him for it."

"Don't waste one second hating Noah, please don't. He's not worth it and I already wasted too much time on him." I considered a moment before saying, "You know, Mom told me once that she had the best part of our dad in us, in Tish and Ruthie and me. And I finally understand that. Millie is the best thing that ever happened to me, no matter how hard it's been to be a mother. But I haven't been single, not truly. I have Grandma and Aunt Ellen, Mom and Aunt Jilly. Even my sisters. They all help me so much, and always have."

"I'm glad. I'm so glad. You deserve that." After a few seconds he added, "I'm sorry that Tess even showed up at White Oaks. I told her not to come back."

"It's not your fault. I'm sorry I was so unreasonable."

"Camille, you weren't unreasonable. Shit, you don't think all this caught me off guard, too? I'm reeling. All I know is that being apart from you is wrong. It's just plain wrong." And then, "We're here."

Mathias slowed and turned right, over a wide, smooth field that appeared frosted with creamy snow. He drove us to the center and then put the truck in neutral, leaving it idling. I unbuckled and scooted over to him at once, any lingering shyness burning away in a flame of need and tenderness and pure, simple wanting. I slid my arms around him; he hauled me onto his lap, pressing his face against my neck, holding me like I'd never known I needed to be held, until him. I hadn't realized a great number of things until Mathias.

I whispered, "Thank you for bringing me out here. It's so perfect."

"Because you're here." His voice was slightly hoarse. "I've imagined you with me so many times. Even before I knew who you were."

"How do you mean?"

He kept his face near my neck. "Do you know that old Travis Tritt song, the one where he talks about how there's a hunger in her eyes that…" He stopped and inhaled, before continuing in a low voice, "That he would recognize the moment he saw her."

"I do." I hugged him all the more tightly. "The one where he hasn't met her yet…and something about the porch swing…"

"That's the one," he affirmed. "That started playing in my head the second I saw you."

"Mathias," I whispered, pressing even closer. "You come out here alone?" It seemed so lonely and I kissed his jaw, his chin, smoothing my hands over his hair, stroking the curls on his neck, letting them glide through my fingers.

"It's peaceful out here," he murmured, shivering at my touch. "Oh holy God, that feels good. And I don't mind being alone, not usually. But these days all I think about is you."

I drew back enough to see his eyes, my hands resting on his wide shoulders, his curved around my waist. He was so serious, after all of our laughter on the way here.

"I think about you all the time, too. In case you hadn't gathered that."

He grinned at my soft admission. "Oh, I did gather that."

Because I was slightly terrified by how much I wanted to make love with him, right here in the cab of his truck, I tried to tease instead, demanding, "I'm starving, where's that picnic?"

His grin widened. "Your wish is my command."

Behind the seat was an insulated food bag, resembling a cooler covered in canvas and with a shoulder strap, from which Mathias pulled two plates, two thermoses, and two containers of food, creating a makeshift little table on the seat between us.

"Wait," he said, as I watched in fascination. He arranged things like a server at a ritzy restaurant, at last producing a single plastic poinsettia with a long stem, which he tucked under the edge of my plate. He lifted his eyes and smiled at me and with my whole heart I smiled back. We sat facing one another, each with one knee bent atop the seat. He reached over the food and the flower and tucked hair behind my right ear.

"Thank you," I whispered. "This is so beautiful."

"You're so beautiful," he whispered back. "So beautiful that it almost hurts me. Let me serve you."

He opened a plastic container to reveal sliced cheese, summer sausage, and crackers. The other contained the cookies he promised, which he arranged on my plate.

"We'll have to share the soup and the hot chocolate," he explained.

"This is *so* romantic," I marveled. "You are such a love."

His eyes lit at my words. He ordered, "I love that, call me that again."

"Are you fishing for a compliment?" I teased, stacking cheese and sausage onto crackers and getting crumbs all over as I ate. It was warm enough in the cab of the truck to shed our jackets, which Mathias tucked behind the seat. He wore his faded jeans that fit him like a cowboy's and a heavy, gray wool sweater that made his shoulders look more powerful and imposing than ever. His black hair fell over his forehead.

"Say it again or I'll start singing," he warned, humming the first few lines of "Twenty-Four Hours of Lovin'," again from *Best Little Whorehouse*.

"I *like* when you sing," I insisted, giggling, marveling anew that someone who made me ache to touch him could also have a sense of humor that so completely matched my own. He was goofy, just like me, the way I acted around my sisters and Clint, people who really knew me.

"You should hear me in the shower," he said, stacking a cracker triple-high with cheese.

"Is that an invitation?" I asked innocently, outright flirting.

He paused with the cracker halfway to his mouth. "You better watch what you ask for."

I flushed and ordered, "Sing."

He obliged, belting out the chorus; as I applauded, he insisted, "That's just a *taste* of what you'd get in the shower."

"How about a taste of that hot chocolate?" I pointed at the thermos.

He unscrewed the top for me, ever a gentleman. "Careful, it's still pretty hot."

I sipped with caution but it was the perfect temperature, warm and sweet.

"Did you put marshmallows in there, too?"

"Of course. What's hot chocolate without the marshmallow snowmen floating in it?"

"Snowmen?"

"You mean your mom didn't make snowmen out of the marshmallows?"

"How do they stick together?"

"Toothpicks, of course. But don't worry, there's no toothpicks in here. Just marshmallows."

"I'll have to try that for Millie," I said, taking another sip. I passed it back to him and as he drank I saw that our lips touched the same spot, just like with the coffee mug in the ice shack.

"There's chicken noodle, too, Mom made some this morning. It's my favorite."

"Are you a little bit spoiled?" I teased, watching as he poured soup into the thermos lid for me. It smelled incredible.

"What would make you say that? Because I'm the baby boy after three girls? That I was an adorable, toothless kid? Or maybe because my mom still does my laundry on Saturdays?" He passed the soup to me with a slow grin lifting the right side of his mouth.

"Thank you." I took the soup from his hands, admitting, "Grandma takes care of laundry at our house, too. But you could if you needed to, right?"

He grimaced, eating another towering stack of cheese and crackers. Mouth full, he said, "Possibly. I think you separate darks and lights or something. It sounds like a pain in the ass."

I rolled my eyes, mouth also full.

"But I can cook the shit out of a steak," he was quick to add. "I am a master on the grill. Or, better yet, over a cookfire. I kick ass over a cookfire."

"Can you make this?" I lifted the thermos lid to indicate the soup. "Because it's delicious."

"No, but Mom's got the recipe in the kitchen. I bet she would love to teach you."

"If you learn with me," I said.

"I am willing to learn anything with you." His eyes were serious and sincere. "Anything at all."

"You are such a love," I whispered, matching his light tone despite the fact that my heart throbbed in my ears. I babbled, "But I do know how to make these sandwich cookies. We made them every Christmas and left them for Santa…"

"Don't change the subject. You called me a love again. I'm just reveling in that for a second here."

My cheeks torched. "Well you are, even if you were spoiled as a little boy."

"I don't suppose you want to come closer after we eat?" he asked, setting aside his plate. "I mean, if you're chilly…I'm pretty warm over here…"

"I'm not chilly," I whispered, keeping a smile from my face with extreme effort. "I hate cuddling, actually."

"Yeah, same here," he said at once, calling my bluff, pinning me with his knowing gaze as he began clearing the way between us, scooping up our plates, capping the thermoses, settling everything on the floor. My heart increased in speed with his every movement; his eyebrows were wicked as he regarded me with nothing between us but the smooth bench seat. I could hardly catch my breath; I was afire. No more than eighteen inches separated us.

His voice was a little hoarse as he suggested, "How about if I just touch your leg? Is that all right? I'll stay over here…"

I nodded, nearly gulping, certain he could hear my heart thrashing. He cupped my left knee, still bent against the seat. His touch there ricocheted straight between my legs and I twitched a little but managed to keep still, letting him tease me inch by inch. He smoothed his palm gently over my knee.

"Maybe you could…" I was embarrassingly breathless and a smile glinted in his eyes. "Maybe it would be all right if you…came over here. With me."

He edged just a fraction closer, cupping my other knee. "Are you sure…"

I nodded.

He eased closer, his warm hands moving up my legs as a white-hot force field built to bursting in my lungs, until our faces were close and he was cupping my thighs; I thought I might die if he didn't come closer at once. He whispered, "Like this?"

His breath was like an intoxicant. And then, because I was no good at guile and because I was overwhelmed by need, I implored, "*Mathias.*"

He threw aside all teasing and took me in his arms, his strong arms that crushed me to his heart, pounding every bit as thunderously as my own. He inhaled against my hair, smoothing it from my temple to press warm kisses there. I closed my eyes and clung to him, fisting my hands around his sweater.

"You feel so good. I really don't hate cuddling. I actually love it."

"I love it, too." He kissed my forehead. And then, sinking his fingers deeply into my curls, he murmured, "Your hair is so soft and thick. I've wanted to put my hands in it since the night I first saw you at Shore Leave."

"You have?" I was delighted by this revelation.

"The moment you walked up to our table that night I had a funny feeling. And by 'funny' I mean fucking amazing. All my instincts were screaming at me that *this girl is for you*. Like I told you the other night, I feel like I've known you forever. I don't know how to explain it other than that. But you looked over at me, standing there holding your pen all set to take our order, and it was like someone snapped a huge fist and coldcocked me."

Emotions stormed my senses, causing tears in my eyes even as I giggled and asked through a choked-up throat, "Did you just say 'coldcocked?'"

He laughed then, too, resting his chin on my hair. He muttered, "Yeah, I also use the word 'shuttlecock' whenever possible."

I laughed harder, pressing my face to his chest. And then I said his name again, because it felt so good on my tongue. Certainly I'd said it countless times in my mind. "Mathias, I felt the same thing that night, like what my Aunt Jilly would call a Notion, when I looked at you."

"I kept trying to get your attention that night." His chest rumbled with his words. "In case you didn't notice."

"I could tell you were surprised to find out that I had a little girl," I whispered, but not in an accusatory way.

"Yeah, I was a little surprised," he admitted. "Just because you're so young to have a daughter. And I was scared then, that maybe you were married or at least in a committed relationship with her dad. I was trying to be all subtle and ask Jake questions about you on the way home, trying to play it cool, but I was so worried, Camille. I'm so happy you weren't with anyone. I'd have fought him, if you were, fought for you. I'd have done anything."

Happiness poured over me like warm, sweet-scented water even as I affected a stern tone. I scolded, "Don't say such things. I thought you weren't a violent man."

"I'm not, usually. But if I thought someone was trying to take you away, I would become the most violent man on the face of the planet. I'm telling you, we knew each other in another life. Probably lots of other lives."

I felt the truth of what he said. It was crazy, overpowering and elemental, this desire to melt into him, to be as close as humanly possible. I

Abbie Williams

lifted my face to kiss his neck, tasting him, and he groaned, shifting with a fluid motion, laying claim to my mouth. I climbed atop and he settled me against his lap, clutching my hips as I gripped his jaw. My tongue swept into his mouth, imbibing the sleek texture of the interior of his cheeks; in turn he tasted me, his tongue voluptuous in my mouth. I took his lower lip between my teeth, lightly biting, then suckling. I pressed possessive kisses to his chin, his nose, his eyebrows, the cupid's bow on his top lip; his eyes blazed into mine with a nearly-untamed intensity. Both of us breathed harshly.

"I don't want...to stop," I gasped, anchored only by his firm grip on my hips. "But I..."

He inhaled a deep breath, as though collecting himself. "I never want to stop kissing you either. Holy shit, woman. But I won't have you thinking that this is all I want from you. I don't want to rush you. You know that, don't you?"

"I do know it," I whispered but did not relinquish my hold; the juncture of my spread thighs was pressed very tightly to him. "I really do."

"*One more*," he groaned, tilting my head into his kiss, one hand buried in my curls as his tongue circled mine and stroked the sensitive skin of my inner lips, kissing me so absolutely that longing beat at me with every breath. I dug my fingers into his hair, smoothed my palms down his neck and over his shoulders, and he made a low, groaning sound and abruptly broke the contact of our mouths, leaning to rest his forehead between my breasts. My nipples had leaked milk into my bra and I was so wet both there and between my legs that a feral part of me, growing ever stronger, envisioned what would happen if I relented to instinct and unzipped and yanked down his jeans.

"Come here, honey." His chest rose and fell with his ragged breathing. He pressed a soft kiss upon my sweater, on the fullest part of my left breast. I could see the pulse beating in his throat as he leaned back, his eyes blue flames. "If you only knew how you look right now. Jesus, I'm afraid that I won't be able to suppress my animal urges."

Shockwaves—equal parts desire and tenderness—struck at me. I bent and traced my tongue lightly over his dimple. "You are a total love."

"I don't know what I did to deserve you, but I'll be grateful until the day I die," he said passionately. "Stay here, in my arms. The lights are already starting," and so saying, shifted us so that we faced the windshield, keeping me on his lap. I linked our fingers and rested them upon my belly; his chin was just at my left temple, my head on his shoulder.

Out in the frozen night, the northern sky put on a hot-pink and neon-green wonderland of a show for us, curling and twisting like living entities up there in the icy-clear black heavens. It was all the more spectacular out here in the country, with no streetlights to dim a thing, no phosphorescent orange glow of a nearby city. We kept the radio low, tuned to the country station out of Bemidji, and Mathias rubbed the backs of my hands with his thumbs. He pressed lingering kisses to my hair, the side of my forehead, and I turned my face against his shoulder time and again, letting my lips touch his neck, inhaling his scent. We talked unceasingly as the lights danced and flared and bloomed like giant wildflowers, intertwining their brilliant colors.

"How did you pick Millie's name?"

"It's supposed to be like Milla, my nickname. Mom has always called me that. And then her middle name is Joelle, after my mom. Millie Jo."

"It's cute, it suits her."

"It does, doesn't it?"

"What's your best Christmas memory?"

"There were a lot of great ones when I was little, but last year with Millie Jo was extra special, since it was her first. She wore this little red footie with curly elf toes."

"She was almost a year old?"

I nodded, smiling. "She opened a few of her presents on her own, but she was more interested in the wrapping paper. Everyone spoiled her and Rae with presents, same as they did last night, but it's so fun to watch them."

"That's Justin and Jilly's little girl?"

I nodded again. "She and Millie are the best of friends. I'm worried that they'll get into more and more trouble as they get older. Mom says they remind her of Tish and me as little girls."

"When I think of you alone last Christmas it breaks my heart," he whispered. "I didn't even get home last year. I couldn't get the time off."

"I already knew your sisters back then." I vividly recalled the night that Tina told me things would be better someday; oh, how I'd wanted to believe her. I turned my face so that my nose rested against his chest and he kissed my hair, nuzzling me.

"I'd already heard about you back then," he murmured. "But I could have found you a whole *year* ago."

"You found me now," I whispered. "That's all that matters."

We watched the lights in silence for a time, warm and cozy in the truck, sharing the last of the hot chocolate, before I observed, "In Chicago, you couldn't even see the stars on any given night. Too much light pollution."

"Do you miss it there? I know that's where you grew up but it doesn't seem right. I mean, I can't imagine you there, in a crowded, dirty city."

"I miss it now and again, the way you'd miss the place you were raised. But when I think back to those days I almost can't imagine it either. Private school, stupid snobby friends, like the guys you talked about from college, who couldn't bait a hook. I hated that pretentious mentality, but I didn't understand how *much* I hated it until I moved here and things changed. Oh God, things changed so much. It's been hard but I'm not sorry any of it happened." Words spilled over words as I reflected on the past two and a half years. "I wouldn't change a thing."

Mathias said, "When I was living in Minneapolis, I was searching so hard for something I couldn't even explain to myself. I only understand it now that I'm home where I belong. I was searching for *you* without even knowing it, until it smacked me in the face when I saw you for the first time."

I whispered, "I was such a mess two years ago. I was so hurt, and exhausted, and struggling to parent a newborn. I never got a minute's peace or sleep, even with all of the help. I started to realize what my mom went through when I was born, back when she was only seventeen. I wasn't the same person then that I am now. I was so naïve and so angry all the time. You probably wouldn't have looked twice."

He shifted us so that he could see my eyes.

"I could have met you at age four and known you were for me. I would have looked twice no matter what."

A lump formed in my throat; instead of replying I rested my lips on his neck.

Holding me tightly, he whispered, "I might not have been here then, but I'm here now."

Hesitant, but wanting him to understand what I was about to say, I finally found my voice. "It's hard for me to trust men. Not just because of Noah, but because of my dad. He had a relationship with another woman for a long time before my mom found out. And the thing is…" I swallowed away the pain of remembrance. "I was always my dad's girl. I looked up to him, I trusted him, only to find out that he'd done such a thing to the woman he was supposed to love. And to us, Tish and Ruthie and me. I felt so betrayed, I can't even imagine what Mom felt."

Mathias was silent, absorbing this; his hands spoke for him, stroking through my curls, the pad of his thumb gentle against my temple. At last he said, "I'm sorry. I can't imagine a shittier thing for a husband to do to a wife. Or a dad to his kids. There's no excuse." He kissed the top of my head, tucked beneath his chin. "Thank you for telling me. I want to know everything about you. Will you tell me everything about you?"

I nodded against his chest.

"And I want you to know everything about me. Ask me anything."

"Who was the poodle girl?" was the question that popped from my lips, before I could consider how rude it sounded to phrase it that way.

Mathias snorted a laugh. "Suzy, the last girl I dated in college, not that there were too many. Three, actually, and that's counting Tess, because we tried to have a long-distance relationship after high school. But to answer your question, that's the nickname Dad came up with for Suzy. To be fair, it was about a perfect description." He laughed again, but softly, wondering aloud, "What would be a kinder way to put it? High maintenance,

I guess. She hated that I wasn't planning to live in Minneapolis. She thought I was crazy not to stay there and make tons of money."

"The morning we had coffee at Shore Leave, after the night we met, I tried to picture you as a business major, sport jacket, necktie, the whole bit," I confessed. "But it just didn't seem right."

"It wasn't," he agreed. "I mean, I did well in school, earned my degree. And I like the thought of running a business, but up here, in Landon, and on my own terms. I'll take over White Oaks for Dad, eventually. I love the lodge. And the thought of sitting in a cubicle day after day made my heart shrivel up." Shifting the subject, he prompted, "You said Noah was the first guy you ever dated." A brief pause, before he admitted, "The thought of him having the privilege of your attention is...not great. And by that I mean I can hardly stand the thought of it."

"Silly," I whispered, studying him at close range, his face just above mine, his eyes so serious. "We only went out for part of that summer. I'd never had sex before him and he's still the only guy I've ever been with... like *that*, anyway."

"I knew I should have beaten him to pulp that night at White Oaks," Mathias growled, almost gritting his teeth.

"If anyone should be beating him to a pulp, it's *me*," I said. "And although I appreciate the sentiment, he's not worth it. He's really not. I know that sounds like a terrible thing to say about my daughter's father."

"Hey, it takes a lot more than starting a baby to be a father."

"After I first found out I was pregnant, all he could say was, 'But I wore a condom every time,' like it was somehow my fault alone. That was his attitude from the first. I was so nervous to tell him but somehow it was even worse to tell my mom. And the same night I told her, I'd *just* found out that she was having an affair with Blythe."

"Talk about shitty timing," Mathias said, kissing my ear, and even though he hadn't intended it, the noise of the kiss was so loud that I giggled and squirmed. And then, oddly, the terrible thing I was about to tell him seemed slightly less terrible. I even considered Noah's perspective for a half-second, realizing that his fear and immaturity had motivated his words more than anything.

"Sorry," Mathias murmured, kissing my ear in the same spot, but quietly. This time I shivered, squeezing his forearms tighter against me.

"But the worst thing was..." I trailed to silence, sighing a little, before trying again. "The worst thing was that Noah wanted me to get an abortion. I felt like he'd hit me hard enough to knock the wind out of me, it was horrible." Mathias wisely remained silent, sensing I would not appreciate any uncharitable comments about Noah right now, even if that's exactly what he was thinking. I continued, gaining momentum, "But you know what? It made me realize once and for all that there was no future with this guy. Up to that point, I still thought I loved him, that I wanted to try and make it work with him. But that comment showed me his true colors. Showed me what he really was and for that I'm grateful. And I hope he thinks of saying that when he looks at Millie, and that it haunts him. I can't think of her as his child, I really can't. She's only mine."

"She's not his, just like you were never his," Mathias said, his voice a little hoarse, as I had already learned it was when his emotions ran strong. "And I'm glad that you realized what a bastard he was. I'm just sorry that he shattered your trust, that he hurt you that way."

"Thank you for listening," I whispered, and confessed, "And to be fair, I still hate Tess. But really I should thank her for being so stupid as to let you go."

"She never had me, not one bit." He cradled me close.

"You smell so good." I inhaled against the material of his sweater. "Can we just stay here like this? Until morning, at least?"

"Yes. You stay in my arms and I'll be your love," he agreed softly. "Nothing seems more right in the world."

Chapter Fourteen

NECESSITY CALLED ME BACK LONG BEFORE DAWN, THE press of responsibilities beyond myself, and Mathias drove us to Shore Leave beneath the velvety-black midnight sky, our hands clasped on the seat between us. He walked me to the door and then kissed me breathless on the snowy front stoop.

"Thank you for the picnic," I whispered, my lips brushing his with the words, as we were unwilling to stop touching and go our separate ways. I clung and he buried his face against my neck.

"You are so completely welcome." He kissed my cheeks, one after the other, then rested his forehead against mine.

"Good-night," I whispered.

"Good-night." And then, with a glint in his eyes, "Tomorrow night I'll have your Christmas present ready for you, too."

"What is it?" I begged, curling my hands into the hair sticking out from beneath his gray wool hat.

"You'll see tomorrow," was all he would say.

"Call me to let me know you got home."

He brought my mittened hands to his lips, kissing each. He promised, "I will. Merry Christmas, Camille Anne."

He climbed into the plow truck, which was still running, growling softly into the cold night. He rolled down his window to blow me a kiss. I watched until he was out of sight, then hurried upstairs to check on Millie Jo, kissing her round cheek as she slept soundly, curled in bed. I shed my jeans but stayed zipped into my coat because it smelled like

Mathias; I snuggled beside Mille and brought my puffy sleeves to my nose, inhaling. No more than five minutes later my phone vibrated.

"Hey," I answered in a whisper, already smiling.

"My truck smells so damn good, it smells just like you," he said in response, husky and sweet. I wrapped one arm around my bent knees, holding close the sound of his voice.

"I was just lying here wearing my coat because it smells like you. Thank you for the picnic. I had such a good time."

"Tomorrow evening seems like a long time away."

"You want to have breakfast?" I asked, warming to the idea; morning was only hours away. "Come over, I'll cook for you and you can hang out with Millie Jo."

"I would be honored." His voice was still hoarse, slightly deeper than normal. "What time? You should hear my thoughts, Camille, I'm sitting here thinking, *Please let it be early.* Because I already can't wait to see you. That's what I'm sitting here thinking in my truck that still smells like your hair."

Mathias. Oh my God, I'm so in love with you.

Breath jammed my throat as I acknowledged what my heart already knew.

"Are you crying?" He sounded appalled. "I'm turning this truck around. What's wrong, honey? Camille, what's wrong?"

"I'm not crying. You just move me so much with your words. My coat smells like your skin and it's like you're here with me."

"I'm coming to get you right now. Dammit. I have to be near you when you say things like that."

I giggled, even as happy tears slid over the bridge of my nose and my right temple, as I was lying on that side. "Come over as soon as you can in the morning. Dawn, if you want."

"Here's the plan. I'll sleep for a few hours and then I'm heading right back to your house. Will your grandma think I'm crazy?"

"She already does," I assured him, giggling more. "I'll make you eggs and bacon. Or pancakes if you want. I'm good at breakfast."

"Pancakes," he decided. "You're good at breakfast and I've got us covered for dinners. We'll be all set. Do you have chocolate chips?"

"Yes. See you in a few hours."

"You're on."

I fell asleep with a smile, waking to the buzz of my phone, which was a foot from my head on the mattress. The room shone silvery with dawn and I knew it was Mathias.

"Are you on the way?" I murmured to answer.

"I'm just heading out the door. Did you sleep all right?"

"I did. And hurry!"

I sat up and the second my feet touched the floor I was up and running. I dashed in and out of the shower, toweling my hair with vigor as I brushed my teeth with the other hand. I pulled on jeans and an old sweatshirt, my warmest slipper socks, and then jogged down the steps just in time to see his truck come around the bend. My heart swelled with pleasure; I felt as glowy-pink as the sunrise just beginning to tint the sky. He parked and I opened both the front door and my arms. And in the next second we were braided together. He put his lips to my hair and inhaled, while I likewise breathed in his scent.

"It must be some sort of crazy primitive thing," he murmured, kissing my temple. "I just crave how you smell."

"I slept with my jacket pressed to my nose. So I know just what you mean." I rubbed my cheek against his chest. "But it's much better in person."

"A hundred times better," he murmured, drawing back to see my eyes. I studied him with absolute joy in the early morning light; he hadn't shaved since yesterday, though his hair was damp and curling, especially along his neck. His eyes were tender in their regard, his lips soft with a smile. He brushed his thumbs over my cheekbones, sending shivers all along my jaw and down my neck. "I'm so happy to be here."

I curled my fingers into his hair and he cupped my face with both hands, marveling at the wonder of what connected us. He brought my lips to his, kissing me with such sweetness, his tongue stroking mine, our heads slanting one way and then the other as we strove to deepen our kisses.

"If he's been here all night we need to have a talk, Camille," Grandma said then, from the stairs.

I squeaked and buried my face against Mathias; he valiantly shouldered arms and said with characteristic cheer, "Good morning. Camille invited me for breakfast, I just got here, I promise. And we were just… we were just…" He faltered a little, making me giggle against him. He rallied with, "We were just saying good morning."

"I'm sure," Grandma said drily. But I could tell she wasn't angry.

I turned to face her. "Breakfast is on me this morning."

"I'll just start the coffee then," Grandma said, giving us a wink as she headed for the kitchen.

Mathias hung his jacket in the entryway, stepping out of his boots to reveal mismatched socks, one gray and one white.

"I haven't gone to get laundry done in a while," he admitted when I poked the gray sock with my toes. He wore his favorite faded jeans and a big old hooded sweatshirt, navy blue to match his eyes. I couldn't stop smiling at him as he helped me make pancakes with chocolate chips. Grandma got coffee perking and then went back upstairs; Millie Jo wouldn't be up for a little while, leaving Mathias and I relatively alone in the warm, sunlit kitchen with its pleasant scents of flour and yeast, maple syrup and coffee. I used this privacy to my advantage, generating excuses to touch him.

"Here, you get the griddle warming." I indicated the stovetop as I rummaged for the mixing bowl.

"Come here first," he whispered, tugging me close, and we regarded each other at close range in the dawn light peeking through the curtains. He pressed a soft kiss flush on my lips. "Good morning."

"Good morning. I missed you."

His blue eyes lit at my words. "I've been thinking about seeing you since the second I dropped you off." He kissed my upper lip, skimming his tongue, and I shivered. "You have a little scar or something, right here."

"That's where Tish bit me when she was little," I explained, pulse thrashing as he gently licked me in the same spot. "It's a bite mark."

"Every little detail of your face is beautiful, your mouth, the colors in your eyes…you get freckles in the summer, don't you? I can see the traces of them on your soft skin…" He trailed little kisses along my cheekbones.

"That feels so good." I was trembling in his arms. "*Mathias…*"

I took his lower lip into my mouth and closed my teeth gently over it; he cupped both hands around my ass and hauled me against his hips, kissing me so thoroughly I was afraid I might just pull him down upon me, right here on the hard kitchen floor. But footsteps thumped upstairs like a herd of miniature deer and we were forced to draw apart. I stole one last kiss, a quick stamp of possession, both of us breathing fast; Mathias groaned a little and said, "I'm sorry, I have no self-control with you. Oh, holy God. Seriously, none."

No more than two seconds later Millie Jo scampered into the kitchen, eyes bright and hair a tangled mess, just like mine always was when I first rolled out of bed. She stopped and planted both hands on her hips, twisting side to side and offering us a smile.

"Morning, Millie Jo-Jo." I bent to scoop her into a hug.

"Good morning, Mama," she chirped. "Morning, Ma-fias!"

"You remember my name?" he asked, patting her back, clearly thrilled at this fact.

"Well, her mama does talk about you a fair amount," Grandma said, breezing in behind Millie. "Have the two of you made any progress on those pancakes?"

Mathias lifted Millie Jo to the counter near the griddle, where he proceeded to help her help me. "Watch, I can crack eggs with one hand," displaying this delicate talent for us.

Millie clapped delightedly. "Now me!"

"It'll be easier when you're bigger," he told her, as she made a mess with her attempts. "It's not easy for little hands."

Aunt Ellen joined Grandma at the table for coffee and the background cadence of their voices was as comforting as a warm bath. Millie was in the process of whisking eggs in a separate bowl, very deliberately, her tongue between her lips as she concentrated. Mathias sent me a wink and then said, "Little one, your mama needs those eggs. You want help pouring?"

She nodded and allowed him to assist her.

"What's your favorite Christmas song?" Mathias asked Millie.

"*Rudolph!*" she belted. "I know all their names."

"Hey, same here! Should we sing it?"

"Yes!" And they did.

After breakfast, Mathias and I did all the dishes; he dried them as Millie colored on the floor at our feet. It was so easy to pretend that we were a family, but I couldn't let myself fall into this yet, not yet. *Too late, way too late not to fall*, I acknowledged. The sky was brightening with a sunny day as we finished the breakfast dishes, and Mathias needed to get to work.

"I'll come get you at seven," he said, as we stole a few good-bye kisses in the entryway. "And dress warm."

"Ice house?" I whispered. And then I couldn't resist, begging, "*More*," and he grinned and kissed me until stars exploded behind my eyelids.

"No, much better," he promised.

Millie and I spent the day coloring and playing dolls; though I was no engineer, I did my best to put together the railroad tracks for her new train. As dusk came creeping from the edges of the yard, she and I helped Aunt Ellen bake chicken and wild rice, while Grandma sipped her nightly glass of crème de cacao (complete with whipped cream garnish) and warmed a leftover pecan pie. I reflected anew, watching my grandmother joke with my daughter while my great-aunt stirred up a pan sauce, humming along with Dolly Parton on the radio, that I would not trade this simple life for anything.

I thought of my dad, longing from the time he was a teenager to shake the dust of Landon from his shoes and make his way in the corporate world, how he'd dragged Mom with him to a city far removed from anything she'd ever known, a place where she was isolated from her family. How painful that must have been for her. How grateful I was down to my very bones that Mom had brought us back here, to stay; even if the choice had been out of her hands at the time, instinct had tugged her home to Landon.

Dad was fairly wealthy these days, I knew; he married Lanny back in 2003 and the two of them had recently purchased a luxurious new town-house, which Ruthie and Tish visited over Thanksgiving break. ("It's big and cold," was Ruthie's observation, while Tish added, "But the view is incredible.") All three of us couldn't help but wonder whether Dad was faithful to this second wife of his, and spent plenty of time discussing it; had our father's choices made him ultimately happy, or not? He sounded perpetually upbeat when we spoke on the phone, which was fairly frequently, but then again, Dad was a successful lawyer—surely he knew how to manipulate his tone, how to choose precise words to create whatever impression he desired. Millie called him 'Grandpa Jackie' and even though Dad made a point to speak often with his granddaughter, Millie probably wouldn't be able to pick him out of a lineup. And for just a second I thought, with true regret, *Aw, Dad.* I loved my father, no matter what. I would be lying if I said I didn't miss him.

"What are you and Mathias up to this evening?" Aunt Ellen asked, drawing me from my woolgathering.

"It's a surprise." I felt a grin spread over my face. "My only clue is that I need to dress warm."

Grandma said, "Wear two pairs of socks, then."

"Maybe I should have a nightcap," I teased, nodding at her drink. "Then I'd be nice and warm," and Grandma swatted at my rear.

"It's just so good to see you excited," Aunt Ellen said.

After supper I dressed in thermal underwear, struggling to tug my jeans over the bottoms. As a concession to Gram, I wore two pairs of socks, and as I buttoned into my warmest sweater, Mathias texted to tell me he was on the way.

"Mama! I see his truck!" Millie shouted from the living room only a minute later, all excited, perched on one of the old recliner chairs near the front windows, her newest doll baby in her arms. I jogged downstairs to open the door, glad I'd bundled so well; Mathias was decked in his full winter gear. He hugged me and then ordered, "One more layer at least."

"Are you going to be walking?" Grandma asked, coming up behind me.

"Not *exactly*," Mathias said. "But we'll be outside for a little while."

"This sounds so mysterious," I said, digging in the closet for my ski pants.

"Please don't freeze," Grandma implored, hands on hips as she regarded Mathias; I didn't dare tell her that the fire that burned between us was so hot there was no danger of freezing.

"Don't worry, I would never let Camille freeze," Mathias assured Grandma, unconsciously echoing my thoughts, and I felt a heated rush, low in my belly, at his words.

"Lift me!" Millie commanded Mathias, tugging his coat to get his attention. He obliged at once, settling her onto his forearm and giving her a bounce. She reached and patted his cheeks, and his eyebrows immediately lifted; I saw the tenderness that came over his face at this unexpected affection from my daughter. She patted him again and pleaded, "Can I come wif you and Mama?"

I could tell he was so charmed that he was about to agree, and so I said firmly, "Not this time, Millie Jo-Jo. It's too cold outside for little girls. Besides, it's almost your bedtime."

She made her pouty lips and wriggled to get down. Mathias watched her scamper over to the couch before turning back to me with the kind of sweet smile that Millie inspired in people. "I think my heart just melted all over the floor. Just the same way ice cream would."

"She likes you," I murmured, giggling at his words.

Just as quietly, he said, "I was hoping her mama might like me a little, too."

"Maybe just a *little*," I teased, though my heart was going like a jackhammer.

"Here, let me help you." He reached for my coat and held it so I could shrug inside, keeping his hands on my upper arms for a moment.

"Kids, you have fun and we'll see you later," Aunt Ellen said as she came from the kitchen.

"Drive safe," Grandma told Mathias.

He nodded seriously.

I bent down to kiss Millie. "Behave yourself."

Millie quit jumping on the couch and gave me a hug. "Have fun, Mama."

Mathias said, "Aw, we'll bring you next time, little one, I promise."

"She won't forget that, you know," I warned as we headed to his truck. He was driving the big plow truck this evening, but with the plow attachment removed. It had such a giant cab that it sat about ten feet above any other vehicle on the road. Mathias opened the squeaky passenger door and helped me inside. Once there, I inhaled the scent of him; this was his space and it smelled delicious, just the way his neck always did.

He jogged around the hood and climbed in loudly, stamping his boots. "I would bring her, but it's so cold. And I really want you to see your Christmas present."

"So where are we headed?" I asked as he drove us slowly back around the lake road.

"White Oaks, first," he announced, all smiley, full of anticipation. In the next second he braked and pulled to the side of Flicker Trail. "Oh my God, come here for a minute first."

I was on his lap, thighs spread, before he could blink. He groaned deep in his throat, running his hands down my back and then lower, fingers splayed wide. I clutched his face and claimed his mouth possessively, heatedly, incredibly. He was so powerful beneath me; even with all of our winter gear in the way, I could feel how hard he was. I tore the hat from his head, overwhelmed by the ferocious need to rip every stitch of clothing from his body as fast as humanly possible.

"Oh my God." His voice was husky, laden with heat. "I promised I wouldn't rush you...oh Jesus, *come here...*"

I unzipped my coat, struggling out of it, his lips following as he kissed my neck, my collarbones, gently cupping my breasts, my nursing bra and layers of heavy clothing in the way.

"Don't stop," I begged and he exhaled in a shuddering rush, kissing the fullest part of each breast before resting his mouth between them, against my sweater. I felt a tremble shudder through him.

"Believe me, I don't want to stop. Oh God, Camille...but I can't take advantage of you like this on the side of the road."

I giggled at little, trying to catch my breath, unwilling to move back to my side of the truck. Besides, his hands anchored me to his lap.

"You're not taking advantage," I disagreed, and his thumbs swept upward, stroking my nipples; I shivered and spilled over between my legs.

"One more," he whispered against my lips, before we managed to separate.

We reached White Oaks not five minutes later, its grand front windows glowing golden and welcoming into the night.

"It's starry," I noticed in wonder, pausing to look up at the sky.

"I thought that was just your eyes," he teased, catching my mitten into his glove. "I told Dad and Ma we'd stop in and say hi before we went."

"Went where?"

"You'll see," was all he would say.

The dining room wasn't weekend-level busy, just a small local crowd playing some pool and drinking tap beer. Elaine and Diana stood behind the bar chatting with an elderly couple while Bull sat near the fireplace with a couple of men from Landon, talking about their winter trap lines; he interrupted himself as Mathias and I entered the dining room decked in our winter gear.

"Hi, you two!" Diana came over to give us hugs. She told me, "Matty has been so excited. He worked like the dickens all day on—"

"Ma!" he yelped. "No giving it away!"

Diana covered her mouth with her right hand as Bull came over and wrapped me in a hug, heartily thumping my back.

"I don't know how he deserves you," Bull said, winking at his son. "But I'm glad you're giving the boy a chance, Camille. I had a feeling about you two, I did."

Elaine leaned over the bar. "Matty, should I tell Tina it's time to... *you know...*"

Mathias made shushing motions, but nodded. "Ma, do you have one of your old snowmobile masks that Camille could borrow?"

I pulled Diana's face mask over my head, the kind that allowed for eyes and mouth to be exposed, nothing else. Awareness beat all along my skin as I studied Mathias in a similar ski mask he donned before we went back outside; the way his sensuous lips and eyes were highlighted made me want to taste his kiss more than ever. He read my mind, bending to kiss me softly, just a brushing of our lips, and my knees trembled.

I whispered, "I feel like a snowman."

"Good, that means you're warm enough. Don't worry, it's not far."

Under the crisp black sky, Mathias held my arm against his side, leading me around White Oaks, where their bank of snowmobiles was parked. "I'm going to blindfold you so that you won't know where we're going until we get there. I'll go slow, so don't worry."

Still mystified, I allowed him to reposition my scarf so that it covered my eyes, smelling the scent of cold wintertime wool. Mathias lifted me into his arms and helped me astride one of the snowmobiles; the seat was cold and hard under me, even with layers of snow gear, and I was glad when he settled immediately behind, warm and solid. He leaned close to my ear, taking my hands into his and positioning them around the handlebars. "I'll be right behind you and we'll go slow."

I nodded and snuggled into him as he fired up the sled. I couldn't help but utter a small sound as he backed us up, feeling blind and out of control, but his arms anchored me, this thighs aligned with mine, and the ride was otherwise smooth as ice. *Just like riding double on a horse*, I found myself thinking. Our bodies shifted as we glided together over the snow, the engine purring quietly beneath us. I could only imagine where we were headed; it was so exciting—and that he'd planned something like this for me was terribly romantic. Less than five minutes later, he slowed our pace and then brought the snowmobile to a halt; in the absence of the engine noise the air retained its perfect, crystalline stillness. I released my grip on the handlebars and cupped his knees.

"Are we here?" I whispered.

"We are." His voice sounded hoarse, like he might have a lump in his throat. He wrapped his arms around my torso, hugging tightly, rocking us side to side. "Are you ready to see it?"

"Yes," I whispered, and he slipped the scarf from my eyes.

I stared, mouth falling open, pelted by emotions the same way I would have been by fists. I brought both hands to my face, gaping in wonder at the sight before my eyes. Mathias rested his hands on my shoulders and all at once I started to cry, the tears hot as bathwater over my chilled cheeks. But they were happy tears, borne of pure amazement.

It was so right.

And then I thought, *Oh, Malcolm…*

"Camille," he whispered, cradling me to his chest.

"It's…so…perfect," I choked out, turning to hug him as best as I could through the dense layers of down between our bodies. "When did…*when did you…*"

"Christmas Eve. I worked all day and into the night. I mucked out the chimney and fixed the window and hauled wood. I cleaned the inside. You could eat off the floor in there now. Come see, honey, come and see." His words were laced with wonder and anticipation, his voice giddy with happiness.

Before us, as we sat together on the snowmobile, the little home-stead cabin was alive in its clearing. Auburn firelight made warm, perfect squares of the windows, dazzling my tear-filled eyes; smoke curled into the clear night sky. I'd never felt more like I was coming home than this moment in time; tears washed faster from my eyes, soaking the ski mask. Mathias stood and helped me to my feet. Because I was tearful and overcome, he lifted me into his arms like a bride on her wedding night and climbed up the porch steps. He reached awkwardly, hampered by his heavy outerwear, to open the door and then we crossed the threshold into our cabin. From this moment forth, I would never think of this place as anything other than *ours*. I tried to look everywhere at once, to fully imbibe the warmth of the little room in the flickering firelight, real-izing that there was a table and two chairs that hadn't been there before, and upon the table was placed a round chocolate cake and a small stack of paper plates. I looked at him, in complete stun.

"Elves. Woodland elves," he said, and I laughed through my tears, hugging him around the neck. We were still in our masks, like two bank robbers, and I was laughing and crying at the same time. Mathias tugged mine over my head, my hair snapping with static electricity, and kissed me with his mask still in place. I clung to him and tasted his kiss, and felt as if all was right in the world—at least, in our little corner of it.

"So, happy birthday, too." His blue eyes glinted with the sparks of tears, even as he grinned wide and warm.

"Thank you." My voice emerged rough with emotion. "In a hundred years I would never have imagined this was my present. Mathias, this is perfect. It's so perfect."

"The cake was last minute, since you just told me when your birthday was last night," he explained, setting me gently to the ground and removing his mask. "I could just stand here and watch you smile, forever. I knew you would love it as much as I do."

"I love it *so* much," I said, hands clasped beneath my chin. I thought, *I love you so much.*

"See the chimney, doesn't it look great?" he rejoiced, tugging me over to inspect his handiwork. The cabin was clean and polished; the mantle and floorboards gleamed. The fire reflected in the window panes and in my heart. He explained, "Tina came out here before we did to get the fire going and set out the cake."

I marveled, "It's like it's never been empty. Like it's been waiting here for us. The whole place feels happy now, doesn't it? It felt so empty when I was here last spring, so sad, but not anymore."

He nodded and our eyes held steady, saying more than any words; I barely heard the other two snowmobiles roar near. He explained, "My family. Some of them, I should say. They wanted to sing to you. I couldn't convince them that we wanted a little privacy. And Dad is beside himself about the cabin. He couldn't be happier."

I was choked up again, unable to release my hold on him. I kissed his neck, his jaw, his chin. "They sing, too?"

Feet thumped up the porch steps, accompanied by the sound of excited chatter.

"They do," he whispered as we turned as one to greet everyone.

Tina and Sam had ridden one of the snowmobiles, Bull and Diana the third. Elaine had elected to walk, as it was such a pretty night, and arrived a few minutes later, just as Tina was arranging candles in the cake. There weren't enough places to sit but as the birthday girl I was allowed a chair; Mathias sat on it first and then pulled me on his lap. He'd stripped down to his thermal shirt and snow bibs; he looked so smiley and disheveled and heart-stoppingly handsome that my fingers tingled to touch him. To be honest, every part of me tingled to be pressed to him. He wrapped both arms loosely about my waist, fingers linked over my belly, and the little space was aglow with warmth and laughter.

Addressing the cabin, I thought, *It's what you've wanted for so long, isn't it?*

And the shiver that overtook me was answer enough.

"You'll need some furniture in here straight away," Diana mused after they all sang "Happy Birthday" to me, as she sliced pieces of the chocolate cake. "A leather couch, a nice entertainment center..."

"Ma, there's the entertainment center," Tina said, indicating the fireplace. Her red hair gleamed in its light.

His mouth full of cake, Sam suggested, "Maybe a bed...a big feather one..."

Everyone laughed and Tina slapped at his arm.

"Son, you done good," Bull said, with gruff affection. He rested a hand on Mathias's shoulder.

"You're right, Dad," Mathias said, looking into my eyes as I sat on his lap, eating a piece of my birthday cake. He smiled softly and repeated, "You're so right."

Chapter Fifteen

THE VERY NEXT MORNING I DROVE MY TRUCK TO THE LITtle clinic in Bemidji and obtained a prescription for birth control pills, a birthday present to myself. "Start them once your period is over and be sure to use protection for at least the first two weeks," the nurse told me, and gifted me with a box of condoms. Just glancing at them on the passenger seat as I drove back to Landon was enough to make my pulse jump and my belly go hollow. I stuffed them deep in my purse before I got home.

Grandma and Aunt Ellen had prepared a birthday supper that included all of my favorite foods—spaghetti with spicy meatballs, garlic cheese bread, three-olive salad, and root beer floats for dessert, never minding the fact that it was eight below zero outside, and that these were technically a summer drink. Mathias ate with us, the two of us interrupting each other as we talked about the cabin, and Mathias's hard work to clean it up and plan a Christmas surprise for me. Aunt Ellen and Grandma listened with quiet amusement, both of them touched at his sweetness, surely observing the naked adoration in my eyes, but I didn't care. I loved him. Sure as the sun would lift to sparkle over the new snow tomorrow morning, I loved Mathias James Carter.

"Mama, when's my birthday?" Millie asked, her face all sticky with root beer float.

"In February," I reminded her, reaching to swipe at the vanilla ice cream ringing her mouth. "Remember? You were born on Valentine's Day, baby."

"Because you're our little sweetheart," Grandma said, winking at Millie.

I indicated the fridge, relating a story often retold, but no less special with each telling. "I was standing right over there. And Auntie Tish and Aunt Ruthie, and Clinty, were all at the kitchen table playing a board game, when suddenly —"

"I poured water on you!" Millie cried, giggling and clapping, and then we were all laughing.

"Yeah, that's pretty much right," I agreed, grinning at my girl, tucking a wayward curl behind her ear. "And then Dodge and Grandma and Aunt Ruthie drove me to the hospital."

Mathias sat with his forearms lining the table's edge, watching my face as I spoke. His gaze was warm and steady. He listened without interruption as I concluded the story.

"And Aunt Ruthie and Grandma watched you be born," I said. "Aunt Ruthie kept asking what I was going to name you but I didn't know for sure until I saw your sweet, little baby face. And then I knew you were my Millie Jo." Tears rimmed my lashes. "For always."

Later, Mathias and I drove over to his apartment at Pine Ridge, which was conveniently empty, as Skid was at his second job.

"I still can't believe all the work you did on the cabin," I said as we lay tangled together on his couch, fully clothed but our hands all over each other. Mathias wore his faded jeans and a threadbare Coca-Cola t-shirt, and had shucked his boots and mismatched socks the minute we set foot inside. His bare feet were warm against mine, beneath the old crocheted afghan he'd settled over us; he'd insisted that I take off my socks so that he could feel my feet against his own. He kept curling his toes over mine, making me laugh.

The television was on in the background, tuned quietly to the local station, which was airing *Back to the Future*, but we weren't paying attention to anything but one another, positioned so that my back was aligned with his front. His warm hand inched carefully beneath my sweater, but no higher than my belly, which he stroked with a soft rhythm, repeatedly curling his fingers against my skin—and I would be a liar if I didn't admit that I felt the heat of that gentle caress on another part of my body. He swept all the hair from the side of my neck, making me shiver and giggle as he pressed kisses to my nape or bit my earlobe.

And we talked and talked.

"This next spring I'm going to make it livable year-round," he said, rubbing his beard-stubbled chin against me; I felt him smile against my neck.

"You won't change it much, will you?" I worried, tilting my head to allow him better access to my bare skin. "I hate to think of it being too modernized, you know what I mean?"

"I do. What I really want to do is add on to the original structure. I'll have to get a permit from the county. I want it to be comfortable, but not too big. And we'll retain the nineteenth-century feel, what do you say?"

"Yes. I think that's important. The cabin was happy last night, wasn't it? I mean, I know that sounds crazy…"

"No, I felt the same. It *wanted* us to be there, like it was waiting for us…"

"For a long time now," I whispered.

His lips were near my ear. "Living in it has been a dream of mine since I was a kid. All those summers I'd lay in there and think about who slept within the walls before me. Then I'd get bitten to shit by mosquitoes, but I didn't care. Sometimes my friends would join me and we'd scare the hell out of each other with stories of ax-murderers who wandered the woods at night." I giggled at this, and Mathias continued, "Skid would remember those summers. One night Elaine and a couple of her friends came sneaking through the woods and scratched on the window, and then ran. I realized that night what it means to have the hair on the back of your neck stand up, like a wolf's. Man, that was scary as shit. The next morning they confessed it, and apologized, but we spent the rest of that summer plotting revenge on them anyway."

"I can just picture you," I said, and I could, exactly. I felt so possessive of him; I wanted to hear every story and know every detail. I wanted every touch and every kiss, and I felt weak with longing for these things.

"We got them really good. We stole their clothes when they were swimming."

"Were they skinny-dipping?"

"Oh, it was sweet revenge. Mom told Dad he ought to horsewhip us, but Dad just grinned and said, 'Boys will be boys.' Isn't that terrible? What a copout answer. But we got away with it."

"No, it's funny. It sounds like something Clinty would do."

"I love how your family seems so close," he said. "I'm glad you've always had that. I know I fight with my sisters but I can't imagine life without them around. These last few years in the Cities, that was the worst part, being away from my family."

"All of them talked about you all the time, about how much they wanted you to move home. And I was missing you too, with all of my heart, I just didn't realize it until I saw you. Until you came home. I'm so happy you came home, Mathias."

His hands stilled their movement. I could feel his heart, the scent of him surrounding me, his skin and his breath. He threaded our fingers, our hands linked just beneath my breasts, and spoke with quiet passion. "You can't know how happy I am to be home, to have found you. Camille, you can't know."

Within my heart, something shifted at the speaking of these words. I closed my eyes and for a time we simply clung; no words were necessary. At last he whispered in my ear, "I want to build the cabin for us, for you and me, and for Millie Jo."

Tears washed over the bridge of my nose to the couch below, and Mathias turned me around in his arms so that he could brush them away. He held my face, studying my eyes as he pronounced, "That's what I want."

"That's what I want, too," I whispered, choked up. "Our little cabin."

Tears glistened on his lashes. "I love that you call it *our* cabin. It is ours. I could never build it for anyone but you. Will you let me build it for you?"

"I'll help you." I was elated at the thought. "We'll make the kitchen a little nicer…and maybe add an indoor bathroom…"

"No more outhouse," he agreed, grinning. "And a couple new bedrooms…"

At the mention of bedrooms (his, complete with bed, was so very close) my blood seemed to catch fire as swiftly as a gasoline spill. Picturing the box of condoms, still tucked in my purse no more than twenty feet away, I heard myself say, "Mathias...I have to tell you something..."

An inadvertent shiver overtook me—and it did not reflect any sort of hesitance, but instead a ferocious, passionate longing to make love with him until the sun rose tomorrow—but he misinterpreted and his expression changed at once, into one of concern. He said, "I love holding you like this. I love it with all my heart. I don't expect anything else. You know that, don't you?"

My face burned hot as a teakettle on a woodstove. I closed my eyes and he implored, "Camille, don't you?"

"I drove to Bemidji today and I..."

"What is it, honey? You what?"

"I got a prescription for the pill." I opened my eyes to find him looking down at me with so much tenderness, so much love; there was no disguising it.

My heart thumped with an all-consuming joy.

"Well," he said at last. And then, gaining momentum, "You know how a pirate must feel when he finds a treasure chest after a lifetime of obsessive searching? Totally priceless, the kind he would lay down his life for, that kind of treasure? This is a hundred times more precious than that. A *thousand*."

I was laughing long before he finished this ridiculous analogy, squirming against his hands, which were everywhere at once, tickling me.

"You think I'm kidding?" he gasped out, laughing too. "Because I'm not. I feel like a man who's just grabbed the log that will keep him afloat, knowing that he'll survive after all..."

"What?" I yelped, breathless with laughter as he dug wickedly into my ribs. "The *log?*"

"I'm just trying to express the depth of my gratitude at this gift—*ooof!*"

I thumped him with a cushion and we rolled to the floor, laughing and struggling (though I didn't exactly fight him away), eventually ending up with me beneath him; Mathias braced on his elbows over me and studied my eyes at close range as we sprawled on the carpet in front of the television set.

All at once somber, he whispered, "It *is* a gift, I'm not teasing you. I want you to stay here with me, right here in my arms. I mean, I know you have to go home to Millie." Searching my eyes, he admitted, "This morning…this morning, right before I woke up, I was dreaming that I couldn't find you, and it was horrible. It was just a nightmare, I know—"

His words called to my mind a dark and unsettled sensation, an intense sense of something I *should* remember and could not…or maybe it was something I did not *want* to remember, even if I had the power…

I said, "I truly believe that it has something to do with Malcolm Carter. He used to live in our cabin, I *know* he did. He was there and then—" I cut short my words, feeling the need to press a hand against the sudden aching in my heart, the anguish in my throat. "And then… something happened. Something bad, I know it. I have to find him. Will you help me find him?"

"Of course I will. There's got to be more clues than we have. We'll ask my dad. If Malcolm's family was here in Landon, what was he doing as far away as Montana when he sent that telegram? That's at least a good half a day's drive from here. What would that possibly equate to on horseback?"

"Over a month of riding, at least," I guessed.

"Most importantly, I think, is *what* was he searching for?" Mathias asked. "You know, it makes me glad to think that Aces was with him. I feel like he loved his horse, you know?"

I nodded adamantly, also believing this.

"Maybe those letters your dad told us about, out in Montana, would have some answers…" Excitement grew in my chest, driving out the ache.

Mathias decided, "Next summer we'll drive out there, you and me. We'll take a week and go. If there's anything to find, we'll hunt it down." Our eyes held for a beat, and then longer, and I felt his heart increase pace, matching mine. He bent and traced his tongue over the tiny scar on my top lip and murmured, "I'm not trying to change the subject, I swear, but sweet Jesus, I want to make love with you so much that it actually hurts. Here I wanted to be this amazingly good guy, the one who didn't push you to do things you weren't ready for, and I'm full of shit because I want to be inside of you at this second more than anything in this world. Oh God…I'm trying so hard to be a gentleman…"

I spread my legs beneath him, unable to stop as he spoke the words *inside of you*, creating a firm cradle for his hips, my arms around his neck. His eyes darkened with intensity and he groaned, "*Oh my God…*"

"You are an amazingly good guy," I whispered, feeling the hardness of him through both pairs of our jeans. My entire body seemed to liquefy with the desire to envelop him. "And you aren't pushing me. I want you, oh God, Mathias, *I want you…*"

He kissed me, tongue claiming my mouth with heated, rhythmic strokes. I moaned and lifted against him, and the intensity of our kissing swelled instantly beyond our control. He rolled us to our sides, pressing his face to my neck.

"We'll wait until you've started the pill. And I hope you know…" He kissed me again, gently parting my lips and caressing with his tongue, a sensual tasting of me that I felt all the way between my legs. I quivered in his arms as he drew back and whispered hoarsely, "I want you to know that I will wait as long as it takes for you to be ready. You know that, don't you?"

"I do. I'm the one who can't wait."

"That is one hundred percent untrue," he groaned. "If I were any less a gentleman, I would be completely buck-ass naked at this moment and so would you…"

I giggled at this, kissing his chin. "I used to think the expression was 'butt naked,' not buck."

His blue eyes blazed. "The thought of you either way is about more than I can handle." He kissed a hot path to the low collar of my sweater; my hips jerked against him and he groaned again, resting his mouth exactly over the spot where my right nipple pressed nearly through the soft material separating it from his tongue; he took it lightly between his teeth through the double layer of sweater and bra, and my breath came in small, panting rushes.

He clutched my hips. "Will you let me—"

Before he could finish asking, I'd already reached to slip down the neck of my sweater.

At that moment a key clicked in the lock, out near the kitchen. Mathias moved swiftly, lifting me to his lap and atop the couch just as Skid clunked into the apartment.

"Hey, guys," Skid said on the way to his room.

Both of us kept quiet until Skid disappeared. And then we were almost hysterical, our broiling desire giving way to helpless laughter.

"Oh God, I'm an animal," Mathias gasped, rocking us side to side. "I'm sorry, sweetheart…"

"Don't be sorry." I wilted against the strength of him, clutching his wrists and bringing his hands beneath my sweater. He immediately cupped my breasts in his broad palms, stroking my nipples with his thumbs, kissing me open-mouthed, hungry and intense.

And again, Skid thumped unknowingly down the hall.

"Goddamn him to hell," Mathias muttered.

"I better get home anyway," I whispered and Mathias held me all the more tightly in response.

"I know you have to go but I'm rebelling against the thought. Can I come and sleep over with you? I can hardly bear to let you out of my sight. God, I sound like a fucking stalker…"

I giggled. "You're not hurting, are you…" Though for whatever reason I suddenly saw the words from Malcolm's telegram emblazoned across my mind's eye. *I miss you all so much I hurt…*

He pressed his nose between my shoulder blades, laughing as he confessed, "I'm not gonna lie…I'm hurting a little. C'mon, I'll drive you home, my birthday girl. But I'm gonna sing to you on the way…"

I insisted, "I get to pick the song."

"Oh, no," he contradicted, and began humming the first lines of "Sneaking Around With You."

"Oh, that's my favorite one from *Best Little Whorehouse*," I said, giggling, and he closed his eyes and really let loose with Burt Reynold's part of the duet.

"Jesus *Christ*, Carter!" Skid yelled from the bathroom. "Put a cork in it!"

Mathias stood, lifting me with him, still singing. He paused to kiss my neck and then continued the song, full-force.

"You're crazy!" Skid shouted, though I could hear him laughing.

And that was the truth; Mathias was exactly my kind of crazy.

Two hours later, snuggled into my bed with Millie snoozing at my side, I reached and opened the top drawer of my nightstand, extracting the picture of Malcolm Carter and Aces. I held it to my heart, as usual, and then clicked on the lamp, squinting against the brightness, hoping Millie wouldn't stir. In the splash of amber-tinted light I tilted the photograph, my eyes roving its surface for the countless time, searching for any sort of clue. I could not help but brush my lips against Malcolm's face, as I had so many nights over the past two years. Malcolm had sustained me for a long time and he would never even know; the ache in my heart returned, full-force, at this thought.

Malcolm A. Carter.

What happened to you?

Tenderness overwhelmed me. I thought, *Sweetheart, my sweet Malcolm, what hurt you? What were you searching for? Why were you hurting? Did you ever find it?*

As I studied the old picture, I didn't have the sense that the loss had yet occurred, at least not in this image. Malcolm's expression and posture conveyed a sense of happiness, contentment even. This was not the photo of a desperate man on an endless search; it was a sharp contrast to the tone of the telegram, which he would deliver sometime in the next year. Silently I implored him, *Why, Malcolm? You're Mathias's ancestor, I know you are. Tell me. Find a way to tell me, please. What were you searching for? What am I missing?*

On sudden inspiration I crept from bed and bundled into my robe before sneaking down to the kitchen, lit only dimly with the last of the embers in the woodstove. I found what I was looking for with little trouble, my fingertips familiar enough with this space that light wasn't necessary. Back upstairs, magnifying glass from the junk drawer in hand, I reexamined Malcolm Carter and Aces. I thought, *He's so handsome. He does resemble Mathias, I can see that now. Same nose, same strong hands, same straight eyebrows. I wonder if his eyes were blue.*

I shifted the tool slowly over the old black and white paper, with its thousand gray tones, fixating over his face, his hands. And then I saw something, the tiniest of details; without the magnifying glass it would not have been visible. Malcolm was wearing a piece of leather tied around his wrist, which I'd noticed before, but clearly my eyes had flowed over it without really seeing it. Upon this closer inspection I realized that there was a word carved into the leather, as though with the tip of a knife. A pulse of exhilaration quickened my blood and rushed my veins; I bent even closer, placing the picture directly beneath the lamplight's glare.

The word was *Cora.*

A beat of awareness. I squinted. Questions swarmed, shoving each other for attention. I debated calling Mathias but he was probably sleeping; he needed to get up at five to start his route. Just as I thought this, my phone vibrated and I smiled even before I leaned to grab it from beside the bed.

Just wanted to say good night and I'll see you tomorrow(!!!)

Hey! I found a name—I inadvertently bumped 'send' before finishing.

That's great news!! For what??

I giggled at his wording, hearing the way his voice would sound as he asked.

A name on Malcolm's wrist! Carved on his leather wristband!

What name?

Cora.

Doesn't sound like a brand name. Wasn't Lorie the girl he was writing to?

Yes, but—and here I gave up texting and pushed the icon to call him instead.

"Hey," he said softly, answering at once.

"Hey," I whispered, warmed through and through at the sound of his voice, all husky and sleepy. He was most certainly in bed. Was he naked? Was the sheet covering him? My thoughts narrowed, focusing only on him.

"Are you in bed?" His voice and this question, so close to what I was thinking, lit a torch low in my belly. He murmured, "Your thoughts are making me blush and I love it."

I giggled then. "I'm just missing you, is all. Are *you* in bed?"

"Oh my God, I miss you, too. I am in bed. I wish you were right beside me. I want to click on the lamp and play the game where I try to decide if your eyes are more green or more gold."

Keeping my voice low, I explained, "I was looking at the picture with a magnifying glass that I remembered was in the junk drawer. I can't believe I never thought to do that before. And then, just now, I spied the name carved into the leather. What do you think it means? Who is Cora?"

"Not his mother. Not a sister, either. I mean, I love my sisters, but I wouldn't wear a bracelet with their names."

"It's not exactly a bracelet…more like a wristband." I studied the strap around Malcolm's wrist. "It's made of braided straps but there's a smooth spot on the top and that's where it says her name. This is so exciting!"

"It is," he agreed. "Can I come over right now?"

"Yes!" I giggled again. "Oh God, Mathias, I would tuck you right into bed with me."

He groaned. "I'll be right there."

"Don't tease me."

"I'll see you tomorrow after work," he promised.

I love you, I wanted to say. Instead I whispered, "I'll be here. Sleep tight."

"You, too, honey," he whispered.

Chapter Sixteen

"Millie Jo made you a cupcake," I told Mathias on the phone. It was New Year's Eve and he was coming for supper, as he had so often this month; I knew Grandma and Aunt Ellen adored him and I appreciated how he took the opportunity to get to know them and Millie at our family dinners. Tish and Ruthie had been over all day, along with little Matthew, who Grandma and Aunt Ellen were watching while Mom and Blythe went for dinner in Bemidji. Uncle Justin and Aunt Jilly ended up staying home because Clint and Rae were both sick, but Matthew crawled all over the downstairs (we'd dragged Millie's baby gate from the attic to block the steps), while Millie Jo followed a step behind and bossed him, quite joyously. Ruthie brought a new manicure set and fixed up both mine and Millie's fingernails; Tish chose to watch and critique instead.

"She made me a cupcake?" Mathias repeated. "I can't wait to see it. But she won't be there, will she? Isn't she having supper with the Utleys?"

She was; Noah's parents had called to ask if she could spend the evening with them. Though it made my stomach feel slightly hollow, I acknowledged that they loved her, too; I refused to begrudge their time with her. Millie adored her grandparents, Curt and Marie; I wouldn't deny her to them, at least not when it was an occasional request. I didn't know if Noah would be there or not; no word from him since the night at White Oaks before Christmas…but no surprise there.

"Yes, they're picking her up at five."

"Shoot. I'll see her tomorrow then. Unless there's two feet of snow tonight, Skid and I are taking the day off."

"Good, you deserve it."

"I'll see you soon," he said, and a beat of anticipation nearly brought me to my knees; we hadn't *exactly* discussed it in so many words, but my period was over and I'd taken the first birth control pill today and I thought that maybe tonight...*maybe we could*...

"Milla!" Tish hollered from downstairs. "Come help me with your kid! She isn't listening!"

"Be right there!" I called. I told Mathias, "See you after work."

Curt and Marie Utley pulled up in their station wagon at ten to five that evening, but to my amazement, who should come walking up the snowy sidewalk but Noah, holding his mother's elbow; Marie was bundled in her puffy red parka, hood up. A twinge of nausea roiled across my gut; what would I say to my daughter? I didn't know if she saw Noah when she visited her grandparents (and it happened to coincide with him being home from college in Madison). I had never asked and Millie had never mentioned a thing. To my knowledge, Noah hadn't actually set eyes on her since she was four months old.

Grandma stood behind me, putting one palm on my elbow in a supportive gesture, leaving Ruthie, Tish, and Matthew in the kitchen, where the girls were talking and laughing about something. She observed, "Noah's with? Oh, Camille..."

Millie darted from the kitchen, crowing, "Gramma Marie!"

"Better answer the door," Grandma said, and I put on my best game face (which is what my dad would have said).

"Camille! Hi, dear." Marie spoke warmly, as though there was nothing unusual or long overdue concerning her son accompanying her to see his child. I'd learned long ago that Noah, as her youngest, seemed to be excused for a great deal of wrongdoing.

Noah studied me with unreadable eyes, but he offered politely, "Hi, Camille. Hi, Joan."

Millie peeked around my legs. "Hi, Gramma!"

I opened the door enough to allow them to enter and Marie bent to scoop Millie Jo close, kissing her cheek. She told Millie, "I have some Christmas presents for you! Grandpa and I were in Kansas at your great-aunt Iris's for Christmas."

"I know!" Millie reminded her. "'Member, Gramma, you called me on the phone?"

"Yes, that's right," Marie said. She rose and enclosed me in a brief hug, and then said to Grandma, "Joan, Happy New Year!"

Grandma said, "Good to see you," and her eyes flickered to Noah to include him in the pleasantry. I looked up at him then instantly away; he stood studying Millie with somber eyes, hands buried in his coat pockets.

"Hi, Noah!" Millie sang out. So I wouldn't *actually* have to introduce the bastard to his child.

"Hi, Millie." It sounded like something had lodged in his throat.

Grandma took control of the situation, affecting her parent voice and telling Millie, "Honey, grab your coat and your boots." Millie galloped to the closet. To Marie, Grandma added, "I have a loaf of that banana bread that you said Curt likes so well, with the coconut flakes."

"Bless you, Joan," Marie said, removing her hood. She was a small, plump woman with the same cleft chin as her son. To my further stun, she suddenly invited, "Camille, would you like to join us? Ben and the kids are over, too, and…"

"Thank you, Marie," I stumbled, interrupting her. "But I have plans this evening."

Marie nodded. "Next time, maybe."

Noah was all but shuffling his feet with discomfort. I moved to help Millie zip her jacket and secured her hat and mittens in place. I hugged her close. "Gramma Marie can call me if you want to come home, all right, baby? But you have fun."

"I will!" she said gaily.

Grandma returned from the kitchen with a bread pan wrapped in aluminum foil, which she passed to Noah. Behind Grandma, I caught sight of my sisters crowding the archway leading back to the kitchen, anxious to see what was happening out here.

"We'll have her home by ten or so," Marie promised.

I hugged Millie and then watched out the window as she held Marie's hand on the return trip to the car. I watched as Marie helped settle her into a car seat and Noah climbed in the driver's side. Grandma put her hand on my back and patted me twice.

Mathias came over at six and entertained all of us with stories of his day spent with Skid, removing piles of snow and ice, sanding parking lots; late in the afternoon he'd trooped out into the woods near White Oaks, along with Bull, to check their winter trap lines. I hadn't yet accompanied him but Mathias had told me all about their winter hunting, which included rabbits, hares, and squirrel. He and his father, especially, liked to test their mettle and hunt as people would have over a hundred years ago; nearly every winter since Mathias was a boy, saving when he was away at college, he'd set winter trap lines along with Bull.

My sisters loved Mathias—mostly, as they confided to me, because he made me so happy. Mathias and I told everyone about the cabin and the plans to rebuild and restore it; I refrained from mentioning Mathias's words about building the cabin for us—as much as Grandma sincerely liked him, I knew she would not be ready to accept such news, and just might lock me in my room for the foreseeable future.

"So, you guys see who can fart the worst in the plow truck? Since you're trapped in there?" Tish was asking, her mouth full, laughing at the same time.

Mathias flushed even as he nodded grinning affirmation. "It's great if you've just eaten a burrito, one of those huge ones from Doggett's gas station, since then—"

"Gross!" Ruthie yelped, giggling.

Little Matthew, in his high chair near Aunt Ellen, banged both palms on his messy tray and grinned angelically at us. His pink-cheeked face was round as a full moon, his head covered in golden curls; when he smiled, he looked just like Blythe. Mathias grinned at him. "Little guy, you agree with me, right?"

"He does not!" Tish protested. "And that's disgusting! Aren't you a college *graduate?*"

Mathias tipped back in his chair, laughing. He managed, "That's a good point."

After supper, we helped Grandma clear the table and put away the food, and then Tish and Ruthie asked if we wanted to watch a movie. Mathias held my gaze for just slightly longer than a heartbeat, asking without words, *What do you think?*

I'd rather be alone with you.

He nodded affirmation, somber, almost stern-faced; saying the first thing that came into my head, I told my sisters, "We're stopping out at White Oaks for a while."

Minutes later, bundled and in his truck, Mathias asked softly, "You want to go to White Oaks?"

I could tell he was trying to leave this decision to me, to be patient, and it was all I could do to say calmly, "Not just now. How about…I thought we could maybe…"

He said, "We could go to our cabin, but Dad and Sam and those guys are snowmobiling and if they saw a fire in there, they might stop in…"

"Is Skid home at your place?" A trembling moved downward from my belly. I was glad it was dark enough that maybe he didn't notice.

Mathias said quietly, "No, he's in Bemidji at his kind-of girlfriend's place."

I looked his way and our gazes collided; there was no trace of a smile on his mouth. My heart just about came through my ribs; I whispered, "Let's go there."

We drove in complete, heated silence. Once there, I waited as Mathias hurried around the hood of the truck to open the door for me. I could feel my pulse like a springtime river, my nipples as firm as cherries beneath my nursing bra; to my dismay, I didn't own a prettier one to wear tonight. He reached and lifted me slowly from the truck, his gloved hands warm on my waist. Once on the ground, he caught my mittened hand in his and led the way up one flight of stairs to his apartment. He fumbled a little unlocking the door and I felt a swell of tenderness, counteracting the anxious energy in my limbs.

"I'm so nervous," Mathias admitted once we were inside. I stood in the entryway as he clicked on the kitchen light, not moving to unwind my scarf or pull off my mittens, just standing still and watching him. Mathias tossed his coat onto the kitchen table, then moved to the living room and began collecting couch pillows and what appeared to be laundry piled on the living room floor. I watched him try to tidy up the space and a fraction of the tension in my belly eased, replaced with affection, a wide, warm rush of it. I crossed the space, tossing my mittens aside so I could touch him with my bare hands, and put both on his back, stilling his frenetic movement. He was bent forward as I did so and I caressed him, spreading my fingers against his sweatshirt.

He straightened slowly and turned, his eyes burning a path directly through my center. I cupped his jaw and he caught me around the waist, hauling my hips firmly against his body. "I'm so glad we came here," he whispered. "Camille. You're still in your coat. And I'm shaking like a teenager."

He was and it thrilled me. I was weak in the knees, too, but so ready for this. I stood on tiptoe to softly kiss his lower lip, and he shuddered and closed his eyes, his arms tightening around me. "I want this so much," I whispered.

Mathias opened his eyes, our hearts matching rhythms. He brought his lips to within a breath of mine and a soft, intense sound lifted from my throat. He reached and gently slipped the band from my ponytail, letting my hair loose. He curled his fingers into it and I could smell his breath, sweet with mint and his own scent, and I could not resist licking his lower lip.

He whispered, "Oh God, you feel good. Can I take this coat off of you?"

"Yes," I whispered, and in response he shifted, lifting me into his arms and carrying me through the living room. He brought us down a short hallway and into the bedroom on the right. Once there, he set me gently upon the carpet and clicked on a bedside lamp. I turned in a circle and observed his space; despite having been in the apartment numerous times, we'd dutifully stuck to the couch to cuddle. The walls were painted a neutral cream, his closet overflowing with his outdoor gear, a tall bureau with t-shirts and underwear crammed into too-small drawers. And his bed, made up with an indigo and forest-green quilt that I recognized from helping him move, pillows sprawled haphazardly.

My pulse beat so forcefully I was sure he could hear it. He caught my hands and kissed the back of each. Then he unzipped my coat and set it neatly aside. I could hardly breathe just watching his eyes, so very serious beneath his straight, black brows as we studied each other; he caught up the ends of my scarf, carefully unwinding it from my neck, placing it near my coat. And then he took my shoulders into his hands.

He said, "Do you know how much I love you?"

Tears wet my eyes even as my heart glowed, a million fireflies springing to instant and delighted life. Though it was the first time he'd spoken the words, I whispered truthfully, "I know it. I do."

"I love you so much my heart feels like it might burst apart. I fall asleep thinking of you, and wake up with you on my mind. Right here," and he indicated his bed with a tilt of his head, keeping my gaze captive in his. "I know you've been hurt before but you have to know that I would never hurt you, not ever."

"Mathias Carter," I whispered, just for the pleasure of speaking his name. I cupped his face and he turned to kiss my right palm. "I love you, oh sweetheart, *I'm so in love with you.* And I've been hurt before but I trust you, Mathias, I trust you with all my heart. I'm so happy you found me."

Tears were in his eyes, too. "Since I was just a kid, I've been waiting to find you, Camille."

He brushed tangled hair from my face, bending to taste my neck with warm, lingering kisses. I tugged him to the bed and we fell upon it, tangled together and squirreling to get closer. His cheekbones were flushed in the golden lamplight, his eyes as hotly blue as the bottom of a candle flame. He grinned, dimple flashing, and I ran my tongue over it, digging my hand into his hair, biting his chin, his jaw, in a fever of increasing need. We kissed deep and lush, legs entwined, hands roving without letup. I slipped mine beneath his sweatshirt, caressing his warm, strong sides as we murmured between hungry kisses.

"I fell in love with you the moment I saw you at Shore Leave, but I realized it when you slipped my ring on your hand that night."

"I knew it then, too, I just wouldn't admit it to myself," I admitted. He grinned and my heart convulsed. I buried my nose against his collarbones, my fingers teasing the top of his jeans. "It's so good to touch you. Oh God, you don't even know…"

"*Touch me*," he breathed, husky and intense, punctuating this demand with kisses. "And let me touch you. Will you let me make love to you? I know you haven't been on the pill long enough but I bought a box of condoms the day after you told me, I have them right here…"

I felt almost sick with love for him, feverish and burning alive, my vision all but swimming; we broke the contact of our mouths only so Mathias could yank the sweatshirt over his head, baring his gorgeous muscular torso, his broad, hairy chest, his wide shoulders that rippled with strength, creating solid ridges on either side of his neck.

"Now you," he whispered, taking my hands into his when I reached for the bottom hem of my sweater. "Let me. I've imagined this so many times, please let me."

With tender, deliberate movements he bared my belly and rested his lips there. I threaded my fingers into the dark curls on his neck, unable to catch my breath. He worked slowly up my body, his nose brushing my blazing skin, tasting me, at last easing the sweater over my breasts. I tensed a little and he immediately stilled his hands, lifting his head from between my breasts, clearly concerned.

I slung a forearm over my eyes. "I might…"

His hands were warm and so reassuring, gripping my waist. He whispered, "Might what, honey?"

"My…breasts…" I spoke in a rush. "I'm still nursing and I might leak milk on you…"

"You thought I would mind that?" He sounded truly stunned and I opened my eyes to his grin. And though I knew he was attempting to coax a smile, to put me at ease, I was overwhelmed by a burst of urgency, erasing any doubt.

"Come here," I begged and the grin fell from his lips.

He kissed me again, tongue delving deeply as I arched against him and he unhooked my bra with skillful fingers. I shifted my arms free of it and a sound escaped his throat, a low groan. He bracketed my breasts with both wide palms, lightly skimming his thumbs over my swelling nipples with a touch both heated and reverent. "Holy God, *you are beautiful…*"

He bent and opened his lips over my right nipple, and just like that I felt a prickling rush and he got a mouthful of breast milk. My left nipple began trickling warm liquid at the exact same instant. I squeaked as he swallowed convulsively and nearly choked. And suddenly we were both laughing. His smile turned wicked and he licked the milk from the inner curve of my left breast.

"It tastes good, really sweet," he gasped, still laughing. "This is *so* erotic…is that terrible of me to say?"

I thought it was erotic, too, even though it was probably wrong to think that. But I didn't care; nothing felt wrong with Mathias. I giggled and writhed as his tongue followed the hot, sticky trails along my breasts. I moaned, "That *tickles…*"

He laughed with my nipple between his lips and we rocked to the side; we were both wearing our jeans and I was still leaking milk as he tried to contain it with his mouth. I would never have guessed that lovemaking could be like this—my body humming and electric with desire even as I laughed hysterically, clinging to Mathias. My right thigh was latched over the side of his waist, his chest hair now sticky from its proximity to my breasts.

"Here," he gasped, breathless with laughter, using the edge of the top sheet to gently clean my skin; of course, this tickled even worse. "Oh God, I'm not helping, am I…"

"Would you…ever have believed…" I couldn't finish the sentence, too giggly, but he understood the gist of what I was trying to say.

"Yes," he murmured, blue eyes ablaze with love; I felt that fire all the way to my toes. "God, yes. With you, I can believe anything." He rested his forehead to mine and our laughter became something else. "My heart is all yours."

"And mine is yours." Tears welled. I hugged him as hard as I could. "I'm getting you all wet…"

He kissed away my tears. "That's supposed to be my job."

Urgency surged anew and I begged, "Help me get out of these," lifting my hips in case he didn't realize I meant my jeans.

He freed me from them in less than a second, his own in the next. I clung to his shoulders as he spread a warm hand on my naked belly and whispered, "Have you ever had an orgasm before?"

I'd given myself a few over the past couple of years, but shook my head, trembling and feverish all over again. Lips brushing mine, he murmured, "Because I intend to give you a few."

I couldn't respond in words as he slipped his hand into my panties, tracing lightly over my skin before slowly deepening his touch, caressing inside as I moaned and lifted against him, tiny, powerful explosions detonating in the wake of his fingers. He took my lower lip between his teeth.

"I love you with my whole heart. I want to bring you pleasure, honey, I want it so much."

"Yes," I begged, hardly able to think beyond the strong, passionate immediacy of him. "Yes, please *yes*…"

I held fast to his back as he continued stroking, biting the ridge of muscle near his neck, quivering beneath him. Sweat trickled over his temples as he bent to my breasts, lavishing them with his tongue; I caught his head in my hands, arching into his mouth. He was breathing hard enough that I almost didn't understand when he said, "I promise I won't…get you pregnant. Not until…you're my wife."

His wife. But even as I rejoiced at the sweet sincerity of his words a sense of loss broadsided me, hard enough that I felt struck by a heavy, unstoppable object; rendered nearly blind by the sensation, I fought against the unexpected notion that we would be separated, and that there was nothing I could do to prevent this.

No, I thought next, fierce with the need to force aside the dread; I begged, "Let me see you," shifting to roll him over, leaning across him and running my hands down his neck with possessive determination, letting my loose, heavy hair stroke all along his chest and belly. I eased him free of his boxers and caught his hard length into my hand. His head fell back and he shuddered with harsh breaths.

"That feels...*so goddamn good.*" He dug his hands into my curls as I bent lower and took him in my mouth. His cock was big, hot and rigid, and I was sticky with warm breast milk, and yet I'd never been so overwhelmed by need. I allowed him as far down my throat as I was able, curving both hands beneath his hips as I swirled my tongue, tasting him.

"Come here," he breathed, sweeping me into his arms and rolling me to my shoulder blades, poised just at the juncture of my legs; I was nearly panting. He said hoarsely, "Condom," and flung open his bedside drawer, rummaging furiously to find the box. He tore it open with his teeth, shook one out, and had it in place almost before I could blink.

"My panties," I gasped, and he grinned. I licked his dimple as he swept the last of my clothing down my legs.

His eyes were blue fire as we clung and I ran my calves along his torso and my fingers over his chest. He demanded, "Tell me once more, oh God, tell me one more time."

"I love you, Mathias, *I love you* —"

He swept one hand down my side, clasping my knee and anchoring it around his hip as he entered my body. We were kissing so hard that my jaw ached but I would have rather died than stop, completely lost in him. He rocked into me, so hard and strong, taking me over an edge I hadn't known existed. He was mine, wild in my arms, his back rippling with muscle beneath my grasping hands, both of us slick with sweat and tangled together. I buried my cries against his neck as he drove into me, clinging with arms and legs, enveloping him in wet heat; he groaned and shuddered hard, falling still and wrapping me close at the same moment, so close that nothing could ever come between us. That nothing could ever separate us.

Mathias...

Time passed; how much, I wasn't sure, and I refused to loosen my grip on him. Mathias trailed gentle fingertips in a pattern along my spine, cradling me to his chest. His heartbeat was slow and steady against my cheek, replete. I inhaled against his sweaty skin, thrilled that I could bring him such pleasure, that he could cause such earthquakes through my body. I slipped one hand down my belly and pressed against my pelvis, where the aftershocks of feeling continued to swell. Eyes still closed, he followed the same path, curling his much bigger hand over mine.

"Thank you for that," he whispered, twining our fingers together. And then, teasing me a little, "I hope it was good for you."

I giggled, my cheek against his hairy chest. "Are you kidding me? You couldn't tell…"

He shifted, shoulders curving protectively over me as I snuggled against him, our fingers intertwined at the slippery juncture of my thighs. I pressed more insistently against his hand, sensing his grin. He admitted, "Well…I had *some* idea…"

"I would certainly hope so." I latched my left leg higher over his hip and he ran his palm along my thigh.

"You're so soft." His blue eyes were lazy with satisfaction. "My sweet woman." He kissed my shoulder, murmuring, "My sweet, sweet honey."

I maneuvered his fingers where I wanted them most at this moment, licking his neck in little hot spots. He made a sound that was part growl, his voice hoarse as he speculated, "Maybe I better call you my *naughty* honey. My sweet, naughty little—"

I bit his chin, urging with my hips.

He rolled over me at once, stroking deeply as I bucked, bursting with such onrushing desire that I was slightly startled. I wanted him to kiss me just where his hand was touching but was too shy to ask outright. I moaned and twisted in an effort to get closer, and he pressed his lips to my temple and whispered, "What is it, honey? What do you want, *tell me…*"

His husky voice sent heat through me just as effectively as his plundering fingers, gliding in and out of my body. I held tightly to his neck and spread my legs further around him. "I want…"

"Tell me." He closed his teeth around my earlobe.

"I want you to…kiss me…here…" I kept my eyes closed even as I felt him grin against the side of my neck. He moved downward along my body, building the throbbing to a shrieking pitch. He took his sweet time, gently tonguing my nipples, peppering kisses upon my belly, at last grasping my hips and spreading my thighs just a little more; I shivered hard, covering my eyes with a forearm. No one had ever done such a thing to me, but I trusted him.

"Right here?" he whispered, and kissed me ever so softly, just a tickling brush of his lips against the flesh between my legs. My hips jerked in response.

"*Yes*," I pleaded, and he curved his hands beneath, lifting me so that he could kiss me again, and again. I didn't even try to muffle the gasping moans that flowed from my throat; he was so incredible. I should have known, could have guessed, but no imagining came close to the real thing, Mathias here with me.

"Oh my *God*," he groaned some time later, breathing roughly. "I've never been so hard in my life. I think I could cut through solid diamond. Jesus Christ."

I would have giggled at his words if I wasn't so out of breath, and slippery-wet; he slid all the way with the first stroke, holding himself deep and still, so very rigid that I couldn't believe he fit.

"You're so good at that." I was still all shivery and he smoothed hair from my flushed face, his eyes so full of love. "Stay here, *inside of me*."

"Always," he whispered back, taking up a steady rhythm. "Always and always."

"I love you, Mathias." Tears glazed my eyes—tears of joy for what we'd found. And even as I spoke I found myself imploring silently, *Please don't take him from me, oh God, please don't take him away from me.*

"I love you." He rested his forehead to mine. "It's so goddamn good… oh my God, Camille…*I love you*."

I wrapped around him, unwilling to relinquish my hold, and it wasn't until much later that we drifted from somewhere up in the bright winter stars, softly back to his bed.

Chapter Seventeen

February, 2006

"I DON'T WANT YOU TO THINK...THAT ALL I WANT FROM you...is this," Mathias groaned, breathless, as we struggled in a rush of frantic need to unbutton each other's jeans. It was a dark winter's evening and we were alone in the ice shack out on Flickertail. Since New Year's Eve we'd made love every moment available to a man with a roommate and a single mom without her own place, full of an ever-increasing hunger, a desire to absorb each other in all ways.

"I don't think that," I assured him between kisses. I loved him so much, craved him so insanely that all sensibility flew swiftly away, on wide, feathery wings. I managed, "It's just that this is so...amazing...*oh my God.*" My head fell back and his teeth were on my neck. "I need you *right now,*" I demanded, as though my body wasn't telling him exactly that, and he kissed me hard and hot.

He shoved everything off the surface of the big wooden barrel, which put me at a perfectly appropriate height for his plans, lifting me atop without breaking our kiss. I held his head, tilting to take his sweet, questing tongue even deeper, assisting him as he worked busily to tug down my jeans and panties enough to free one leg, still clad in a knee-high woolen sock, which he then hooked around his hip. Breathing harshly, he tore his mouth from mine to whisper, "You'll get splinters..."

I giggled, even though splinters in my ass were the last things I was worried about right now. He ripped off his coat and settled it under me, then pulled my mouth back to his, uttering a husky sound deep in his throat—his lovemaking sound, I knew, one that I'd heard many beautiful times by now. I reached to yank down his jeans just enough to free his cock.

"Hurry," I ordered, and he shifted to impale me as I moaned again. "You feel so good...don't stop...*don't stop...*"

We thrust together and I clutched his shoulders to keep from getting bucked right off the barrel. I buried my cries against his neck and he groaned and came a little, I could feel the hot burst of it, happy not to have a condom in the way.

"Not yet..." he murmured, slowing his pace. He grasped my hips and tilted me to a slightly different angle, deepening each movement, plunging again and again; sweat trickled over my temples and between my breasts. He grinned, his eyelids lowered in seductive bliss; he hadn't shaved in a couple of days and his stubble was dark and raspy, totally sexy, giving him the appearance of someone perhaps a little dangerous, maybe a sailor who'd been out to sea for months...

"Oh my God...*Mathias...*" I gasped, coming so hard against him that I nearly fell off the barrel. He held me steady, driving hard before he was at last overcome. I rested my forehead on his chest, vibrating with pleasure. He bit my earlobe.

"Were we too loud?" I worried against his thermal underwear. He was radiating heat, hotter than any furnace. I inhaled almost greedily, absorbing the scent of him; it was a primal, animal thing, this craving for another person that overrode all else.

He kissed my tangled hair, stroking it away from my sweating forehead. "I think we're safe, honey-love. It's pretty loud out there."

I caught his jaw into my hands and he tipped forward to kiss my lips, my nose; my legs remained locked around his hips. I whispered, "We're so naughty."

"Yes, we are," he agreed, nuzzling my neck. "And I love it."

I kissed his ear, then bit it. "I love being naughty...really, *really* naughty..."

His dimple deepened as his hands came around my hips; I ordered, "I want to ride you...*lay down...*"

He hurried to oblige my demand, and then we were laughing and struggling to get completely out of our jeans and to position something under us, so there was a barrier between Mathias and the ice, our bodies intertwined in this dark, cramped, heavenly little space. He managed to get his coat angled just right. "Come here, honey, come right here."

I straddled him, bracing on his powerful chest as he uttered a low cry and clutched my hips. Our motion knocked the leg of one of the camp chairs into the hole in the ice but it was too big to fall in completely, and neither of us paid any attention. I tore off my coat and his hands went under my sweatshirt, cupping my naked breasts. I curled forward to kiss his jaw, slowing our rhythm, licking his hot, sweating skin, closing my teeth around his chin; he gasped, shuddering violently, as a fountain seemed to explode inside of me…and at that exact instant there was an insistent knocking on the ice shack door. I squeaked and collapsed atop his chest, my static-wild hair falling all around us while Mathias struggled to gather his wits, rolling so that I was safely hidden beneath his big nude body.

"Hang on!" he rasped in the direction of the door, muffling his laughter as he whispered to me, "Shit. I can't move after coming like that. I'm useless right now. I hope it's not a burglar…"

"It's Tina!" she announced cheerfully from right outside, maybe six steps from us. "Sorry to interrupt! Matty, Glenna got the snowmobile stuck and so we need your muscles."

"Jesus *Christ*," Mathias muttered, hiding his eyes behind one hand. I smothered my giggles, wiggling into my jeans, tugging down my sweatshirt; when he couldn't manage to haul his own jeans back in place, I helped him, neither of us trying to stifle our laughter now.

"What's going on in there?" Tina demanded, and I pictured her standing there in the dim, snowy night with her hands planted on her hips.

"We're coming!" I called, trying to infuse a sense of apology in my voice, to no avail. Once we'd managed to get to our feet, Mathias caught me close for one last kiss, hugging me and rocking us side to side. Against my hair he muttered, "I'm sorry my family is such a pain in the ass."

"They are not," I scolded.

We answered the door to Tina's knowing smile. She was bundled in a silver and blue snowmobile suit, holding aloft a travel-sized propane lantern. She regarded us; we were flushed and disheveled, clothes askew, undoubtedly guilty. Tina raised her right eyebrow. "Hi, you two. I know that look."

"What look is that?" Mathias practically growled at her, and she rolled her eyes.

"Happiness," she concluded, punching his shoulder. "That's what look that is."

"She's right," he said later as we drove back to Shore Leave through the glittering cold night, our fingers linked on the seat. Before I could respond, Mathias elaborated, "What Tina said. I've never been happier in my life."

I squeezed his fingers in mine, his strong hand that held me so securely, that had touched every last inch of my skin many times by now. I admitted, "It sometimes scares me to say such things out loud, but I agree completely."

"Don't be scared, honey," he said softly, bringing my hand to his lips and kissing it before holding it to his cheek; my heart caught on something sharp at his words.

"I don't mean to be." My throat ached as he turned into Grandma's driveway. The outside light glowed in welcome.

Mathias parked and said, "Come here." He held me close for a long time, stroking my hair; at last he whispered, as though to earn a smile, "My beard doesn't scratch you, does it? I've been so lazy and content I haven't shaved in three days."

"Not one bit. I like it," I whispered, storing up the feel of him for all night when we'd be apart. We hadn't yet been able to spend the night together, as I felt far too guilty being away from Millie Jo that way. Despite the fact that Millie liked Mathias enormously I wasn't ready to make the decision to move out of Grandma's house, dragging Millie from the only home she'd ever known. And then a spurt of panic flared in my gut, the thought that Mathias might get tired of waiting and that I would be without him; why did that unspeakable sensation plague me? I hated it—and the most horrible part was that somehow it felt *familiar*. As though I'd been torn from him before this moment.

Stop it, I ordered. *He's right here, and you're being completely irrational.*

"I can't bear to drive away every night and leave you alone," he murmured, sensing the direction of my thoughts to some extent. And then, startling me, he said, "God, this is terrible, but I'm going to say it anyway."

"Say what?" I asked, alarmed, clutching his elbows, closing my fists around the material of his parka.

"I was just going to say that even though we're taking precautions, I'm sitting here thinking I wish you were pregnant with my baby. Then we could get married next month."

"Mathias *Carter*," I whispered, half-scolding, though I was deeply touched at his sincerity. I drew back to see his eyes, his dear, handsome face. "I would love to have your babies. But I want to be married first, and married for a while. It's not easy to have a newborn, even with help, as I well know." We had talked about getting married since New Year's, the night we'd made love for the first time. It seemed so natural, so right; I would marry him next month, baby or no. But Millie took precedence in my thoughts; I couldn't rush into something without considering how it would affect her. And Mathias, endearingly romantic as he was, truly didn't truly realize the hardship that accompanied a child.

But what if...

The sensation of loss stabbed at me; I fought the urge to grit my teeth.

What if you wait and something happens...

Stop it!

Mathias was saying, "I know, sweetheart, I'm sorry. I agree, I really do. I just get carried away."

I debated telling him what I feared but didn't want to come across as irrational as it would no doubt sound; instead I whispered, "Don't be sorry, love. And I want a big family just as much as you. I can't imagine not having a bunch of kids around our table." I thought suddenly of the evening Millie was born, sitting at the kitchen table with Tish and worrying that my baby would never have a brother or sister, that she'd be lonely as a result. Even if I hadn't articulated it at the time, the thought of never finding someone I loved—never finding someone to share our life with—had loomed like a devastating storm, bent on complete wreckage. Tears stung the bridge of my nose, blurring the sight of his face. I spoke using the nickname I'd created for him, the one that no one but me used. "I once thought Millie would never have any siblings and it about broke my heart, Thias. My life would be so different without my sisters, it would be completely different…"

"Honey, we'll give Millie as many little brothers and sisters as she wants." He amended quickly, "Down the road, I mean. And I love that you just said 'our table.' The table I'm going to build for us in our cabin."

Tears slipped from beneath my eyelashes even as I smiled in joy at the picture he painted; I vowed, *We will live there, I swear this. I won't let anything happen.*

I whispered, "A *big* table."

Hours later, I had a dream.

The winter woods were impenetrable in this hour of deepest night and I was lost within them. Snow fell, icy upon my skin, silent and unceasing; I wore no protective gear and in fact when I looked in the direction of my feet I observed that they were bare, their prints creating damp depressions in the unforgiving layer of snow upon the ground. Pine boughs loomed near my face, laden with clots of ice, forcing me to brush them aside with fingers growing ever more numb as I plundered forward; I sought my home with a desperation I'd never known.

It's just around that bend.

Don't stop walking, don't stop moving.

He's there, just ahead, don't you see him?

But I cried, *I can't, I can't see a thing!*

Far from where I stood, I thought I could discern the shape of a candle flame, flickering to guide my way, as though placed in a window. I thought, *If I can just get there, I'll be home.*

I longed for home—I was so close, *he* was so close, but I was lost in these freezing woods, the way dense with impassable trees, mounds of snow engulfing my legs to the thigh, even as I struggled to free my body from the depths. My clothing was tattered and I was a mess, skinny and starving, dirty and ragged, half-frozen. I was near the end, I had no doubt. I needed to keep moving and yet as I watched, the candle flame grew weak, wavering as though a stream of cold air strove to extinguish its meager light.

No, oh God, no…

Please don't burn out before I get there…

I've traveled so far to get here…farther than anyone could ever imagine…

Using my elbows to brace my weight, I fought against the terrible pull of the cold, the urge to sink into the downy drift and simply die. I couldn't die before I saw him one last time and I begged, using the last of my strength to scream.

Malcolm! Please hear me, Malcolm Alastair Carter!

Snow filled my mouth, rough and shockingly cold, cutting off my attempts to cry out. My eyelashes grew coated with icicles, my face hardening to glass. I sobbed, *Malcolm…*

And then a whooshing breath, blessedly warm, sounded in my right ear. Overwhelmed with grateful relief, I knew it was Aces High; our good boy, our horse, here to save me in the end. I thrashed free of the snow surrounding my arms, the ice that would have cut off my last link to this life, and felt the solid immediacy of the chestnut horse, the familiar warm bulk of him; if Aces was near, Malcolm was not far behind, I knew this. I sobbed, *Aces, you found me, thank God, you found me. Where is he? Is he with you?* I reached to curl my fingers into the gelding's coarse black mane, to lift myself to the safety of his broad back, tears warming my frozen cheeks…

But at the last second I felt the earth give way beneath my feet and I fell—*and fell*—a soundless scream, the last trace of who or what I had been.

Chapter Eighteen

"MILLIE JO, YOU'RE TWO YEARS OLD TODAY!" I HUGGED HER close as we woke to find rosy morning sunlight streaming through the dormer windows. Of course it was sunny today—it was my daughter's birthday. I could hear birds singing right outside the window. "Do you hear the birdies? They're wishing you happy birthday! It's your second birthday! You're two!"

"Two?" she repeated, as though asking a question. She rolled to her back and gave me her crinkly-eyed grin. I scooped her into my arms, cuddling her snuggly little body close, clad in her footie pajamas, her bottom squishy with a soggy diaper. Her curls brushed my cheek.

"I love you," I whispered into her wild hair. "I love you so much, baby girl."

"I wuv you, Mama," she said, then wriggled free of my arms and squirmed to her belly to slide off the bed. I heard the phone ring downstairs and a minute later Grandma called from the kitchen, "Millie Jo! Grandma Marie is on the phone for you!"

Millie went running; I followed more slowly, shuffling into my robe and wool socks. Downstairs, I helped myself to a cup of coffee, leaning my hip on the counter as Millie talked to Marie and Grandma fried bacon. Aunt Ellen sat at the table, kneading bread dough. Listening to Millie chatter to her grandmother, I thought about what I'd learned just last weekend; apparently Noah had dropped out of college and moved home with his parents. Uncle Justin, who'd talked to Noah's older brother, Ben (and then told Aunt Jilly everything, as she told me), explained that Noah's drinking was out of control and Curt and Marie were attempting to get him into a rehab clinic in Bemidji; he'd flunked out of school and subsequently lost his partial scholarship. I felt only pity, and mild revulsion; this shitpile Noah was creating of his life brought me no comfort, no satisfaction.

I thought about Noah's appearance at White Oaks just before Christmas and how he'd confronted me, drunk and appearing shameful. But then again, he'd stood up for me to Tess, if only fractionally. Maybe he possessed a few redeeming qualities after all. I thought, *Dammit, Noah, be a man. Be a man and get your act together, and be a father to your child.* I wouldn't keep Millie from occasionally seeing him, as long as he was sober; he needed to prove that he could be worthy of her. I'd long ago given up expecting him to be worthy of *me*, but it was fathoms more important for him to be a decent father. I could live with that.

The entire family had celebrated Millie Jo's birthday last night, everyone converging on Grandma's house for a fried chicken dinner, with a layered chocolate cake for dessert—Mathias, Mom, Blythe, Matthew, and my sisters; Aunt Jilly and Uncle Justin, Dodge, Rae and Clinty—the whole bunch, loud and boisterous, excited to celebrate, just as always. Aunt Jilly was pregnant again, which she'd only just announced, and this time I was the one with a Notion; the moment I touched her belly last night I'd known, "A boy."

Aunt Jilly covered my hands with hers, gorgeous blue eyes glinting. "That was my first thought, too." And then she continued to study me, the sort of gaze I knew well, full of compassion and love, but with intense speculation at its heart. She whispered, "What is it, Milla? What's wrong?"

I shook my head, wishing I could explain, wishing I knew how to express what troubled me; I'd been unable to sleep well the past week, disturbed at the necessity of closing my eyes, fearful of what I might encounter if I dared to let myself dream. Though the exact details escaped me, were lost in the recesses of my memory, merely the sense of the darkness I'd encountered lately while sleeping kept me in a state of insomnia.

Aunt Jilly let her soft touch move beneath my chin, almost as if I was still a little girl; a shiver jolted my spine, a recognition of her full concentration, the expression on her delicate pixie face growing ever more focused. I imagined the finely-wrought wires of her thoughts entering into my mind, seeking answers. She closed her eyes, gentle fingertips brushing my face like someone reading Braille; at last she whispered, "You're scared." Her eyes opened and I blinked at the power of her gaze, her understanding. It was far beyond my own abilities. A small shock, similar to the spark of static electricity, flashed from her fingers to my skin; both of us startled at the sensation.

"But you don't know of what," she concluded, and I heard the notes of quiet alarm in her voice, even if she hadn't intended that.

I grasped her hands and clung, the two of us alone in the warm, sweet-smelling kitchen with the muted sound of the dishwasher in our ears; pans and bowls were piled in the sink, requiring extra soaking. A single candle burned on the counter, casting Aunt Jilly's face in lambent patterns of light and shadow, ever-changing. The living room was near to bursting with our family—our men and children, our sisters, everyone who loved us—and yet both of us felt the sudden chill in the air, the sense of danger just beyond our reach; beyond our control.

"What do you think it is?" My lips felt wooden with fear.

Aunt Jilly drew a breath, squeezing my hands, with conviction. She requested quietly, "Let's not talk about this with anyone, all right? Not until I can get a stronger sense of what's wrong." She exhaled slowly, our gazes holding fast, then lowered her voice another notch to explain, "Justin will be so worried if I tell him something is wrong, and I don't want him to worry. At least, not before I understand the nature of the worry."

I nodded, in complete agreement.

"You're in love with Mathias," my aunt whispered. "And he's in love with you, I can see that even without my extra senses."

I nodded again, almost too afraid to confess to it, to admit to my own happiness. Before I could bite the words from existence, I begged, "Don't let anything happen to him."

Aunt Jilly's brows lowered in confused concern. She was about to reply when Rae and Millie Jo darted into the kitchen, seeking our attention; my aunt said, "We'll talk more about this, I promise. Try to get some sleep tonight."

And I had, a few hours' worth, at least.

Marie Utley had called earlier in the week to ask if Millie might come to their house on Valentine's Day to celebrate her birthday with them; at first I'd been selfishly reluctant, but Marie explained that her older sister would be in town for the day and would love to see Millie. And so it was that I bundled up my daughter in the late-afternoon of her second birthday, allowing her to go with Marie and Curt; Noah hadn't accompanied them this time, to my unspoken relief. I watched them walk over the crunchy snow to their station wagon, the low sunlight sparking red on the ends of Millie's dark curls, sticking out beneath her pink wool hat with its puffball top, and suddenly felt a small, sharp stab of unease. I reeled a little, blinking, and the feeling slithered away. Millie turned back to wave and I blew her a kiss, reminding myself that she would be back early. The Utleys only lived a few miles outside of Landon, on their dairy farm.

It's just because it's weird that she's not with you on her actual birthday. That's all.

But I watched until their car was out of sight.

"You'll be done by nine or so?" Mathias asked about an hour later, and my heart soared to hear his familiar voice over the phone; I tried to pretend that the lingering agitation in my gut was just my imagination. He added, "Happy Valentine's. You all right, honey?"

He knew it was hard for me to let Millie go with her grandparents on her birthday.

"I am. I'm headed to the lodge right now but I should be done by nine." I hadn't worked at White Oaks in a month but agreed when Tina asked if I would help out on Valentine's Day. I told him, "Tina thought it would be an early rush tonight."

"I'll meet you there as quick as I can. I hate not taking you out to dinner on Valentine's." Because it was a Tuesday, he had plow work as usual. "And I have *such* a good present for you, honey."

"You do?" I caressed the phone as though it was a part of him. "What is it?"

"It's a surprise," he insisted, and even though I could tell he was grinning, the knot of fear in my belly seemed to pulse, enough that I inhaled too sharply. He heard this and asked at once, "What's wrong?"

"I don't know," I admitted miserably, longing to be able to explain just exactly what it was I feared so much, but I could hardly explain it to my *own* satisfaction. "I had a bad feeling, earlier when Millie Jo left. Like something's wrong but I don't know what."

"You want to go and get her? I'll drive you over to their house right now," he said. "I know you've had something on your mind, honey, I can tell."

Of course he could tell; I assured him, "I'm all right." I didn't want to be melodramatic, or an alarmist; besides, I really did have to get to work at White Oaks. I drew what was meant to be a calming breath. "I just didn't get enough sleep last night."

"Are you sure? You don't sound sure."

"I love that you can hear that." I took a moment to appreciate this fact; I wished I could shake aside this lingering fear. I reassured myself that Millie was just fine, that Mathias was all right…everything was all right…

Except that somehow it *wasn't* and I was overwhelmed by the urge to beg him to come over at once, to let me put my eyes and hands on him, in that order.

Stop it, I reprimanded, struggling to draw another full breath.

"I love you," he said in return, and I forced away the ridiculous sense of doom. "I'll head over to White Oaks just as soon as I'm done with work and do a quick check on our trap lines. Dad didn't get a chance yet today." He paused and said softly, "And I'll get a fire stoked in our cabin, honey, for later."

"That's perfect," I whispered.

"Those are for you," Tina said as I hurried into the dining room at White Oaks twenty minutes later, tying my black server apron into place. She indicated a vase situated on the bar, a gorgeous cluster of sunflowers, indigo irises, and the little azure stars of aster blossoms, spilling in a luminous array of yellow and blue. The vase was ringed by a heart made of individually-wrapped caramels, my favorite kind, handmade at Farmer's Market. I blinked in surprise, then smiled widely, burying my face in the blooms. A small note in Mathias's handwriting read, *This isn't your real present but I hope you like it anyway. Love, Aces.* He'd drawn what was meant to be a horseshoe and I giggled, even as tears wet my eyes.

"Smitten, that's what," Elaine observed, leaning over from the other side of the bar and patting my forearms. Her eyes shone into mine as she pronounced, "Flat-out in love."

"I love him, too," I whispered, bringing the note to my lips.

"Matty arranged those on his lunch hour today and told me I better not let anyone touch a thing until you saw it."

"You two are obnoxious," Tina teased, snagging me around the waist with one arm, squeezing me briefly close. "And hey, I'd like to be in charge of your wedding."

I giggled again, swiping tears with my knuckles, carefully tucking the note into the pocket of my apron; Tina kissed my cheek. I tightened the band on my ponytail and likewise pulled myself together, as the dining room was already bustling with locals dressed in their Valentine's finery. We were steadily busy for the next hour; work kept my mind occupied, and I reached time and again to caress the note in my apron, running my fingers over Mathias's words as I had so very many times over Malcolm's, seeking reassurance; at one point I found myself wondering if Aces was in the corral outside, letting my imagination drift and tangle into daydreams. But it seemed as if the horse *should* be waiting outside, no matter how crazy or illogical.

I waited on Eddie and his wife, Alice, along with their middle daughter and her husband, and had just rung in another bottle of wine for their table when my gaze flashed to the last of the sunset, framed by the wide front windows. The oak trees on the far bank stretched their sharp, bare limbs into the piercing golden light. I blinked, disliking how they seemed to stab at the sky. The lacy amber frost decorating the glass sent shards of blinding light straight into my skull. I reeled this time, seeing the same scene superimposed on the backsides of my eyelids in a muddy purple hue; for a strange, slow-paced moment I struggled to remember exactly what year it was and had to grip the edge of the bar to keep my balance, terribly frightened by this sensation.

"Oh God, you're pregnant, aren't you?" Elaine's worried voice cut through my haze; she darted around the bar to my side, ignoring clamoring customers, bolstering me around the waist. "Here, let me help you."

"Pregnant?" I repeated dumbly, focusing on Mathias's sister as her blue eyes, so very like his, studied me with concerned certainty.

Elaine assured, "It's all right, hon, I'll help you sit down. Oh jeez, you look exhausted. Are you going to throw up? I know just how you feel…"

"I'm not…"

Elaine did not hear my weak protests. "Oh God, Matty is going to be *so* excited. I mean, I know it's all so early for you two, and all of that, but he's already been talking to Mom about when you guys have your first baby and what a great dad he'll be—"

"Camille, you're pregnant? Oh, how exciting!" cried Lynda Doggett, whose family ran the gas station. She immediately spun around on her barstool to congratulate me, enthusing, "This is wonderful news. I love to see a young couple getting started. Ellen and Joanie must be thrilled! When will the wedding be?"

Oh, dear God. Already this was out of hand. As politely as I could manage, I told Lynda, "I'm not pregnant," but she was already passing the news to her husband, seated on the adjacent barstool and chatting with another couple, the Henrys, who lived about a mile from Curt and Marie.

"Are you sure you're not?" Elaine asked, peering into my face.

"Yes," I insisted, gently moving from her exuberant grasp; she didn't seem inclined to believe me and so I said, "I honestly hope to be pregnant with Mathias's baby someday in the future, but I'm not just now, I promise you."

The sun disappeared over the horizon just as I spoke, drawing the brilliance of the fire-hued light from the etchings of frost in the window and my lungs simultaneously emptied of air. It struck me as ominous—that the light would disappear exactly as I spoke about the future—as if to dare to do so was the worst tempting of fate that existed; worse yet, I had the sense that I should have known so much better. The band of fearful tension in my chest tightened like a cinch strap held by a brutal hand.

Elaine's face was pale. She demanded, "What's wrong?"

I shook my head in wordless distress, fumbling the cell phone from my apron pocket; there was a missed call from Aunt Jilly but I called the Utleys' house at once, hardly able to breathe past the lumping in my throat. A minute later, Marie assured me that Millie Jo was just fine, having fun with her cousins, currently enjoying birthday cake with ice cream.

Marie's voice sounded distant and tinny in my ear as she unconsciously repeated Elaine's question, asking worriedly, "What's wrong, dear?" But I'd already disconnected the call, trembling now, pressing the icon to call Mathias. The line rang—once, twice, my heart seizing painfully in each tiny eternity between rings. But he didn't answer. When his voicemail picked up instead the encroaching twilight leaped inward, into White Oaks, into my heart. Not yet understanding why, I knew only that I must move as quickly as my feet would carry me. I chucked my phone on the bar counter and ran for the front doors.

"Camille!" Elaine chased after me.

"Bull!" I yelled, knowing he must be here somewhere. I flew, breath coming hard and tight, knowing I must find Mathias's father; he would help me. "*Bull!*"

Bull and Diana stood chatting near the front check-in desk, in the oldest section of White Oaks, the part built in the 1860s, in which Malcolm Carter must certainly have walked and breathed and lived. Desperate with purpose, I thought, *Help me, Malcolm. Please, please help me. Where is he? Where's Mathias?*

"Camille, what's the matter?" Diana cried.

"It's Mathias," I gasped, ribs hurting as I clung to the edge of the check-in desk. My coat was all the way back in the kitchen, hanging near the door that opened onto the parking lot, but there was no time. I grabbed an unfamiliar parka from the nearby coatrack, stuffing my arms into it. Bull didn't ask for an explanation, instead reaching for his own coat and hat, his gloves.

Diana demanded, "What's going on?"

Elaine said, "Mom, come on!"

The four of us ran into the dusk, the air as static as the interior of a snow globe, cold stars glittering to life as if flung by a careless hand across the charcoal sky. Fear overrode all else in that moment, sharpening my senses. I turned in a circle, listening as hard as I could, attempting to discern logic from the buzzing void of fear in my head. Mathias was in danger. He needed me and he needed help—

But where was he?

"Mathias is in trouble," I said, hollow with cold sickness at this truth, gripping Bull's coat sleeves in both bare hands; though I hadn't a hope of shaking him, I tried anyway, desperate to convey the seriousness of my certainty. Bull looked deeply into my eyes, attempting to pry the answer straight from my mind, but I could tell that he believed me and I nearly wilted with relief. I insisted, "Where would he be, right now? Where would he be at dusk, right now?"

"The northern trap lines," Bull said grimly.

"Yes," I recognized, breathless with the need to go, to get to him.

Rippling into action, referring to Landon law enforcement, Bull ordered, "Diana, call Charlie and Mikey, tell them to meet us on the north side." And then to me, "C'mon!"

We ran, snow crunching beneath our feet. The borrowed parka flapped at my thighs; I wore no boots, no other outer gear, but paid no heed, instinct narrowing my focus to a thin corridor. The presence of danger had made itself known to me, purposely or not, and I thought, *Hold on, sweetheart. Hold on, we're coming!*

Tears froze on my cheeks. I fell, skidding over ice on my stupid shoes, but scrambled up instantly, hardly losing stride. We reached the snowmobiles. Bull straddled one and I clambered behind him, grabbing his waist as he fired it to life, its beam cutting the darkness like a light-house beacon. I clung to his bulk as we roared into the woods, Bull following the trail that led roughly a mile and a half, to the far side of Flickertail Lake, the less-populated north shore where the Carters laid their winter trap lines; as we flew over the hard-packed snow, he hollered his son's name, the two of us sweeping our gazes over the trail, looking for any sign. Bull slowed as we came to the clearing where they often parked and there was Mathias's plow truck, cold and quiet, snow dust-ing its dark windshield. My teeth clenched in a grimace of pain; Bull hardly slowed the sled before I flew from it, scouring the truck for signs of him—how I hated the sight of the empty cab, ominous as a body. I screamed, "*Mathias!*"

Bull killed the engine and said decisively, "We'll walk the line, c'mon."

In the distance I heard the wail of a police cruiser rushing from down-town, but other than that sound, Bull and I might have been alone in another century; I followed Mathias's father, ragged with dread, the both of us yelling for him, Bull sweeping the narrow path—far too confined to continue on the snowmobile—with the beam of a powerful Maglite he'd grabbed from the compartment beneath the seat of the sled. I stepped in the boot prints Bull left in the knee-high snow in order to keep up with him, caught in a backlash of horror—something about this cold, wild searching was all too familiar—the sense of being too late, no matter how strongly I rebelled against the notion. I fought aside the fear, snow cascading into my shoes, stinging-cold against my face as our passage caused pine boughs to spill their burden, miring my ankles. The temper-ature descended swiftly now that it was dark, the air with a late-winter bite that ensnared the entire north woods. And Mathias was somewhere in it, unable to answer us.

Bull stopped so abruptly that I crashed into his back; he directed the flashlight beam at the ground, breathing heavily as he scoured evidence. "He was here not long ago. See here, there's his boot tracks." He looked outward into the darkness, bellowing, "*Boy!* Can you hear me? Where in the hell are you?"

Perhaps two hundred yards behind us, back in the clearing, car doors slammed.

"Let's go!" Bull ordered, and the reassurance of his steady presence lent me strength; he gripped my elbow, hauling me along with his determined stride.

"Carter!" A distant yell rolled to our ears and I recognized Charlie Evans, Landon's senior police officer. "You out here?"

But Bull wasted no time responding, the two of us intent with purpose. I heard it just as Bull did; he stopped again, tense and crackling with energy. I clamped down on my next inhalation, listening with all my might, as was Bull, and there it came again, the sound of labored breathing belonging to neither of us, the sound of hurried passage somewhere ahead. Bull swung the light and then exclaimed in what could only be described as fury. Effectively trapped behind his broad back, I could not see what motivated his anger and fear surged into my throat as swiftly as vomit. Bull dropped the flashlight, which sunk into the deep snow, plunging us into abrupt darkness, but this did not stop him from lunging forward with a roar, charging between the pine trees. I fumbled for the light, fingers scraping madly for its long metal handle, desperate to know what was happening, trying to piece together any sort of sense from the sounds.

Another voice, unrecognizable to me, yelped in pain.

Bull was fighting someone, grappling so fiercely that tree trunks seemed to be crashing to the forest floor.

My fingers curled around the solid length of the Maglite and I swung it upward like a weapon, its beam bouncing erratically, highlighting the unbelievable image of Bull locked in combat with a stranger. But then I saw Mathias sprawled perhaps ten running paces from the path, on his back, eyes closed, and all else disappeared; I was conscious of nothing but getting to his side, desperation swelling into every vessel, every cell in my body.

"*No*," I gasped, falling to my knees beside him; I'd dropped the light in my haste to get to him but regretted the stupidity of this inadvertent action, as I was now rendered blind. My hands were on his face, which, as I'd caught sight of it only seconds ago, was bleeding from a gash on his forehead. "Talk to me, oh God, Thias, talk to me." Trembling and frantic, I instinctively sought the pulse in his neck and crumpled in relief, feeling it beating against my fingertips. Somewhere just beyond where Mathias lay on the ground, sprawled unconscious and with arms flung to the sides, his father battled whoever had done this to him—whoever it was, and for whatever unfathomable reason, that struck Mathias in the face.

"I'm here, I'm here," I babbled, stretching full-length against him, trying to combine the heat of my body with his, slipping careful hands beneath his head to cushion it from the snowy ground. His gray woolen hat was askew, his hair soft in my fingers, his cheeks cold; as my eyes adjusted to the dark, I could see the trails of blood along his face, appearing black against his pale skin. I sobbed, "What happened? Sweetheart, what happened?"

The sounds of vicious conflict vanished as suddenly as they began and Bull was at my side; he dropped to a crouch and demanded in a voice not to be argued with, "Mathias! Can you hear me?"

Mathias groaned and a ragged whimper of relief tore from my throat. Snow and ice cut into my knees; tears ran like heated water, dripping from my chin. Other people were fast approaching, additional flashlights cutting a swath through the black night. I couldn't maintain any sort of composure now, weeping, unwilling to release my hold on Mathias.

His gruff voice uncharacteristically gentle, Bull said, "Honey, let me lift him," and I eased back so that he could gather his son into his brawny arms; Bull stood and shouted, "Evans! We're back here!"

I dogged Bull's right elbow; he carried his son as though Mathias was still a little boy and not a full grown man taller than his father, hurrying but taking great care. Charlie, Mike Mulvey, and two township firemen met us roughly halfway back to the clearing and the cacophony of voices swelled beyond understanding. No questions could be successfully answered in this moment, but everyone attempted to ask them, all at once. Bull finally yelled, "Goddammit! My boy needs attention!" and without further ado, we were speeding toward Rose Lake in the back of a Landon Fire Department truck.

Mathias came to on the way to the hospital as Otto Sorenson, Eddie's oldest son and a local first-responder, directed a penlight into his eyes, searching for signs of concussion. I sat with hands braced to retain balance in the fast-moving vehicle and leaped to my feet at the sight of him alert, immediately almost falling to my knees. Mathias shoved at Otto, whose hands effectively pinned him flat on the cot, not yet aware that his father and I were near; he rasped angrily, "Where the hell am I?"

"Son, we're here," Bull said, leaning into Mathias's line of sight, helping Otto to keep him stationary as he struggled to sit upright.

"What the hell happened? Where's Camille?" and his voice bordered on frantic as he spoke my name; I stumbled as close as I could; the fire truck rumbled over the snowy ground, making it difficult to stand.

"I'm here," I said, clasping the hand he reached for me, dying to feel his warm skin. He tried again to get to his elbows.

"Carter, I'm going to have to ask you to keep calm," Otto ordered, not unkindly. He continued, "Someone clocked you in the head, I'm guessing with a weapon." He leaned closer to Mathias. "Can you remember anything? Do you know what happened?"

Mathias did not remove his gaze from me, his eyes moving over my face as though I was the one hurt. I clung to his hand, planting my feet to keep from lurching at the icy ruts in the road. I hastened to say, "I'm all right, love, I'm just fine." I wanted to beg for details as Otto had, to understand what had just occurred in the forest—despite evidence of a furious fight in the snow and Bull's bleeding nose, into which he'd unceremoniously stuffed a tissue—the man who'd caused all this harm was absolutely nowhere to be found. Mike Mulvey and two additional cops were still searching the area.

"I don't…" Mathias's voice emerged gruff and hoarse; he sounded just like Bull. He cleared his throat and tightened his grip on my hand, threading our fingers. His gaze moved to his father's face and he whispered, "Dad, I don't know what happened."

Bull's expression was as tender as I'd ever beheld it, nearly painful in its vulnerability, and as a parent, I understood completely. He could have lost his son this night, his only son, the joy of his life. My heart clenched at the thought, then expanded as though to burst through my ribcage. Bull rumbled with quiet intensity, "Someone attacked you. I would have killed him if he hadn't disappeared. Son of a bitch *disappeared*."

"He ran away?" Otto guessed, resuming his examination with the penlight. He speculated, "You're gonna have a hell of a headache tomorrow, Carter. You're decently concussed and you'll need stitches, but you're lucky."

"What happened, sweetheart?" I wanted to put my hands on his face, to wipe away the blood streaking darkly along the sides of his nose, drying now as the gash on his forehead coagulated, but I didn't want to impede Otto's inspection.

Mathias's gaze shifted up and to the left as he considered. Otto dabbed an antiseptic wipe to the wound and Mathias flinched a little—I did, too, just watching—and Bull curled a hand over his son's shoulder. Mathias murmured, "I got to the trail just at sunset, no more than an hour ago…" He drew a slow breath and continued, "I've walked those lines since I was a kid and never in my life felt worried, or unprepared, out there. I had my skinning knife but I must have dropped it when he hit me —"

"When *who* hit you?" Otto asked. "Who the hell would attack a man walking his trap lines?"

"I don't know, I didn't see his face," Mathias said. "He came from the side, to my left, I think. I heard him just before I saw a branch coming at my head."

"He was young, no more than your age," Bull supplied, shifting position, his free hand unconsciously balling into a white-knuckled fist. "Tall, thin, light-haired. No coat. I would have strangled the bastard to death but he disappeared. He didn't run away. I swear on my life he vanished from my grip like goddamn smoke. Suddenly I was holding onto nothing."

I studied Bull, a horrible shiver slithering over my spine. I knew he wasn't exaggerating; I understood he spoke the truth, however implausible. Bull suddenly reached and took my hand, bringing it to his lips; he kissed my knuckles and said roughly, "You knew something was wrong. You saved my boy."

Tears swelled, streaking my cheeks. I moved into Bull's embrace and wept against the solid strength of his chest, this man who would be my father-in-law one day soon; though nowhere near as skilled as Aunt Jilly at sensing the future, I believed this to be true. Bull cupped my skull with one big hand; his scent was similar to Mathias's and therefore familiar to me. I heard him tell Mathias, "Your woman knew something was wrong, you should have seen her, son."

"Oh God, come here, honey," Mathias said, hauling himself to an elbow. I cupped his jaw, my vision blurred with tears and blinded by the sight of his face. He clutched my wrist in his hand, gently stroking with his thumb, and acknowledged softly, "You knew something was wrong earlier." I nodded, and he rested his cheek to my belly as he lay on the cot while I stood as close as I dared, wrapping both arms around my waist.

Otto observed, "We're here."

In the half hour since our arrival at the Rose Lake hospital, Diana, Tina, Glenna, and Elaine had all converged. I'd called Grandma, and then Mom, to explain what was happening; Grandma and Aunt Ellen headed over to the Utleys' to pick up Millie. Bull and I were forced to relinquish Mathias in order for stitches to be administered to his forehead, and sat together in the waiting room; Charlie Evans showed up just ahead of the rest of the Carters, pulling Bull and me aside to explain that they'd found Mathias's truck keys and skinning knife close to where he'd been lying, and something wholly unexpected resting at the base of a nearby pine tree, as though flung from a careless grip: two heavy, rectangular bars of what Charlie believed, at least on sight, to be gold.

Bull's eyes crinkled at the outer corners as he repeated, "Gold?"

Charlie appeared as mystified as anyone; I studied his lined, jowly, darkly-tanned face for any clue as to what he might be thinking, vividly remembering the night, close to three years ago now, that he'd shown up at the cafe to cart Blythe to jail. My dad had been at Shore Leave that same evening, acting like an asshole and goading Blythe to fight him. Charlie asked Bull, "Do any such things belong to your family? Was Matty carrying it on him? Might someone have known and tried to rob him?"

"My son wasn't carrying gold," Bull said. "It was the other fellow's, it had to have been. That's why he was pawing through the snow when I swung the flashlight his way."

"Let's sit, Carter, I better take your statement," Charlie said, just as Diana and her daughters flew into the waiting room, their high-pitched fright preceding them like a flock of flustered birds.

Bull gathered his wife directly into his arms, where she burrowed close, weeping. He murmured, "It's all right, baby, he's all right."

I told Grandma I would be spending the night in Rose Lake, and much later sat at Mathias's bedside, my elbow resting on the mattress, my hands on his chest; he stroked through my hair with his left hand. Shadows ringed his eyes and he appeared ghostly-pale, the gash on his forehead held closed with ten precise stitches. Bull slept in the waiting room, feet propped on an adjacent chair; Diana and the girls left with promises to return in the morning. Mathias and I were all but alone in the small hospital room, lit with the dim glow of a lamp clamped to the metal headboard.

His eyes glinted as he whispered, "So, we're having a baby, huh?"

I smiled at these words, as he'd intended; after all the insanity of the past few hours, we found room to laugh at his mother's announcement. Apparently the rumor had been given wings at White Oaks earlier this evening, starting with Lynda Doggett congratulating Diana on the big news. Diana arrived at the hospital wondering when I was due, asking what she could do to help with our wedding plans.

"It's Elaine's fault," I complained, glad for this moment of levity; we'd reached no satisfactory conclusions regarding the events in the woods, or what to make of the aftermath. I just thanked all the powers that be for the fact that Mathias was safe, that he hadn't been hurt worse than he already was; at my words, a smile tugged at his lips.

"It got me all excited," he confessed. "I want it to be true."

"It will." I shifted closer to him, wanting to crawl right up on the narrow hospital bed. "It will before we know it, sweetheart."

"I didn't get to give you your present," he said, caressing my cheek.

I hadn't meant to cry any more tonight but tears stung. I turned my face toward his palm, letting my lips rest against the warm strength of him; I whispered, "You know I don't need any present but you."

"Come here, honey." He eased to his elbow. "I want to taste your mouth."

A shuddering sigh, one of pure need, escaped on a breath at his urgent words; our lips met flush and he parted mine with his tongue, catching my jaw in his hand and tilting my face into his kiss, claiming my mouth with such intensity, such possessive passion, that I lost all sense of time, swept willingly along on currents beyond my control, recognizing the necessity of being together, of loving him. Behind my closed eyes I beheld sights I did not fully understand, but in that moment of kissing him, understanding was unnecessary; only feeling was required. And what I felt was so right—a satiation of all the terrible waiting, the aching desire to find him, to feel him, to get my arms around him—simply to *see* him, when we'd been kept apart, waiting to find each other, for so very long.

Aces High stamped his hooves, waiting for us in the near-distance, a low-slanting sun shining over his chestnut hide, drawing forth its tints of red and bronze. The western horizon appeared jagged with mountain peaks, the tallest frosted with a layer of snow, knifing into the mauve breast of the evening sky. Grasses grew rangy and golden here in the foothills, crackling and stirring all around our camp. Kindling was stacked into a small teepee in preparation for the colder night hours and we kissed without end near the shallow fire pit, my hands in his hair and his nimbly racing to untie the row of lacing along the back of my dress; when he drew slightly away, our breath ragged, his eyes burned with an untamed fire that sent a pulse thundering between my legs. I spread my thighs in resolute invitation, begging, *Hurry, I need you…*

I need you, Malcolm…

And he kissed me all the more deeply in response.

Chapter Nineteen

A WEEK LATER, MATHIAS SAT AT MY SIDE, MY ENTIRE FAM-
ily, as well as Dodge, Bull, and Diana, gathered for Sunday dinner at
Grandma's house; I'd helped Aunt Ellen add leaves to the dining room
table to accommodate everyone. The woodstove crackled with warmth,
the kitchen replete with the scents of slow-cooked pot roast and glazed
carrots, biscuits and rich dark gravy, cinnamon strudel for dessert. Mathias
ate with one hand resting on my thigh; I kept my fingers threaded with
his. Millie Jo insisted on claiming the chair on Mathias's other side, sitting on her knees and maintaining a constant flow of chatter with him; at
one point she rested her cheek to his upper arm and I could almost hear
his tender thoughts, silently promising her that he'd be her daddy, that he
and I would give her a half-dozen little sisters and brothers.

Tish, Clint, and Ruthie sat just across the table from me—we had
claimed one end for ourselves in a version of the "kids' table" from the
old days—the three of them ladling out the latest gossip from Landon
High, news both trivial and comforting; Tish was at the top of the senior class, aiming for valedictorian and a scholarship to the University
of Minnesota, while Clint ducked his head, casually evading when
asked what he planned after graduation. Ruthie, despite numerous de-
nials, was apparently in a relationship with Hal Worden, one of Liz
and Wordo's triplets.

"He calls our house about ten times a night," Tish informed, her
mouth full; I loved my sisters dearly, especially the fact that while Tish
was a 4.0 scholar and bound for a career in law, she still barely knew the

difference between mascara and eyeliner. I reflected that before she left for college I would have to help her shop for some actual lingerie, and coax her out of the habit of exclusively wearing sports bras. She hadn't yet had a boyfriend, preferring boys as actual friends, nothing more, but I knew that would change the moment she met the right guy.

"He does *not*," Ruthie protested weakly, giggling as Tish mimed someone making exaggerated kissy-lips into a phone.

Clint, who sat with his forearms surrounding his plate, like usual, offered, "If he's bugging you, Liam and me will kick his ass, Ruthanna-banana."

"Yeah, like that's real smart," Tish said, with plenty of disdain; she and Clint never quit. Referring to Hal Worden's older half-brother, who was also a senior, Tish added, "Then Jeff would kick *your* ass."

"Jeff couldn't take the both of us," Clint fired right back. His eyes glinted with teasing. "Just because you and him were making out all over the parking lot after the hockey game last weekend—"

I was not about to let Tish evade this startling and hilarious news. In my best big sister voice I demanded, "What's this?!"

Tish actually went red across the cheekbones, hiding her scorching face behind a sip of soda, sending us all into gales of laughter, relishing this opportunity to pick on her, fair or not.

Ruthie contributed delightedly, "Yeah, Hal told me Jeff was all day-dreamy and walked right into the front door when they got home that night. Like, without opening it first."

"Why am I just hearing about this now?" I grinned wickedly at Tish and she glared in my direction. "I want all the gory details!"

"I hope he took out his mouth guard first," Mathias said solemnly; Jeff was a goalie for Landon High's hockey team, for which Mathias played center in his own high school days.

"And his headgear!" Clint whooped, prompting Tish to snort.

"Like he wears headgear in the daytime!" she said.

"So, you've seen him wear it at night?" I couldn't resist pestering.

We'd drawn attention from the other end of the table; Mom leaned our way to say, "It sounds like I better have a talk with Liz in the near future."

"Yeah, those Worden boys are trouble," Aunt Jilly said, winking at Tish.

Dodge was sitting beside Aunt Ellen; I realized that I always thought of them as a couple, even though technically they were not—at least, not openly. But somehow they seemed *right* together. Dodge bellowed, "What's this? Do I have to take a strap to my own grandsons?"

Uncle Justin said, "Yeah, since you were so opposed to taking a strap to your own son."

Everyone laughed at his teasing; Dodge said, "But I taught you a thing or two didn't I, boy?"

I loved how Dodge called Uncle Justin *boy*, just like Bull called Mathias; I found it oddly endearing. I imagined Mathias referring to our sons that way someday, and a burst of love for him prompted me to lean and kiss his jaw. He grinned, bringing my knuckles to his lips and kissing the ring he'd placed on my finger only a few days ago.

Diana said to Mom, "We'll have to go shopping together, Jo."

Mom smiled at me with absolute love, the same way I smiled at my daughter. She said, "You're right, we'll have to plan a trip to the Cities."

"Tina already requested scarlet for the bridesmaid dresses," I said, thinking of the night after Mathias was released from the hospital; I'd insisted he come to Grandma and Aunt Ellen's house, so that I wouldn't have to leave his side.

"I don't want to spend one more night without you in it," Mathias told me as Bull drove us back to Landon from Rose Lake that afternoon. We'd been in the backseat together, holding hands, and he spoke these words in his father's presence with no hint of embarrassment, or qualms; he was simply adamant in this decision.

My eyes wet with tears, I nodded agreement, bringing his hand to my cheek. His forehead was discolored by a raw purple bruise, the gash upon it stitched in black thread. The force of the blow had also blackened his eyes and the doctor determined after a thorough examination that someone had not only struck his face, but then proceeded to drag him along the ground; the multiple lacerations along his lower back were proof of this action. I could not dwell for more than a second on what might have happened that night in the woods if not for the sense that alerted me, the warning that something was wrong, and Bull's willingness to listen, to take seriously my demands for his help that night. Further, I was certain that Malcolm had somehow communicated this danger to me in the first place, had somehow, some way, called to me across time. And I could never be thankful enough.

That first night we'd eaten a quiet supper with Grandma, Aunt Ellen, and Millie Jo; Aunt Ellen prepared a pot of chicken soup and buttermilk biscuits. Exhausted, we'd retired to bed early, just after tucking in Millie. Grandma had lugged the toddler bed from the attic and adorned it with fresh sheets, placing it in her room for the night, so that Mathias and I might be allowed a little privacy. We'd already decided that once Mathias felt up to it, we'd move into the little apartment above the garage, where Aunt Jilly and Clint used to live. I changed into my pajamas in the bathroom—of course I wouldn't dream of having sex in my bedroom while my grandma and great-aunt, not to mention Millie, were in their rooms just down the hall—and besides, Mathias and I needed nothing more than to hold each other, at least for this night.

I returned to my room to find him sitting on the bed in a t-shirt and boxer shorts, grinning at me despite everything. Holding his gaze in mine, I quietly eased closed the door and then planted both hands slowly on my hips, letting an answering smile overtake my face.

"Sweetheart, this may have been the most extreme thing you could do for us to spend the night together," I joked.

"C'mere," he murmured, reaching, and I flew, restraining myself from bounding across the mattress and diving against him. He caught me close and took us to our sides; I latched a possessive leg over his right hip, though carefully, bracing on one elbow and regarding him in the lamplight. I could not study his face enough to satisfy the need, and I knew it was the same for him. No words, as none were necessary just now; instead, we spoke with touches, caressing each other with nearly unceasing motion, tracing the bone structures beneath each other's skin, as though sculpting clay. I longed to believe that all danger was behind us, that we'd overcome the worst of it, but I could not deny its presence, like a small, terrible knot deep in my belly. So many questions yet unanswered—no trace of the attacker, no hint as to whom the gold bars, apparently minted in Denver in 1876, belonged—but I shoved aside all my worries, so grateful to be here with Mathias, his body aligned with mine, when I'd spent so many nights longing for him so badly that it was physical pain; even before I'd met him, it had been so.

I finally whispered, "I decided Millie was old enough to stop nursing."

I hadn't nursed her to sleep in two nights, as was our usual custom, motivated by my decision that two years was a perfect age to discontinue the habit. Millie was more than old enough; I was reluctant to stop only because to do so seemed to signify the end of something unutterably special between us, almost indefinable. Maybe I felt that it symbolized that she would no longer need me quite as much.

Mathias skimmed one hand along the curve of my hip. "Why's that?" he whispered, smoothing hair from my face, tucking it gently behind my ear. "Doesn't it help her sleep?"

"It does. That's the only time she nurses anymore. But she's a big girl now and I think that it's time." I admitted, "But it hurts to think of not sharing that with her anymore."

"You don't need to rush anything, honey. You can get her right now, we'll make room."

"I know," I whispered, my hands on his chest. "But it's time. I shouldn't feel like it means she won't need me as much."

"Hey," he said, softly but intently; I could feel the words rumbling in his chest as he spoke. "Millie still needs you with all her heart, honey. She's your baby and she'll always be your baby." He studied my eyes in the dimness of the quiet room. "And I need you, Camille, with all my heart. I need that look in your eyes that says I'm crazy but you love me anyway. I need your smile, and your arms around me, and your sweet, tender soul. Oh God, I need you," and he punctuated this with a soft kiss, full on my lips. "So don't go thinking that we don't need you, not for one second."

I wrapped him close to me. Mathias pressed his lips to my shoulder. "Do you know how much I love you? Tell me that you know."

"I know it," I said, choked up all over again.

The next morning, before Millie woke up, we examined Malcolm's picture anew, using the magnifying glass in the rosy, early-morning sunlight, which struck Malcolm and Aces, gilding them with radiance. For a second, they almost seemed alive. As though, if I rose and crept to the window, the two of them would be down in the yard, looking back up.

"Malcolm," I whispered. But I realized that I was referring to Mathias; I'd called him *Malcolm*. I set aside the picture. "We have to find him. We *have* to. I know this."

Mathias spread his hands protectively over my back. The dawning sun grazed his black hair, lit the gold in his eyes; I understood that he was part of Malcolm, that he would not exist here in 2006 without Malcolm having existed in the nineteenth century. He whispered, "We will, honey. We will do everything we can. We have those letters, out in Montana…"

"This summer," I said, rife with determination.

"Whatever happened to him, we'll find out."

And so it wasn't until many days after Valentine's that Mathias was able to bestow upon me the present he'd intended. After we'd eaten dinner at Bull and Diana's we took one of the snowmobiles directly to our cabin, parking near the front porch. Inside, I lit the candles we'd placed around the little room and then helped him load wood into the old stone fireplace; the process was delayed significantly because we couldn't stop kissing. At last, a small blaze joined the candles in warming the room, leaping over the walls and painting our faces auburn.

Mathias shook out the queen-sized down comforter I'd pilfered from the attic at Grandma's, spreading it before the fire so that we had a soft place to sit close. Once this was done, he helped me from my ski pants and puffy coat, and I helped him from his, and then we were kissing again, me straddling his lap, his knees bent behind me, both hands wrapped around my waist.

"I want…" he murmured.

"Tell me just what you want," I whispered, kissing the side of his neck, biting his earlobe, and he shivered. We'd refrained from making love while in the bedroom at Grandma's house and the deprivation of the last week was keen in our blood, our every touch.

"Honey, I want to give you your present," he whispered, kissing my throat, fingers spread over my back. "Before all the blood flows away from my head that is."

I giggled and moved primly from his lap.

"Close your eyes for just a minute," he said, and I did, my heartbeat increasing in intensity with each breath.

I listened as he moved from the blanket and rummaged for something in his coat pocket; I heard the scrape of a zipper and then he knelt before me once more and closed one hand around my left, lifting it to his lips. He whispered, "Open your eyes."

Upon my palm he set the ring from this very cabin, the one that he found behind a stone in the fireplace. His voice was husky with emotion. "This is yours. When I was little I told my sisters that someday my wife would wear this ring and I want you to be my wife. I need to know that someday soon your name will be Camille Carter." His eyes drove into mine and tears flowed down my cheeks. "I love you with my whole heart and I know that I've loved you long before I met you. I am yours, and you are mine, and I don't know how I know this to be true, but it is."

"Mathias," I said, almost a sob. I took the golden circle into the tips of my right fingers and slipped it at once over my ring finger, where it fit perfectly, as before. He made a sound in his throat and brought my hand to his lips, kissing the ring, before I threw my arms around him and clung. I said against his neck, quoting the inscription on the ring, "My heart is yours for all time. And I know that for truth."

He rocked against me and we tumbled back to the blanket, where in the firelight we stripped one another of all pieces of clothing, slowly, kissing each inch of bared flesh. Wordless, intense, never taking our eyes from each other. I felt removed from myself, completely melded together with him, to the point where we no longer seemed to possess names; our names mattered not at all. *Him. His. Mine.* He was mine, and I was his, and nothing more mattered.

He joined our hands, linking our fingers, bracing them just above my head as I curved my legs about his hips and took him within me, gasping as his hard length filled me to bursting. And we made love without saying a word, quiet and shattering and intense. At some point I shifted and clung to his shoulders, my forearms curled beneath his arms, gripping securely as he buried his face against my neck. We grew slick with sweat, heat flowing between us, spilling from between my legs as he kept on and on, unceasing, and my body responded like nothing I'd ever known. I shuddered with release, repeatedly, our breath harsh and our hearts beating in a frantic double rhythm.

I love you so, he told me without words.

I responded in kind, *I love you. I will be your wife.*

You are my love, Cora, and I will never leave you.

You are mine, my true love, Malcolm. I trust you.

And in the darkness we held fast, on and on.

Excerpt from Wild Flower

Camille's voice woke me and I sat up too fast, reeling, reaching blindly into the humid darkness of a July night. The blood in my veins thundered like water over a falls. Only a second earlier my niece had been clutching my arm, screaming and frantic, and now all I could hear in the void of silence surrounding my eardrums was the violence of my heartbeat.

Oh God, what is it, what's wrong? Camille and Mathias were still in Montana. I closed my eyes and concentrated for all I was worth, trying to discern a shred of an answer. Sending the thought with as much force as I could muster, I pleaded, *Camille, tell me*!

Beside me, Justin woke and rolled to wrap an arm over my lap.

"I'm here, baby." His warm hand curved around my right thigh.

"I'm scared." My voice was high and hoarse. The only time a sense of foreboding had ripped through me so fiercely was the long-ago winter night my first husband, Christopher, had died.

Justin collected me close, his protective embrace easing some of the rigid tension in my body. "I'm here, Jilly-honey, it's all right."

I clung, feeling the worried pace of his heart against my cheek, slowly regaining a sense of calm. I whispered, "It's not that."

He smoothed loose hair from my flushed face. "Is it Rae? Clint?" The hall light clicked into existence as Justin assured himself that our children were both safe in their bedrooms down the hall; seconds later he was back, gathering me against his warm, bare chest. He stroked my pregnant belly in small, comforting circles. "What is it, Jills? What's happening?"

"It's Camille." I pressed all eight fingertips to my forehead. I moaned, "Oh God, I was just dreaming of her and Mathias. Something's wrong..."

Against the backdrop of my closed eyes a picture wavered into existence, a horizon in the distance, etched with the outline of a low-slung, jagged-edged mountain. For a fraction of a second I could see Camille plainly through what appeared to be misting rain; despite the dark night around her, she was momentarily highlighted by a rending in the cloud cover and a milky spill of moonlight gilded her long, wild hair. She was screaming one word, in a refrain of hysteria.

"Mathias."

Printed in the United States
by Baker & Taylor Publisher Services